Felicity Pulman is the novels for children and Shalott trilogy, The Janna Mysteries and *A Ring Through Time*. *I, Morgana* is her first novel for adults, inspired by her early research into Arthurian legend and her journey to the UK and France to 'walk in the footsteps of Arthur' before writing the Shalott trilogy. Her interest in crime, fantasy and history (both Australian and European) inspires most of her novels – and often necessitates travelling for research purposes, which is something she loves to do. She has many years' experience talking about researching and writing her novels both in schools and to adults, as well as conducting creative writing workshops in a wide variety of genres. Felicity is married, with two children and five grandchildren, all of whom help to keep her young and techno-savvy – sort of! You can find out more about Felicity on her website and blog: www.felicitypulman.com.au or on Facebook.

First published by Momentum in 2014
This edition published in 2014 by Momentum
Pan Macmillan Australia Pty Ltd
1 Market Street, Sydney 2000

Copyright © Felicity Pulman 2014
The moral right of the author has been asserted.

All rights reserved. This publication (or any part of it) may not be reproduced or transmitted, copied, stored, distributed or otherwise made available by any person or entity (including Google, Amazon or similar organisations), in any form (electronic, digital, optical, mechanical) or by any means (photocopying, recording, scanning or otherwise) without prior written permission from the publisher.

A CIP record for this book is available at the National Library of Australia

I, Morgana

EPUB format: 9781760081379
Mobi format: 9781760081386
Print on Demand format: 9781760081393

Cover design by Raewyn Brack
Edited by Kylie Mason
Proofread by Hayley Crandell

Macmillan Digital Australia: www.macmillandigital.com.au

To report a typographical error, please visit momentumbooks.com.au/contact/

Visit www.momentumbooks.com.au to read more about all our books and to buy books online. You will also find features, author interviews and news of any author events.

I, Morgana

Felicity Pulman

momentum

PROLOGUE

I am an old woman now. My bones creak and scrape together like bare branches in a winter wind. I ache with longing for my youth. When I notice my reflection, I am aghast at the vision of the hag who looks back at me. I mourn the passing of who I was, and everything I could have been. More than anything, I long to reverse time. Throughout the years I have tried and tried to do this, without success. Now, even my most potent spells and incantations cannot transform me into the young woman I once was, with all my life still to live. With age, my magical powers have all but deserted me. Once I was desired by men; now I am disregarded by all and loved by none.

And I ask myself: How has it come to this, when once the future looked so bright and full of promise? And I swear a sacred oath to the gods, whoever they may be, that if only they would grant me my life anew, along with the wisdom I have learned so painfully, I would not make the same mistakes again. I would not lead us all to destruction.

But the gods are deaf to my prayers and to my promises. All I can do now is call for parchment, cut my quill, and tell my story. I shall start at the beginning, because that's when the first seeds of doom were sown: when I was a child and believed I had the power to make the whole world new.

CHAPTER 1

"Look at me, Merlin! Look at me." I twirl and twirl, giddy with delight, bubbling with laughter as the earth turns around me and my hair flies into my eyes.

"Well done, Morgana! You must concentrate now; think about being a bird. How will it feel when you are flying?"

I close my eyes and I try, I try so hard, because I know how much it'll please Merlin if I succeed. Around and around I spin, the world gone dark around me, the air swishing past.

"Open your eyes, Morgana! Look about you. See that raven? Remember what I told you? You have to think that raven, *be* a raven."

I am a raven. I am a raven. I am Merlin's raven. I am! I am a raven flying, flying high, soaring into the sky, riding on the wind.

I think it. I will it with all my heart, my mind, my soul.

Something shifts. Something changes. The air feels cool against my cheek, my black feathers ruffle in the breeze. I look down as a little girl dissolves into light and shadows, and I know that I am free!

Merlin knows it too. I can see him down there, shading his eyes from the sun as he stares up at me. I feel such exultation, such triumph, I could almost burst. I am Morgana, Merlin's raven, and I have the whole realm in my power. All that I can see below me will be mine one day. I know that's true because my father has willed it, and Merlin has promised me.

He's waving at me now, beckoning me to come down, for I have proved myself to him. But I am gone beyond him. I am intoxicated with joy, with the sensation of flying and the knowledge that at last I have unlocked the secret to shape-shifting. Now I can escape from my earthbound body and become anyone or anything that takes my fancy. And so I fly on, for the first time able to look down on the land that one day will be mine, and on the people over whom I shall rule. Beyond the spit of land on which our castle stands is the dark blue ocean, buffed into sharp waves by a brisk wind. It's a ragged coastline of jagged cliffs, marked by the foam of breaking waves at their base. The sea hides a multitude of broken dreams, ships coming close to harbor but caught by waves and tide instead, and torn to pieces on the cruel and unforgiving rocks below the surface.

Bells ring out as I fly over the abbey. Obeying their urgent summons, the monks of Tintagel hurry to Mass in their great stone church with its cross at the summit. In my bird's mind I pull a human face at them, for their love of the Christ is not for me. I put my trust in Merlin's magic, not the will of the god they worship.

On a whim I fly onward, to the place where my father died in battle, for I have never been allowed to see the place where he fell, just as I was not allowed to see his dead body, nor was I able to mourn him openly, as a daughter should.

Once I come to the battlefield, I alight on a branch and look out across the bare scrubby grass that lies baking in the glare of the sun. I try to imagine how it must have been: my father's troops trying to defend our territory against the soldiers of the High King; a battle that ended in the death of my father, Gorlois, Duke of Cornwall. My heart fills with sorrow as I recall the events that led to that moment.

It all began when my father was summoned to London to pay tribute to the new High King, and made the mistake of bringing his family with him, for it was then that Uther Pendragon fell in love with my mother and she with him. I remember how awed I was by the magnificence of the High King's palace and the presence of kings and nobles from across the southern country. We'd walked along the banks of the River Thames, my father and I, while he'd announced his dreams for my future.

"I shall not make any arrangements for your betrothal, Morgana, not yet. There is time enough to choose a worthy consort to be at your side, but it is you I shall name as my heir, and it is you who will rule Cornwall in my stead. I'm putting my trust in you, Morgana. You must take care of my realm and rule wisely and well. You must not fail me in this. Do I have your word that you will do as I ask?"

His words had so filled me with excitement that I'd stopped walking and faced him. I'd crossed my hands over my heart and sworn an oath that I would never let him down, and that I would do all that he asked of me, and more.

My father had laughed then—not at me, but with relief, because he knew that I understood the gravity of his charge. And I saw the love and pride that shone in his eyes when he presented me to Uther, the High King, as his heir.

But there are other things I remember about that time. How Uther followed my mother, Igraine, around his court, seizing every opportunity to take her hand and press it to his lips for a lingering kiss. At the time I'd thought it a mark of his respect for us, but later I understood that Uther loved my mother. I also remember the growing tension between my father and mother that culminated in a bitter quarrel and led to our hasty departure from London.

Just six months after that, my father is dead and my mother remarried.

I shake my glossy feathers into smoothness, as if I could at the same time shake myself free of memories. Conscious of time passing, I look out over the battlefield once more, and mouth an anathema against the man who caused my father's death. Then, with some trepidation, worried I may have lost the knack of it, I launch myself off the branch. I spread my wings and my body lifts up into a current of air that will blow me toward the forest and Merlin.

My flight takes me over the castle and I look down at its inhabitants, tiny as ants as they swirl in patterns around the courtyard, going about their business. I fly closer so that I can see them more clearly, for I am intrigued to find out what people might do, how they might act when they believe themselves unobserved.

I see my mother, and my heart catches in my feathered breast. She is sitting in her private arbor. With her is Uther Pendragon. As I watch, he places his hand on her stomach and leans over to kiss her cheek. She laughs, and puts her hand over his—and I realize the significance of what I see. Looking at them now, at the way their joined hands stroke the curve of her belly, I understand that soon I shall have yet another rival for my mother's love.

How I hate Uther Pendragon! I hate him for the way he took my father's place so soon after he was killed. That he loves my mother beyond reason, I have no doubt. But I blame him most bitterly for my father's death in battle and for seizing our kingdom. I also blame him for taking my mother away from me. These days she has eyes only for him.

If only I knew how to do it, I would strike Uther Pendragon dead! And my mother's unborn child with him. Merlin has promised to teach me more tricks and more magic than mere shape-shifting; he's promised to give me all the gifts

I shall need to rule a kingdom. I don't want another rival for Merlin's affection. What I really want is to change things back to how they were; to turn back time and have power over life *and* death, and that's what I would learn from him.

A sudden thought strikes terror into my heart: What if my mother bears a son, what then? I fly back to Merlin as quickly as I can and, as soon as I've transformed myself, I question him.

He gives me a fond smile. "You have nothing to fear, Morgana. Remember: your father has named you as his heir, even if Uther has usurped your position for the moment. But I believe you have an even greater destiny, for while Uther dabbles here with your mother, he is neglecting his duty as High King. The kings of Britain are jostling for power, leaving our country disunited and increasingly vulnerable to attacks from across the sea. You have courage, and intelligence, and you have shown great aptitude in the magical arts. I believe that when the time comes, and with my help, you will have the strength and the knowledge to unite all the tribes of Britain and bring them under your protection so that we may live in peace and prosperity once more."

I take comfort from Merlin's words, for they justify my father's trust in me. But Merlin has not yet finished.

"A word of warning," he says, and now his voice is stern. "When I bid you to return from flight, or to do anything else, I expect you to do as you are told. No!" He raises his hand as I open my mouth to argue. "I know it is a temptation to fly further and to test yourself, especially when you are new to shape-shifting, but you must always respect your magical powers, Morgana, and use them wisely. You are six summers grown now; old enough to obey my instructions as well as learn from me."

"Of course I shall do everything you ask, Merlin." I am so grateful for the mage's reassurance of my destiny that I will promise him anything. I am also grateful to have escaped a long lecture. Although I love Merlin, and will do anything to please him, I do hate it when he's cross with me!

Merlin is something of a mystery to me. He has power, I know that—the power of a mage steeped in magic—yet he is not a member of our court. My mother has become a devout Christian since marrying Uther, and anything to do with the occult has been banned. But Merlin and I have always met in secret, right from the very first when, by chance, I escaped my nurse and my sister, and ran into the forest beyond the castle looking for adventure. Merlin found me—or perhaps he knew I would come that day and so he waited for me? I know not, but since then we have always met in the forest, and I have told no one about what he is teaching me.

He looks a bit like an elderly owl, with tufty white hair and piercing eyes that seem to see right through me. I know that he believes in me, for he cares for me as a father would. And I try to please him in everything, for there is much I can learn from him, lessons I need to understand if I am to fulfill the shining destiny he has promised me. I am determined to do well, to be the best. I am determined to justify his faith in me, and fulfill the oath I swore to my father.

*

After Arthur is born, I wonder why I ever felt such hatred toward him. He's the sweetest thing I've ever seen, smiling up at me and gurgling with joy whenever I come into the room. I cuddle him when he is fretful, and at night when he's going to sleep, I sing him into the dark. In every way I try to give him the love and comfort we both need, to compensate for our mother's preoccupation with Uther and her indifference to us. I've come to resent Igraine, and I hate her new husband. But my heart has been stolen by this child, who loves me without reserve just as I love him.

As Arthur grows older it becomes increasingly difficult to leave him behind when I meet Merlin. I am fearful that he might innocently betray my secret, but my usually placid and biddable little brother puts on such a tantrum when I try to get away that I eventually relent. Once begun, I continue to bring him with me, all the time warning him that I'll cut out his tongue if he ever says Merlin's name. Even though I have no intention of carrying out my threat, Arthur believes me and so, whenever he sees Merlin, he sticks out his tongue and slices his finger across it. And I smile and nod, and give him a cuddle to compensate for scaring him.

Arthur follows me everywhere, trying to copy whatever I'm doing, often with amusing results, especially when it comes to magic. Shapeshifting comes easily to me now but not to Arthur. At first he rolls himself into a little ball and squeaks like a mouse, really believing that's what he is. He tries so hard, but he keeps crashing into the wall when he attempts to run down a mouse hole. Finally he catches his hand in a mouse trap while trying to steal a piece of cheese—a painful lesson for him! He's not much better at transforming himself into a rabbit either, even though he keeps trying.

I must admit I enjoy showing off to Arthur, who is always impressed and who always begs for more—even when I once turned myself into an irritating fly to torment him! Sometimes I become a pet for him to play with: a puppy, a pony, a cheeky monkey full of tricks. Sometimes I secretly help him perform magic, just to see the joy on his face when he thinks he's able to do what I can. And I pretend that his favorite cloth rabbit can talk, although I often need to hide my mirth when Arthur confides in his rabbit without seeming to realize that he is also confiding in me. But speaking as Arthur's rabbit gives me a further opportunity to comfort him if comfort is needed, and to gently guide him in the ways of the court. Keeping Arthur amused with my magic tricks is more important to me than obeying Merlin's exhortations to use magic sparingly, and only when necessary.

On one occasion, I transform myself into a raven and ignore Merlin's cries to come back. I swoop down on my mother and Uther, circling closer and closer, avoiding their flailing arms until I manage to deposit a dropping on Uther's head. How sweet that moment is! What pleasure it gives me! But my pleasure turns sour when Merlin begins his lecture. "The knowledge of magic is dangerous when used without wisdom," he warns.

How can he accuse me of lacking wisdom when I'm always so quick to learn whatever he teaches me? I'm so annoyed that I flounce off, even though Merlin has promised to initiate me in the use of sacred herbs and their magical properties.

Then Arthur tells me Merlin has started to teach him magic, really teach him magic instead of just letting him watch and play at it, so I give Merlin a pretty apology. He says he's glad I've come to my senses and we go on as usual, with one difference: Arthur is part of the lessons now. Not that I mind, not really. I'm so much better and so much quicker at everything than he is. Nevertheless, I listen carefully, and practice until I have perfected each new challenge. But it worries me that Arthur is becoming closer to Merlin. I know I am Merlin's favorite, his most gifted pupil. As much as I love my little brother, I intend to keep first place in Merlin's heart, always.

Merlin has told me that one day he hopes he will be able to teach me how to traverse time, although he warned me, with a cackle of laughter, that he, himself, has been unable as yet to master the art. I'm excited by the possibilities; I dream of what I might achieve, determined as I am to go beyond Merlin's abilities and do what he cannot. My ambition is to turn back time; to keep my beloved father safe and the usurper, Uther, out of my mother's bed.

Of course, there's also my younger sister, Morgause, but I don't feel close to her at all. She spends her time in the company of my mother's attendants, liking nothing better than to dress up and play at being a great lady. She boasts about Lot of Lothian and the Orkney Isles, the prince from the north to whom she is already betrothed. She prattles endlessly of the castle she will live in, the sumptuous clothes and costly jewels she'll wear, the delicious delicacies that will grace her table, and the troubadours and players who'll flock to her court to entertain her. I have no interest in such things, nor do I share her small ambitions. So we exchange nothing beyond pleasantries. She has no idea where Arthur and I go when we disappear, nor does she know anything of what I'm learning. She wouldn't understand even if she did. Merlin and I both know that.

Learning magic from Merlin is always a challenge, and sometimes there's more than one lesson to master. I discover this when he decides to teach Arthur and me about tree lore. The first thing he shows us is how to write the ancient Ogham alphabet, which he says is still used by the Druids in a world unknown to us. Arthur struggles to remember the signs, but I quickly memorize the horizontal, slanted and vertical lines that are cut into wooden posts or trees, or even carved into stone, conveying messages that may be read only by initiates. We move on to other forms of magical script, and it becomes a game between us, with Merlin leaving messages for me to decipher regarding when and where we'll next meet.

Once I've mastered the runes (and after Merlin finally gives up on trying to teach Arthur), we learn more about trees. Merlin starts his lesson by telling us about the ash.

"It was once thought that all mankind emanated from the ash," he says. "The ash is therefore considered to be a sacred tree, a symbol of the life force. We call it the 'tree of the world' or *Yggdrasil*, for it spreads its limbs over every land

and forms a link between the spirits in the world above, the dead in the world below and our own land of the living. Stories from across the water tell us that Odin hung himself from an ash to receive wisdom, while Nemesis carried an ash branch as a symbol of divine justice. Spears made from the ash are invisible to the enemy, and may be used to inspire an ecstatic frenzy." He pauses a moment. "That's especially useful in times of battle," he adds dryly. "When you've embarked on a killing spree, you usually don't have too much time for rational thought."

Arthur is already engaged in a mock battle, lunging with a pretend sword and raising his arm to block a pretend blow. He's no longer listening, but I am fascinated that a tree I've always taken for granted can have such a history and such magical properties.

"How do you know all this?"

"I have been there and heard the stories."

I frown. In all the time I've known Merlin, I've never seen him embark on a sea voyage to anywhere. So how can he …? I give a little grunt of amusement. Merlin has no need of a boat to travel anywhere! I swell with pride to think that, once I have mastered all he can teach me, neither shall I.

Merlin is still lecturing. "In Britain, we use the ash for spells of rebirth and new life, especially when it comes to the protection of children and to ensure longevity. The ash is also used in the cure of fever and liver complaints, and to aid digestive upsets."

He clicks his fingers to summon his wand, which he then waves in front of me. "This is made of ash," he says, and points to the symbols carved in a spiraling pattern along its length. "When you reach thirteen summers I shall give you your own wands, Morgana. You will need an ash wand for healing, which will become the greater part of your practice, but it will also give you protection, health and prosperity."

"And the power to work magic," I remind him.

Merlin smiles. "For that you'll need a wand of hazel. But you've already acquired enough skills to begin working magic on your own account. You have no need of any wands just yet."

"But I want a wand!" I'm not prepared to give up such a valuable instrument, not having come so close to acquiring it.

"And one day you shall have all three," Merlin promises, and lays his hand on my head. "The wand of greatest power is the wand of oak, for the oak will help you gain access to Otherworlds, worlds beyond our imaginings." He is gazing over my shoulder, and I wonder what he's looking at. The sacred island of Avalon, about which I've heard him speak, but have never seen? Or is he looking beyond, to those places across the water with which he seems so familiar?

"One day this kingdom will come under threat as never before," he says, his eyes still fixed on the line where the earth meets the sky. "A great horde from across the ocean, barbarians who covet our land, will invade our shores and try to take from us what is not theirs to possess. Several raiding parties have already come, but there are watchers on the lookout and beacons ready to be lit, both to give warning and to summon help. So far we have managed to repel them. But once Uther dies, you need to be ready to take his place and unite the kingdom in order to fight off the invaders who will surely flock to our shores once they hear of his death."

"I'm ready now, Merlin."

Merlin blinks. His gaze focuses on me almost as if he's seeing me for the very first time.

"It was my father's wish that I succeed him after his death. Uther may have usurped my father's position, but he cannot undo my destiny," I say fiercely, unsettled by his strange expression. "That's why I'm learning all I can from you, Merlin! Together, we'll be more than a match for any invaders. We'll crush them as if they were just so many ants!" I grind my knuckles into the palm of my hand to illustrate my point. "We'll drive them back into the sea and then Britain will be safe forever."

Merlin is no longer looking at me. His gaze has settled on Arthur.

"No!" I shout, not sure why I'm protesting or even what I'm protesting about. "Look at me, Merlin! Look at me! I can do everything you ask of me, and more. I know I can be the leader Britain needs when the time comes. And I promise you that I will honor your teaching in everything I do. I shall be a wise leader, and a strong one. I shall protect everything we hold dear, with my life if necessary."

The old man removes his hand from my head. "We shall see," he says.

I shiver at his words; an icy dread settles on my heart, so heavy I can scarcely breathe.

"It's my birthright!" I protest, growing angry now. "You promised me, Merlin." I grab him and give him a shake. I've never dared touch him before and I am surprised how frail his arms feel within my strong grip.

The force of his power and his anger smash through me like a thunderbolt. At once I snatch my hands away and take a quick step backward, touching my forehead in a sign of obeisance. "I beg your pardon, master," I murmur. "Please forgive me."

It isn't often that I address him so, but the mage will not be mollified. He banishes me from his presence and I feel the scorching breath of his anger reaching out to me through many days and nights before he sends for me once again. When our lessons resume, I am cautious and extremely polite. Our falling out is soon forgotten in the thrill of learning how to tell time and direction from the sun and the stars and how to communicate with birds and beasts, among other useful and often magical abilities and tricks. Finally, to my joy, Merlin gives me three wands: ash for healing and protection; hazel for the power to work magic; and oak to help transport me to the Otherworlds I long to visit. But this provokes the first serious argument between Arthur and me.

"Can I have some wands?" he begs.

"No, Arthur!" It is inconceivable that my brother, who is so inept when it comes to performing magic, should also be given these symbols of power.

"But I want them. It's not fair to give them just to you!" Arthur's face is red with frustration, but Merlin just laughs and tells him he can have them when he's older.

Merlin might laugh, but his words strike dread in my heart.

"Why should Arthur have any wands at all? You know he'll never be able to perform magic as well as I can."

Arthur scowls at me. "I can do magic if I have some wands."

I stare at my little brother, and realize he's no longer so little. He's old enough now to think for himself, which makes him old enough to understand once and for all his place in our future.

I turn in appeal to Merlin. "I need these wands because I am the one who will inherit this realm, and maybe rule all of Britain one day. Therefore I am the only one who should have them."

"But you're only a girl!" says my brother.

I curl up my fists in rage and frustration. Arthur has taken to watching the knights and their squires training in the tilting yard, practicing their wrestling holds and their sword play. I should have realized when I caught him fighting shadows with a broken stave that he might also mimic their opinions.

"I may be a girl, but that won't stop me. My destiny is to rule our kingdom," I say, trying to hide my annoyance.

A fleeting smirk crosses Arthur's face. "You can only ever be a queen, Morgana. But I'm a boy. And I'm going to be king one day, so I'll rule the *king*dom. That's why I need wands too." He tries to grab them from my hands, but I am too quick for him. I hold my wands high in the air, out of his reach.

"Merlin!" he shouts, and stamps his foot.

"Not now, Arthur." The mage places his hand on Arthur's shoulder to calm him. It doesn't prevent my brother from sticking out his tongue and glaring at me. I try to ignore him, but I am troubled. It was our father's wish that I inherit his realm. I have no intention of breaking my vow and handing it over to Arthur.

"He's young, he'll understand when he's older," I tell myself, trying to settle my spirits so I can concentrate on Merlin's next course of instruction: how to fashion a magical cloak of invisibility.

Our lessons pass without further fuss from Arthur, but sometimes he looks at me and in that brooding stare I know he has not forgotten. I suspect he has not yet accepted his fate, but I know this is something he must come to terms with in his own time. To make much of it now would only look like gloating; it would harden his heart against me. I couldn't bear that. And so I am affectionate toward him, as usual, and he still reaches out to me when in need of something.

I work hard to win Merlin's praise and esteem, learning my lessons well and practicing diligently all that he can teach me. I am determined that, when the time comes, my destiny will not be in doubt. It consoles me that Arthur is having trouble keeping up with us. On this day he lags behind as Merlin leads us to an unfamiliar part of the forest and shows us the herbarium he has created around a bark hut at its center. I am curious about this hut, for I do not think he lives there: there is no sign of a bed or storage space for his clothes, or a supply of food or anything else of that nature. Instead, there is a workbench and a fireplace, with pots and receptacles of various sizes.

"This is where I brew my healing potions," he tells us. "And this is where I shall teach you all that I know, Morgana. And Arthur," he adds quickly, as Arthur catches up to us, and scowls at being left out.

We go outside once more, and Merlin begins to talk about his plants. "These are the herbs of healing," he says, and shows us agrimony, betony, and woundwort. "Comfrey will help to knit broken bones together," he tells us. "And this is valerian, for nervous complaints." He moves on to a tall plant with fern-like leaves, clusters of small white flowers, and a terrible smell. "This is hemlock," he says. "It's poisonous, so you must use it with care and very sparingly. It's good for pain relief. Poppy juice is even more effective, but again must be used with care." He walks over to a patch of bright red flowers that commonly grow wild in the fields, and demonstrates how to gather their seeds to make a soothing syrup. At the center of the patch stand some white-flowering blooms on tall blue-green stems. He plucks an unripe pod from one of them, and slices it open. He points to the milky juice oozing out. "I shall also show you how to prepare this, for it is excellent for pain relief. But beware: too large a dose will bring oblivion and even death."

There are many plants to remember, all with their different uses, and not only for healing for some also have magical properties. We return to Merlin's garden many times, and learn their appearance and purpose one by one. Some have a use in the kitchen, such as tansy. "It's used as a strewing herb to repel insects," says Merlin, who shows us also the fragrant and flavorsome herbs used in the preparation of food. I listen, and I write down the names and particulars of every plant he shows me so I won't forget. I am not allowed near the kitchen gardens at home; my mother considers it beneath me to learn the art of healing, or how to cook and flavor food, for we employ others to do such things for us. But I want to learn and so I press Merlin to tell me what else he knows of the practice of medicine, such as the importance of balancing the humors for wellbeing, the efficacy of leeches and how to set broken bones. I watch carefully as he shows me how to brew, blend and concoct the creams, lotions and potions that will ease pain and bring relief to the sick and injured. And when he sees I have a knack for this, he invites me to make use of his hut to prepare remedies of my own. I know that Merlin is pleased with me again for he praises my diligence and smiles at me like a fond father, especially after I tell him that castle servants are starting to visit me in secret, seeking a cure for their various maladies.

Arthur sulks because he can't remember the names of the plants, and is in a total muddle over their uses. I suspect it's because he is just not interested; it's the techniques of fighting and killing rather than nurturing and healing that hold his attention now. I sense that he's withdrawing from me. He's spending more and more time with the pages, with the squires, and even with the knights when they're not too busy to tolerate him. He is growing up fast, and turning toward the world of men.

Arthur's interest sparks again, however, when Merlin speaks of the strange arts, the first of which is harnessing the power of the lodestone to turn base metal into gold.

"I shall need to know how to do this when I am king," he tells Merlin.

I'm about to remonstrate but Merlin's laughter and upraised hand forestalls me. Instead, I glare at Arthur, and he scowls back at me. Merlin doesn't notice; he's busy assembling what he needs for the demonstration. But he doesn't show us how to accomplish this transmutation.

"I want you to try, Morgana," he tells me. "If anyone can succeed, you can."

At once, Arthur pushes in front of me to stand at the table. Merlin draws him back.

"Let Morgana do it," he says, and begins to recite instructions from an old book that he sometimes uses, while I try to follow them. To my chagrin, I fail to achieve the desired result: the base metal stays as it always was.

"It's not working!" I turn to Merlin in frustration. Arthur sniggers. Merlin comes closer to inspect my efforts.

"To some, those who value riches above all else, this knowledge is the Grail," he says. "I wanted you to try, Morgana, so that you would know it cannot be done. Nor is it possible to find the elixir of everlasting life, which is another Grail that others may seek." He gives a sudden wild cackle of laughter. "Some people search all their lives for this Grail, the Sangreal they call it. But none has ever found it, and they still die when their time has been spent. No one has ever managed to turn base metal into gold, or create such an elixir."

"Not even you, Merlin?" I am sure he must have succeeded, for he is so ancient! A hundred summers at least, or even older. But Merlin merely smiles and taps the side of his nose.

At our next lesson, and because Merlin deems me old enough to understand, he begins to introduce me to Otherworlds beyond my imagining. Arthur tries to come too, but he has trouble moving into the unknown, fetching up short each time, as if an invisible wall has stopped him.

"Can't we just leave him behind?" I ask impatiently, but Merlin says, "It might be helpful if he can see what you can see, so that in time he will learn everything you know." His words send a frisson of foreboding down my spine, but he looks so stern that I am afraid to argue.

But finally, even Merlin is forced to accept defeat and so we go adventuring together without Arthur.

I like the first Otherworld we visit best of all: there I meet magical and mythical beasts like fierce gryphons, airy phoenixes, winged wyverns and fire-breathing dragons. I make the most of the time I spend with these strange and wonderful creatures. I look into their minds and hearts, I learn how to communicate with them, and I interrogate Merlin about their habitat, their natures and their magical qualities.

A silvery white unicorn becomes my special favorite, for he allows me to ride on his back. Aleph is faster than any of the horses in our own stable so that once we are in motion it feels almost as if we are flying. When I ask him if unicorns can fly, his long lips curl into a smile but he does not reply. Nevertheless, I live in hope that one day we might fly together. I feel sure that all the worlds as we know them would then be revealed on our travels.

I found the castle in uproar when I returned after our first visit to that Otherworld— everyone had been out searching for me. Although we were only with the magical creatures for a little while, some days had passed in real time and I was missed. Arthur, the little sneak, had even broken our pact and told our mother that I was with Merlin. Fortunately, no one believed him.

Still, I had to come up with a quick explanation. I remembered Arthur's wet nurse, of whom I was fond but who had been dismissed once Arthur no longer needed to suckle at her breast. She lived in a village some distance from ours and so I told everyone that I'd gone to visit her, at the same time making a pretty apology for not warning everyone that I would be away for some time.

Now, I always find some excuse for my absence before Merlin and I go adventuring to Otherworlds, for I am never quite sure how much time will pass in our own world while I am away. Nor am I ever sure whether the Otherworlds I explore with Merlin are back in time from ours, or in the future, although some of them seem very similar. For example, there is a world where Druids still hold power over the realm, although their world looks much like our own. But their ways are different from ours and, as always, I learn what I can from them, along with whatever Merlin can tell me.

There is also the magical Isle of Avalon, the Isle of Apples, a place of great power and mystery, situated as it is at a confluence of several overlapping Otherworlds. Merlin had told me about it—and about the priestess Viviane who rules over it—and finally I saw it for myself. A tor towers over the isle, but this tor also forms part of an Otherworld called Glastonbury, where a great abbey is located.

There are no tribes in Glastonbury; the country is united and is ruled over by a king. But even the king pays heed to the priests of the man they call Jesus Christ. We know about him in our own world, and our priests conduct Christian ceremonies, but Merlin tells me that Christian churches are far more widespread here. This Glastonbury cathedral is also much taller and far larger than any abbey I have ever seen, with soaring stone arches supporting the walls, and beautifully carved statues to decorate it inside. There are even precious colored-glass pictures in some of the windows. The ceremonies are elaborate and mysterious. I suspect this world is more advanced than ours, even though the inhabitants appear to have no knowledge whatsoever of magic. But it is impossible to say, for their calculation of time is different from our own, and so all I can do is look, and marvel, and learn what I may.

On one occasion in this Otherworld I manage to escape Merlin and I run off on my own to explore the marketplace. A jongleur stands beside a cross at the center with a crowd around him. He is holding everyone spellbound with his recital. Curious, I come closer to listen, for we also have jongleurs and entertainers in our world and I am always eager to hear their stories.

It is a pleasing tale of knights and their ladies at a court called Camelot, and of the knights' adventures against dragons and Otherworldly beasts. I wonder if the jongleur has also visited Otherworlds or whether this is a fancy of his own invention, and I question him afterward.

"Have you ever seen these dragons and unicorns of which you speak?"

He looks puzzled. "No, my lady. Everyone knows such fabulous beasts exist only in legend."

"And where is this Camelot with its knights and its courtly adventures? Is it real and of this world, or is it also a legend?"

The jongleur looks at me for a long moment. "I believe that is something you need to find out for yourself, my lady." He bows, and turns to talk to someone else.

I am torn between wanting to stay and question him further, or returning to the abbey, where I left Merlin looking over an old manuscript in the great library. Finally, I decide it would be best not to risk incurring Merlin's wrath, and so I reluctantly leave the marketplace.

To my relief, Merlin hasn't missed me. Indeed, he continues to praise my efforts to please him. I take comfort from this for, when he is not in Merlin's presence, Arthur continues to taunt me about being a girl, which he insists makes me unfit to rule a kingdom. I realize ambition has awakened in him, but he is clever enough not to plague me in front of Merlin. Instead, he spends all his free time at the archery butt and the tilting yard, learning how to become a warrior, and he boasts of his growing prowess. I ignore him, content in the knowledge that I have Merlin's support, and that my intelligence coupled with my ability in the magical arts will prove far more important for the safety and future of our kingdom.

I can feel my power growing as I learn all manner of spells: to transform, to bind and to release. The only spells Merlin cannot teach me are the spells I want most: to travel back in time to wreak revenge on my enemies, and to have the power of life—and death—over them. I have one particular enemy in mind, and I hate him with a great passion, a hatred that grows stronger as I grow older. My relationship with my mother has descended into indifference but toward my stepfather I am openly hostile. I provoke and defy him at every opportunity, despite Merlin's command that I must rise above my petty grievances and make peace with my family. Somehow, being with Uther brings out the worst of my temper, always.

The best times are when Uther goes off hunting, or parleying, or else takes to his bed, for there is some unknown malady that keeps striking him down. If I had the skill, I would ensure that the malady became terminal. As it is, there seems little I can do to defeat my most hated enemy, but that doesn't stop me searching for the means to bring about his downfall.

*

After long months of winter, a hunt is planned. I beg my mother to allow me to accompany the men, for I am almost losing my wits being shut indoors with the ladies, being made to spin, stitch and weave, and other such womanly things. But my mother forbids me to go.

"Why? I've always gone hunting with the men in the past. Why do you prevent me from doing so now?" I am close to tears; I am desperate to be free.

"You are sixteen summers grown, Morgana; old enough indeed to be a wife and a mother. It is not seemly for you to ride out with the men."

Beside her, Uther nods in agreement. My hands curl into fists.

"It is time we found you a husband worthy of your position, but there is still much for you to learn before you can become a wife," my mother continues.

"My father said I should choose my own husband—when I inherit his realm."

Uther looks as if he is about to speak, but my mother quickly shakes her head.

"I've already learned all the skills needed to run a household," Morgause says, looking smug. She sits on a stool close to our mother, her usual position as our mother's favorite.

"Morgana could learn a great many things from you, Morgause."

I make a rude noise in the back of my throat. I would rather visit the Isle of the Dead than take instruction from my sister!

"I *will* go!" I say loudly. I can tell from Arthur's expression that he longs to come too. "I can take Arthur with me. He's old enough now to go hunting."

"No! Neither of you is to go." Our mother sends a glance of appeal in Uther's direction. He is reclining along the seat beside her. Although he is still recovering from his latest bout of sickness, he has announced that he will lead the hunt come morning.

"You'll do as your mother says," he growls.

"I won't be confined indoors with the women," I shout. "I will not!"

"Then I shall lock you away, for you will not come with us," he says.

Furious at being shamed by him in front of my mother's ladies, I turn on him. "I hate you! I wish you were dead!"

"Morgana!"

My mother's appalled whisper is drowned in a roar of rage from Uther. "You are a rude and undisciplined young woman, Morgana. It's time you learned how to behave as befits your position in this household. And I shall make it my duty to teach you. By soft words, if that is possible, but by the whip if it is not."

"I'll never bow down to you. Never! I'd rather leave this court than let you rule my life." Even as I say the words, I know it's a vain threat, for I would never turn my back on my realm and my people. But Uther pounces on the idea as a cat pounces on a mouse.

"I wish by all the saints you'd do exactly that!" He sounds angrier than I've ever heard him. "God knows, our lives would be so much easier without having to listen to your waspish tongue and put up with your disobedience. In fact, we'd have been spared a lot of trouble and heartache if you'd never been born at all."

Aghast, I look to my mother for support. But she stays silent, and reaches to stroke the hair from Uther's forehead.

"Your mother is right; it is time you were wed," Uther continues. "One of my subjects will do—someone old enough to keep you under control and who lives far enough away from here that we'll no longer be plagued by your tantrums."

"No!" It is a cry from the depths of my heart, but my mother nods her agreement.

"It will be for the best, Morgana. It is your duty to your family to marry well and become a good wife and mother."

"It is not my duty to marry and breed! My duty is to inherit this kingdom, as my father promised me, and to rule it wisely and well. I swore an oath than I would do as he asked, and that I would honor his faith in me. I will *not* betray his trust."

Arthur has been sitting quietly beside Uther, but now he stands to confront me. "Our father is dead, and Lord Uther has taken his place. He is the High King of Britain, and you must do as he says."

I am so angry, and so hurt by Arthur's callous disregard for my rights, that I cannot speak. Instead, I raise my hand to slap him hard. But he catches my wrist, and holds my hand steady. I realize that his time practicing at the tilting yard has been well spent, and that his strength is equal to mine. We stare at each other for a long, heartbreaking moment.

"Go to your bedchamber," Uther commands. "You will stay there until you have learned obedience."

"I won't go! You cannot banish me as if I was still a small child."

"You will go. And you will be locked in until I give you leave to rejoin us. I hope that by then you will have remembered your manners and that you will at last behave in a way befitting the daughter of a High King."

I begin to shake with fury; the words pour out of my mouth in a flood of hate. "I am no daughter of yours, Uther Pendragon. Nor are you the rightful king, not of this realm! My father would never have treated me as you have done, nor talked to me as if I was some common kitchen maid. He loved me! And I would have done anything for him. Anything at all. But not for you, Uther. Never for you. I swear on my mother's life that I'll—" But my threat is cut short as, at a nod from Uther, I am seized by two of his men and dragged from the solar.

Their grip is painful on my arms, but I will not cry mercy. Instead I maintain a dignified silence, even when they push me through the open door to my bedchamber, sending me sprawling. I pick myself up, stalk to the door and slam it in their faces. I am seething with rage—and something akin to panic.

As I pace restlessly around my room, thinking through what has just happened, I come to some painful realizations. Arthur's betrayal is one. How greatly I once loved him—and how I fear him now. Ambition has wakened in him. If he can, I know that he will grab the crown that is rightfully mine, and Uther will support him. My mother, too, has turned against me. By not speaking out on my behalf, she has forfeited any last shreds of my love and good will. My heart is full of vengeance against them all, but most particularly against Uther. All my hopes and my dreams now count for naught, for he has made it clear he has no intention of honoring my father's wishes. He has full power to direct my future, and I fear what he has in mind.

I fall onto my bed and pound my feather pillow in utter despair. I cannot allow this to happen. I swore an oath to my father. Somehow I must find a way to fulfill my destiny.

The thought comes to me: What about Merlin? Can I ask for his help? I stop punishing my pillow and roll over onto my back to ponder the question. It has been some time since we last met; he has been rather evasive of late. But he, too, has promised me a golden future. Would he support me in my bid to stop Uther arranging my marriage and exile from the land that is rightfully mine?

On further reflection, I shake my head. Even if Merlin had the courage to speak out on my behalf, he is not accepted at court. Uther would pay no attention to anything he might have to say.

Magic, then? I sit up, and consider it. Persuasion won't change Uther's mind, I know that full well. Can I convince Merlin to help me devise a spell?

I shake my head. He has lectured me on the need to use magic wisely and only when necessary. I believe that the time is now, but Merlin might not agree.

I stand up and begin to pace once more. I know Uther will waste no time in getting rid of me by any means at his disposal—so perhaps I should get rid of him first? I stop abruptly, and a smile spreads across my face as I wonder how I might use my magic to achieve this without any blame being laid at my door.

The long hours of darkness drag on, but by the time the stars fade into the light of early dawn I have still not come up with a plan that will best suit my purpose.

As soon as the hunting party is assembled in the courtyard, I transform myself into a swallow just like the one nesting on the roof outside my window. Once free from my prison I begin to follow the hunt, flying high above the men on their horses, feeling a savage delight that I have managed to defy my stepfather. Yet I am also puzzled. Even though the hounds are in hot pursuit of a fox, the men following Uther seem to be dressed more for a battle than for a hunt. And there are so many of them, far more than would normally be invited on a hunting expedition. Not only that, they carry all the appurtenances of battle, most of them with shields, swords and lances along with their bows and quivers full of arrows. It's as if they are expecting to meet trouble along the way.

I fly on, determined not to concern myself with minor details. My mind is wholly bent on how to get the better of Uther, although I am still debating ways to achieve my aim. Can I perhaps turn myself into a fox to put the hounds off the scent and lead the huntsmen astray? But I am afraid of being chased and possibly caught. In my imagination I feel sharp teeth shredding my flesh to bloody scraps. I wince, knowing that I can't risk it. But how else can I spite Uther, who is leading the charge? Can I become a gryphon, or a dragon perhaps, something to frighten his horse enough that he'll be thrown and maybe injure himself, or even die? Or what if I change myself into something fiercesome enough to eat him? The idea is tempting, but I am afraid I might not have the power or skill—or even the will—to carry it through. Another thought stops me: If I try to assume the guise of a creature from an Otherworld, might those real creatures attack and punish me for bringing their guise out of safety? Could I try to summon them here to my cause? But I have not attempted this before, and I am not sure they would come at my bidding. A further thought makes me hesitate: even a gryphon or a dragon can be captured and slaughtered by my stepfather and his men. It is too great a risk. Depositing a dropping on Uther from on high would be safe. But that's a child's trick, and I am no longer a child. Besides, it is not serious enough to punish him for his treatment of me, nor will it change his mind about ordering my future.

An idea stirs in my mind. As I think it through, I like it more and more. Excited now, I fly ahead of the hunt into the heart of the forest, looking for an open space where I can shape-shift into something else.

I alight on the ground and become myself once more, but only momentarily. Calling on all my powers, I quickly transform into an enormous oak tree. I tremble with fear and excitement as I listen to the sounds of the hunt drawing near. I close my mind off to everything but the fox, and I sing it toward me. Even through its panic it responds, fleeing straight to the shelter of the mighty tree, desperate to escape. The hounds chase after it, closing in on their prey. Uther leads the charge in their wake. But then I hear a murmuring behind me, the soft footfalls of men and horses, a clink and a chink as if swords are being unsheathed.

I cannot allow myself to be distracted, not with my quarry coming so close. I steady my gaze on Uther, who is still charging toward me. I wait, readying one of the tree's many limbs in preparation. I've already chosen the branch that will become my instrument of justice, and have asked the tree I have become if I may make the sacrifice without harm to my mortal self. I've never attempted such a thing before but I take comfort from the fact that if I succeed, no blame can ever be laid at my door. *Stay steady, stay in control*, I warn myself. *Do not act too soon, or too late. The wrong timing will wreck everything.*

I hold the heavy branch strong and steady in my mind, ready to let it fall on Uther as he passes by in the hope that it will smash him into the earth. The fox races past my tree with the hounds in pursuit, but Uther abruptly checks his mount and holds up his hand in warning. The huntsmen abandon the chase and circle around Uther, lifting their swords and shields in readiness. Uther's steed paws the ground uneasily. I will Uther to come closer, but instead he begins to organize his men into formation, using hand movements to indicate silence.

I remember the muted sounds behind me, and suddenly realize what is really happening. Uther must have had warning of a raiding party and, under guise of a hunt, has prepared his men for battle. No wonder I wasn't allowed to accompany them! I keep as still as I can, hoping that no one will pay any attention to me or understand that the tree close to them is not all it seems. But my leaves rustle as I quiver with the knowledge that the enemy is already near.

Uther and his men are armed and ready, and they wait in silence. They've forgotten all about the fox for they have a new prey now, one that is far more deadly. The marauders charge from their hiding place in the forest and rush upon the waiting soldiers with a ululating battle cry loud enough to freeze the blood and turn strong men into mewling infants. But Uther's warriors stand fast, meeting steel with steel and blow with blow. The earth reddens with the blood of the wounded and dying; the air resounds with their screams. Thuds and buffets, the clash and clang of weapons, grunts and shouts and curses as the men fight; the fierce battle rages around me, while I hold my breath and keep still. I am frightened to move so much as a leaf in case the tree suffers damage that might have unforeseen repercussions on my own body. Uther's men—some of them my own father's warriors—are as brave as lions and strong as bulls. Slowly, inexorably, they cut their way through the raiding party, decimating their ranks. Accepting defeat but not capture, the marauders turn and flee.

With the enemy on the run, Uther's men pause to regroup and catch their breath. But I notice an armed invader wheel around and turn back. It seems to me he is a harbinger of doom, and I am suddenly filled with anxiety. I try to shout a warning, but manage only a leafy rustle. Uther can't see him. He is facing his men, and their eyes are on him as he congratulates them on their prowess. Their cheering covers the sound of the approaching rider who, with dagger drawn, leans sideways out of the saddle and stabs Uther in the back. Struck dumb with horror, Uther's men are too slow to stop the assassin from regaining his seat and racing off to rejoin his brothers-in-arms. When Uther's men finally come to their senses, they set off after him with a roar, leaving their king alone to die.

Too afraid to show myself, to intervene or help, I watch as the terrified horse wheels and stamps and does its best to shake off its burden. Uther topples out of the saddle, but his heel catches in the stirrups and his head hits the ground. He makes a feeble gesture, trying to free his foot perhaps, or calm his mount. But the steed continues to buck and kick until finally it is free. At once it takes off at a gallop, while Uther lies in a pool of his own blood and breathes his last.

I look down on him, my mind churning in a giddy whirl of elation mingled with regret—and fear. My wish has been granted, but did I really want Uther to die or did I just want to change his mind and at the same time teach him a lesson about power? Now that he is dead, I find it hard to believe that I ever wished him quite so ill.

The soldier huntsmen return. While I'm quite sure that Uther is dead, one of the men confirms it after feeling his chest for signs of a heartbeat and listening for a breath. He breaks the sad tidings to the assembled company, and I watch as a litter is quickly improvised and the bloody body of my stepfather is laid upon it.

I'd thought to feel triumph as the cortege moves away, accompanied by the lamentations of Uther's companions. Instead, my fear grows as the implications of his death become clearer. It is only chance that the king's blood is not on my hands but, even if I'm not responsible, the end result is the same: the kingdom has been left without protection.

I shiver at the thought of what Merlin would say if he ever found out what I intended. With an effort, I calm my trembling leaves and make a solemn vow to myself that he will never, ever find out the part I almost played in Uther's death.

And yet with Uther dead, and my mother no doubt prostrated with grief, my future is no longer in doubt, for surely Merlin will agree that it is time for me to seize my birthright and rule over south Britain? If I am wise and strong enough to fulfill our dreams for the future, I shall then go on and bring all the realms of Britain beneath my sovereignty, and so make our nation great. My spirits rise in wild elation as I realize that this dream is now almost within my grasp. I feel a surge of power; I am desperate to be gone. But I know that I must stay until the last straggler has left the scene. I need to be sure there is no one around to spy on me, in case the observer understands what's happening when I transform myself first into Morgana and then into a swallow to fly back to my bed. I can only hope I have not been missed. Once I have been freed from my prison, I shall profess myself ignorant of all that has befallen the unlucky Uther. I shall join my mother, and all the others in the castle, and I shall pretend to mourn him.

Conscious of time passing, and fearful that, even now, someone might be unlocking the door of my bedchamber to find me gone, I finally transform myself and quickly check for signs of damage. To my relief, there are none. I am about to become a swallow once more when a large eagle alights on the ground nearby. As I pause to rethink my strategy, for a swallow would be no match for an eagle, a well-known voice drives all thought from my mind and shrivels my heart with fear. The eagle has resumed its human form.

"That was ill-done, Morgana."

I tremble as I stand before Merlin. He seems taller somehow, powerful and terrible in his wrath as he glares down at me.

"You stupid, stupid girl," he says softly. "You could have inherited a great kingdom but, by your own willfulness and vengeful thoughts, you have squandered your birthright."

"But I was just watching. I didn't do anything!" I'm hoping to bluff my way out of this, but I quickly realize that Merlin can see right through me and that he knows everything.

"Even though it was not your hand that struck Uther down, the intention was there. You would have killed Uther without thought for a kingdom left unprotected at a time of great peril, all to satisfy your own desire for revenge. And at such a cost! You have known only peace and plenty in your life. Did you ever pause to think how we shall fare if the invaders defeat us? They will swarm over our lands, stripping us of our wealth, our possessions, our crops and animals, our homes and our livelihood. And do you know the price they will exact in order to keep themselves safe? They'll kill our men—and our children. And they'll seize our women—yes, even you, Morgana, especially you—for their own pleasure. Our kingdom will become theirs, at the price of our blood and our liberty.

"And now the death of our king has left us vulnerable to these predators; it has extended an invitation for them to invade us without delay. Our way of life will come to an end, unless we fight for it. You would have extended that invitation on your own account even without that marauding party today. For shame that you have so little regard for human life, Morgana! For shame that you have so little regard for your family, for your people and for your kingdom!"

"I'm glad he's dead," I mutter, stung by Merlin's criticism and anxious to defend myself. "He was going to go against my father's wishes, and stop me inheriting my birthright. Worse, he threated to marry me off to one of his old retainers. He said that he'd make sure it was someone who lived far away so I ... so ..." I take a deep, shuddering breath. I will not let Merlin see me cry. "He's dead—and I'm not sorry!"

"You should be," Merlin says sternly. "Being a ruler is not only about being strong and having a knowledge of magic.

It's also about diplomacy, the art of negotiation and the gift of persuading others to see your way. Above all, it is about having a clear vision for the future of this country, and the courage and determination to bring it to fruition."

I know I am in the wrong, and I hate that I've been caught out. I can think of only one way to redeem myself. "I can change the future if only I can change the past. Teach me how to cross time, Merlin, and Uther will live to fight on against the invaders." Even through my distress I am angry that the mage seems to hold me responsible for what he has foreseen after Uther's death.

Merlin shakes his head. "You can change nothing," he says, "for our time is now and what's done is done. I cannot move backward or forward through time—and neither can you, Morgana, for all you might think that trying will make it so."

"Then continue to instruct me so that I can learn wisdom enough to save us all." I can't help feeling impatient with the old man. Uther is dead. Surely the future is all that matters now? "I swear I'll be a good leader, Merlin. I swear I'll do all in my power to repel the invaders and make our kingdom strong."

Merlin looks at me with a strong and steady gaze. But his eyes are hard as flint. "No," he says softly. "You are too wayward, too unreliable. I have long suspected it, but I hoped that under my tuition you would learn to let your mind guide your heart rather than the other way 'round. Your deed this day has proved my error in believing that change is possible." He shakes his head, staring past me into the distance, seeing something there that seems to give him comfort, for his expression softens into almost a smile. "But perhaps it's not too late after all. There is one other ..."

I am filled with dread. "Who?" I ask, although I already know the answer.

Merlin folds his arms and presses his lips together.

"You can't mean Arthur!" I shout. But Merlin won't look at me.

"You can't choose him over me!" I am panicking now; I am determined to change Merlin's mind. "Arthur's too young. He's not ready; he'll never be ready. He doesn't understand magic. He can't do half the things that I can."

"I have enough magic for both of us."

"But he's slow. How can he rule a kingdom when he takes forever to make up his mind about something, anything at all, let alone something really important?"

"He's slow because he looks at every angle of a question, he doesn't just follow his heart or act on impulse, as you do. He's steady. Reliable. He may be young, but he is high born and he has the good of our nation at heart. He is also fast acquiring knowledge of the art of war that will help to keep us safe. He has a sense of duty and of justice that seems to be lacking in you, Morgana. He will listen before he speaks and think before he acts."

"But he's not the rightful heir. I am, by the will of my father, and by your will too, for why else would you have schooled me so diligently in magic and in the ways of the world?" I will not let my little brother usurp my position without a fight.

Merlin shakes his head. His next words pierce my heart with an arrow's deadly sting.

"Perhaps this day was destined all along, to show me my error in trusting you, for 'tis true the brilliance of your fool's gold has blinded me to the true worth of the gold that might yet save our kingdom." His eyes lose focus as he stares past me. "Perhaps this is why Uther begged me to change him into the likeness of Gorlois while your father was away waging war against the High King's men?" he mutters. "I should have realized earlier that it wasn't only because he wanted to lie with Igraine and slake his lust. It was so they could make a child together, a child destined to be the one true ruler of all Britain."

"No!" I clap my hands over my ears so that I will not have to hear any more. The world stands still as Merlin's words echo through my mind. "You tricked my mother into lying with Uther so that Arthur could be born to take my place?" I back away from him in my terror. I can hardly speak for the pain of Merlin's betrayal. "Did you also ensure that my father would be killed in battle so my mother could marry the High King, and make Arthur their legitimate heir?" Having trusted Merlin in everything it is hard to believe that he could have acted against me, and against my father, with such treachery.

The mage stays silent, and I understand why. I am filled with rage, and a pain so vast that everything around me turns black with my anger and despair.

"I'll pay you back for this, Merlin, I swear it. Even if it takes forever, I'll make you regret what you've done!" My throat scrapes raw as I scream my threat aloud.

But Merlin is not here to hear it. He has disappeared. And I am left alone.

CHAPTER 2

As I'd feared, my absence from the castle was noted, although the rumpus following the news of Uther's death meant that I was not reprimanded for it—at least, not at first. Finally, my mother sends for me. As soon as I appear, she begins to berate me for my insolence; worse, she tells me that she intends to fulfill Uther's wish that Arthur inherit the crown, and that I must marry and go to live far away.

At that, my bitterness spills over. "Arthur is a bastard. He was conceived by trickery and out of wedlock. He has no right to my realm!"

"What?" My mother puts her hands to her ears in a vain effort to block what she is hearing. But I've given Merlin's words some thought and I know that what I am saying is true.

I raise my voice. "Merlin told me. He said that he'd changed Uther into the likeness of my father because Uther lusted after you, and wished to lie with you. Did you never wonder how it was that on the last night of my father's life, while you lay with him, he was also killed waging war against Uther's men?"

"No!" she whispers. "No, that's not how it was. He was killed after he'd been with me." Her face has gone deathly pale. I wonder if all along she might have suspected the truth. After all, she must have noticed some differences between husband and usurper in the intimacy of the marital bed. But if so, she is not prepared to admit it.

"Get out of my sight," she hisses. "I will not hear these lies."

I do not see her again after that, for she breaks down in a storm of weeping, and thereafter keeps to her bed with only her ladies in attendance. Everyone thinks she is distraught over Uther's death—only I suspect the true cause of her distress.

I had hoped, after the care and affection I had bestowed on Arthur, that love and loyalty might prompt him to acknowledge my right to inherit the realm of my father even if not the whole of Britain. I should have known that his ambition, once awakened, would grow to a sense of entitlement, and so it has.

I am present, though concealed, when he meets with Merlin in the forest, and Merlin tells him of his destiny. I witness his joy and, for one fleeting moment, his absolute triumph that I have been put aside and that he has won the crown, before he composes his face into due solemnity as befits the occasion.

"I always told Morgana she couldn't be a queen and rule a kingdom, but she wouldn't listen to me," he says proudly.

"It is up to you to convince her that you are a worthy choice, even if you are still but a child," the old man mutters. I wonder if he is having second thoughts, for he seems a little shamefaced about it all.

"She will soon find out that I am more than her equal," Arthur boasts.

"Do not underestimate her, Arthur. She may be proud, and she may lack judgment, but she is also talented and very clever. If you can win her goodwill, she may help you rule the kingdom wisely and well, at least until you are old enough to rule alone."

Arthur's happy countenance becomes a scowl. "I have you to help me, Merlin. I shan't need Morgana."

"She can help you when I am not here."

"No." Arthur lifts his chin in defiance. "She's always telling me what to do and ordering me about. I won't have it. This kingdom was my father's, and now it is mine. And I will make of it what I must, without Morgana's help."

Merlin looks at him and shakes his head. I know then that my fate is sealed. He hasn't told Arthur why he's changed his mind about me; perhaps he knows that I'm hiding close by, and is trying to spare my feelings. Nevertheless I stay hidden for a long time after they leave the forest, trying to find consolation for all that I have lost; seeking comfort for my raging, grieving heart.

In the days that follow, I realize that for Merlin it's as if I no longer exist. And for me, it feels as though I have lost another father as well as the kingdom.

*

Merlin may have decided my fate, but it soon becomes clear that everyone at court still believes that I am my father's heir and I do my utmost to foster that belief. Arthur, of course, is furious that no one will take him seriously, and Merlin finally resorts to trickery in order to persuade them all. One morning, a sword appears in the castle courtyard. It's thrust into a huge rock up to its hilt, and it quickly becomes apparent that none of Uther's men is able to draw it out. Even I, using all my power and all the magic I have learned from Merlin, am unable to shift it by as much as a hair's breadth. Not that I let Merlin see me try! I go in secret, at night, and I twist and tug until my hands are bruised and bleeding, but Merlin's magic ensures that the sword won't budge.

As word of the sword spreads, it becomes quite a competition. Barons and kings begin to flock from all parts of Britain to try to retrieve it, for it is a handsome weapon. The fact that it's embedded in stone speaks of its magical qualities, while its hilt, which is set with precious jewels, is sufficient to grace any nobleman's armaments and promises a potential fortune for any landless knight. It is indeed a possession to be coveted, but all who come fail in their attempt to release it from its sheath of stone.

With my mother still in seclusion, it falls to me to receive them graciously and play the hostess. And of course I try to deflect them from the sword even while I ponder its purpose. I preside at high table, and arrange feasts and amusements for their entertainment, although my efforts are undercut by Arthur, who struts around demanding their attention.

Once there are enough important noblemen at court, Merlin sends out word of a tournament, with a huge prize to be won at the end of it. I suspect that the prize is only an incentive to keep the noblemen in attendance and that Merlin has more than a tournament in mind. Although I've had no dealings with the mage since the day he turned away from me and set his course with Arthur, I know him well and I fear his cunning.

I realize that the game is in play when Merlin comes to court and, for the first time, appears in public at Arthur's side. He announces that the sword embedded in the stone is a test, and that only the true-born High King of all Britain will succeed in pulling it free. Of course this is a signal for knights and kings alike to redouble their efforts, all without success. The tournament, so Merlin says, will settle the question once and for all.

To my amazement (and Arthur's disgust) he is deemed not old enough to take part in the tournament. Instead, he is assigned to his friend Sir Kay as his squire, and so it becomes Arthur's responsibility to arm him. But Kay's sword inexplicably goes missing, and it doesn't take me long to understand why when—in front of several noblemen and to their great surprise—Arthur pulls the magical sword out of the stone and hands it over to his friend to use.

I have to admit it's a good trick; I admire it although I hate what happens next, as all those present, prompted by Merlin, fall to their knees and proclaim Arthur the High King of all Britain.

News of this miracle spreads. The tournament comes to an abrupt halt as everyone rushes to the stone to witness it for themselves. Time and again Arthur is asked to replace the sword and pull it out. Some of the barons, and several of the attendant kings, ask him to replace the sword so that they themselves can have another try at freeing it. None succeeds, save Arthur. Finally, there is a great commotion as they all assemble to kneel before him and swear an oath of fealty.

But for all that, I hear some muttering among them later. Not all are happy about having a mere boy as their ruler. And I play a part in their doubting. After Arthur's triumph, I leave the court. I travel east across the southern country, reminding kings and barons that I am my father's rightful heir by birth and training. And I ask for their support against Arthur, the usurper. While in their courts and households I discuss with them the vulnerability of the kingdom caused by the death of Uther, and the dangers of installing a young and untried boy as king. We discuss battle strategy, and the overriding need for unity to combat the threat of the growing numbers of raiding parties landing on our shores. I do my best to bind the men to my cause.

At the same time, I use my knowledge to help the women of the court with healing, and birthing, and any other domestic tasks I am called on to perform, for I believe women wield a greater influence than is generally acknowledged. Although I'm usually received with suspicion at first, by the time I leave each demesne I know that the inhabitants, both high and low born, are coming around to my way of thinking.

All is going well, and I am garnering support, until Arthur realizes what I am doing. I am staying with Bagdemagus, King of Gore, when Arthur sends a company of guards to bring me back to the castle. Although I appeal to Bagdemagus, and he is sympathetic to my cause, in the end he will not gainsay Arthur's command and so I am forced to return, in ignominy and as a captive, to Tintagel.

When I am brought before my brother, I find Merlin standing beside him. I face them both and my anger spills over.

"How dare you arrest me and drag me back here like a common criminal!"

Arthur takes a step backward, seemingly unnerved by my fury. I am tempted to try to transform him into the mouse he once wanted to be, but a glance at Merlin changes my mind. I glare at him before turning my attention back to Arthur.

"Not content with usurping my kingdom, you now treat me like the lowliest and least worthy of your subjects."

Perhaps taking comfort from Merlin's proximity, Arthur draws a breath and puffs out his chest. "*My* kingdom, Morgana. Mine, despite what you've been telling my people as you've travelled around spreading your poison. If you were anyone else, I would have you tried for treason and locked away—or even beheaded. As you are my half-sister, I shall forgive you this once. You may continue to live here quietly in my castle where I can keep watch over you. But have no doubt about what will happen to you should you try, in any way, to undermine my right to rule my kingdom at any time in the future. Death will be your fate, for the safety and the unity of my kingdom are paramount." He glances at Merlin, as if seeking his approval. The mage nods slightly, and Arthur smiles.

I am speechless with rage, and with pain. If I were a man, I would challenge Arthur to a duel. My fists clench in impotent fury. Merlin frowns a warning: *Say nothing, and accept your fate.* But I will not—not ever! Nevertheless, I bow in obeisance to my brother before leaving the room. I may be beaten—for the moment—but I will wait, and I will watch, and eventually, I will reclaim my kingdom. I intend to fulfill my promise to my father; I intend also to have my revenge on all who have betrayed me.

To ensure my obedience, Arthur sends heralds around the southern country to announce that Merlin is his adviser now, and to quote the mage's prophecy: Only he, Arthur, has the power to keep the kingdom safe, and once the invaders are routed, he will found a new kingdom more bright and glorious than any that has come before. At the same time as praising Arthur the heralds belittle me, pointing out that I, as a mere woman, have not the wits, courage, strength or skill to rule, or to protect the kingdom against the raiding parties that continue to beset us. People believe what they are told, and they all turn against me.

My heart hardens with hatred even while I am forced to admit that, if our roles had been reversed, I might well have done exactly as Arthur has. Nevertheless, his treatment of me is a grievous hurt considering how close we once were, and how I loved, sheltered and protected him when he was a child. I am furious at being thwarted in this way; I am full of bitterness and resentment. I cannot forgive Merlin for his betrayal of all I hold dear, nor can I forgive Arthur for so willingly stepping into my place, usurping my position and my heritage, and denigrating me in the eyes of all those who once looked up to me. I shall never forget their treachery. And I vow to myself that I will never trust anyone ever again.

While Arthur becomes the acclaimed lord and king of the southern country, Merlin becomes his puppet master. The pity is that no one else can see what's really going on. Merlin is too clever for them while I, who was once schooled by him and can see behind his tricks and spells, have been cast aside—by Merlin, by my once-beloved brother, by my mother, and also by my stupid sister. Morgause is no longer at court, having wed Lot of Lothian and gone off to the north, where she's given birth to her first child and is expecting another. My mother has also departed; she has taken refuge with the nuns at far away Amesbury Abbey. Apparently she professes great piety although her prayers would choke in her throat if there was any justice in this world or the next.

I am left alone at court, carefully guarded and watched by Arthur and his men lest I continue my campaign to destabilize his rule. Mostly, the courtiers ignore me, being more concerned with demonstrating their loyalty to Arthur than showing friendship to me. It is a sad and lonely time, but the flame of my anger keeps me warm, and vigilant. Although I know I could become a bird and fly to freedom if I chose to do so, I am not sure where to go, for this is the only home I know and it is mine by right. Of course I could marry someone, as Arthur has pressed me to do on more than one occasion. But while marriage would give me a home, it would also signal the end of my dreams for the future. And so I conduct myself with decorum while I wait, although I sometimes fly about the castle in the guise of a swallow, to garner information and keep an eye on what is going on.

Finally, an opportunity arises for me to take action: Arthur announces the date of his coronation. "Of course you'll come, Morgana, as will my mother and Morgause, but Merlin will attend me. You may sit to the side, with the women," he says. The pain is so great it is as if rats gnaw at my vitals. What hurts most is the thought that the oath I swore to my father has come to naught.

I make a silent vow that I will not go to witness his triumph, this celebration that marks the loss of my kingdom. I begin to pack up my belongings while I wait for my chance to escape. I select everything with care for I will have to carry whatever I take on a journey of many miles, for I need to disappear from Arthur's sight.

When the day that Arthur will assume my crown finally dawns, I take advantage of the flurry and bustle of preparation and unobtrusively make my way out of the castle. A shawl over my head and shoulders disguises me along with the large bag I am carrying as I hurry down to Merlin's cave by the sea. Although he now lives in the castle, I know well that he still visits his cave; I have seen him going there while I've been flying about prying into everyone's secrets. Merlin had never invited either Arthur or me to visit him there; in fact, I am sure he believes the location of his real home is a secret, for he always took care to meet us somewhere within the forest glade. But I have learned how potent knowledge can be, particularly if its source is secret or magical and I am more determined than ever to learn all that I may of our world and of the Otherworlds beyond. I know that Merlin has the tools to help me achieve my ambition, and I plan to find them.

The cave is disguised and protected by its narrow entrance, a thin crack in the rockface that is almost obscured by twining vines. Inside, the cave is large and dry, and it contains all that Merlin needs to practice his magical arts. There is a fireplace close enough to the entrance to allow smoke to escape, although no fire burns now. An iron rack is placed above it, on which stands a pot half filled with water. Merlin's bed—rough sacking stuffed with straw—is rolled up to one side. A handcarved table and a stool stand in the center, giving a limited view of the ocean beyond. The table is littered with scraps of parchment, a bowl of ink and a quill. I glance at what Merlin has been writing. It is some sort of journal, but I have not the time to look through the musings of that treacherous mage. I am more interested in a shelf that stands at the back of the cave where it is protected from wind and rain. It is made of sea-weathered wood and piled high with scrolls and several bound books. I recognize one of the books, and pick it up. It is so ancient it is falling apart, but it is full of the lore and wisdom of time long ago, when the way between the worlds was open, and all things were known. I'd seen Merlin use this book in the past for his spells and I know that much of what he taught me has its origins here. I place it in my bag, fair recompense for all that I have lost. I know that there is so much more to learn and I pray that I will find the answers I seek within it. My greatest ambition is to master moving forward or back in time: what revenge I shall take once I can do this!

The other writings hold little interest for me; I already know much of what they contain. I turn my attention to the oaken chest that squats below the shelf. It is locked, but I say the spell of undoing and raise its lid to survey the contents. As I'm going through Merlin's collection of magical paraphernalia, a small chunk of rock with purple crystals at its heart catches my eye. Amethyst; the stone of healing, the stone of meditation and psychic ability. I'm not sure of its other powers, but when I pick it up I feel its warmth. Its energy thrums through my fingers and I know that I must have it. Doubtless I shall find a use for it in time.

The third thing I take is a pack of thin wooden tablets. They are cracked and splintered with age, the illustrations etched on them smooth and in some places almost obliterated from long use. I don't know their purpose but I find them attractive, for each tablet bears a different design. Some are numbered but none are named so, although each tablet seems to carry a special meaning, I am unable to decipher what it might be. But I am sure that I shall find out, given time.

I wrap the objects carefully and stow them away in my bag. I need to hurry now, to put as many miles between me and my prison as possible. I hoist my bag onto my back and climb up from the cave to follow the track to the forest and the road beyond that will lead me east.

As I trudge the weary miles it occurs to me that I am now a fugitive. I have no home, and no friends who might shelter me. I have my father's gifts in the form of jewels, plus some coins to help fund my journey, but at present I have no food, nor anything to drink—I had not thought to bring provisions. I am quite alone in the world and I have no plans for the future other than flight. I curse myself for not having the foresight to plan my escape more carefully.

As the sun slips down the sky and the day begins to darken into night, I pass a small homestead. A horse is tethered in the field, and I hide nearby. Once the moon rises and there is enough light to see what I am doing, I draw water from the well to slake my thirst, and then mount the horse and gallop away, holding tight to its mane for there is no saddle and no bridle. I leave a silver penny beside the gatepost in payment.

During my flight I ponder where to take refuge, for I need somewhere that Arthur will never find me. After discarding several options, which include going to my sister or to my mother at Amesbury Abbey, I decide that some other abbey will do very well as a hiding place, and so I turn north in the direction of Glastonbury. I have been told that a new Christian abbey has been built there, and I'm hoping that it may be as great as the abbey I visited with Merlin in that Otherworld that so closely touches our own. It was a place of great learning and I long to see it again, but first I must learn the secrets of what I have stolen from Merlin, for without him I've been unable to visit the Otherworlds of my choice. Once I have mastered the trick, I mean to visit that great abbey, and also the Isle of Avalon, for I am sure there is far more for me to learn than only the magical arts of an aging mage.

I spend several weary days on horseback. On several occasions I need to hide after I spy Arthur's soldiers out looking for me. Finally, to aid my disguise, I ask a peasant woman to exchange her rough garb for mine, and leave with her my horse. It is easier to blend into the crowd after that, but still I make haste to reach the abbey, for I shall not feel comfortable until I am safely within its walls.

As I approach the Tor, I see the new abbey at its feet. I pause a moment to survey my new home and, for a few heartbeats, my courage fails me. How can I resign myself to a life locked away with a community of women, a life to be spent in prayer and contemplation?

My mind and my heart shriek out in denial. "This is only for a short time, just until the hunt dies down," I mutter in an effort to steady myself. I become calmer as I remember that I can also disguise myself, become anything I want and so may leave the abbey at any time I wish. Nevertheless, my heart is heavy with foreboding as I approach the abbey, and the small priory that is attached to it.

Once at the gate, I ask to speak to the prioress. The young novice eyes my rough tunic, now more ragged than ever after my long and dusty journey, and is about to refuse when I hand her a coin to change her mind. She bobs her head and opens the gate, but it takes another coin before I am admitted into the presence of the prioress.

"My name is Anna. I am from a land far away, and I am in need of sanctuary," I tell her. She surveys me thoughtfully, her gaze moving from my face to my rough peasant's tunic and on down to my hands, which bear no marks of scarring or the calluses of hard work. I hurriedly thrust them behind my back.

"Some soldiers visited the priory two days ago. They come from the court of King Arthur, and they travel in search of his sister, the Lady Morgana. I believe the king desires her presence back at Tintagel," she says.

I say nothing; the silence lengthens between us.

"They seem determined to find her," the prioress adds at last.

"Pity the lady if they do, for the palace has become her prison—or so I hear."

Another long silence ensues. Finally the prioress nods. "May I suggest, Anna, that if you do have any connection to the royal court, you keep it to yourself, both for your own safety and also because it would be best if the sisters don't hear of it lest it turn their minds from the sacred to the secular."

"Thank you." Tears spring into my eyes: from gratitude; from relief. And also from this simple act of kindness that tells me I shall be safe here. I knuckle them away, but I know she has noticed. "Thank you," I say again. I am uncertain what I should call her. Mother? Prioress? She gives me no help in the matter, but summons the almoner and instructs her to take me to the guest house.

"Yes, Prioress." The nun bobs her head in obeisance, and my question is answered.

*

The new abbey is far smaller and less decorative than the abbey I remember visiting with Merlin in the Otherworld. But it does have an impressive library, and I feel sure there will be much I can learn here. In my first few weeks, I explore the library. I also study Merlin's book, for I am determined to revisit the Otherworlds of my youth, and there I find some of the answers I seek. A plan begins to form in my mind, but first I need permission from the prioress.

"You wish to create a new garden of your own design? But why? There is already a herbarium attached to the priory."

"I have some knowledge of the healing power of plants, and I also know much of their other uses," I explain. "There is a far greater variety of plants that may be grown to provide the priory—and also the abbey—with everything we need, from medicaments to food." I cannot tell the prioress what other purpose I have in mind for the garden. I can only hope that my argument is compelling enough. "I'm prepared to choose the plants and see to their placing myself," I tell her. "And I'm prepared to pay workmen out of my own funds to till the soil and do any rough work that is needed."

Perhaps the prioress senses the urgency of my need, or perhaps she is persuaded by my argument of self-sufficiency; whatever the reason, she gives me the agreement I need, with an added boon: the promise that the lay sisters and even the nuns will help me in their spare time.

Designing and constructing the garden becomes a popular pastime at the priory. I think we all welcome the chance to be outside in the open air, creating something beautiful. Working on the garden gives me some measure of peace and a sense of self-worth, while the hard physical labor that accompanies its creation means that I fall into bed each night too tired to brood or do anything other than sleep.

I am proud of my design, which is unlike any I have seen elsewhere. The garden takes the form of an enormous wheel within a square, divided into triangular segments, each housing plants for a particular purpose. Many of the herbs and flowers I plant have more than one use, so the same plants are to be found in more than one segment, all blending into a harmonious whole. In the center of the circle I devise a flowery mead, lush grass spangled with sweet violets, primroses, cornflowers, wild strawberries, poppies and other colorful wildflowers. At its heart is a fountain, its cool splashing water providing refreshment on hot, thirsty days. There are benches of turf close by, so that the sisters may rest their weary bodies and aching feet.

Having discovered how important fruit and vegetables are in the monastic diet during the time of Lent, in the largest triangle I plant an abundance of such things as leeks and a variety of coleworts, fava beans and peas of various types; root vegetables such as onions and turnips; and savory pot herbs including rosemary, thyme and parsley.

In the physic garden segment are all the herbs I already know about, for I plan to help pay for my lodging in the priory by treating the sick and the injured with my medicaments. Time has proved that I have some talent in this, and besides, I enjoy experimenting. I know that I shall find a sense of achievement while creating my lotions and brewing my decoctions.

In another segment, I put in plants of use about the household: alecost and several other herbs for brewing and flavoring ale; dyer's bugloss, chamomile and others for dying cloth, along with pot marigold, which is also used for coloring food; there are tansy, rosemary and other pungent strewing herbs to sweeten floor rushes and repel insects; soapwort for cleansing; flax for sewing and making cloth, plus many others besides.

In the four corners left outside the circle, and for the benefit of the nuns and the prioress, I create small spaces dedicated to the Virgin Mary, for I have discovered how very important she is in their life and worship. I seek out those bushes, like May, and the flowers that once were sacred to the old gods and have been renamed and dedicated to Christ's mother, such as the Madonna lily; the blue "Eyes of Mary" that the common people call forget-me-nots; "Mary's crown" or cornflowers, representing the mantle of the Virgin's cloak; yellow mullein or "Virgin Mary's Candle'; "Our Lady's shoes" that are actually columbines; "Our Lady's gloves", or foxgloves of folklore; purple "Madonna's herb", and many others. Each private herber has a turf bench for solitary rest and quiet contemplation, and is cut off from the main garden by a sheltering screen of fragrant Gallica roses, a symbol of divine love that scent the air with their sweet perfume.

On three sides of the square surrounding the garden, I establish a range of fruit trees, apples, pears, plums and cherries, that will give the beauty of their blossom in spring, shade in summer, fruit in autumn and sunlight through their bare branches in winter. On the fourth side I plant a variety of prickly bramble bushes and canes that will yield fruit such as blackberries and raspberries but that will also act as a barrier against intruders—and aid me in my quest. Winding pathways link one garden bed to another, and these are framed with a sturdy lattice over which grow clinging vines of honeysuckle and roses or grapes, providing shade and a sweet and juicy treat in summer.

The garden takes a while to establish, but the plants grow quickly and the sisters praise my efforts. They tell me how much they enjoy visiting it, how greatly they appreciate the beautiful flowers as well as all the plants that may be put to practical use. I know they make use of the quiet herbers for rest and as a welcome relief from the relentless presence of others. In fact they're so pleased with me that they do not remark on my absence when I sometimes go missing. They cannot know that parts of the garden are hidden from their eyes. For, while I am laying out the garden, with the help of Merlin's book I am also plotting secret ways to take me to a part of it that no one else will be able to find.

The first secret way I create takes me to the ancient spring that lies beneath the fountain at the heart of my garden. It was probably once a shrine to the old gods, but when the new abbey and priory were built it was turned into a fountain; I adapted this to my design, and to my purpose. I used my wands to cast spells and now, when I walk widdershins and recite the chant that I found in Merlin's book of magic, I come to the ancient spring. I make offerings and, in reward, I sometimes catch tantalizing glimpses of the future—or perhaps it's the past—when I look into the water's rusty red depths.

Voices speak words that sometimes resemble the language of the church, but there are others that I cannot understand at all.

On one occasion I see a young woman looking back at me: mouse-brown hair and a plain, rather solemn face. I look into her greenish-gold eyes, and see a mirror reflection of myself. "Who are you?" I whisper, trying to contain my excitement for I can't help wondering if perhaps she is me, but in some Otherworld or at some time into the future.

"Morgan," she answers. "Who are you?"

"My name is Morgana."

"Morgana." The word is echoed on a sigh as the vision fades.

I do not see her again. Instead, I hear a wailing chant that is beyond any words I know. The sound of it prickles the hairs on the back of my neck. There is danger here, a form of madness. I can sense it even if I do not understand it. By keeping still and quiet, I can feel in my heart the passion behind what's being said, although there seems such a depth of hatred and rage, such a roaring and shouting, that I am shaken with terror and a deep sense of foreboding that this can only lead to the end of our world as we know it. I long to know more, and fear it too, but for full understanding I suspect I shall need patience and a great deal more time.

Perhaps this is the most important lesson I am learning during my time here in the priory. Patience, as I struggle to understand. Patience, as I try to see a way to fulfill my dreams.

My other secret way is the portal I have made in the bramble hedge that forms one side of the abbey garden. No one else can enter this way, for their path is blocked by thorns. I use the same chant to open this portal but I have not yet fathomed all its secrets, although I hope in time to find a way through to the Otherworlds I long to visit.

Meanwhile I am learning about the man they call Jesus, for his followers are becoming more widespread across the realm and it's in my interests to find out how they think and what they believe. Even Arthur, so I have heard, now carries a cross on his shield. I suspect it's to honor our mother, who, I'm told, repented her sin of lying with Uther before they were wed, and has now died of grief and remorse. I feel some vindication that she acknowledged the truth behind Arthur's conception, although my brother is still acclaimed as the heir to my kingdom.

As well as learning about the Christ, I am also learning about a past that I never suspected. There are a few scrolls and books at the priory but many more at the abbey library, ancient writings from Greece and Arabia with much of interest concerning both our world and what lies beyond. I owe my thanks to the prioress for ensuring I have access to whatever texts I want, and to the brothers at the abbey for helping me to read and understand them. I know they expect some largesse in return, and so I give them a gold ring that once belonged to my father, but that is too large for me to wear on any of my fingers or even my thumb.

There is a good reason for my industry. Although I enjoy learning for its own sake, it is my belief that if I have more knowledge than Merlin, I shall be able to outwit him when the time is right. I haven't forgotten my promise to punish him for his betrayal—of my father and of me—and the harm that he has done. Arthur too. They have taken what was mine, my birthright, and I will not rest until I have wrought vengeance on both of them.

To my delight, I finally solve the secret of Merlin's crystal. The spells of the garden and my secret ways were cast with wands of ash, oak and hazel, under a full moon. All of these spells I found in Merlin's book, but it says little about how to access paths to Otherworlds and other realities, perhaps assuming a knowledge that I don't have. When I visited some of these worlds with Merlin at Tintagel, he never showed me just how it was done. This is a trick I've had to learn through trial and error, and I've discovered that Merlin's crystal is the key, along with the need to also carry some portion of an oak tree, either my wand, or even a leaf or a twig, when I venture forth through the bramble bushes.

One of the worlds I return to is the island of Avalon, the sacred isle of healing guarded by the high priestess Viviane and her acolytes, all of whom worship a being they call the Mother Goddess. Viviane is also known as the Lady of the Lake because of her habit of bathing naked in the lake in the center of the isle under the light of the full moon. She claims the moon's power fills her with radiance and enhances her magical abilities. I have noticed she allows no one else the same privilege, or opportunity for improvement. Indeed, she guards her magical arts just as jealously as the Christian priests guard their mysteries at the high altar. To me, the rituals at the shrine of the Mother Goddess seem to be as hierarchical and narrow as the rituals of the Christians in their church; only the gender of the being they worship is different. But I respect their knowledge of the natural world, and I am learning all I can about the magical healing properties of some of the unfamiliar herbs, flowers, trees and bushes that grow in the wild there. On each visit I secrete some of these magical plants under my cloak to bring back to the priory, for it gives me great pleasure to make use of the knowledge and skills I have learned in Avalon to heal the sick and bring relief from suffering in our own world.

I have also returned to the world of the Druids. I'm beginning to think that the seed of Arthur's destruction may lie in this world, for it is similar to our own in appearance and in almost everything else except that in this Otherworld it is the Druids who have the power over the hearts and minds of the people. I spend more and more time there, where I am known and revered as the daughter of an Otherworld king. I am learning high magic from the Druids while plotting how to take my revenge on Arthur and Merlin. Several years pass by while I bide my time, and learn what I can, and wait for my hour of triumph.

*

When word comes to the priory that a great battle has been waged against the invaders from across the sea, and that Arthur's army is camped close by, I know it is time for me to act. I have learned not only how to shape-shift into other creatures but also how to take on the appearance of someone else. It has been a great source of amusement trying out various personae in the places where I am known. I have become an old crone, a young boy, a priest (with a most unholy tongue!) and a juggler. With this last, I'd thought to entertain the sisters with some songs and juggling tricks, but there was such consternation to find an unexpected stranger in their midst that I found myself quickly bundled outside the gate, and had to fly back inside disguised as a swallow.

Now the time for experiments and playing is over. This time I assume the guise of a young woman, beautiful enough to tempt Arthur to abandon his troops and follow me to the Otherworld of the Druids, where people are ruled by a man they call Myrddin. Before I leave the priory, I inspect my reflection in the blood-dark water of my scrying pool. I am content with what I see: a slim, shapely form clad in a silken gown the color of the ocean. My eyes sparkle with desire; my red lips invite temptation; my hair gleams like a river in the moonlight. I know that I have made myself irresistible to all men and, briefly and fiercely, I wish I could always stay as young and beautiful as I am today. But I suspect, if Merlin's book is to be believed, that my transformation can last no longer than a year and a day.

I cast a final lingering glance at my reflection, but I cannot see myself. Instead I hear the shouts of battle and the screams of the dying, while a barge, clad in the black of deep mourning, sails slowly upriver. Before I can decipher any more, the vision has vanished and the water becomes still.

I feel uneasy, but shrug away my misgivings, anxious to be gone.

I have chosen the night of Samhain for my revenge on Arthur. It is the night when hearth fires are doused and homes abandoned. The night when the dead walk and no one is safe. The night when, in this Otherworld I have come to know, a new fire is lit for fortune in the year ahead. It is the night when stones are cast to tell who will live and who will die. This is what the Druids believe, and this is what I'd have Arthur believe too.

When I reach Arthur's camp I am shocked to see the toll the battle has taken on his troops; young men look old before their time, their eyes betraying the horrors they've witnessed. The stench of spilled blood mingles with the scent of their cooking fires. An uneasy quiet pervades, broken only by the jingling harness of a restless steed and the occasional muttered oath. Confident that I can take care of myself if necessary, I walk among the men. I use my skills and what limited resources are available to help the injured, giving relief where I may, for their wounds are terrible. As I minister to them, I indulge in flirtatious banter in the hope of easing the burden of their memories. But it is Arthur's attention I am after. Soon enough, he joins the growing band of warriors ringed around me, each of them hopeful of catching my favor for the night.

He is a grown man of twenty-one summers now, tall and come into his strength, although I can see he has been wounded; a bloodied bandage is bound around his left arm. Having learned much of healing from the priestess of Avalon and the infirmarian at the priory, I know enough to tell that the wound is clean and is not deep enough to be dangerous. I smile at Arthur, and he smiles back at me. I recognize that smile from his childhood; it is a brave smile, one that covers a knowledge of hurt and harm, of doubts and fears. A smile that rips my heart into shreds.

When first I devised my plan, I did so with hatred and a desire for revenge; it seemed eminently sensible. Now I am not sure I can go through with it. I call on Merlin's early teaching to help me. *You have to think that raven,* be *a raven,* he'd said. I have to remember that I am no longer Arthur's sister, Morgana. Instead, I am a beautiful young woman, ripe for seduction by a young and handsome king. I have no past and, after tonight, no future either.

I take his arm and say softly, "I can see that you are hurt and in need of comfort, my liege. I pray you, walk with me a way for I have remedies to heal your wound and ..." I pause, eyes downcast and eyelashes fluttering demurely, "... and I am willing to do what I may for you in any other way you desire, sire." I raise my face and our eyes meet. In that instant I know he has understood my meaning, and he is mine for the taking.

I lead him back to the priory and the hawthorn hedge, and silently say a special chant that I hope will open the portal wide enough to admit strangers. I pass through and, to my relief, Arthur is able to follow me. Together, we walk through an avenue of trees so closely growing that their leaves form a green tunnel over our heads. Arthur is not aware that we have just left behind all that is known to him as the Otherworld opens before us. There is a crowd pressed around a great bonfire, just as I had been told there would be on this night of nights, and I lead Arthur toward it. He shivers with the wind on his back; its icy breath frosts our noses and ears and I press closer to him for warmth.

Myrddin, the Druid priest, is a tall man, with long flowing hair and a nose like an eagle's beak. He raises his arms to the sky. The fire lights his face, throwing into relief his stern features and the coarse strands of his long gray beard.

"Oh Dark One, Lord of Death, grant us a boon this night and let us walk in safety," he intones. "Take none of us for your sacrifice, for we are few in number and we live in desperate times. Our land trembles under the tread of rapacious invaders. Their warriors nip at our heels. Our men are brave but when they leave to fight our enemies, our homes and our livelihood depend on children and the courage of women. The winter will be cold and hard for all of us. Seek what ye will, Lord of Darkness, but protect our land and leave our people in peace, we beseech thee."

He bends to raise a mighty branch of oak. Sweating with the effort, he thrusts the log onto the sacred bonfire. It flares up, crackling and spitting its fury. The wind carries sparks high into the dark night, fireflies to light the path walked by the dead.

"Who is this priest?" Arthur whispers. "I have never seen him before."

"He's someone new, come to Glastonbury from across the sea." I hope my explanation is enough to lull any suspicions Arthur may have.

Two acolytes stagger forward, their shoulders bowed under the weight of a huge stag. Its feet are bound but it struggles still, wild with panic in the face of imminent death. Reverently, the acolytes lay the beast at the priest's feet.

The Druid raises his hands in blessing over the stag. "We give you this offering with a full heart and a prayer that you will protect Riothamus from the swords of our enemies. Our hopes rest in the power of his right hand when it is raised to protect us against them, and we pray that you will keep him safe this night and until the threat against our land is over."

From the sheath slung at his waist, Myrddin draws a ceremonial dagger. With a swift movement he slits the animal's throat, and raises the bloody knife to the sky.

"Who is Riothamus? Where are we?" Arthur sounds somewhat anxious.

"Riothamus is you, Arthur; it's just his way of saying your name. Hush, now, there's nothing to fear. This priest has brought new ways to Glastonbury from across the water. It seems they do things differently there." It is almost the truth, after all.

I touch his arm and try to distract him from Dryw the Vatis, who watches intently as the animal staggers and falls into a pool of its own blood. He makes a single thrust down its belly and its guts spill out. It is Dryw and the Vates who interpret signs and make predictions, and now they all crowd around to divine the future from the beast's death agony and its looping entrails. Once the divination is over, the animal will be cast onto the fire to placate the Dark Ones who walk the land. And in the morning, the ashes will be raked and fortunes told from the charred bones. This is a yearly ritual, similar to what country folk used to do in our own world, so Merlin once told me, as was the life-reckoning of the stones that will come next.

"This is the night when the dead walk," I explain. "And this is the new way to keep ourselves safe."

I believe that the dead do walk, and I am sure Arthur does too, no matter that he professes to follow the Christian faith. Every year I pray to see my father Gorlois so that I can tell him the things that have come to pass since his untimely death. Perhaps this year, in this place, I shall finally meet him again.

Arthur shivers and edges closer to the fire. Does he hope to see Uther? Surely that usurper cannot rest easy in his grave!

I look upward, seeking the souls of the dead in the dark sky. Above my head circles the silver ribbon of fiery stars that, in Avalon, light the way to the temple of the Goddess. I close my eyes and, for comfort, I try to sense the presence of the Great Mother.

I feel Arthur's movement beside me, and hear the soft words of his prayer. "Keep us safe this night, oh Lord." He steals a glance at me, and his breathing quickens. "Let me acquit myself with valor against our enemies, and let me survive to be a leader for my people, for there is so much to be gained if only I can find a way to unite us all against our common foe."

I wonder if his words are for his God, or designed to impress me, and I burn with hatred that his position is not mine. But I know what he says is true, for Merlin's dire prediction at the time of Uther's death has now come to pass. Waves of invaders have been landing on our shores and Arthur's subjects, divided by petty arguments over land and property, look almost beaten.

"This is not a night for worrying, my liege," I say softly, and touch his hand, the hand that once I'd held to guide his first uncertain footsteps. Memories flood my mind and I am overwhelmed with a love so strong it almost chokes me. My resolve weakens; I am ready to abandon my cause. Until Arthur speaks again.

"It is true that it is my destiny to lead my people to a final victory."

My destiny, I rage silently. *My people, my victory!*

But Arthur is still talking. "So my mage has promised me, and yet victory seems unattainable. I have heard that the usurpers from across the sea are waiting only for Samhain to be over, waiting for the dead to lie safe in their graves once more before they come after us again."

He turns to me, a frown creasing his forehead. "Please understand, lady. It is not that I'm reluctant to fight, but these skirmishes are futile. They achieve nothing but a heartbeat's breathing space. And every time the invaders land on our shores, it seems they take more of Britain under their control." He heaves a deep sigh. "If only I was able to call all our people together. As one fighting force we would be more than a match for the invaders, we could vanquish them once and for all."

He has seen what I have long known, but I cannot tell him that. Instead, I smile and step closer. "I can see victory in your eyes, my liege, and I trust what I see. But hush now. Banish the shadows and dismiss your fears. Tomorrow you will be born anew, but tonight …" I snuggle closer and look up at him.

To my great relief, Arthur puts his arm around me. I feel him tremble as he draws me close, and I wonder if he has ever lain with a woman. I can read in his face all his longing and desire, emotions that I hope are mirrored in my own expression. But I am distracted by the thought that I, too, am untutored in the arts of love. True, though I've lived as a maiden I've experienced desire and, safe in my virginal bed, I have experimented with ways to appease that desire. My skin tingles at the memory; my nipples harden and I feel a hot ache in my groin that, tonight, nothing but a man can assuage. I am on fire to experience sexual delight and for that, I need to become who Arthur thinks I am: an unknown young woman whose only thought is to pleasure a king. I have transformed my appearance; now I must transform my mind to become the bewitching temptress Arthur believes me to be. I cannot afford any more thoughts of our close kinship for I know my courage will fail me if I allow myself to remember Arthur as a child.

And so I close my eyes and, just as I might will myself to become a bird or some other creature both in thought and in appearance, so I imagine myself into the mind of a young woman, moonstruck at holding such power over her liege lord yet wanting most desperately to please him. I go inside my mind, and only when I am truly ready do I allow myself to look once more at my king.

"Tonight is just for us, my lord, to do as we wish. You have only to tell me what it is that you desire." My voice is soft and as sweet as the music of a fairy harp.

Arthur catches his breath. "My greatest desire is to lie with you, lady." He blushes at the admission. "But I do not even know your name," he adds hurriedly.

"Tonight, of all nights, there is no need for names between us. Yet we must cast our names into the fire, for our life and fortune depend on it." I take two small pebbles from my purse and hand one to Arthur.

"Come, my lord. Inscribe your name on this pebble, as I have already inscribed mine. Then shall we cast our fate together—and with good fortune begin our future this night." I touch my breasts and then slide my hand downwards so that he will understand my meaning. Even these simple gestures increase the fire that rages within me, an itch that I am desperate to assuage.

Arthur takes the stone and, with the point of his dagger, inscribes his name upon it. He doesn't know, as I do, that there is danger in this. While tonight we shall all feast, dance and make love to drive away the darkness, so our fate will be determined by the spirits who walk behind our backs. In the morning there'll be an anxious sifting of the stones to find the ones inscribed with our names, for our fate is sealed if our stone has disappeared.

Some of this I explain to Arthur. He looks frightened as I take his stone and cast it into the fire, along with the stone I have marked with my real name.

"Come with me." I take his hand to lead him away, far enough to afford some slight privacy but not too far, for it isn't safe to be alone among the spirits of the dead.

"Nay, lady. It grieves me, but I cannot lie with you."

I stare at him, unable to believe his words for his body tells me that he wants this union as much as I do. "But I desire you above all others. Will you not please me in this?"

He shakes his head. "I, too, desire you above all others and would make love with you all the night long if I could do so with a clear conscience. But I realize now that I have little to offer you except myself. If I should die in the battles to come, another king will be chosen to take my place and you will be left without honor, or a husband to protect you."

I am impressed by Arthur's sense of chivalry, even though I saw little of it before his coronation. But no, I cannot, *must not,* think of that now. Instead, I must concentrate on changing his mind, for my future depends on it.

"Have courage," I reassure him. "You are the *dux bellorum,* the leader of battles, but you must cast your net wider to find men willing to fight on your side. You will find them if you send envoys throughout Britain to speak on your behalf, trusted men who will take the time to explain your vision when they sound the call to arms. With you as their leader, our people will unite behind you and drive the invaders howling into the sea like the curs they are." I know this to be true even though it pains me to say it. I have seen his victory in the sacred scrying pool. What I don't know is whether Merlin has also seen this, or whether his words were merely wishful thinking, designed to reassure himself that he made the right decision when he chose Arthur over me. I know in my heart that I could do what I'm urging Arthur to do, and I could have done it sooner, because I, too, am capable of uniting our people and leading them into battle.

"Who are you, lady, that you can make such a confident prediction?" Arthur looks wary even though I can see he's taken some comfort from my words.

"I am someone who has your safety and the safety of our country at heart. Trust me, my lord, the future is glorious. But tonight ... ah, tonight ..." I slowly lick my lips and watch Arthur's eyes darken with desire.

We move away into the shadows. Arthur spreads his cloak and we lie down together. At last, his lips meet mine and, in that first touching, all thoughts fly away into the darkness.

Yet Arthur is clumsy. He fumbles with my clothing until, in an agony of impatience, I sweep off my gown and tug down his breeches. There in the darkness we couple like peasants, Arthur so impatient that he spills his seed before I have time to take my own pleasure. I lie beside him, fuming, as he falls into an exhausted slumber. I am on fire with wanting and, as I have so often before, I seek once more to satisfy my arousal. But being with Arthur has made me realize that there is more to loving than what I've previously experienced. I cannot quench the longing that torments me.

I let Arthur sleep, and watch until dawn begins to lighten the sky with its golden glow, chasing the dead home to their unquiet graves. I've waited long enough.

"My liege." I brush his lips in a kiss while my hand creeps down to arouse him once again.

He wakens with a start. Without giving him time to think, I cover his body with my own. His erection pierces my center and I moan in delight, hardly feeling the pain as he thrusts deeper. In a single movement he rears up and pulls me over and under him. His body pulsates against mine, bringing waves of pleasure. I am lost to everything, aware only of the sensation of skin against skin, and a hot throbbing that is gaining momentum, demanding release. "Yes," I moan. "Yes, yes ..."

Arthur gives one last shuddering thrust and lies still. But my body cannot be governed by my mind. It demands satisfaction. I continue to move against him, yearning and desperate for relief. But his thrusting erection has deflated; it lies inert and useless inside me. For Arthur it is over and no more is necessary. He moves off me and I lie rumpled and vulnerable beside him, hating him.

"Have I pleased you, my lady?" he asks, as he hastily dresses himself. I know he is looking for reassurance that his prowess as a man equals his prowess as a warrior and king, and I hesitate, torn between telling him the truth and fostering his self-delusion.

"Yes," I say at last.

He fumbles with the laces of his breeches, then stops to stare down at me. I follow his gaze and see what has caught his attention: my thighs are stained with the blood of my maidenhead. I am conscious that its loss pains me more than the physical discomfort of our coupling. I wait for him to comment, but he turns away and continues to lace up his breeches.

I sweep up my gown and pull it over my head, rearranging my face in the privacy afforded within its folds. "You are a potent lover, Arthur," I lie as I pull my gown into place and smooth my hands down its fabric. I look at my brother, and catch the self-same smirk of satisfaction he wore when he found out Merlin had changed my destiny, and he would take my place and become king. I bite my lips together, needing the pain of it to hide my hatred.

"Will you come with me to court, lady? I would see you again—if the stones have spared us."

"No, my liege, I regret that I cannot." Arthur has fulfilled his purpose and I will not lie with him ever again. Remembering his performance, I make a silent vow to myself to choose a more skillful lover next time. If there is a next time. I have been so caught up in my plan to ruin Arthur that I have ignored what else will happen here. Arthur will live; I have scried the sacred pool and seen his coming victory. But what of me? Although I have looked for signs, I have never seen any indication that I will succeed in taking back what is rightfully mine, or that I shall one day rule a kingdom. I wonder if I'll even live long enough to raise my son to the destiny I have chosen for him: the son who will turn on his father and rule in his place.

I rub my arms for warmth, and to hide the fact that I am trembling and fearful of what lies ahead. "Come, let us see what the stones show us of the year ahead," I suggest.

The Vates are already at the fire, salvaging the bones and fanning the hot coals into flames to give fire to the villagers for their hearths. As they go about their business, Myrddin sifts the stones while those present wait anxiously for their names to be called out. Each name called is punctuated by a cheer as a year's reprieve is granted.

"Arthur Pendragon!"

Arthur's taut shoulders relax. He turns to me, grinning with relief. I wait for my name to be called, for I'm hopeful that I shall be spared for a few more years at least.

"Morgana."

"My sister! I didn't know she was here!" Arthur looks around the assembled throng. I am surprised how eager he seems, how excited as he scans the crowd for a familiar face.

For a moment I am assailed by a terrible misgiving, a premonition of disaster. I am tempted to stay still but, finally, I inhale a deep, steadying breath and begin to walk away from Arthur. As I go, I allow my deceptive guise to fade away, transforming myself once more into the sister Arthur recognizes. I hear his gasp of horror as he comes to understand what I have done. I quicken my pace and, before he has a chance to come after me, I have vanished from his sight. I don't look back but instead weave the enchantment that will lead him back to the realm he knows.

My fingers stroke my stomach as I anticipate the future, the child who is already beginning to form there, the son of our union.

CHAPTER 3

It is a surprise to be summoned by the Prioress and told that an envoy has arrived with a message from the king demanding to see me. I know she has prevaricated on my behalf on several occasions over the intervening years, but it seems that this time is different: he has had word that I am here, and has threatened to search the priory and the abbey until he finds me. All this the prioress whispers to me, along with an apology, before she leads me to her parlor where the man is waiting.

I have not met him before, but he bows with all the respect due to the king's sister and hands over a parchment scroll. I am nervous, but try to hide the tremors in my hands as I unfurl it to read what is on Arthur's mind.

Arthur bids me wait upon him at his new court called Camelot. There is no reason given for his summons but I know that, as the king's subject, I am forced to obey. As I think through what this means, I am struck with terror. How has Arthur found me? What has he been told? Blood pulses through my body. I feel giddy; my palms begin to sweat.

I had thought to hate the instrument of my revenge, the child I made with Arthur, and was utterly unprepared for the rush of love I felt for the tiny babe when first I held him in my arms. Mordred. He was such a bonny baby that I lost my heart to him completely. After his birth I hung over his cradle, tickled him and made him smile. I rejoiced in his first baby words: "Mma-mma." He said them over and over. I don't know if he was just making random sounds but to me they sounded as if he already knew me for who I was. His mama. Later, as he learned to speak, he called me "mother." He is the one person in all this earth whom I love unreservedly, and for whom I would give my life. And he is mine, all mine. I know Mordred loves me as I love him. So my first reaction on reading Arthur's message is blind panic.

Unbidden, a passage from the story of Christ comes into my mind: the story of how Herod the king ordered all boy babies killed after listening to a seer foretell that a newborn babe would one day bring about his downfall. If I know that passage, so too will Arthur, whose court continues the tradition of worshipping Christ that he learned from our mother, Igraine.

But even if he has heard of Mordred's birth, how can Arthur know the purpose I have in mind for our son? Fearing the worst, I question the messenger.

"Did the king say why I am to come to court?"

"No, my lady. He just bid me bring you this message with all speed."

"And what of Camelot? Is aught wrong there that the king requires my presence?"

"No, my lady. We have all settled happily into the new court." The messenger pauses for a moment, then ventures timidly, "Perhaps it is only that the king wishes to show his new stronghold to his sister?"

"Perhaps." The thought gives me some comfort. But still I ask, "Does the king wish anyone else to accompany me?" If Arthur expects me to bring Mordred, he will be disappointed.

I would rather die than take my child into that nest of wasps. I offer up a brief prayer of thanks that Mordred is safe with his favorite Sister Agnes in the garden. There is nothing here in the parlor to betray his birth or his presence in my life. And I shall keep the messenger ignorant if I can.

"He mentioned no one else, my lady. He said only that I was to find his sister, the Lady Morgana, and bid her come with me, and that we should make haste."

"Pray return at once to the king; offer him my compliments and good wishes and tell him that I shall make all speed to follow you to Camelot."

"But, my lady, the king bade me wait and escort you, so that I may show you the way."

"I already know the location of Camelot," I say brusquely, and dismiss him. In fact, I have spoken the truth. On hearing tidings of the new court being built at Arthur's behest, I transformed myself into a hawk and flew off to find it, for it is not so very far from Glastonbury. I'd seen an impressive castle set within extensive bounds. I'd hovered over it for some time, observing the comings and goings of the lords and their ladies along with the myriad servants who take care of their needs. I'd waited until I'd seen Arthur, unable to explain even to myself why that was important to me. Once I'd glimpsed him, looking hale and happy in the company of some of his men, I left. I haven't returned since.

But this is the first time I have heard the name of Arthur's stronghold. A memory of my visit to that Otherworld at Glastonbury so long ago comes into my mind: the jongleur who'd spoken of a court called Camelot. A shiver of foreboding prickles my skin. Camelot is indeed real. I know I can find the court easily enough on land, for what they call the causeway of the giants is really just an ancient track that leads to the site of the abandoned fort upon which Arthur has built his new royal demesne. Perhaps I can pretend to lose my way, and not attend Arthur at all? Yet his command is clear and if I don't obey, I know that next time he will fetch me under guard.

Feeling deeply troubled, I hurry into the garden as soon as the messenger is safely out of sight. My heart lifts at the sight of my child, and I hold out my arms to him. His face splits into a huge smile as soon as he notices me and, breaking free from Sister Agnes, he runs into my embrace. I sweep him up and smother him with kisses, and he winds his arms around me and nuzzles into my neck.

I look into Mordred's shining, innocent face, and my courage fails me. I cannot set him against his father; I cannot use him as my instrument of revenge. I know that now. Although I am determined to start teaching him all I know, I make a vow to myself that he must never know the truth of his birth, nor must he sense my hatred of his father. He has his own destiny ahead of him, and I want him to be happy. In no way must I influence him to tread the bitter path that I follow. I must find some other way to punish Arthur, and Merlin too.

These thoughts are followed immediately by others. Six years have passed since our coupling and in all the time since I'd fled Arthur's court, I had believed my whereabouts a secret. I heard nothing from Arthur nor did I expect word from him, for only the prioress knows—or suspects—my true identity here. In all that time I've been living in the priory's guest house, first as a single woman and later with my child. The nuns, although disappointed by my lapse from grace, allowed me to stay on after Mordred's birth and continue my studies. Even though I don't join in their worship, I am grateful to them for giving me shelter and for not asking questions regarding Mordred's father. But now that Arthur knows where I am, it is imperative that I take Mordred away from the priory, both for his own protection and for mine. The priory is too close to the new court to guarantee Mordred's safety if Arthur should decide to remove him. I suspect too that the good sisters would make the most of my absence to influence an innocent boy in the ways of their Christ.

I need to find somewhere to keep him safe, at least while he is so young and so vulnerable. I need also to find an explanation for his existence. If not Arthur, who shall I claim to be Mordred's father? I cannot keep Mordred's existence a secret forever. When Arthur finally hears of his birth, and perhaps even interrogates Mordred himself to allay any suspicions, he must not hear the truth.

I dream up and discard several possibilities until I find a solution. It brings a smile to my face. I shall tell people that, in a moment of weakness, I tumbled in a field with a handsome young shepherd. Such disgraceful behavior must surely work in my favor, for why should I make up a story that can only bring me discredit? And there'll be no reason for Arthur to fear the child of a man of such lowly birth. By promoting my so-called disgrace, I shall keep Mordred safe. I decide that I must first confess to the prioress my lapse with the shepherd. I probably should have thought of it before. The prioress will believe what I tell her, and may pass it on if questioned by Arthur. Not even Arthur would dare to doubt the word of a holy servant of God.

After a great deal more thought, and putting aside Arthur's instructions to make haste, I pack up our belongings and journey instead to the kingdom of Lothian, to ask my sister Morgause if she will look after Mordred for me. I tell her that I would like him to learn something about service in a royal court. I cannot resist embroidering the lie I've prepared regarding my son's father, for I can tell from her sour and discontented expression, and from the way she treats Lot, that her husband is a sore disappointment to her.

"We bedded in a field of daisies, with the sounds of birds and bells and the bleating of lambs to serenade our love-making," I say. "Such a lusty young man! He was not easily satisfied, but every time he took me, I experienced a degree of pleasure I never thought possible. Small wonder that we've bred a young lion between us." I look fondly at Mordred, who is busy tormenting Gareth. Morgause's youngest son is a few years older than Mordred but I can see that he is a gentle boy, and has obviously been treated as the baby of the family.

"Lion he may be by nature, but low born for all that," Morgause snaps, and hurries to separate the boys. I hide a smile for I can see the envy beneath her scorn. I only wish that anything of what I've said was true! Whatever Lot's shortcomings, Morgause is in a far better position than I, for her sexuality has some outlet for expression: four sons bear testimony to that. But since coupling with Arthur, I have nightly gone alone to my bed, my needs unassuaged except by my own devices.

"Take good care of Mordred for me," I beg her. In my heart, I know she will, for I've observed her to be a good mother. Even so, I wait for a few more days to make sure she treats my low-born child kindly, and also to ensure that Mordred settles happily with his cousins. It is only when I am fully reassured that I take my leave.

Saying goodbye to Mordred is difficult enough, but witnessing his distress as I turn my horse to gallop away is almost unbearable. I want to run back to him and take him in my arms, and tell him I shall never leave him, never. But our safety depends on my going to court and telling lies, and so I steel my heart and call out to him my promise that I shall bring him a special surprise on my return.

Under escort from Lot's men—and grieving—I journey to Arthur's new court, still wondering why I've been summoned, and still apprehensive. Once safely at the gate house, I pay off the men and dismiss them, for I do not want anyone at

Camelot to know from where and under whose protection I have journeyed. In spite of a light, misting rain, the courtyard is crammed with people coming and going. I look about with enjoyment, relishing the noise and bustle after the quietness of the priory and the long journey from Lothian. Merchants and traders push and shove for position, their trays and carts piled high with everything from fish to loaves of bread, from bolts of finely woven fabric to rough baskets crammed with anything that could possibly be wanted or needed by a royal household.

Knights jostle past on their way to the tilting yard, attended by their squires. I hail one of them, and am in turn greeted by Sir Kay who sends his squire with word of my arrival to the king. While I wait for Arthur to receive me, Sir Kay makes some enquiries, and then he and Sir Bedivere personally escort me to where I shall sleep, on the excuse that they can show me some features of the new castle along the way. I must admit that what I see impresses me.

The Great Hall is larger and longer than any I have yet encountered. At its center is an immense round table surrounded by chairs with elaborately carved arms and padded with comfortable cushions. The shutters are open to let in the light from several huge windows. Rich, beautifully embroidered tapestries depicting wild creatures and hunting scenes adorn the stone walls, a fitting decoration for the feasts, which must always include the results of the huntsmen's kill: the boar, deer and birds that will grace the table. The round table and chairs are the only furniture in the room.

"This is where we sit while we conduct our business with the king," Kay tells me, puffing up his chest importantly. "But the hall is large enough to accommodate everyone at Camelot, so additional benches and tables are brought in when we dine."

We walk on. I look about me with great curiosity, impressed not only by the finery but also by the calm and order that seems to prevail throughout the castle. The women's solar is well appointed, with colorful hangings to brighten bare stone walls, and padded cushions to add comfort to benches and stools. A couple of windows, protected by thin layers of shaved horn, add a welcome brightness to the room and illuminate the ladies' industry. They look up from embroidery frames and looms as we pass, and bob their heads in acknowledgment without pausing in their labors. The soft notes of a lute follow us down the corridor.

I am relieved to find that I am not expected to share either a bed or a room with other women from Arthur's entourage, for I have grown used to my own company in the priory. I gaze in appreciation at the soft feather bed that dominates the small sleeping space allotted to me. It will be an especial treat after the narrow, straw-filled mattress on which I sleep at the priory. What loving might one have in such a bed! I hide a smile as I ponder the possibilities, for the one thing Arthur's court does not seem to lack is lusty young men.

In the days that follow, I am treated with some respect—and great caution. I realize that no one is quite sure of my standing and my status becomes increasingly precarious as I wait for my first meeting with Arthur. I may be living in unaccustomed luxury, but I'm certainly not enjoying my stay here. Arthur keeps sending his excuses and, despite my apprehension, I resent the slight. I even wonder if perhaps he now regrets sending for me and is afraid to face me.

Arthur's Camelot is a wonder though, and I explore it thoroughly. I discover that it was built to celebrate Arthur's greatest victory against the invaders after what I (and Merlin) foretold came to pass. Britain is at peace at last and I suppose I should credit Arthur with bringing it about, although it was my suggestion that enabled him to do so. Perhaps invigorated after his night with me, Arthur sent envoys around Britain and men came from everywhere to fight the usurpers in a series of battles that culminated in the last and bloodiest of them all at Mount Badon. The enemy were routed, and they fled in ignominy and in terror. Fighting together against a common foe served to unite the people of Britain, and Arthur has taken steps to ensure that each tribe has a representative here at court. He has shown some wisdom in this—but I could have achieved the same outcome if given the chance, of course.

I also come to understand more of one of Arthur's innovations. Bedivere tells me that Arthur and his friends and advisers at court sit around the great round table to deliberate matters of state, each in his own named chair. It seems that Arthur believes that being seated in the round makes everyone equal and gives everyone an opportunity to speak his mind. It's an idiotic idea, but typical of Arthur, who was ever unable to make up his mind about anything. For all the fancy words and explanations, I suspect that having a round table means that, rather than showing leadership, Arthur probably waits for someone to tell him what to do! I know things would have been different under my rule, so different, and I curb my tongue with difficulty.

I renew old acquaintances at court, although I try to avoid Merlin. He seems to be everywhere, Arthur's mentor and adviser in all things. Inevitably, our paths finally cross. I can hardly hide my apprehension as I bend my knee to him in obeisance.

"Merlin." I lower my head so that he cannot read my face. At all costs he must not discover what I have done in my attempt to bring about the downfall of Arthur.

"Lady Morgana." He is coolly polite. I take my cue from him. We exchange a few pleasantries and I walk on, shaking with the release of tension.

The tone of that meeting sets the tenor of our encounters in the future. I haven't forgotten my vow to bring him down, but I am prepared to wait. In the meantime I watch him closely. I show respect—and ever so gently I interrogate him to find out how much he knows, or thinks he knows. It soon becomes clear to me that he either suspects nothing of my theft of his property, or is unwilling to confront me with his knowledge. Nor does he seem to know of Mordred's existence, or the means of his birth. This removes my greatest worry, for it means that Arthur has kept our liaison secret. It comes as something of a revelation to realize the limits of the great mage's powers: that while he knows a great deal about magic he has so little understanding of the human heart. Silently, I make a vow never to fall into the same trap.

I wait for Arthur to send for me. I fume at the delay, wondering if this is Arthur's doing or if Merlin has advised against the meeting. Eventually I run out of patience and decide to pack up my belongings and leave Camelot. The next dawn heralds the day of the feast marking Pentecost. From all the preparations underway, I can tell that this will be a very special occasion indeed. I change my mind: I shall give Arthur one last chance. If he doesn't send for me during the day I shall take leave of him at the feast, shame him in front of the whole court if necessary. Whatever the outcome, I intend to turn my back on him, and on Camelot, until the time comes for me to take my place as head of the realm.

Arthur and his favorites are seated at the round table to dine, the knights in their accustomed places, but space has been made for their ladies to sit beside them. Other members of the court sit at benches ringed around the great table. I am seated at one of these, the only woman without an escort. I am deeply conscious of the lack, and of the pitying glances that come my way.

Feeling tired and dispirited, I survey the scene. The Great Hall is aglow with candlelight. The ladies in their silken gowns gleam like butterflies among the more soberly dressed men. Sparkling crystals and precious gems adorn wrists, fingers and throats. Gold and silver tableware reflect the candlelight, adding luster. The excited buzz of conversation almost drowns the sweet tones of a lute and the voice of a minstrel who sings louder and louder in order to be heard.

Forgotten and ignored by all, I find it hard to share in the gaiety. Because it is Pentecost, Arthur announces at the beginning of the feast that he is expecting something wonderful to happen: apparently this has become the custom for every feast at Pentecost. Everyone cheers his words, while I sourly surmise that perhaps the wonder will lie in his final acknowledgment of my presence.

I reflect that, where once I had joy and a sense of purpose in my life, now I have nothing. Unwittingly or not, Merlin shattered more than my ambition; he also shattered my life and my reason for being. I look around the room and recognize that I feel nothing for those gathered around me. I care about nothing except my son, Mordred. He is the one light in the darkness and desolation that I inhabit, and I determine to leave, to reclaim him without delay.

The sudden loud knocking of the steward's staff upon the wooden floor jerks me from my reverie, and stops the minstrel mid-verse. My pulse quickens, although I cannot say why. A man steps into the Great Hall. He is dressed in a simple tunic and breeches, denoting his lowly status. Apart from the steward, he is unattended. A sigh of disappointment rises in a wave around me. But the man shows no fear or awe as he approaches Arthur. Once close enough, he bows deeply and then straightens to face the king.

"I am Launcelot du Lac, son of King Ban, and I am here to serve you, sire." He bows again, seemingly unaware of the collective gasp that echoes around the silent hall. Everyone has heard of Sir Launcelot du Lac from across the sea, for his exploits have been sung by bards, and even by the minstrel who entertains us this night. The bravest of knights have been defeated by Launcelot, but he is also credited with winning battles against unworldly beings as well as showing himself a chivalrous knight to any damsel in distress.

I watch intently as Arthur bids him welcome. And then Launcelot turns, and his eyes meet mine.

I was once in the forest in a thunderstorm; a bolt of lightning split the tree under which I was sheltering, and blasted me into the air. But that was nothing to how I feel now as we face each other, as our hearts, our minds, our souls collide with such impact that it seems we have fused into one.

He feels the shock of it too, I know he does, for he stands still for several long moments as we stare at each other. And then he walks to where I am sitting, ignoring Arthur's invitation to join him at his side. I move along the bench to make room for him, and he sits beside me, his thigh touching mine in a searing promise for the night, and for the future.

While I appear composed, inside my heart sings like a nightingale. All my senses have sparked into brilliant life. I am acutely conscious of Launcelot's regard as he bends his dark and admiring gaze on me. I know I can inspire awe among those who respect my learning and my skill at healing, but I hardly dare believe that I can inspire the admiration of this one man above all others, this man whose opinion I would most value and whose love I would most cherish, when there are so many more beautiful ladies at court who would take him in a heartbeat if they could.

"You have heard my name, lady; may I hear yours?" he asks.

"Morgana, daughter of Gorlois, Duke of Cornwall. I am half-sister to the king." I give my name freely for I want no pretense between us. Indeed I believe I would give him so much more than my name, if he but asked for it! For a moment I am tempted to weave a love spell, just to make sure of him. Perhaps I should even transform myself, as I did in order to lie with Arthur? But I want this man to love me as I am, and for that reason I vow there will be no spells, no magic involved in our relationship.

And then I realize, to my infinite dismay, that there can never be full honor and trust between us either, for Launcelot must never find out that I coupled with Arthur and we made a child together. I must needs proceed with caution, and be always on guard. There is great sadness in the thought. But I smile and say, "May I welcome you to court, sire."

"I am pleased to be here safely at last," Launcelot responds gravely. "I must confess that there were times along the road when I thought I might never arrive, when I feared for my very life."

"It sounds as though you had a dangerous and difficult journey, sire." I touch his hand, feel the thrill of it run through my body. "Pray, tell me something of your travels." I listen intently as Launcelot begins to recount tales of knights errant on quests, of ladies in need of rescue, and his encounters with the Questing Beast, that elusive creature with the head of a snake and the body of a lion, whose presence is heralded by the baying of forty questing hounds. I watch his lips form the words and all the while I long to feel the touch of those lips on mine. Each adventure sounds more difficult and bloodthirsty than the last, so that by the end of his recital I marvel at his prowess in managing to stay alive against such great odds.

"I give thanks that you are safely here," I tell him. "But, sire, what brings you to Camelot?" I don't mention that I, too, have only lately come to court and that I really have no place here. No doubt he'll find out soon enough.

"I have come to serve the king." Launcelot gazes into my eyes. "And to serve you too, Lady Morgana, if I may?"

As understanding comes, I flush with painful embarrassment. Launcelot has a reputation for being chivalrous to women. Having seen that I have no companion at table, he is offering his services, nothing more.

"I have no need of a knight to serve me." My voice is harsh, grating with disappointment. "I have power and status of my own."

"I beg your pardon if I have offended you, lady." Launcelot looks startled that his offer has been so ungraciously declined.

I wonder if I have been too touchy, too hasty in my reply. "There is no offence taken, Sir Launcelot. But I prefer to meet you as an equal, not as a damsel wanting protection."

"I never for one moment doubted that you could not look after yourself, lady." Now he sounds amused; his eyes reflect glittering points of candlelight, and a warmth I cannot fault.

"That being settled between us, tell me about your home across the sea." I am eager to hear more of the real world, the world beyond my home at Tintagel, the priory of Glastonbury and Camelot. True, I have caught glimpses of unknown places in my scrying pool and I have seen the stalls at the great markets, where foreign traders sell furs, spices, glassware and fine pottery as well as strange birds and animals. I long to know more of these countries beyond my ken.

But Launcelot instead turns the conversation back to Camelot and the exploits of the knights in residence here, saying he wants to know all I can tell him. We pass a pleasant evening together, marked by a flirtatious banter that threatens my cautious heart. I wonder if he will suggest that we bed together and what my response will be—or what it should be—if he does. I know that I want him both as a lover and as a friend. But past experience pricks my desire with doubt. Everything I've ever loved and valued was taken from me when Merlin switched his allegiance to Arthur. Everything save Mordred; him I will hold fast with all my power. They will not get my son.

But Launcelot's first allegiance is to his king; I have just heard him make his pledge. Where will that leave me, if he is forced to choose? If I give my heart to him; if I give him my love and my allegiance, will he also betray me one day?

It is such a risk, my heart fails at the very thought of it. Better not to savor delight in the first place, I think, for having once tasted the sweetness of loving Launcelot I will surely die if I lose him. And yet a sense of destiny pulls me into the dance of love he is weaving around me, and I know that I am already helplessly ensnared.

I am saved, of all people, by my brother.

"Morgana?"

Launcelot and I are so engrossed in each other that we are unaware of Arthur's approach until he stands before us. Arthur nods to Launcelot, who returns his gesture with a small bow. With difficulty, I raise my eyes to meet Arthur's steady regard, afraid of what he might reveal in front of Launcelot.

"My liege and brother," I greet him.

"Thank you for answering my summons to wait on me at Camelot," he says, ensuring that I understand the difference in our status. "If you will excuse us, Sir Launcelot, my half-sister and I have something we must discuss."

Arthur's demand means that I am forced to bid Launcelot farewell and take my leave. I badly want to stay, for the very thought of making love with Launcelot sets my blood roaring and if I leave now, he may set his sights on another. Frustrated and annoyed, I walk behind Arthur as we retire to his private chamber.

For one awful moment, as I look at his bed, I wonder if he has brought me here to prove himself as a lover once more. But he waves me toward a small stool while he seats himself on a handsomely carved chair. All this display is to remind me of his kingship, no doubt, and to reassure himself that he has won the crown.

"I cannot help but remember the circumstances under which we last met, Morgana," he murmurs. At least he is not going to pretend to have forgotten what has passed between us. "I trust there were no ... consequences as a result of our union?" Arthur continues.

"None at all, sire," I reply, keeping my eyes downcast lest he read the truth there. My doubts about using Mordred as my instrument of justice have been reinforced during my time at court. Even though I begrudge it, I have seen for myself the love and respect that Arthur commands from his people. I love my son far too much to risk his life in the bloody conflagration that must surely follow if he challenges Arthur for the crown on my behalf. Nevertheless, my longing to claim my birthright is unassuaged, the flames fanned higher after Arthur's treatment of me during my time here in his new court.

I drag myself back to the present. Arthur is still speaking.

"... grateful that you have accepted your lot, and sequestered yourself at the priory. Even so, Morgana, what happened between us must never be spoken of again. It would shame me, and it would greatly upset my wife."

"Your wife?" I speak without thinking. "Are you wed, Arthur?"

"You haven't been paying attention," he chides me with a frown. "I have just told you that I intend to take a wife. Guenevere, daughter of King Leodegrance. Once the agreement is signed, I shall send for her. Perhaps you would care to stay on at court for our wedding?"

"Yes, I shall stay. But only if I can be spared from the priory," I add hastily, needing time to calculate if this would be in my best interest. My mind is spinning with new possibilities. I smile at him, surprised that he seems to have forgiven my deception so readily. "Thank you, Arthur. Let me think about it."

Arthur's eyes narrow. "I meant what I said about keeping our liaison secret, Morgana. I have no idea why you acted as you did. Perhaps you would care to explain it to me?"

Unable to give Arthur the real reason, I think quickly. "It was a momentary lapse, Arthur, brought on by the peril of the night," I say softly. "Not wanting to disclose my whereabouts to you, I came to the battlefield in disguise, with the aim of doing what I could to help with the wounded. As you know, I have some skills in the art of healing. But when I witnessed the terrible harm done to your army, and when I saw your utter despair, I realized that you were more in need of comfort and encouragement than anyone else. And who better to provide both than—"

"You tricked me into lying with you!" Arthur's tone is savage.

"I had not intended it to go so far, and I have regretted it ever since." While I cannot regret Mordred's birth, now that I have met Launcelot this is most definitely true.

"Merlin was right when he said that you were always too quick to act, and too slow to think through the consequences. You were kind to me in our childhood years and I cannot forget that. But nor can I forget—or forgive—your tricks and your treachery. And I warn you, if any hint of what we did together is made known, I shall at once deny it as the ravings of a madwoman. And you will be removed from court and kept under guard in a place of safety for the rest of your life. Be in no doubt that I mean what I say. Give even the slightest hint, and I'll not hesitate to take steps to ensure that you will disappear forever."

I am so angry I could shove Arthur's tongue down his throat. How dare he threaten me with banishment from my own kingdom! Again I keep my eyes downcast so he cannot read my hatred.

"I am so sorry, Arthur. I swear no one will ever hear what happened between us on that night of Samhain." It is a relief to know that at least our vows guarantee that Launcelot will not learn the truth.

He nods. Making a visible effort to regain his equilibrium, he says, "We shall not speak of it again. But remember my words, Morgana." The hard edge is back in his voice. "I shall regard anything that comes between me and my queen, or between me and my kingdom, as a threat to be dealt with—and deal with it I shall."

He makes a dismissive gesture with his hand, just as if he is sending away a lowly goose girl. I am white hot with rage, and I clench my fists tight to contain my anger as I stand up and march to the door.

"Good rest and God be with you, Morgana."

Arthur's words take me by surprise, and I reply without thought.

"May the gods be with you,
And bless you this night.
And hold you, and guard you,
till morning brings light."

It is my own cradle song, composed to allay his fear of the dark and a familiar ritual from his childhood. I regret it the moment the words slip out. Not trusting myself to say anything further, I carefully close the door behind me, although what I really want to do is slam it so hard it will fly off its hinges.

I am still seething as I walk across the courtyard. At least I've been given my own sleeping space and do not have to share with those women who are either too young to marry, or too old to hope for an offer. My fists clench and unclench as I fantasize about punching Arthur in his smug and smiling face and I am well prepared and able to defend myself when a figure steps suddenly out of the shadows and touches my shoulder. I swing my right fist and hear it connect with a satisfying crunch, but before I can follow up with a blow from my left, both of my arms are seized and held in a tight embrace that brings me face to face with Launcelot.

"Lady," he breathes. "I beg your pardon if I frightened you—but you have certainly proved beyond doubt that you are well capable of protecting yourself."

Shock keeps me speechless for a moment. Then a blinding fury sweeps over me and I push my hands against his chest in an effort to set myself free. At once Launcelot releases me and steps back, sketching a small bow by way of apology.

"I was so sorry that our pleasant interlude together was interrupted," he says smoothly. "I waited to waylay you in the hope that we might continue our ... conversation?" His eyes in the moonlight promise so much, but I am still furious and in no mood for loving.

"Leave me alone!" I hiss, thinking that this is the way of all men: first Arthur imposing his will, and now Launcelot. I want none of them. I turn on my heel and stride away, rather regretting my hasty action as I recall the sweet sensations I felt earlier.

"Lady?" I hear his soft voice behind me as I pause at the door of my bedchamber.

I turn to him. He reaches across me to open the door and gestures for me to go through. I feel a spurt of disappointment that he seems merely to be seeing me safely to my bed, but then he follows me inside and closes the door behind him. It is the first time I've ever been alone with a man in a bedchamber. The silken bedhangings are drawn back; the fat pillows and fur blanket invite us to comfort and rest, but I stay standing, facing Launcelot. My heart is thumping, but whether from fear, or anger, or desire, I can no longer tell.

He raises a hand and smooths a tendril of hair from my eyes, tucking it behind my ear with a gentle touch. I blink, unused to—and almost undone—by such a loving gesture.

"You were happy while we were dining, but something has happened to upset you." Launcelot's tone is as soft as his touch. "Do you want to tell me what it is, Morgana? Perhaps I can help you put things right again."

To my horror, tears well hot and heavy behind my eyes. I have learned to steel myself against hatred, scorn, rejection, even indifference. But Launcelot's loving concern is more than I can bear. I try to blink back my tears, but they begin to slide in a steady stream down my cheeks.

Launcelot draws me into his arms and holds me close. He doesn't say anything, just drops soft kisses onto my hair as I begin to weep in earnest. I am crying for everything I have lost, for everything I haven't allowed myself to mourn before. I cry also for all the mistakes I have made that threaten to blight my life even further. And all the while he holds me, until my tears cease and I am mistress of myself at last. I pull out of his embrace and sink down onto my bed, wiping my face and nose on my kerchief. I am all too conscious of how my ravaged face must look after that storm of weeping, but it cannot be helped. In truth, I feel a little better, for my tears have purged my anger and bitterness, at least for the moment.

"It is ever my role to console a damsel in distress," he says, attempting a smile and a light tone. But he cannot disguise his concern as he adds, "I pray you, Morgana, tell me what ails you. It distresses me to see you so unhappy. You are born to laughter and joy, not to this bitter weeping."

If only I could confess my past to Launcelot; if only I could start again! But I cannot, and I sigh with bitter regret. "My brother and I had a slight quarrel, and it upset me," I say. "But it is over, forgotten. Thank you for your concern and for your patience, Sir Launcelot. I really am quite recovered now."

There is a momentary awkwardness between us. Conscious that we are alone in my bedchamber, I wait for him to decide on what will happen next. Perhaps he, too, is waiting for a sign from me.

When none comes, he bows again. "God be with you this night, and pleasant dreams, my lady." And within a heartbeat he has opened the door and is gone.

I strip off my gown. Clad only in my shift, I slip into bed. The sheets are cold, and I hug myself in an effort to keep warm. And in a while, with my arms around me, I imagine that I lie with Launcelot and that his arms hold me tight. My body begins to heat until the wanting becomes unbearable. As has happened in the past I try to pleasure myself, to ease the ache. But desire has a name and a face now, and with Launcelot full in my mind, I weep with emptiness and regret.

CHAPTER 4

Thoughts of Mordred keep tugging my mind back to Lothian. I long to see my beloved child again, although secret reports from Morgause indicate that he is thriving and is enjoying the company of her own sons, Gawain, Gaheris, Agravaine and Gareth. I tell myself that Mordred has had little enough to do with boys and men, staying with me in the convent as he has, and that some time without me will be good for him, will show him how boys and men behave, and that this will help him grow into his own manhood.

So I tell myself, but in truth I cannot tear myself away from Arthur's court and from Launcelot. After those first tender moments we shared, I wait impatiently to be alone with him once more. Not for weeping this time, but for what I tell myself will be my real initiation into womanhood, my union with Launcelot. I am determined that sooner or later it must happen; I cannot bear to leave Camelot before he beds me. But now that Launcelot has come to court, it seems that Arthur cannot have enough of his company; they are either out hunting together or attending to other affairs, while their nights are spent carousing in the Great Hall until the hour is late. Launcelot and I never have a chance to be alone together, to speak in private and explore the attraction that leaped between us right from the start.

My plans are further thwarted when Arthur sends Launcelot to fetch his bride to him. Frustrated and angry, for I am sure Arthur has sent him on purpose to get him away from me, I am almost ready to leave Camelot until I realize that to do so will give Arthur the victory. And so I stay, and amid the busy preparations for the coming nuptials, I stitch a sumptuous gown of royal blue velvet that I embroider with pearls and gold thread. I am determined to look beautiful for Launcelot at Arthur's wedding.

Without Launcelot at court to distract me, I become aware of a new danger: that a bride for Arthur could mean the death of my hopes of claiming what is rightfully mine. Should they make a child together, that child would inherit the kingdom—unless I'm prepared to confess Mordred's true parentage. But that I can't do, at least while Arthur is alive, for he has already made his thoughts on that matter quite clear.

Mindful of my need to protect Mordred from his father while also safeguarding my claim to the crown, I try to devise a way of ensuring my best interests. After a great deal of thought, I finally find a solution. I have learnt that, shortly after becoming king, Arthur was given a new sword, this one even more beautiful and more magical than the one he pulled from the stone as a result of Merlin's trickery. The new sword is called Excalibur and all at court know that while Arthur possesses it, he can never be harmed or defeated in battle. I alone suspect the sword's real provenance: that Merlin himself formed it, perhaps with the help of the high priestess Viviane of Avalon, for it seems she was at court at the time the sword appeared. I know also that, while the sword itself possesses an Otherworldly strength, it is the scabbard that imbues it with the power to keep Arthur safe. If I wish to have a chance of overthrowing Arthur, I must remove his magical protection.

And so as well as stitching my new gown, I surreptitiously weave a new scabbard to house Excalibur, using my magical arts to match exactly the design and jeweled ornaments of the real scabbard. One of Arthur's knights, Accolon, has set himself to woo me, although I have no interest in him at all. I suspect he has no real interest in me either, other than believing that a liaison with me would lead to an enhancement of his own status. Nevertheless, during Launcelot's absence I lead him on with smiles and stolen kisses and the promise of my hand, until I am sure that he will do as I ask, and exchange my false scabbard for the real one when no one is looking.

I know that Arthur is unlikely to use his sword unless threatened by hostile invaders or a fiercesome creature, and I settle down to wait. But I am impatient to reclaim what is mine by rights, and I begin to wonder if I might conjure up a dangerous creature or situation in order to force his hand. I am about to put my idea into action when I hear the shrill blaring of a hunting horn that heralds the arrival of visitors to the castle.

A glance over the parapet sets my heart leaping: Launcelot leads the party. By his side is a beautiful young woman with bright golden hair. I feel a stab of jealousy, yet Launcelot seems largely unaware of his ward. He gazes around the courtyard, his expression anxious as he scans the crowd gathered to witness his approach, then looks up to the parapet. I raise my hand in greeting, hardly daring to hope I am the one for whom he is searching. I watch his body relax back into the saddle as he returns my gesture.

Greatly reassured, I hurry down to meet him. My first impression of Guenevere proves correct. I can see, from the lustful glances of Arthur's entourage when they think their king isn't looking, that they are all completely captivated by her beauty. But she is entirely smitten with Launcelot; her eyes, the color of deep blue gentians, are fixed on her escort with a look of adoration. I turn my attention to him, needing to allay a lingering fear that he is as taken with Arthur's bride as are the rest of her escort.

To my great relief he seems indifferent, for after handing her over to Arthur's care, he leaves the crowd gathering around both of them and comes straight to where I stand, half hidden in the shadows.

"My love. I have longed to see you again." He wastes no time in drawing me toward him.

"Launcelot." I can only murmur his name before his lips claim mine. He grips me harder, pulls me closer so that I am immediately aware of the length of his hard body pressed against me.

"I have missed you so," he says. His kiss deepens. I open my mouth to him, feel his tongue enter and explore with tantalizing darts and licks. My body opens to him, yearning for him, and I clutch him tight, feeling as if I am drowning.

How long do we stay locked together? I cannot say, but it is a shock when he suddenly thrusts me away from him. My knees buckle and I almost fall, but he cups my elbow and hauls me upright.

"I can't wait any longer," he groans. "I want you, Morgana, as I've never wanted a woman before. But if we stand here any longer, I swear the whole court will witness our coupling."

A savage delight sweeps over me as I hear his words and understand that his need equals mine. "Come to my bedchamber tonight," I whisper.

"No!" He shakes his head.

"No?" I stare at him, wild with anger and disappointment. I turn on my heel to hurry away before he can witness my devastation. I am fully determined to leave him, to flee the court, when he takes hold of my arm and draws me further into the shadows.

"I won't come to your bed, not here, not where everyone spies on everyone else and tattles to the king. Come with me to Joyous Garde, my dearest heart. If you say you wish to leave the court, and I follow you a day or two later, none will know where we have gone or that we are together. And that is as it should be, for I will not have anyone whispering about us or spreading rumors. We can be alone in my castle, my darling, just the two of us, with the freedom to do whatever makes us happy."

I nod my agreement, while a blazing happiness sweeps away all my doubts. At the back of my mind is the thought that it is a very good idea to leave the court so that the false scabbard cannot be linked to me when Arthur falls. Added to that is the need to get away from Accolon, who no doubt will come to claim the reward I have promised him should Arthur die. Launcelot's offer serves my interests as well as my heart.

"I shall leave just as soon as I may," I promise. "I'll wait for you on the night of the full moon. You'll find me beside the two ancient oaks close to the abbey at Glastonbury."

"I shall count the hours," he says, and takes hold of my hand. "Wear this ring as my pledge that I shall come to you, and make you my own." He slips a thin gold band onto my littlest finger. It is almost unnoticeable among the many jewel-encrusted rings I wear. Perhaps that is his intention, for it would be hard to explain a ring of betrothal or of marriage when no vows have been exchanged in public. This is his private vow and I give him one last kiss for it.

With a singing heart, I leave the shadowy alcove and venture out into the sunlit courtyard, closely followed by Launcelot. Half dazzled by the light, I stop a moment to shield my eyes, and feel Launcelot's hand grip my arm to steady me. I become aware that the courtyard is still crowded with courtiers, Arthur and Guenevere among them. Her searching glance moves from me to focus over my left shoulder, and she smiles with the innocent, open face of a girl in love. At once I shift away, but Guenevere has already seen where Launcelot's hand rests, and has drawn her own conclusions. Her smile darkens to a frown as she studies me more closely. I hurry away from Launcelot, lowering my head to avoid Guenevere's searching gaze. I am anxious to pack up my belongings and leave, for I cannot bear to wait a moment longer to be alone with him at last.

And yet, once away from the thrilling urgency of his presence, questions return to torment me. I know he's anxious to bed me, but why this need for such secrecy? He's given me a ring; we could live openly as man and wife, and yet we steal away like fugitives. He hasn't mentioned marriage or our future together. Why? Does he intend this to be just a temporary—and private—liaison?

I shrug the doubts away as I fold my possessions into a bag. After all, I don't see the need for the trappings of marriage; even less will I honor the convention that binds a woman to the will of her husband. This is not for me, especially as I believe that Arthur's kingdom by rights should be mine. While there is a place for a man by my side, I certainly have no intention of sharing my throne.

It is too late to leave Camelot for night is drawing in, and so I am forced to sit through the sumptuous feast that has been prepared to welcome Guenevere to court; forced to watch, from my lonely bench, how all the eyes of the court are focused on the fair-haired beauty who sits between Arthur and Launcelot. It is clear that Guenevere is well aware of the attention she commands, for every action seems staged for her audience: the delicate gestures of her small, white hands; the toss of her long golden locks; the fluttering of eyelashes as she turns from Arthur to Launcelot, with a look that suggests she will never tire of watching him. Finally her attention shifts to all seated around the large table. I notice that her smiles are designed not to encompass her admirers but as a screen to search for me. Her gaze moves past Arthur's favorite knights and their ladies until she locates me on my lonely bench outside their charmed circle. A genuine smile lifts the corners of her mouth as she observes my lowly position. Thereafter, her attention seems entirely taken by the man at her side.

Although I know Launcelot's true feelings for me, it is an effort to keep my composure. Somehow I keep smiling; somehow I endure the long night alone. As soon as morning dawns, I complete my preparations and then go to the hall to break my fast. I am about to leave Camelot when my brother summons me to attend him. Thinking it best to keep on side with him, I obey his command. As soon as I enter his solar, Arthur stands to welcome me. He takes my hand in his and escorts me to a seat beside him, before dismissing all those who wait on him. There is a silence between us as they bow and shuffle out.

"I want you to know that I have forgiven you for your trickery, Morgana, but I also want to make amends," he says, once we are alone. I wonder if he is referring to the way he's usurped my throne and I warm slightly toward him. "I realize you've been hiding in a priory this long while," he continues, "but I think it's now time for you to have a home of your own. To this purpose, I propose to give you an estate, along with a castle—although of course you'll always be welcome here at court," he adds stiffly.

For a moment I am lost for words; my brother's gesture has taken me completely by surprise. Even so, I need to make sure that he will not repent his magnanimity and so, after thanking him, I question him regarding the castle's name and whereabouts, and ask him to sign a deed that names the Castle Perilous as mine. As he signs and seals the parchment, it occurs to me that perhaps Arthur's generosity is dictated by the need to have me settled as far from the court as possible so as to keep our secret safe.

"Guenevere is concerned for your future, just as I am," he says awkwardly. "Now that you have an estate of your own, she has begged me to arrange a prestigious marriage for you, Morgana. We believe King Urien of Rheged will make an excellent husband for you."

Urien of Rheged! I would sooner walk over hot coals than marry that old man. I'd rather drown myself than submit to his embrace. How dare my brother and his child bride presume to meddle in my affairs! A moment's reflection brings understanding: that this, of course, is Guenevere's ploy to get me away from court and keep me apart from Launcelot. It seems that I have underestimated the guile that lurks behind that innocent, lovely face. A slow rage begins to simmer in my breast.

"Urien won't do at all, brother," I say sweetly, thinking of the plot I've woven that concerns Urien's son, Accolon; thinking too that soon enough I shall be free of both Arthur and his meddling wife-to-be. "There are others at your court who are far more worthy of marriage to the king's sister; others who are far more to my liking than Urien of Rheged. And I shall certainly inform you of *my* choice, once I have made my decision."

Launcelot, not Urien! My heart leaps with joy, with the knowledge that we shall soon be together despite Guenevere's machinations to keep us apart.

"But I am not ready for marriage yet," I say hastily. "With your leave, I wish to return to the priory for a time. I have been away too long already."

I face him, daring him to refuse, but he says only, and with a trace of disappointment that I could swear is real, "I'd hoped you would stay on and attend my marriage to Guenevere, Morgana."

"I shall do all in my power to return to court in time for it," I assure him, although I have no intention of honoring my promise. But it seems enough to satisfy Arthur, for he nods in agreement and even kisses my hand in farewell.

I collect my belongings and hurry to the stables where I direct a stablehand to saddle my palfrey. I am determined to leave Camelot without further delay, in case Guenevere is tempted to meddle further.

There is one last hurdle that I had not anticipated. As I prepare to ride through the gates of Camelot, I hear someone call my name. The voice is too faint for me to identify its owner, and so I rein in my mount and turn to see who is calling me. It is only when he is close, too close for me to flee without causing suspicion, that I realize it is Accolon who pursues me. Trying to conceal my alarm and dismay, I look down at him, and frown as he snatches my hand and holds it to his lips.

"You were going away without bidding me farewell, lady?" His face is red and sweating with exertion; the accusation I read in his protruding blue eyes is matched by the tone of his voice.

"I was not aware that I needed your permission to leave Camelot, Accolon," I say coldly.

"I thought we had an understanding, Lady Morgana." His tone is as icy as my own. I am suddenly afraid that the man whom I'd thought of as my tame lapdog may yet prove to have the claws of a lion.

"I've given it much thought and I believe it is best for me to leave Camelot at once," I say, adopting a more conciliatory tone. "There must be no hint of suspicion that Arthur is in any danger, or that we are in any way connected to each other."

Accolon eyes me, still suspicious. "And so you have decided to let me bear the consequence of betraying the king on my own?"

"Only because I know that you are a man of courage—and wisdom. Arthur will use his sword when danger next threatens. He is a king—and a brave warrior. It may be that the changed scabbard will make no difference to the outcome of the contest, but either way, no blame can ever be attached to you—or to me, if I am not here. Once word reaches me of Arthur's death, believe that I shall waste no time in coming to your side with the reward that I have promised you."

It is partly true, for indeed I shall waste no time returning to Camelot. But I alone shall claim the crown—and the kingdom—on my own account. It has not been spoken of between us, but I know that when Arthur dies, Accolon is expecting to win my hand and also the crown. What then shall I do about him if, or when, it comes about? I curse myself for not thinking that far ahead. Somehow I shall have to silence him; I cannot afford my part in Arthur's downfall to become common knowledge. But I hide my doubts and fears and instead smile sweetly as I bid him farewell.

"Do not kiss me again," I say sharply, as he seizes hold of my hand once more.

A movement on the parapet catches my attention, and I screw up my eyes against the sun to see more clearly. I had stood up there to watch Launcelot escort Guenevere through the gates and now it is Guenevere's turn to watch my departure. A deathly chill steals over me as I notice how she leans over the parapet in order to see me and my companion more clearly. Accolon is still holding my hand, and I snatch it free of his grasp.

"Go away!" I hiss. "For our safety, you must pretend there is nothing between us, that there has never been anything between us." I wheel my mount around and dig my heels against its flank. Without a backward glance, but with a heart torn between fear and anticipation, I leave Camelot.

CHAPTER 5

It is difficult to find the words to describe our happiness at Joyous Garde—a place most truly named. On our arrival I was unsure of myself, for I was tormented by thoughts of other women Launcelot might have brought here in the past, until he assured me I was the first and only one. The castle itself is quite small by Camelot's standards, but with extensive grounds that, in a high tide, are severed from the mainland so that we live almost on an enchanted isle of our own.

Most days we go riding, for pleasure but also to inspect the fields and boundaries of Launcelot's estate. Sometimes we hunt. Other times we stay closer to home, walking through the formal gardens and flowery meadows that surround the castle. Often we visit the hawks and hounds, the stables, byres and sties, the brew house and bakery, the smithy and every other part of Joyous Garde, including the homes of those who live and work here, for Launcelot is determined to see how everyone has fared in his absence. It becomes apparent that his estate has been neglected and has fallen into some disrepair, and so we decide to replace his steward. Several men are brought in for interview—and also for my inspection—after which we discuss our choice. Although I don't know these men, Launcelot assures me that he values my opinion for, he says, while he can assess a man's capacity for work and organization, only I can assess a man's heart and willingness to take on responsibility for the lives of others.

This marks the beginning of our partnership. We discuss everything after that, from the family disputes in which he is asked to mediate, to plans for the sowing and reaping of crops for the seasons to come; from the brewing of ale and the ordering of provisions to who should be promoted to new positions or downgraded for reasons of infirmity or incompetence. It is the first time I have been actively involved in the work and organization that go into ordering a well-run estate, and I glory in the fact that I am useful to Launcelot, and that he trusts and values my judgment.

There are times—so many times—that my heart is torn in two by thoughts of Mordred. I worry about my son, and I long to go to him, yet I cannot find a compelling enough reason to abandon Launcelot other than to tell him the truth—and that I cannot do. Even while telling myself that soon I will find an excuse to absent myself for a time, still I always have reasons to delay my departure.

One is the construction of a new garden to service Launcelot's demesne. On my instruction, the existing garden is being extended and replanted with those herbs most useful for concocting remedies and potions, for I intend to teach his tenants some of the skills I have learned from the infirmarian at the priory and the great healers in the Otherworlds I've visited. I am happy to share my knowledge for I know how much can be achieved if knowledge is matched with a healing touch and the correct treatment.

But our nights together are mostly responsible for delaying my departure, for they bring me the greatest joy. That first night with Launcelot—my heart still catches at the memory of it. We arrived late in the afternoon after four long days in the saddle. I was weary and, I must admit, somewhat apprehensive about the night to come. After the huge disappointment of Arthur, I wondered if it was always like that for women: a man pleasuring himself and then rolling over to slumber, leaving his lover aching and unfulfilled.

The first thing Launcelot ordered on our arrival was hot water and refreshments to be brought to the room we would occupy. I looked at the big bed that took up most of the space, and wondered if he would take me there and then, and how I should respond if he did. In truth, I was not in the mood for love, feeling grimy from our journey and utterly exhausted. Instead, Launcelot bade me rest, and indicated a comfortable, cushioned chair. He sat close by, and we sipped spiced wine and nibbled on sweet pastries while a large tub was carried up to the room and placed in front of the crackling fire. Servants arrived in relays, bearing jugs of hot water, steaming and fragrant with rose petals. Candlelight gilded the ripples as water splashed into the tub and the level began to rise. Finally, Launcelot dismissed the servants with a flick of his wrist. He stood up, and gave me his hand to help me rise.

"There's nothing to fear," he said. I felt mortified that he had sensed my lack of desire and was about to brazen it out, but he put a finger to my lips and I knew then that he had experience enough for both of us.

He held me close to him, and so we gazed into each other's eyes for a few moments. My mouth was dry, and I moistened my lips with my tongue. As if waiting for this signal, Launcelot removed the veil from my hair and untied my girdle. I stood passive under his touch, unwilling to break the spell he was weaving about me as he slowly began to unlace my gown. It slipped to my feet, and I stepped out of it and out of my shoes. Launcelot's fingers on my skin sent shivers of delight through my body as he helped me take off my pleated undertunic and more intimate garments. Finally, I stood naked before him. Still he did not caress or fondle me, but instead loosed my hair so that it fell around my face and over my shoulders. He looked at me then, a long and watchful stare that heated my body almost to melting point.

Still holding my gaze, he unbelted his girdle and began to unlace his tunic. I watched, mesmerized, as his broad chest and muscular arms were revealed to my wondering gaze. I was finding it difficult to breathe. I had thought to undress him as he had undressed me but, when it came to it, I couldn't move, I could only watch and marvel as his naked body was finally unveiled. I could see he was as aroused as I now was, and yet he made no move to push me down on the bed and have his way with me. Instead, he stepped into the bath, and beckoned me to join him.

As I lowered myself into the golden water, it lapped around me like a balm. I lay back and closed my eyes, feeling my muscles relax into looseness. I breathed in the fragrant steam.

Launcelot picked up a cloth, dipped it into the scented water, and began slowly and gently to wash my face, my arms and breasts, dipping the cloth into the water before moving on to my stomach, marking a trail of hot desire as he moved downwards. I wanted to beg him to stop, to take me there and then when he paused a few moments to gently stroke and probe. I thought I would die with wanting, but I kept my eyes closed and silently waited for him to complete the cleansing ritual.

Surely we must consummate our relationship now—I opened my eyes, ready to abandon all pretense.

He had dipped the cloth once more into the water and was silently mopping his own face with it.

I could no longer stay still; I needed to match him with my own actions. And so I took the cloth from him and began the tantalizing path of exploration downwards, moving from the dark thicket of the hair on his chest over his flat stomach and on, taking special care to caress his arousal as part of my ministrations. He groaned, but still he made no move to mount me. And so I dipped the cloth once more and continued, taking delight in the feel of skin and hair under my fingertips, although I was growing more nervous by the moment.

Finally, he took my hand and we stepped out of the tub together. Surely now, I thought, as he moved toward the bed. But it was only to fetch a towel, with which he tenderly patted me dry. By now I was shaking with fear, and with desire. I snatched up a dry towel, impatient to complete this dance between us, but he seized it from me and quickly rubbed himself down.

I could bear the delay no longer, and so I lay on his bed, and waited for him to fall on me and ravish me as Arthur had done. But he did not. He settled down beside me and began to kiss me. His mouth covered mine; his tongue darted and flicked, and I moaned and tried to shift under him so that he could fill me where I longed to be filled. Instead, his mouth moved downwards, fluttering kisses onto my breasts, onto my stomach and downwards until I opened myself wide to him, felt his tongue enter and tease me until I began to shake and thrust against him and again and again until I came to climax with a final glorious explosion of release.

It took me a few moments to realize what had happened, and then I was overcome with shame. I had done to Launcelot what Arthur had done to me; taken my pleasure without thought or care for him. "I'm so sorry," I whispered, but he kissed me again, stopping my words. I could taste myself in his kiss. Full of remorse, I moved my head away and, in turn, began to kiss his nipples, his stomach, feeling desire ignite once more as I came down to his erection. More than anything I wanted to love him as he had loved me, and give him the pleasure that he had given me. I touched his swollen penis, felt it throb within my fingers and then, with an agonized groan, Launcelot covered me and thrust himself inside. I felt myself melting into him as he pushed deeper, until it seemed that we had become one, rising and rising on spirals of infinite joy and sensation until I cried out in a shuddering climax, and felt the spurt of his seed inside me.

Passion spent, still we cleaved together, one body, and one heart. And so we slept, and woke, and made love, and slept again.

Each time we come together seems more delightful than the last for, as the days pass, so we have come to know each other's bodies as intimately as our own, and we find new and diverse ways to pleasure each other. I cannot tell Launcelot how superior a lover he is to Arthur, but I can tell him in so many other ways and gestures that he is everything to me, both as a lover and as a friend. And I wait for him to speak of the future, our future. But he does not. However, I take it as a measure of his regard for me when he commissions a series of tapestries to be woven to my design to adorn the walls of our hall.

"But what scenes shall I choose?" I ask him.

He smiles at me. "That is for you to decide, but you must be in all of them. There should be at least four tapestries, one for each wall, so that I can see you at every turn."

Four scenes from Joyous Garde? The castle itself? The garden? The river? The ocean beyond that surrounds us at high tide, and then retreats once more? Or something more magical than that?

I recall the Otherworlds I have visited, both with Merlin and on my own. And I remember the silvery white unicorn I befriended, along with many other marvelous creatures I encountered. I look at my new pet, a puppy abandoned by its mother and adopted by me. It follows me everywhere. There is also the little monkey that Launcelot bought for me as we passed through a fair on our way to Joyous Garde. Ideas start to stir, and for the next few days I scribble busily on scraps of parchment until I have the theme and the designs sorted out to my satisfaction.

"What have you decided on?" Launcelot asks when I bid him summon the seamstresses for consultation.

"It's to be a surprise. You'll have to wait and see."

I keep a close eye on the work as it progresses. There are ten seamstresses, all of them skillful and quick with their needles, and all of them sworn to secrecy. I think the tapestries will turn out well and I wait impatiently to see them whole.

Seasons change, and change again, and I am happier than I have ever been. True, I was happy as a child, before my father was slain. But this is a happiness that goes far beyond childhood, for Launcelot treats me as a friend and as an equal by day, and with a passionate and tender love at night. And yet a nagging question lurks always at the back of my mind: Am I right to trust Launcelot when everyone I have ever loved in the past has betrayed me?

The other thing that troubles me is Mordred. I miss my son, sometimes with an ache that is hard to hide. I wonder if he is fretting without me, and I try to console myself with the thought that he has his cousins to amuse him, and the care of a loving surrogate mother in Morgause. I tell myself also that he is of an age when high-born children are sent to friends or relatives in noble houses elsewhere, to become first a page and then a squire; to learn courtly manners but also how to hunt and ride, and to master the arts of war. I would have had to send him away soon enough, for I want my son to grow up as a man, and with a manly sense of duty. He would not have learned any of this in the priory.

Thus I rationalize my desertion of my son, but still his absence pains me. Whenever Launcelot asks why I seem so pensive I long to tell him, but always I hold back. Each time

I try to speak, something stops me. Perhaps it is because I know I shall have to tell him a lie, and I cannot bring myself to do that. And yet my silence is also a lie. I call myself a coward, yet I do nothing, and say nothing, hoping that somehow, some time, I will find a way to be truly honest with Launcelot without jeopardizing the happiness I have found here. Meanwhile I make excuses for my inattention: that the sultry weather has brought on a headache, or that I have had a bad dream.

The seasons change again, and the day comes at last when the tapestries are finally complete. They are all and more than I had hoped, for the seamstresses have added touches of their own: wildflowers are scattered like stars across their dark red backgrounds. Launcelot's coat of arms adorns the draperies. Other creatures, hares and baby lambs, keep company with my young whippet and pet monkey. A lion on one side balances the unicorn on the other. All these changes were sanctioned by me, and I am delighted with the result. I am impatient to witness Launcelot's reaction.

Once I am sure that he is out and busy with affairs around the estate, we carry the tapestries to the hall. There are six of them, and I summon several workmen to help with their hanging. And then we walk around, the seamstresses and I, marveling at how well they have turned out. I congratulate them and give them my heartfelt thanks, with a purse of silver to add to their wages as a token of my gratitude. When I hear Launcelot calling for me, I run to greet him. "Come and see." I drag him into the hall. He stops on the threshold, his eyes wide with wonder. Slowly, he paces from tapestry to tapestry, inspecting each in careful silence. I pace with him, wishing that he would say something. Anything. I worry that he is displeased, and I can't think what to say.

"Don't you like them?" I whisper at last.

"My love!" He turns to me with a quick embrace. "They are a wonder. A marvel! I've been trying to perceive their meaning. I'm not quite sure, but I think I'm beginning to understand."

I exhale the breath I hadn't realized I was holding. "Tell me." I smile at him. "A kiss if you guess aright."

"Only a kiss?" His answering smile ignites a heat that spreads through my body.

"Only a kiss if you don't get it right," I amend.

"Then I shall have to consider my words very carefully." He takes my hand and moves to stand in front of the tapestry nearest the door. "I see you are in all of them, as I requested. The likeness is amazing, Morgana." He squeezes my hand, and is silent a moment. "I suspect these depict the five senses. In this one, you are gazing in a mirror that reflects this strange creature here."

"It's a unicorn," I tell him.

"A marvelous creature indeed. So this panel represents sight. Am I right?"

I nod, and we move on. "And here you are playing a positif, while a maidservant works the bellows. So you are listening to music. Sound, or hearing, yes?"

"Right again." I lead him on to the next tapestry. "What about this one?"

"A maidservant is offering you a piece of confectionery. Taste?"

"Indeed." It delights me that Launcelot has been so quick to understand my meaning. I point to the next tapestry. "What does this tell you?"

Launcelot looks at the hands in the tapestry, one of which rests on a standard adorned with his coat of arms while the other caresses the unicorn's horn. "Touch?"

I nod, and point again.

Launcelot frowns and walks closer. "There is only one sense remaining, and yet there are still two tapestries that need deciphering. But I notice that in this one you are weaving a garland of flowers, and that you have just taken a scented carnation from your maidservant's basket. So this one denotes the sense of smell? But I confess, Morgana, much as it pains me to lose our little wager, I cannot fathom what to make of this last tapestry."

"Look more closely." I drag him across to the last panel, largest of them all. I touch the inscription embroidered in gold on the blue pavilion behind the depiction of me and my maidservant.

"*À mon seul désir*," Launcelot says slowly. "My only desire?"

"My only desire is you, my lord," I tell him. "You are in my heart, my mind and my soul. My body is yours. My only desire is to please you in every way you can imagine. I see the heart as the sixth sense, the heart that makes sense of everything else."

Launcelot is silent as he scrutinizes the pretty scene with its heartfelt motto. I wonder what he is thinking. I wonder if now, at last, he will propose marriage. He turns and takes me in his arms. "And my only desire is to please you, beloved," he murmurs, and his lips find mine in a long and loving kiss.

*

There is no proposal, not then nor in the months that follow. And yet I know that Launcelot loves me as much as I love him. It is evident not only in our passionate coupling, but in the many small acts of thoughtfulness, caring and kindness that mark our days. I tell myself that I am content; nevertheless I begin to wonder how much longer I can stay away from Mordred.

At the heart of it is Launcelot himself. I cannot bear to leave him, to say goodbye, for I cannot be sure when I might see him again. I torment myself with questions. Would he stay on here without me or would he return to Camelot? And if he did, might someone else capture his heart in my absence, someone like Guenevere? I try to reassure myself that my fears are groundless, for he tells me often enough that he loves me and certainly I have constant proof of his desire. Our loving is so sweet that I find it impossible to put an end to it.

Finally, the time comes when I know that we must talk about the future. Despite my precautions I have missed one course, and I live with a growing delight that I do not voice until another month passes by with still no sign of "the flowers", as common people call the menses. I am waiting for an opportune time to tell the good news to my lover when a messenger arrives from Arthur, summoning Launcelot back to Camelot. I listen in dismay as Launcelot reads the message out to me.

"*I beg you to come back to court, for I need my friends about me at this time. An attempt was made on my life. Fortunately it was unsuccessful, but Sir Accolon was killed and now the court is buzzing with rumors.*"

Accolon! My dismay grows as Launcelot continues to read out the details of Arthur's slaying of Accolon. How Accolon had provoked a quarrel with curses and slurs on Arthur's governance and reputation, and had drawn his sword, tempting Arthur to retaliate.

I close my eyes in dread. Accolon must have grown impatient; must have thought to bring me back to Camelot by catching the king unawares, and killing him. But why is Accolon dead and Arthur still alive?

"*It seems that by some chance the magical scabbard as well as my sword Excalibur were exchanged by Accolon for his own weapon and scabbard. Unfortunately I did not notice the switch, and it was only by good fortune that I was able to wrest Excalibur from Accolon's grasp and in turn pierce my attacker through the heart.*"

Lancelot frowns at me. "This is a dreadful business, Morgana. Who could have thought such treachery could lie hidden and unsuspected in Arthur's court?" His voice is heavy with foreboding as he reads on.

"Accolon is dead, but the matter has not ended there, for it seems there was more to this attempt on my life than the ambition of one man."

A deathly coldness creeps over me at the realization that Accolon must have talked to someone, told the truth about what he'd done, and my part in it too, no doubt. I bow my head, not knowing what to say or how I might defend myself while Launcelot continues.

"Everyone knows that the scabbard of Excalibur has magical properties, but not everyone has the knowledge or the skill to weave a replacement so similar that I had no notion that it was not genuine. People are saying that there is dark magic involved in this affair and, with your help, I would like to investigate this matter further."

Launcelot stops abruptly, although I notice his eyes continue to skim the parchment. "What else does it say?" I ask, although I dread hearing the full extent of what Arthur knows. Launcelot coughs, and reads aloud once more.

"My wife joins with me in begging you to return to Camelot. Since you escorted her from her father's home, she has always thought of you as her special champion. She was immensely distressed that you were not present at our nuptials and asks as a personal favor that you do not disappoint us in this."

I hardly hear the closing salutation from Arthur, I feel such relief—and anger. And jealousy. Guenevere! When I first looked down on her, I realized she had eyes only for Launcelot, but once again I have underestimated her ability to connive and plot to get her own way, for it seems she will stop at nothing to bring him to her side. Is Arthur blind that he cannot see what lies behind his wife's request?

But of far more importance to me is the next question: Will Launcelot obey his king's—and Guenevere's—command?

I look to him for the answer, and find him assessing me with a long and thoughtful stare. My jealousy is forgotten as I struggle to interpret what he is thinking. Now is the time to tell him that we are to have a child, I think, but this thought is immediately followed by another. I will not shame Launcelot into a proposal of marriage. If we are to wed, the suggestion must come from him, and I must be sure that he means it.

"I have to go," he tells me. "I have to obey the king's summons."

"Then I'll come with you." Better to be there to defend myself against gossip if need be. And defend Launcelot against Guenevere, if it comes to that.

"No, Morgana. I cannot have you with me. I must go alone." His refusal hits me like a slap across the face. Speechless, I stare at him.

He takes my hand. "You know I love you." He begins to play with my fingers, twisting the ring he has given me around and around. "And I know that you love me in return."

"Of course I do!" After all we've been to each other at Joyous Garde, how can he doubt it?

"Have you wondered at all why our liaison has been conducted here rather than at Camelot?"

"Yes, I have." I am about to go on to tell him that, no matter what else he may hear about me, I truly love him and trust him above all others. But he forestalls me.

"While I was at Camelot, I heard several stories about you." Launcelot keeps on twisting the ring around my finger; he won't look at me. "People said that you and the king are at odds with each other, and that you desire his position for yourself."

"It was my father's wish that I succeed him as his heir."

"But Arthur is the son of the High King—and a man. His claim is therefore far greater than yours."

Do all men share this disdain—nay, this *contempt*—for a woman's ability to rule? Is that why Launcelot dismisses my claim to the kingdom so lightly? Can he not see how his words thunder in my ears?

"And so to protect your good name and your standing with Arthur—and his queen—you have taken your pleasure with me, but in secret and at no risk to you," I say coldly, coming at last to understand my place in Launcelot's life.

"No, it's not like that. There is always gossip at court, stories circulating about who is doing what and with whom. I give them no credence because I prefer to make my own judgments about the situation." He coughs, and clears his throat. "But Guenevere told me, before I left the court, that she had seen you with Accolon and that your behavior suggested that you were more than mere acquaintances. I dismissed her words as idle mischief-making, for I know well that you love me. But now that this has happened, you must understand that my first allegiance is to your brother, my king. I cannot jeopardize his friendship, particularly at this time when he trusts me to find out who was responsible for this attack on his life. That is why you cannot accompany me, Morgana. I must be seen as a man with no ties and completely impartial in this matter, both for my sake but also, my darling, for yours."

"But you do have ties, whether or not you acknowledge them in public. All that we have shared here, our happiness, our life at Joyous Garde, tie us together." I will not tell him what else binds us together, not now, but I grasp his hand with both of mine. "You know that Guenevere's accusation is baseless. Please, take me with you to court."

The rightful heir to the kingdom should not have to beg for favors. I resent being put in this position yet the truth is stark and clear. As things stand, I am nothing and nobody unless I have Launcelot at my side. Together, we could face the court and fight for my good name. His presence would protect me against the slander and gossip of Arthur's courtiers and his queen. He could give me a position in Camelot as the wife of the best, the fairest and bravest of all Arthur's knights—if only he would agree.

"No, Morgana. I cannot acknowledge you unless and until I am able to prove your innocence in this affair."

Even though I know myself to be guilty of all that he suspects, nevertheless I am consumed with rage that, after all his words of love and all we have shared together at Joyous Garde, he will not acknowledge me for who I am: his wife in all but name, and the mother of his unborn child.

So be it. I snatch my hand from his and face him. "Look at me," I command, and so he does. I read in his expression such grief, such torment, that my courage almost fails me. Yet I force myself to continue. "Let me be sure I understand you. On the basis of the lying, slanderous tongues of the court, you are putting me aside to hurry back to Camelot, to Arthur—and the queen."

"I'm not putting you aside, I'm just asking for your ... discretion. For the moment."

"Until you can prove that what everyone is saying about me isn't true?"

"Is it not true, Morgana? Do I have your word on that?"

I open my mouth to give him the assurance he wants—but I find that the words stick in my throat. "It depends on what they're saying," I prevaricate, hoping this will be sufficient to divert him. Launcelot subjects me to another long stare before handing me the message from Arthur. He has omitted to read aloud the passage that directly concerns me and that is of most concern to him.

> *People are saying that there is dark magic involved in this and, with your help, I would like to investigate this matter*

further. It seems that my half-sister Morgana might well have had a hand in it. She is skilled in magic, having been trained in her early years by the mage, Merlin, who led her to believe that she was the true heir to the kingdom until she proved that she was unworthy. More, she is known to have had a liaison with Accolon, and may well have persuaded him to do her bidding in order to bring me down. As her kin, I am unable to conduct the investigation, which is why I'm asking you, as an impartial observer, to see to it yourself.

I can feel the blush of shame burning my face as I crumple up the parchment and throw it on the ground. "What they're saying about me and Accolon—that's not true," I say fiercely. "I never had a liaison with Accolon, no matter what anyone, including the queen, might say."

"No?" Launcelot raised one eyebrow. "But what about the false scabbard, Morgana? You've never told me that you have a knowledge of magic and otherworldly matters. What do you know about the scabbard's provenance—and what else haven't you told me?"

I cannot answer and so I turn away, knowing that I have lost Launcelot's trust and that things can never be the same after this. I want to howl my misery aloud. Once again, and more than ever, I wish for the power to turn back time so that I can make everything clean and pure between us. But it is too late for that; my fate was sealed when first my mother, then Merlin, and finally Arthur, betrayed me. A flash of bright, hot anger dries my tears as I come to a bitter understanding that once again I've been betrayed by someone I love. Launcelot was my lover, but he could also have been my husband and the father of our child. Instead, he has turned his back on me in his haste to find favor with Arthur and the queen. And for that I cannot and will not forgive him.

"Go and do Arthur's bidding then, and I wish you well of it," I say.

Without further words, or even a farewell kiss in parting, I walk out of the room and down to the stables, not even waiting for my belongings to be packed. I am appalled at how quickly our joy has turned to ashes, but I keep my head held high and my chin uplifted while the groom saddles my palfrey and makes everything ready for me. The tide is out, so I can ride across the causeway rather than wait for a ferryman. I am glad of that. I do not want Launcelot to witness my distress.

My eyes stream with tears as I ride away from Joyous Garde. I wonder if Launcelot is watching me from the parapet as once I watched for him. I steel myself not to look around for one last glance of my beloved, and I ride on until the castle is out of sight. To take my mind off my despair, I try instead to focus on my immediate future.

My first thought is to go to my sister Morgause and reclaim my son. My heart, a solid rock in my breast, softens slightly at the thought of seeing Mordred again. Together, we can go back to the priory and take shelter from the world. I can have my baby there; we shall be safe. It is a tempting thought, yet one that leaves me feeling strangely dissatisfied until I realize that unless I make some effort to redeem myself, I shall for ever afterward be known as Morgana, the betrayer. For Mordred's sake, and for the sake of my unborn child—and yes, to shame Launcelot—I need to fight for my good name and reputation.

Going to Camelot feels like the right course of action, for I have never run from a challenge in all my life. If I am at court, and if I can convince Arthur of my innocence, I can punish Launcelot at the same time. I will not have him back in my bed: not now, not ever. I intend to make him regret that he ever doubted me, especially when he finally understands that he has lost me forever.

As I have lost him. Grief shudders through me; I howl my misery aloud. I whip my palfrey into a gallop, but I cannot outrun my despair. I know that I will live with this loss until death brings sweet oblivion.

But I cannot think of death, not now, not while there is a new life growing inside me. I press my hand against my stomach, imagining the child forming within. Another child without a father. Another story to invent. What shall I say this time?

There is some ease to be found in stoking my anger against Launcelot, and against all those others who have stolen my destiny and laid waste to my future. I determine that Camelot will be my destination, because I need to settle matters there. I won't forget or forgive Launcelot's disloyalty, nor the conniving and faithless queen who perhaps may be used to my own advantage, now my carefully wrought plan against Arthur has gone awry. Instead of going to court and throwing myself on my brother's mercy, can I instead find some other way to bring him undone, some way that can never be traced back to me?

Mordred? I thrust that thought aside. Although it was my original intention, I know that I cannot use my child to punish Arthur. Not Mordred. Not this unborn child either. Once more I caress my stomach, seeking to reassure the babe within of my goodwill toward it.

If I go to court, if Launcelot sees me growing great with child, will he realize that the child is his, or will he suspect that Accolon is the father? I wince at the thought. I have never lain with Accolon, but I have seen that Launcelot has lost faith in me. So he might well credit Accolon as the father rather than himself, even though the timing of the birth should leave no doubt in the matter. Does a man know about this sort of thing? I shrug, doubting it. Launcelot will believe whatever it suits him to believe. But I do not want him, or anyone, to know that I carry a child.

My head spins with ideas until I finally settle on a plan that I hope will answer my desire for revenge and, at the same time, give me the power I need to rule the kingdom in Arthur's stead. My first task is to change my appearance. There are several things I need to accomplish, but I know my mission will be impossible if I go to court as Arthur's sister. More, it would be excruciating to meet Launcelot under such changed circumstances. I cannot bear to see his face should he learn the full extent of my treachery, so my disguise will be part of ensuring that he never will; that no one will ever find out the truth behind Accolon's attack on Arthur. Nor must anyone associate me with anything that happens to Arthur in the future.

And so I change my appearance to resemble one of the high priestesses of Avalon, a lady whom I particularly admire. Niniane is sweet natured, but very powerful, second only to the high priestess Viviane. I am in awe of Viviane, but I am comfortable with Niniane, who has lived in our world for a time and who understands our ways, unlike most of the neophytes and guardians of Avalon, all of whom are female. Their way is not for me; my time with Launcelot has convinced me of that. Indeed, I wonder how the more worldly Niniane puts up with the catfights and jealousies inevitable among a company made up solely of women. I am sure living in Avalon is no different from living in the closed world of the priory, and there I have seen at firsthand how favoritism and backbiting can sour even the most devout believer. It is one reason why I kept myself apart from them all.

I begin to weave the magic that will transform me, not into Niniane exactly, but into something akin. I shall say that I have come from Avalon to visit Camelot, having heard of the wonders of Arthur's court. I know enough of my brother to understand that my flattery will win his trust and that he will not question me further. Of course, if he should ask me about Avalon I can certainly satisfy his curiosity.

I grow taller, and my hair changes in color from mouse brown to silvery gold. My eyes lighten to pale gray, which I hurriedly change to dark blue as I recall Viviane's penetrating stare. She, too, has gray eyes. I give myself a heart-shaped face—I have always wanted one of those! And, while I am indulging myself, I curl my straight hair into luxurious waves. I set a gold band on my brow, like the ones all the sisters wear in Avalon. Finally, and because I don't know how long I'll be in Camelot, I devise a flowing gown in a filmy fabric shading from silver to blue and mauve, colors that shift and change and that, I hope, will detract from and hide my growing stomach if it turns out that I need to stay in Camelot long enough that the baby will start to show.

From time to time I pat and massage the slight mound of my belly, seeking consolation from this growing proof of my love for Launcelot and his love for me. My heart splinters into pieces at the very thought of what else lies ahead if I carry out my plan. Launcelot has put his suspicions, and his duty to the king, ahead of his love for me. In turn, I could give him a lesson in love and loyalty, a lesson that would have the potential to split Camelot in two and that would certainly lose him the love, respect and friendship of his king and the knights at court. At the same time, I would repay those others who have wronged me, who have set me on this path of vengeance—a path that only I can reverse. If I have the resolve to put the rest of my plan into action, I know I could make them all repent the past, and beg for my good governance, the governance they should have recognized right from the start. And so I tell myself that no matter what the cost may be, I must continue with my tricks and deceits, and leave the outcome in the lap of the gods—and the judgment of those whom I intend to test.

Sometimes my power to change other people's lives worries me, but I console myself with the thought that of them all, it is Launcelot's future that is of the most concern to me. Will he see through my tricks and deceits? Will he have the wisdom and strength not to fall into my trap? If he is the man I once thought him, then his honor may yet be salvaged—and perhaps my happiness too.

And so, despite Launcelot's betrayal and my desolation at his abandonment, and despite the failure of my latest plan to remove Arthur from the throne, my courage is high when, at last, I ride through the gates of Camelot and into Arthur's court.

CHAPTER 6

Confident in my disguise, the first thing I do is request an audience with Arthur. To my annoyance, I find Guenevere sitting beside him. I have my story prepared and know it is persuasive enough to convince Arthur. I am not quite so sure about his wife. Having underestimated her in the past, I shall not make the same mistake again.

It is the first chance I've had to really study her, and I make the most of the opportunity. At such close quarters, my first impression of her youth and beauty is reinforced. Yet there is something to mar her expression, some discontent and, when she turns to her husband, there is acid in her tone as she chides him for not calling for refreshments to welcome me. My brother does her bidding, while apologizing for his lack of courtesy. I want to tell him to act like a man and a king; to remind him that organizing refreshments is women's work, but I keep silent, knowing that I can learn more through observation and holding my tongue.

"Pray, be seated, lady. You must be tired after your journey." The request is sweetly civil, but Guenevere betrays herself when she turns to her husband. "Arthur!" she snaps. "Draw up a chair for our guest."

Interesting. I remember how unsatisfied I felt after bedding Arthur, and feel a momentary sympathy for the queen. It would seem that there are no children of this union as yet. That thought brings much comfort, while also suggesting several interesting possibilities.

"Now, lady; tell me who you are and how I may serve you?" Arthur ignores his wife's command. He settles back into his seat, and pats her hand as if soothing a fractious hound.

I open my mouth to give my assumed name. If I had done so, I would have been doomed, for the door opens to reveal Viviane of Avalon. She strides in, gives me a long assessing stare, and then goes to stand behind Arthur, forming a protective presence at his back. I can tell from Guenevere's sour expression that the lady isn't welcome here. Another interesting observation to think about later. For now, I am busy revising my story, trying to come up with something convincing that doesn't involve Avalon.

"My name is Nimue, my liege," I say, and sweep into a deep curtsy.

"You are welcome to Camelot." Arthur holds out his hand. I take it and kiss it.

"I come from a faraway realm, but your fame, and the news of your court, has reached even the Isles of … of Annwyn." It is the name of one of the Otherworlds that I have visited in the past. Too late, I wonder if the Lady of Avalon also knows of Annwyn. I look beyond Arthur and find her staring at me with narrowed eyes. I wonder if she can see through my disguise. To my infinite relief, she does not challenge me.

"Why have you come to Camelot?" Guenevere asks. She smooths away a crease in her gown and primps her hair. I read in her gestures all the signs of an insecure girl needing reassurance. And she will get it—but not from her husband. My heart quails at the thought of what I propose to do. But it is not time, not yet. And hopefully, never.

"I've come to see for myself the wonders of your court," I say humbly. "And to serve you in any way I can, for I have heard of the recent attempt on your life and it may be that I have information that will be of interest to you."

Arthur nods, and motions toward a bench. He turns to Viviane. "Pray, will you take a seat with us, lady?" To my relief, for I am not sure how long I can endure that questioning stare that stabs like a sword, she relinquishes her post behind Arthur and helps me drag the bench closer to the royal couple. We sit down, and she is no longer in my line of sight.

"I am greatly indebted to the Lady Viviane, who is able to see something of the future, and who came down the river to my court in order to warn me that my life was in danger," Arthur tells me. "It seems that King Urien's son, Accolon, stole my sword and scabbard and left imitations in their place. He provoked me to a quarrel, and would have killed me but for Viviane's warning to be on my guard. Fortunately, I was able to seize Excalibur from Accolon and, instead, I slew him."

"Do not forget, sire, that it was your sister Morgana who wove the scabbard that tricked you into believing that Accolon's sword was your own," Viviane murmurs.

I grit my teeth, wanting to choke her. But this is my chance to speak on my own behalf. "You are greatly mistaken, lady," I say sweetly. "I am in the confidence of the Lady Morgana, and I know how much she loves and respects you, sire. She would never try to harm you."

I can read the disbelief on Guenevere's face. It is sweet to think of the fate I have in store for her. "As for Accolon of Gaul, he was ever a liar and a braggard," I continue. "The Lady Morgana has told me how he followed her around while she was here at court, promising her that if only she would lie with him, he would conquer the world in her name and make her his queen. She said she laughed at him when he told her that, sire. Rather than stay, lest it encourage his foolish ambition, she bade him farewell and left your court. Never for one moment did she dream that he would try to make good his boast. She was devastated when she found out what he'd done. And she gives thanks that he did not succeed."

"You are saying that my sister is innocent of the charges that have been laid against her good name."

"On my life, sire!" I put all my heart and feeling into the oath. I can tell that Arthur believes me. But I am fairly sure Guenevere will not want to think well of any woman, particularly someone she perceives as a rival for Launcelot's affection. As for Viviane, she sits upright and silent beside me.

"I am pleased—and very relieved—to hear of my sister's innocence," says Arthur. "But where have you seen her that you seem to know so much about her, for she vanished from my court many, many moons ago?"

"She is living quietly at a priory not so very far from here. I … I took shelter there on my journey to your court and, when I saw how distressed she was by the rumors that have come to her ears, I stayed on a few days more to comfort her. She begged me to put her case forward on her behalf. It would relieve her mind greatly if I could tell her on my return journey that she is absolved of all guilt, my liege."

"And so you may." Several servants now stand at the door, bearing jugs of spiced wine and plates of honey wafers. Arthur beckons them forward and they lay out the refreshments. Hungry and tired after my long journey, and feeling an immeasurable relief, I lick my lips in anticipation. But it seems I am not yet out of danger.

"Nimue? You bear a marked resemblance to the Lady Niniane, to whom I have left the care of my demesne in my absence." Viviane is scrutinizing me with those big gray eyes that seem to see and understand everything.

I shake my head and assume a modest expression. "I am but a humble damsel, my lady; I can claim no kinship with anyone from the sacred Isle of Avalon."

"How do you know I come from the sacred isle?" Viviane retorts sharply.

I think quickly. "The Lady Morgana mentioned you to me; she spoke of your power and your gift for seeing the truth." I hold my breath as I say this for, if my magical powers are not greater than Viviane's, now is the time for her to reveal her knowledge of my true identity. But she stays silent. I feel a flash of triumph as I continue, "The Lady Morgana and I spent a great deal of time talking together."

I turn to Arthur in appeal; I will not deal with Viviane again unless I have no choice. "My liege, she sought me out once she knew where I was bound. I cannot tell you how greatly her heart and mind have been affected by these foul rumors."

Guenevere gives a delicate sniff. "Why then does she not come to court to speak for herself?"

The queen is someone else I need to watch out for, I remind myself. "Your sister fears your wrath, my liege," I say humbly, still addressing Arthur. "But, if you forgive her, you may wish to send for her yourself?"

"There's no need for that, Arthur." I am grateful that Guenevere has put that notion to rest although it's fairly clear that Launcelot's expected arrival is behind her words. It seems she will do anything to keep me out of his way. And she will attain her heart's desire soon enough, I think savagely, although the price she will pay is beyond her calculation.

"You forget that some questions regarding this affair have not yet been answered, my liege." Viviane's quiet voice alerts me to further danger. "Who wove the false scabbard, if not your sister Morgana?"

This time I cannot speak, for to do so will betray more knowledge than I should possess. Arthur shifts in his chair, looking uncomfortable. The silence lengthens until I am forced to break it.

"Surely there are other seamstresses in your court, sire, skillful enough to weave a copy for a man whom they might well covet as a husband?"

"Skillful enough to make a copy, perhaps, but not skillful enough to weave magic into it."

"Was magic woven into it?" I meet Viviane's searching glance with a shocked expression. "Was not the trick dependent on merely exchanging the one for the other?"

"Of course it was," Arthur said impatiently. "I was wrong to blame my sister. I was wrong to suspect her of this right from the start."

I glance thoughtfully at my brother, whose sword within its magical scabbard lies close to his hand. I have other plans for it now. He will not be able to find it again once I have finished with it.

"Perhaps, sire, you should not listen to the lies of the court but rather make up your own mind about what happens here in your demesne?" I cannot resist the rebuke but, as I watch Arthur's face darken in anger, I am sorry I have spoken.

"Hold your tongue, lady," Guenevere spits like a small, angry kitten. "You do ill to speak so disrespectfully to the king." It seems that, while it is quite fitting for her to shame Arthur in public, no one else is allowed to do so.

"I humbly apologize, my liege," I say hastily. "I assure you, I meant no disrespect."

Arthur nods. Viviane says nothing, and I am glad of it. Having accomplished what I set out to do, I am anxious now to flee their presence. And so I make an excuse that I need to wash after my long journey, and with great relief I take my leave.

After my ablutions, I visit the castle gardens, saying that I have heard of their magnificence and wish to see for myself what makes them so memorable. Once there, I stroll about in seemingly aimless fashion, picking sweet strawberries to eat, and a selection of flowers and herbs that I fashion into a pretty posy. In themselves the plants are relatively harmless. Combined, they become effective for my purpose, but what will really give my potion its power hereafter is the incantation that I shall recite during its concoction. I am more determined than ever to secure the kingdom for Mordred, if not for myself, and I am prepared to use all my magical arts to ensure it. What I most need now is some privacy to prepare the infusion for the queen, for I know she will ask for it sooner or later.

I wait for a chance to talk to Guenevere through a lengthy dinner the following noon. It comprises an array of courses the like of which I've never seen before: roasted swan and hedgehog, porpoises and an assortment of sea creatures, some in a variety of shells that for the most part take quite some getting into and for very little reward. It is clear that Guenevere has set her seal on Camelot, and on its kitchen in particular. But I dine well and with enthusiasm; I am always prepared to try anything new.

During the meal we are entertained by a juggler and then a magician, who performs a series of tricks that I find so laughable I am sorely tempted to show off a few of my own. He is followed by a poet with a lute, who gazes at Guenevere with soulful eyes and sings ballads to her beauty and to the splendors of the court. It is nauseating, but I can tell she is swallowing it down as greedily as a pig at the swill bucket.

When Arthur excuses himself from the table to attend to the steward who has been hovering by his side for quite some time, I move from my seat to sit closer to his wife.

"Lady, I apologize for my rudeness earlier," I say, willing to humble myself if it serves my purpose. "I can assure you it was not intended as a judgment of the king. Rather, it was a reflection of my eagerness to keep faith with the Lady

Morgana, who trusted me to bring her message to the court and, most particularly, to her brother."

Guenevere looks down her nose at me. Flattery, I remind myself, and begin to praise the dinner and the beautiful queen who presides over it. Finally, when I think she has thawed sufficiently, I broach the true purpose of this conversation.

"Forgive me if I speak too freely, madame, but it saddens me that as yet you have no child to bless your union with the king."

Guenevere draws a quivering breath. Tears glimmer in her eyes and she dashes them away. I know how hard it must be for her, knowing that the whole court is watching and waiting for her to produce an heir, and commenting on her failure to do so. And I feel a moment of shame as I begin to tell her the story I have prepared.

"While living on the island of Annwyn I learned much of herbs and their properties, and also the healing arts … including a way to encourage a reluctant womb to bear seed."

I have Guenevere's full attention now. She clutches my arm. "Can you help me, Nimue?" she whispers.

I smile at her. "It would be my honor and a privilege, your majesty." And so we make an arrangement to meet later, under cover of night, and she gathers up her ladies and leaves the hall.

I linger, for I've noticed that in his hurry to attend to his steward's request Arthur has forgotten to take both his sword and its scabbard. They stand propped close to his seat, according to custom, for no knight will sit down to his meat fully armed. I click my tongue, tutting that he can be so careless after having so recently survived an attack on his life. Once I am sure that I am unobserved, I nudge the sword to my side and unsheathe it before placing it under his chair as if kicked there by a careless step. With the magical scabbard hidden within the folds of my dress, I stroll out of the castle grounds, telling the guards that I need to visit the water meadows and there pick some special herbs at the queen's command. They cannot know that I already have what I need, and Guenevere's name is enough to guarantee that they will not question me further.

By now it is late afternoon; the setting sun tinges meadow grasses, flowers and reeds with a ruddy glow. Moorhens bob and cluck, and rooks call raucously from their nests. I hurry beside the water channels until I reach the deep spring that feeds them. There I pull the scabbard from where I have concealed it and hold it for a moment in my hands. Doubt assails me, but I know that it is too late now to change my mind and leave the future to unwind along the unknown spool of life. Camelot's destiny is cast, its doom sealed by the betrayal of Merlin, and Arthur, and Launcelot. With no further time for regret, I cast the magical scabbard into the water. I watch it arc through the air, watch it splash down, float a few moments and finally sink into the depths. Arthur's protection has gone forever. Now, he is as vulnerable as the poorest churl in his kingdom.

For the first time since the messenger called at Joyous Garde, I feel my spirits quieten into a semblance of peace.

Mindful of my excuse, I pick a selection of wildflowers on my stroll back to the castle to replace the posy I gathered the day before. Their fragrance sweetens my corner of the room I share with the castle's unwed ladies. It is there I take shelter while making the utmost of the uproar over the missing scabbard that has erupted throughout the castle and that keeps everyone else away. I quickly brew the magical potion that will ensure that Guenevere will never bear a child. I utter the incantation that will bind it, and then hide the flask where no one will think to look for it. Having already submitted to a search of my own belongings, and an interrogation regarding my departure from the castle, which I explained away with the posy of flowers, my innocence in the affair has been accepted. I offer to join in the search for the missing scabbard, and my search is as diligent as that conducted by anyone else. To everyone's amazement but mine, the scabbard is not to be found anywhere at all.

*

Once darkness falls, I hurry out into the garden to meet Guenevere as arranged. She is seated on a turf bench screened by a woven trellis. Red and white roses spill over and around it, adding their rich perfume to the spicy scents of rue, sage, marjoram and other fragrant herbs planted among the flowery mead nearby. She half rises to meet me as I arrive, and then settles back as if remembering that she is the queen and I merely a lowly subject, even if I do carry in my hand the means to achieve her heartfelt desire.

I feel a flash of shame as I offer the flask to her. I, too, had once known joy, reveling in the world and my place in it. Now I have traveled further than I could ever have imagined along this road of deception and revenge, all with the intention of bringing despair and even death upon those who have wronged me. I tell myself that the queen is not really of that ilk; she has done no more against me than any woman in love and therefore she should not be part of my plan, but then I remind myself of her poisonous gossip regarding Accolon and me. More important by far: her very presence and her potential to produce an heir threaten my son's right to the crown. Besides, I need her, for she is my instrument, the means by which I shall perhaps bring them all undone.

And so I hand over the flask with the instruction that she drink the potion now so that I can take it away with me. To protect myself, I shall destroy the flask and deny everything if I am ever asked—but I do not tell her that.

She hesitates, the flask held to her lips. "And you swear this will help me conceive a child?"

"Unless God wishes it otherwise, madame," I say smoothly, knowing that once she drinks, she will never conceive a child with Arthur. If God can be blamed instead of me, so much the better.

She nods, but lowers the flask again. "What's in it?"

I hear the suspicion in her voice, and I hurry to allay it. "It's a love potion made from herbs, your majesty; something that will render your love-making more pleasurable and ensure that a child results from the union."

Her expression sours. "The king treats me like a brood mare," she says furiously. "Slaking his own appetite is all he knows how to do. Do you really think this will help?"

"I give you my word," I say, hiding a smile. Poor, unfortunate Guenevere. "It's important, my lady, to maintain a loving relationship with your husband if you wish to conceive a child," I add, thinking to use Arthur's incompetence as a lover as a further excuse when the queen demands to know why she is still barren.

Quickly, as if steeling herself to the act, Guenevere swallows the contents of the flask and hands it back to me. "My thanks, Nimue," she says, and licks her lips. "It tastes quite pleasant." She sounds surprised.

"Remember, madame: a passionate relationship will ease conception."

"Is that why I've been unable to have a baby?" Guenevere asks innocently. "Is it because Arthur doesn't really love me, he just wants an heir?"

I try to reassure her. "I am sure the king has fallen under your spell, as have most of the court. It's your duty both as wife and queen for that love to bear fruit. My potion will help to smooth your path."

"My thanks and gratitude, Nimue." Guenevere pulls a few coins from the purse at her waist and holds them out to me. Greatly offended, I am about to refuse until I realize that a humble traveler would be glad of the coins. So I take them, and thank the queen as graciously as I may.

"Nimue, are you able to see the future?" Guenevere blushes, and gives a nervous giggle. "I cannot believe I am asking such a thing, but can you tell what lies ahead for me?"

How shall I answer? Yes, I have seen many things while scrying the sacred pool. I have seen a black-draped boat of mourning—but not who rides in it. And although I am plotting Arthur's downfall, I know not if I shall be successful or even how or when his death will come about. I have seen naught of Guenevere because I have not looked for her. Nor have I had the opportunity to look for Launcelot. I feel a ripple of panic that causes me to catch my breath. I knew nothing of him, or Guenevere, when I last searched the sacred pool for answers. Should I go back to consult it before carrying on with my plan? I brush away my concerns, too impatient to brook any delay. Launcelot is due at court and I want to be here, waiting for him.

I conceal my misgivings with a cheerful laugh. "I have not the gift of prophecy, majesty, if that's what you are asking. All I can do is attempt to grant your wishes through my knowledge of herbs and healing." It isn't quite the truth, but it will do. And I am curious. "What is it that most concerns you?"

She giggles again, and raises a hand to hide her blushes. "Nothing of importance," she says, and hurries away. I watch her retreating figure and my mind spins with possibilities. Her need for a child would be obvious even to the blind, but I suspect that it is not only to provide an heir for Arthur. Guenevere wants a child to love, to hold in her arms just as I once held Mordred. I am shaken with pity, but it is too late now to regret what I have done.

Guenevere's need has also opened afresh my longing to see my son, but I am determined to stay on here, both to punish my lover for abandoning me and also to put in place my further plans for bringing about Arthur's ruin. My mind hardens against her.

I am nervous about meeting Launcelot, for I know how painful it will be to see him again. To while away the time until he arrives, I decide to attend to some other unfinished business. Merlin. To my surprise, he is nowhere to be found at court. A casual enquiry elicits the information that the old mage is still around, but that he's retired from court and is living in a cave not too far from Camelot. No one seems to know where it is, and so my first task is to change from Nimue into a bird so that I can fly in ever-increasing circles around Camelot until I find out where Merlin now lives. To conserve time and energy, and also for my own protection, I become a large eagle.

As always, I relish the freedom of flight, and I take the opportunity to first spy out what is happening in Camelot itself. I see Arthur and Guenevere walking in the garden together. She is stroking his arm in a loving manner and, judging from the way he turns to her, I suspect that their next attempt at baby-making will come about sooner rather than later. I fly further, until I notice I have come close to the abbey at Glastonbury and the priory where I used to live. Realizing I have flown too far in that direction, I am about to turn when, to my surprise, I spy Launcelot's entourage. In my feathered disguise I cannot resist flying closer. Launcelot rides alone. I am pleased to see how morose he looks. His escort follows behind. There are none of the jokes and laughter usual between men who are on a long ride and seeking to pass the time. This looks more like a funeral procession. I take a savage satisfaction from the scene as I turn away and fly on.

I spot a thin plume of smoke emanating from a woody thicket and swoop down to investigate further, but not too close for I am afraid that, if Merlin is present, he might see through my disguise. I shudder as I remember how I turned myself into a tree, and the consequences that arose from that one act. And I wonder if, instead of appearing as Nimue as I'd intended, I should instead meet him as I truly am and take my chances. But no. Even though I have tried to build a bridge between us, I know Merlin trusts me as much as I trust him. Better I try to trick him, if I possibly can.

A bird's eye view from a distance confirms that I have guessed aright, and I memorize the way to his sheltering cave on my way back to Camelot. There I complete my transformation back to Nimue, taking comfort from the fact that I am in human form, that Merlin has not seen me for a number of years and that he may well be tempted by a beautiful young woman.

Even so, when I come to his cave I approach him cautiously, ready to transmute myself and fly to safety if need be. He is sitting outside, warming himself at a small fire, for the evening has turned cool. Beside him sit several woodland creatures: a family of badgers, a fox, two rabbits, and a long-eared owl that perches comfortably on his shoulder. I look from the owl to Merlin, amused at the owl's resemblance to its master: tufted "ears" pricked for information; amber eyes bright and all-seeing; a sharp beak set in a lugubrious face that culminates in a whiskery gray beard.

"Greetings, Merlin," I say, lowering my tone in the hope he will not identify my voice.

He peers up at me. I see the film of milky white across his eyes, the signs of incipient blindness. I breathe a small sigh of relief and continue with the story I have prepared. "My name is Nimue." I pause, waiting to hear if he will contradict me, but he does not. "I have come from afar to meet you for I have heard great tales of your power and magical abilities. I wish to learn from you, Merlin, if you will only teach me."

"Nimue?" His voice is as creaky as an old door. "Come closer, child, so that I can see you."

I come close, and put down the basket I carry before kneeling at his feet. To my horror, he thrusts his face close to mine and inhales my scent. Apparently he does not remember me, for he stands, raising me with him. He begins to pat me down, as if his fingers can tell him what his eyes cannot. His hands pause at my breasts. I squirm at his touch, but try to conceal my aversion. He lingers to fondle me for a few moments, before his hands move on. I stay frozen, unsure how to extricate myself without causing offence. I need to win his trust before I can act against him.

His hands rest on my stomach. "You are with child." It is not a question.

I nod, realize he probably cannot see me, and whisper, "Yes, Merlin."

To my great relief, he stops handling me and draws back. "I once taught a child," he murmurs. "A virgin. I can only teach the young and innocent, Nimue."

"What happened to the child?" I am curious to know if Merlin feels any regret over his treatment of me.

"Morgana." He gives a low chuckle. "She was ever my favorite, but so wild, so headstrong. She understood the magical arts like no other I've ever known, but there was still much I could have taught her. If we could have worked together, discovered those secrets still undisclosed to me, I believe we might well have conquered the world as we know it." He breaks off and clears his throat. His expression has turned hard. Unforgiving.

"Morgana could have been a great leader if only she had the patience to learn, and the wisdom to use her knowledge with humility and generosity. But she stole from me the sources of my knowledge and power, took them before she was ready, before she was skilled enough to understand all that she had taken. And now I fear that her ignorance will undo us all."

I am silent, caught by the regret I hear in Merlin's voice, and by the unsettling sensation that our world is beginning to spin off course because of what I have done. I need to defend myself even to this old man. "You say she was just a child. Why did you not give her a chance to grow to adulthood?"

"She was too proud, and too wilful. I could not trust her. And now I fear great harm might come ..." Merlin's voice trails off. He looks away, off into the distance, seeing visions that even I cannot see.

Merlin is right to say that I am proud. And what is wrong with that, pray? One needs confidence to lead a nation; a ruler is nothing without pride. But to say that he could not trust me, when I would have done anything to please him, and to secure the throne? That is a false accusation, and I shall not let it pass.

"Why could you not trust her?"

Perhaps there is too much passion in my voice, for Merlin blinks and comes back to himself. "She did not use her powers wisely, for the good of all. So I found another who was better suited to take her place," he says firmly, in a voice that resembles the Merlin of old. He bends to pick up a small log from a pile nearby, and throws it onto the fire. He pokes it into place with a long stout stick.

"What did she steal from you, Merlin?" I have to ask, although I am afraid to show too much interest lest I give myself away.

He pauses in the tending of the fire; his filmy eyes look up at me. "Three things. She is clever enough to decipher the purpose of two of them, but the third ..." He gives a low chuckle. "I doubt she has the wisdom to see what should be plain in front of her. If she can but find the key she could read the future and, perhaps, even change it—if it's not too late." He turns to give the fire a savage poke with his stick.

If Merlin refers to the pack of decorated wooden tablets, he is right. And yet they seemed to fly so easily into my hand while I was searching his lair that I was quite sure I was meant to have them and that they were part of my destiny.

"Why are you here, Nimue? What do you want from me?" His voice sounds harsh. Unforgiving. I am afraid that I have missed my chance, and I set myself to woo him, to assuage his dark imaginings.

"I came to ask if you would teach me, Merlin," I say humbly. He raises his fist and brandishes the firestick at me. I take a hurried step backward. "Yes, I am with child but I am still anxious to be your pupil, if you will have me."

"I will not," he growls. "I teach only the very few who are worthy, those who are high-born enough to make a difference to those they rule and who I know will use the magical arts wisely in their service. And you fail on all counts, Nimue."

I cannot give up, nor can I show my disappointment. "Then, if you cannot teach me, Merlin, may I at least stay here with you for a time? Perhaps I can help you?"

"I doubt there is much you can do to help me, lady, unless you think to trick me into helping *you*. And that I will not do." He sinks down onto his seat, and turns his face away from me.

He knows who I am! I am sure of it. But I can't resist testing him. "Where is Morgana now, Merlin?"

There is a raucous squawk from the owl. I jump, wondering for one insane moment if I have been transformed by Merlin. I pinch my hand, just to make sure I am still Nimue, and am relieved to touch skin rather than feathers. The old man chuckles, his good humor apparently restored. He leans forward and sniffs the air. "She is everywhere," he murmurs.

There is no more time. I have to act. And so, before Merlin can stop me, I shoo away the creatures that sit around him. I clap my hands together hard to dislodge the owl, and catch its beak in a glancing blow. It fluffs up its feathers in protest but doesn't budge. No matter, I think. He can keep the owl for company.

"By what right do you dare chase away my companions!" Merlin struggles to his feet, his joints creaking in protest. Living rough and with not enough food has taken its toll. I feel a momentary pity for the once great mage.

"You have a new companion to take their place, Merlin. I am here to do your bidding. But I don't understand why you live alone out here in such rough conditions? Surely there is a place for you at Arthur's court?"

"Not since he wed Guenevere." The old man's voice is bitter. "Arthur and his men follow the new way of Christ but there was also room for the old ways until Guenevere came along. She distrusts anything she doesn't understand, or that the priests can't explain to her. Although I offered to show her something of my magical arts, she took fright and banished me from Camelot. And so I found a refuge out here in the forest. The king still visits me from time to time, but no one else knows where I live. Which leads me to wonder how you managed to find me, Nimue?"

I berate myself for not anticipating the question. "I ... I followed my instincts, Merlin." It is the best answer I can come up with. Not giving him a chance to question me further, I ask, "May I see inside your cave?"

"So that you can pry into all my secrets?" The old man might look frail but he hasn't lost his wits, or his sharp tongue.

I give a carefree laugh. "Not at all. I thought to start helping you by making things tidy. And I can prepare a meal for you. See, I have brought a basket of food with me. A ham, some smoked fish and a pot of honey. Bread. And fruit."

The old man licks his lips. His stomach growls in anticipation. I hand over the basket and he grabs it with greedy urgency. He pushes ahead of me to take it inside, hunger driving his footsteps. I linger, waiting until he is safely across the threshold, and then I begin to utter aloud the spell of binding, a spell that will seal the cave and keep Merlin locked within it forever.

I hear his roar of rage from within, and know that he has recognized the words I am chanting. And so he should, for they come from his own book, the one I stole from his cave so long ago.

Before I have time to finish the chant I hear the sound of rushing wings. Luck—or instinct—makes me turn aside. A hard beak strikes my head; sharp talons rake my neck. I should have known Merlin would use all the magic at his command to avoid my binding spell, and I curse my stupidity for not anticipating this attack. I snatch up the firestick and swipe it at Merlin's owl, but I am unable to dodge its lacerating beak and claws. I beat the air again and again until, finally, a lucky strike connects and the owl falls limp to the ground.

The owl's attack has given Merlin the time he needs to defend himself. I hear the cry of a mighty eagle as it swoops down from the branches of a nearby tree. I swiftly utter the spell of transformation and fly into its path, talons outstretched, with buffeting wings and a sharp beak designed to tear and kill. We fight viciously and in silence, Merlin and I, while the ground below becomes spattered with gore. I swerve and drop to avoid a raking claw; it would have blinded me if I had not escaped in time. I retaliate with an upward thrust at his feathery belly, and taste his blood on my beak.

Finally I sense that Merlin is weakening. I gather all my strength for one last savage attack, drawing blood and feathers both, until at last my adversary drops. Down I swoop, picking up the limp body with my talons and dropping it into the cave. The eagle is still breathing, but I don't stop to see if it will live or die, nor do I wait to see if Merlin still has the power to transform himself once more. I am eager to complete the spell that will seal him inside the cave forever.

My task done, I assume the guise of Nimue and take a few steps back to assess my handiwork. I cannot see the barrier and so I approach the mouth of the cave for I fear that something has gone wrong with my spell. Even now I don't trust Merlin to stay where he is, for he has shown me that he still has a few magical arts to call on. I try to step into the cave, and discover that the spell has worked. The seal is in place but it is transparent, made of fine crystal. Using Merlin's own wand of oak, the strongest spellbinder of them all, I utter the incantation that will keep the seal fastened through eternity.

The cave begins to shimmer with light and slowly disappears in a shower of sparkles, until there is no sign of it, nor of Merlin. I close my eyes, exhausted from my magic-making and sickened by the unexpected battle that has left so many painful marks upon my human body. But I feel also a great sense of release. I vowed to punish Merlin, to have my revenge on him, and I have kept my vow. At last he understands the consequences of his action in handing the kingdom to Arthur and not to me. And he will regret it for all time.

CHAPTER 7

My satisfaction over Merlin's defeat lasts until I arrive back at Camelot, having taken shelter along the journey to clean and heal my wounds. The talons and beaks of the owl and the eagle have left deep lacerations on my body and I require all my craft and care to heal them. The delay gives me time to compose myself. Although I am pleased that I've kept my word to repay Merlin for robbing me of my rightful heritage, going into a battle unto death with my once loved and revered mentor has upset me far more than I expected.

I know that further trials await me once I am in Camelot, and as I enter the gates I steel myself to meet the first of them: the return of Launcelot. But I discover that he has still not arrived, and I wonder at the delay. I cannot say anything but I am anxious. Has he fallen into the hands of brigands; is he even now lying in a field somewhere, with his throat cut and ravens feasting on his blood, his eyes, and on the mouth that kissed me? I shudder, and press my hand over my stomach, seeking some small comfort from the child within.

With an effort, I turn my fevered imagination to something far more likely—that he has been diverted by the sorts of adventures he seems to enjoy: rescuing damsels and defeating dragons and slicing off the heads of those he perceives as his enemies.

Several new knights have joined Arthur's court and I am astounded to recognize three of them, although they are now full grown into manhood. It is all I can do not to fall on them with hugs and kisses, and beg them for news of my son. Fortunately I remember in time that I am no longer their aunt Morgana. I smile in welcome as they introduce themselves, and question them as delicately as possible so that they will not find out where my true interest lies.

Gawain is the eldest, and he is the one to whom I turn with my questions. But I soon discover that, while he is considered a lion in battle, he is something of a mouse around women. A few monosyllabic answers establish what I already know: that they are the sons of King Lot and Queen Morgause of Lothian and the Orkney Isles. Thereafter I address Gawain's brothers, Gaheris and Agravaine, hoping they will give me the news I long to hear.

"Are there just the three of you or do you have other brothers who will come to grace the king's court?"

"Gareth is our youngest brother; he is still too young to come to Camelot." Gaheris is the most handsome of the brothers, but there is an air of wildness about him that I mistrust. He does not look at me as we converse; instead his gaze flickers like lightning around the room.

"So there are just the four of you?" I hope he will take the hint. But it is Agravaine who answers.

"We have a young foster brother, Mordred. His mother abandoned him, so he has made his home with us. Fortunately for him, my mother dotes on him as he dotes on her, but I suppose he will come to court too. Eventually."

"Mordred?" I echo faintly, feeling a rush of dread as I come to understand the sentiments underlying Agravaine's words. "And ... and is he well? Mordred?"

"He's very well," Agravaine answers. He is shorter than the others, while his girth and his cheerful demeanor betray his enjoyment of the good life. It is clear that he also relishes passing on scandalous stories. And so I turn my attention to him alone.

"Is he happy? Does he miss his mother?" All the brothers look at me strangely. "It's … it's hard to grow up not knowing a mother's love," I add hastily. "I suppose he dotes on your father too?"

"Our father is dead," Gawain says bluntly. "He was killed by Sir Pellinore."

"But—why?" I feel a twinge of sympathy for my sister, quickly dispelled as I remember the state of her marriage.

Gawain shrugs and glances sideways at the tilting yard. "We're needed for practice at the quintain," he mutters, and hurries away.

Agravaine lingers. I look at him, thinking that perhaps his wagging tongue is his greatest weapon as well as the source of his greatest pleasure. I suspect he uses it both to demolish people's reputations and to relish his food, for I am quite sure that he prefers a seat at the dining table to a seat on a horse.

"Pellinore was an irascible fool and always too quick with a sword," he tells me. "The knight was ever after the Questing Beast, and in his anger at his constant failure to find and dispatch it, he tended to seek a quarrel with any he might happen upon. In this case, there was a melee. Pellinore struck our father's horse in the neck. It went down, taking our father with it. And while my father was down, that mangy cur killed him. But we have sworn to take our revenge when next he crosses our path."

I am silent for a few moments as I contemplate the ways of men. For them, revenge and satisfaction lie at the point of a sword.

"Would you like to come and watch us at the quintain, Nimue?" Gaheris interrupts my thoughts. For once he is looking directly at me; I read the hot lust in his eyes, and I quickly excuse myself.

As I watch him strut away, followed by a reluctant Agravaine, I mull over what I have been told. I am happy to hear that Morgause dotes on Mordred, it means she is taking good care of him. But surely he cannot have forgotten me so soon? I do a hasty calculation, and am appalled to discover just how long, in fact, I have been away from my child. Almost four years!

I reassure myself that just a few more weeks won't change anything, and settle back in the castle, at Arthur's invitation, to wait for Launcelot's return to court. I need to be sure that I no longer love Launcelot; that his betrayal, his treachery, has killed my love forever. And yet a sweet heat runs through my body at the very thought of him. He must arrive soon. I have to see him one last time.

But here my thoughts tend to leap and skitter like crickets. I have a trick to play on Launcelot. And Guenevere. A trick that will affect the fate of Camelot. I just don't know if I have the courage or the will to carry it through.

To my dismay, I learn that Guenevere and Arthur have not given up on their plans for me—that is, for Morgana—when I happen upon them in the garden and hear them talking.

"If what Nimue says is the truth, I must send for Morgana," Arthur says, as they come to a discreet bower and sit down on a turf bench.

Curious, I wait until they are settled and then creep closer to listen.

"She needs to be here while Launcelot conducts his investigation. I am sure Nimue tells the truth as she knows it, but Morgana should also be present to defend her good name."

"Surely we should rather listen to the Lady of Avalon's advice? Whether it can be proved or not, she believes

Morgana is behind Accolon's attack on you." I clench my fists as I listen to Guenevere's girlish, venomous voice as she continues. "You tell me your sister has knowledge of magic, and that makes her dangerous—to you, to me, and potentially to all our court. Besides, she's also disruptive. You know she tries to attract the attention of your knights—and of any man who crosses her path. Look how she poisoned Accolon's mind against you. Please don't send for her, Arthur. We don't want her here."

"It will only be for a short time, my darling." Arthur sounds triumphant. "When I last consulted Merlin, his advice was for me to arrange a marriage for her that will take her to the furthest part of our kingdom. I spoke to Morgana some time ago about your suggestion of granting her a castle of her own, and arranging a marriage between her and Urien of Rheged. At the time she rejected the notion out of hand, but I am convinced now that this is the best, the only solution to our concerns, and so I shall insist on it. She will see the sense of my suggestion, I feel sure of it. And it will be good for her to have a husband and his household to take care of; it will give her something to do."

Guenevere claps her hands in appreciation. "Rheged is a thousand days' ride from here," she observes, with such deep pleasure that I want to smack her.

"Not quite as far as that, my love." Arthur smiles indulgently. "But far enough to keep her from troubling the court while, at the same time, I shall make sure that the old man sees it as a gesture of my good faith and patronage, as well as my trust in my sister's innocence in this matter of Accolon's attack, and his consequent death. If Morgana is as penitent as Nimue says she is, she will do as I say."

Crouched behind the hedge of thorny roses, I seethe with bitterness. I cannot leave my hiding place without Arthur and Guenevere seeing me, so I must wait. But their words lead to kissing, and then to other matters. I close my ears to the sound of their loving, and mull over what I have heard. After the first shock wears off, I have to admit to a grudging admiration. I had not suspected Arthur capable of such craft in matters of state. But Urien! My whole being revolts at the thought of living with him as his wife. Bedding with him. Sharing with him all that I shared with Launcelot, which once was a delight but with Urien will become a penance.

And yet. My fingers touch my belly. I gently stroke the small bump. The baby is growing, and I need a father for it most urgently.

Urien is old, so old that perhaps he can be beguiled into believing the child is his. He is certainly too old to try to tame me. Could Arthur unknowingly have devised both my escape, and also my salvation? Rheged is nothing like a thousand days' ride away, but it is far enough that I may stay there in safety, with Mordred and the baby, after my task here is done. I can shelter there until I am summoned to assume my rightful place as head of the realm and savior of the kingdom.

*

The long days of waiting were broken by an unexpected adventure that quickly became the talk of the court. While Arthur and his knights were out hunting, they encountered a giant—or so the credulous would have you believe, although it seems to me that the warrior only grew in height to appease Arthur's wounded pride at being bested in combat. The giant told Arthur he would only spare his life if he could find the answer to the question, "What is it that women most desire?" and bring it back to him within a week.

Arthur came home to interrogate the court, and received a variety of answers: gold, jewels, a handsome lover, a good husband, wealth and status. I could have told him the true answer but I did not, for I doubted he would believe its simplicity. Besides, I was intrigued to see how it all played out; it was my hope that, all being well, the giant might carry out his threat without my having to do anything further to bring about Arthur's death.

Finally, and as requested, Arthur took all the answers he'd heard back to the giant. Along the way he encountered a loathly lady. Reports as to her extreme ugliness vary, but all were agreed that the poor dame was bent and hideous, that she had but one eye and only a slit for a mouth, and that her hair was gray and bedraggled. But she claimed to know the true answer to the giant's riddle, which she would only tell Arthur in exchange for a boon. And he, without asking any further questions, agreed to it. And so she whispered in his ear and he told the giant, who roared with rage but was forced to spare Arthur's life because the answer was correct.

You would think the ninny might have shared this wisdom with the others in his party, but he did not. Instead, he returned to the old hag and agreed to carry out whatever she might ask—and what she wanted was for a young and handsome knight from Arthur's court to marry her! Arthur returned to court in a great bother, and finally Gawain, fool that he is, put himself forward—or was pushed into it—when no one else would agree to the crone's request.

We all witness Gawain's return to Camelot with his poor, deformed bride-to-be riding in front of him. Everyone at court falls silent; all are embarrassed by her appearance, for surely no woman should suffer such deformity and live. Everyone pities Gawain to the depths of their souls. Everyone except me, for when I gaze at the poor wretch I suspect there is some magic afoot, and I wonder at it.

Guenevere, to her credit, and perhaps because of the debt Arthur owes Gawain, makes much of the creature, whose name is Dame Ragnell. She takes her away to bathe in scented water, and arrays her in a costly gown, one of Guenevere's own, but nothing can conceal the dame's loathsome appearance.

I wonder even more about magic after we break our fast the following morning. I expect Gawain to appear gaunt and haggard after sharing his bride's bed, and yet his eyes are bright and there is a spring in his step, although his bride is as ugly and deformed as ever. Indeed Gawain appears so much more lively and mirthful than usual that I cannot help but take him aside to question him in the hope of satisfying my curiosity.

It is a strange story. He tells me that, utterly cast down and unable to face his bride, he sat staring at the fire burning in their room while wondering how he was going to endure the night.

"She spoke to me then," Gawain says. "She asked if I could not bear to look on her face—and when I did, I beheld such loveliness that I was struck dumb with it! I swear, Nimue, she is more beautiful even than the queen! But I could weep at what has happened to her, for she says that she and her brother, the giant encountered by Arthur, have had an enchantment put on them by an evil lord. She says that she is doomed to be fair for one half of the day, and hideous for the other, and that only I can free her of the spell—but I need to choose the right answer to be successful."

"The right answer to what?"

"I cannot say, for she did not tell me the riddle. But she has asked if I would prefer her to be beautiful by day—when all will see that I have a beautiful bride—or by night, when I may have joy of her. When I asked for her beauty at night, she wept most bitterly for she knows she is an object of scorn and loathing to others; she says she would prefer to appear beautiful before them. But if I grant her wish, I shall have no joy of her at night, while knowing that other knights at court will lust after her by day, and try to win her affection. What then if she should decide she prefers another to me?" Gawain looks wretched at the very thought of it. "I've never been much use around women, Nimue, but I would be loath to lose my wife to another having seen how comely she is, and how sweet her nature."

I revise my opinion of the giant of Arthur's imagining; it seems that magic really is afoot here, and I wonder who has instigated it.

"Can you help me, Nimue?" Gawain implores. "Can you fathom an answer that might remove the spell?"

I am almost sure I can, if it is the same answer that Arthur was seeking only a day or two ago. And so I tell him, and hope that my guess proves correct.

The answer comes as a radiant Ragnell appears beside Gawain when we meet for dinner. There is a buzzing around the table as everyone asks who the dame is, and it is Gawain who says, in triumph, "This is my wife, who had a curse placed upon her, although the curse has now been lifted."

He brings Ragnell over to me after we have dined, to thank me for my help in breaking the spell. It seems I guessed the right answer to both the giant's question, and also to what lay at the heart of Ragnell's request that Gawain choose when she should appear beautiful: "What is it that women most desire?" I told Gawain to suggest the lady choose according to her own will, for indeed, isn't that what all women would prefer?

I am fond of Gawain; he is perhaps my favorite nephew, and it pleases me to see that he is happily wed, and to someone who will be good to him, and who will help him be more at ease among both his fellow knights and their ladies.

*

A blast of a hunting horn tells me that my waiting is finally at an end. Once more I hurry to the parapet to watch

Launcelot's arrival. As if drawn by an invisible thread, he looks upward in expectation, and his eyes meet mine. I stand there, brazen in my disguise, and watch with great satisfaction the disappointment that flashes across his face before it smooths into lines of indifference.

"We had hoped to see you at our court some weeks ago, Sir Launcelot." I arrive in the courtyard just in time to hear Guenevere's greeting. There is a slight waspishness beneath her sweet tone.

"My apologies for my delay, lady. I … I mislaid something and needed to find what was missing before I could obey the king's summons."

Mislaid something? Does he mean me? Not sure whether to be angry or amused—or flattered—I wait to hear more.

"You are here now. That is all that matters."

I can see, from the way Guenevere takes Launcelot's arm to lead him into the solar, that she is already establishing an intimacy between them. I grit my teeth as the queen sweeps past me without making any effort to introduce us. While it suits me to have Guenevere think of Launcelot as her possession, it grates my heart raw to see them together. But I follow them into the solar, and witness Launcelot's introduction to those knights already gathered there and who have not yet made his acquaintance. To my dismay, for I had not foreseen the consequences until now—Morgause's sons are among them, with all their knowledge of their aunt's downfall and the child that resulted from it. But there is little I can do other than push myself forward and curtsy before Launcelot, hoping to take his attention and distract him from the gathered assembly. More than anything, I want to restore my good name, to witness his regret and, hopefully, recover his regard.

Now I have a chance to look more closely at him, I note how gaunt he looks. There are new lines of strain on his face, and a bleakness in his eyes that perhaps only I, who know him so well, can recognize. It would seem that my abrupt disappearance has taken its toll, and I feel a sharp stab of regret that such a love as we shared has come to this.

"The Lady Nimue," Guenevere says coldly. "She brought us news of Arthur's sister, Lady Morgana."

Launcelot's body stiffens and stills at the mention of my name. I feel a momentary pleasure that I still have that power over him, made sweeter when I realize that Guenevere has also marked his reaction. But my satisfaction turns to bitter ashes as soon as Agravaine butts into the conversation.

"Morgana is our aunt," he tells Launcelot, before turning to me in accusation. "Why did you not say that you know her?"

"I don't know her, not really," I answer. "The lady is now living quietly at a priory where I happened to take shelter for some days. She has been accused of a terrible crime, but I have helped the king discover the truth of the matter: that she is innocent." I look Launcelot square in the eye, glorying in his manifest discomfort.

"So you say, but we have only your word for Morgana's innocence," Guenevere snaps. I wonder if she suspects that Launcelot was my lover. It is clear, from the way she is looking at him, that he is already far more dear to her than her own husband. And from her words, it is also apparent that she will let no rival stand in her way.

"Our mother has always believed that Morgana is not to be trusted," Agravaine says, perhaps trying to earn favor with the queen. "In fact, she was heartless enough even to abandon her own son. She left him with my mother and simply disappeared."

"Morgana has a son?" Launcelot's face turns pale as curd.

"Yes, indeed. He was conceived under a hedge with some churl, I believe. It's a family scandal." Agravaine smiles, while I want to throttle him. How I wish I'd had enough sense to ask for his silence on this affair. As it is, I can only stand impotent with fury as he prattles on about his saintly mother and how readily she took in my motherless child and made him her own. And then I become aware that Arthur has joined us, and that he is listening carefully.

"Who is this churl who sired Morgana's child?"

Agravaine stammers to a halt, perhaps aware at last that he is slandering the king's half-sister. "I ... we know not, sire. All she told my mother was that she lay with a shepherd boy, and that a child was conceived."

"And how old is this child?" Arthur's voice is quiet; the whole court has hushed to hear the answer.

"Ten or eleven summers, I believe." Agravaine cannot know what lies behind Arthur's question; none of them knows, except me. And my worst fears are realized when Arthur turns to the Orkney brothers. "I bid you go fetch your mother, Gaheris. And the boy. I want them both to come here to my court."

"I did not know that the Lady Morgana had given birth to a child." Launcelot looks sick and shaken.

"And with a lowborn churl at that!" Guenevere smiles with malicious glee. "Who would have thought it, after all her airs and graces while she was at court? It is time for her to wed, husband, for her wantonness sullies the reputation of decent women everywhere. A good husband will keep her in check, some good knight with lands far distant from here. We have already suggested Urien of Rheged as a suitor. The king believes him an excellent choice."

It takes all my self-control not to launch myself at Guenevere and scratch out her eyes. How pleased I am that I have given her the potion. Truly, it is no more than she deserves. I wait for Launcelot to contradict her, hardly aware that I am holding my breath as I give him this one last chance to be my champion.

"She seems to bring trouble in her wake, I grant you," he says slowly. "But rather than condemn her to a loveless marriage, perhaps you should leave her at the priory? It might be the best place for her—she'll be away from the temptations of the world and she'll have the good example of the nuns always before her."

"It suits me to have her wed to Urien," Arthur contradicts, going on to detail why the marriage would be seen as an act of good faith on his part.

"And an old husband would have a steadying influence on Morgana," Guenevere chips in, with a quick sideways glance at Launcelot to see how he's taking the suggestion.

He nods gravely. "Rheged is certainly far enough away from court to prevent any further temptation or lapses from grace."

Bereft and furious, I can hardly bear to look at them. I hate them both: Launcelot for betraying our love, for wanting me far away from temptation and for equating my love for him as a lapse from grace. And Guenevere, for her lies and her simpering morality. Their words have sealed their fate. But underlying my anger is a fluttering panic. I carry Launcelot's child; I must think how to keep it safe. And Mordred too. Arthur is bound to find out the truth—and then what? Two things I know for certain: I must be here at court when Mordred arrives, but he must know me as his mother, Morgana. At the same time, I must think of some way to see this through to a conclusion that will contribute to Arthur's downfall, while keeping me safe.

The course of action I have devised will fulfill some of my requirements, although the very thought of it wrenches my heart and almost stops the breath in my body. Do I have the courage to see it through? Every step is laden with sorrow as I walk down to the water meadows to pick flowers and herbs for a second concoction, one that may prove far more dangerous and will have far-reaching consequences. At the back of my mind is the thought that it will be to Launcelot's and Guenevere's blame if my trick succeeds—but despite myself, I pray that it will not, for it will be Launcelot who, at the end, holds the fate of the kingdom in his hands and who may yet save it if he proves to be all that I once thought him.

After my seemingly innocent posy is gathered, I again prepare the brew in secret. I cannot stop my tears from falling as I utter the incantation, this time to ensure that Launcelot will fall as desperately in love with Guenevere as she is with him: a love so strong that it will last until the day they die. Imagining Launcelot in love with anyone other than me is lacerating, but I try to reassure myself that he may be too wise to fall for my trick; that he may prove strong enough to withstand my magic. But if not, there is some comfort in knowing that while he and Guenevere may yearn for each other, they will also suffer the torment of never being able to consummate that love, for they put their lives in jeopardy if they break their oaths of love and fidelity to the king. Thus Launcelot will learn the true meaning of love and loyalty, and of the heartache that results when one is in conflict with the other, while Guenevere will learn that it is not always possible to gain whatsoever she covets. At the same time she may also discover how easy it is to lose her honor and reputation.

My chance comes at dinner the following day. Guenevere takes great care to seat Launcelot beside her while I have been relegated to a seat some distance away. But before we sit down I persuade the lady on Launcelot's other side, an elderly dame and therefore perceived as no threat by Guenevere, to change places with me. And so, to Guenevere's annoyance, the three of us dine in close proximity to one another. On my other side is Viviane. I would rather have any other table companion, but this is an opportunity I have to take. I am shaking with nerves as I produce the silver flask that contains my potion, and place it on the table as the young pages begin to lay out our meat and pour the wine. Will Viviane recognize it for what it truly is—and if she does, will she interfere? I wait until the knight on her other side engages her in conversation before turning to Launcelot and Guenevere.

"This is a special honey mead brewed by my own hands and brought from my home in Annwyn," I say softly. "I have been saving it for a special occasion, and I can think of nothing more deserving than your arrival at court, Sir Launcelot." I remove the stopper from the flask and, waving aside the page who darts forward to pour more wine, I pour out a measure of my own concoction into a cup that I set between them. "Your good health, sire." I raise my own cup in salutation. "And for you, lady, may you live long and prosper, and your children, and your children's children after you."

A brief flicker of Guenevere's eyelid tells me that she understands my words. She will not dare refuse my gift. The future of the kingdom depends on her giving Arthur an heir. She takes a sip and sets the cup down. Launcelot stretches out his hand for it—and in that moment, I change my mind. I cannot say anything, but I stare at him with desperate appeal. He glances at me, and I hear his quick intake of breath. I wonder if I have been recognized.

He sets the cup down, but Guenevere picks it up once more. She looks at him with shining eyes, and holds the cup to his lips. "Will you not share this drink with me, my lord?" she whispers.

Launcelot hesitates, and then obediently takes a long draught of the nectar. And I straighten my spine and brace myself against what is to come.

They take turns to drink my potion, sip by sip, their growing intimacy clear to me if not yet to the court. Finally, Launcelot sets down the empty goblet and turns to Guenevere with such a look of love that I snatch up my own cup and quaff the wine down. It is like swallowing shards of glass. Guenevere meets his gaze, and a small, self-satisfied smile curls the corner of her rosebud mouth as she reads in his eyes what she has always longed to see. She leans toward him, and stops abruptly as she becomes conscious of her surroundings once more. And I ... I cannot tear my eyes away from the knowledge dawning on Launcelot's face: that he loves this young woman and will have her if he can.

It is only then that I awaken to the danger I have unleashed. With my preparations I have ensured that Guenevere will never bear a child to Arthur. More to the point, although I know she has always loved Launcelot, all would have been safe while he still loved me. With this new potion, I have ensured that Launcelot now loves her, and that they will love each other until the day they die. I grip both hands across my stomach in deathly fear and remorse. Will the spell of barrenness I've cast on Guenevere extend to a liaison with Launcelot, if they should ever dare to consummate their love? Or will she, like me, bear Launcelot's child? I have no way of knowing, nor can I undo what I have done, for in drinking the potion they have become irresistible to each other. Their fate is sealed—and possibly mine as well. All I can do is await the consequences, and hide my anguish as best I may.

"Who are you really, lady?"

A soft voice on my other side awakens me to further danger. I turn to Viviane, smoothing my face into a mask of indifference.

"I am Nimue from Annwyn," I tell her.

She shakes her head. She is not looking at me, she is watching Launcelot and Guenevere laughing together. "What have you done?" she murmurs.

I snatch up the silver flask and hide it within the folds of my gown. "I have done nothing other than come to Arthur's court to honor him—and to tell him of the Lady Morgana's dismay over the calumny being spread around the court about her."

"My belief is that you were sent by Morgana to corrupt the king and drip poison into his ear."

"Morgana is ever the king's loyal sister." A flash of inspiration prompts me further. "If you continue to spread these false accusations about her, I shall go to her and suggest that she comes to court herself so that she can speak for her own good name."

"Do that, Nimue—if that is who you really are." Viviane is looking at me closely now, her eyes searching my disguise. "I think that's a very good idea indeed."

*

And so I take my leave of the court. I long to visit Mordred, to reassure myself of his wellbeing, but there is no time for that. I console myself with the thought that he will come to court soon enough, in company with my sister, who I hope will help me allay Arthur's suspicions. I shall see my son then. My heart fills with joy at the thought of our reunion.

I turn my mount toward the priory. I intend to stay there for a few days, so that I may search my scrying pool for glimpses of the future. I'm anxious to find reassurance that my plans will bear the fruit that I desire. But once I am there, I discover that no matter how hard I try, the water is always so troubled that I can only glimpse flashes of movement. If there is any message, it is rendered meaningless. I wonder if I am being punished for my meddling, but there is nothing I can do about it.

Finally, when I judge enough time has passed, I return to Camelot in my true guise. I discover that Launcelot is holding some sort of trial into the affair of the fake scabbard and the death of Accolon, and he requests me to appear before him so that he can hear my evidence. I comply with his request, defiant and strenuously denying all of the accusations that have been put before him. For his part, he is apologetic, seeming sorry that the affair reflects so badly on a reputation that is already mired in scandal. He is polite, courteous—but no more than that. It is obvious to me, and possibly to all the court by now, that he and Guenevere are smitten with each other. The trial seems a chore to him, an annoyance that takes him away from the queen, and he dismisses me and discharges the affair without a result and, more important for my purpose, without a stain on my character—or so he says.

Nevertheless, I am left in no doubt that my supposed liaison with Accolon and my tumble with the shepherd have been much discussed by all the court, albeit in whispers behind hands and with many half-suppressed titters that I am supposed to ignore, just as I am supposed to ignore the rudeness of those who turn and hurry away at my approach so they will not have to sully their good names by having anything to do with me.

Mordred and my sister have not yet arrived in Camelot, but Urien of Rheged is there, having come to court in an attempt to clear his son's good name, and also to bury him. There are bridges to build between us, and I determine to make the most of my time, with Arthur's assistance, to weave my future. But before I can do anything, I am summoned by Arthur. To my relief, he is alone. He pats my hand in the manner of an elderly uncle.

"About your marriage, Morgana," he begins.

I cast my eyes heavenward, knowing already what he is going to say, and wondering how I might turn it to my advantage.

Sensing my impatience, Arthur hurries on. "I know you believe Urien of Rheged is unworthy of you, but I beg you to reconsider your position." He stops, perhaps waiting for my reaction. I remain silent. "He has come to court to cause trouble over the death of his son, Accolon. He says that the boy was bewitched by you and therefore he should be forgiven for the harm he caused while under your spell. More, he says that I, as your brother, should make reparation for the loss of his only son and heir. I have assured him of your innocence, as has Launcelot. But if I can convince him that he has your love and that you would make him a good wife—" Arthur breaks off when I am unable to stifle a snort of bitter laughter. "If I can offer him marriage to my sister, it will enable me to buy his loyalty. It will help repair the rift between us caused by Accolon's death," he finishes in a rush.

Despite my resentment at being used as a pawn by Arthur and his queen, I know that the marriage makes sound political sense. But for the moment I keep hidden the fact that it might also suit my needs, for it can only work in my favor if Arthur believes himself beholden to my good nature. The question is, can I persuade Urien to forget the past, and my tarnished reputation, and believe in Arthur's dream of the future?

"Very well," I say.

Arthur blinks in surprise. Obviously he has not expected such an easy victory.

"I shall do as you ask, since it is you who request the favor," I add.

"Thank you, Morgana. I understand he is not your first choice for a husband. I am in your debt."

And I'll make sure you remember it. "Of course it depends on whether Urien will have me as a wife," I say, "but I shall speak to him, Arthur. The matter will be better arranged if I give him an explanation regarding Accolon's behavior, and if he thinks my willingness to marry him comes from me rather than from you."

"You are right as always, Morgana." Arthur smiles his relief. "I shall leave it all in your hands."

"By your leave, I shall seek him now." I cannot waste time, for my belly is beginning to show the presence of a child. Soon enough even the loosest of garments will not be able to hide the signs of my pregnancy. I stand up, bow to my brother, and walk out of the room.

I realize that Arthur hasn't raised the topic of my bastard-born child. Perhaps he believes that I'm not aware of what he has found out. Perhaps he wants me out of the way, so he can interrogate Mordred on his own. I shall not allow that to happen, but it's a matter to be dealt with on another day. For now, I have the future of my unborn child to consider.

I go in search of Urien, and find him drowsing under a tree in the orchard. I ask him if he would care to escort me around the castle garden. He looks somewhat surprised but, after I flutter my eyelashes and glance at him flirtatiously, he arises and courteously offers me his arm. And so we commence a decorous progress along the pathways, pausing here to sniff a rose and there to admire some ripening fruit. He is somewhat flinty and stiff at first, until I say what needs to be said.

"I was so sorry to hear of the death of Accolon. It must be a great grief to you." I pat his arm in sympathy. "But I feel I owe you some explanation of this sad affair. Just between us, sire: your son desired us to wed, he set such great love upon me." Here I pause, and modestly lower my eyes. "But he was too young for me, and so I told him often enough. Believe me, sire, it was a great dread to me to hear what he did in my name, and for my sake." I raise my hand to wipe away a non-existent tear and utter a little whimper for good measure.

Urien takes the bait as I hoped he would. "Do not trouble yourself further over my son's deeds, lady," he says, and places his arm around my shoulders to comfort me. "He was a rash, hot-headed young fool. I can quite see why a woman of your … sensibilities would look to someone older and with more experience to guide her, and show her the ways of love."

"Indeed, sire," I say fervently, "you understand me only too well. Where the son could not go, the father ..." I break off and give a delicate sniff.

Urien draws me closer. We continue to walk while I question him about himself and make flattering comments about his deeds, and generally worm my way into his affections. By the end of it, I know we understand each other and that it is only a matter of time before he asks Arthur for my hand. We part with great satisfaction on both sides.

Launcelot's closure of the trial has reinforced my innocence, although the question of who wove the fake scabbard for Excalibur has not been addressed. No doubt the old man still believes that Accolon was enticed into the act somehow, but I hope that I have allayed his suspicions. I know that Arthur will also reassure him on my account. Also in my favor is the fact that it is believed I was absent from court when the scabbard went missing a second time.

To assist my wooing of Urien, he—or Guenevere, perhaps—has ensured that we sit together when we dine. As dinner is served, I continue my seduction. In fact, I had come to know Urien slightly during the time Accolon pursued me. He suffers from a sore back and stiff joints, and so I made up a rubbing lotion that I helped him to apply. Unlike his son, Urien has courtly manners and a wry sense of humor, often at his own expense. I gaze at him, wondering how it will be when we are wed. Marriage may come sooner or later but, for my purposes, I need to make sure that he beds me, and quickly.

At the thought, I glance involuntarily at Launcelot. As always, he sits on one side of Guenevere while Arthur sits on the other. I watch the flirtatious banter between the two as they explore their growing love for each other, and I wonder if Arthur is blind as well as stupid. Watching Launcelot look at Guenevere the way he once looked at me makes me want to howl like a wolf, but it is too late, now, for regrets.

Of far more importance are my survival and the survival of my children, and the need to clear the path to the throne—for Mordred, if not for me.

I turn back to Urien, and this time all my attention, my flattery and wiles, are for him and him alone.

"I so enjoyed our walk in the garden," I tell him demurely. "Perhaps we might walk there again after dinner—if the day stays fine?" I hesitate. "It is hard to speak in private here, with so many courtiers around to observe us."

I wonder if he understands my meaning. His hand fumbles for mine, and he gives it a quick squeeze. I think he knows what is on my mind, although my courage fails me at the thought of the probable outcome.

And so it comes about. We meet, we stroll through the garden until we find a private bower, and there, after some awkward fumbling, he takes me. I close my eyes, and think of Launcelot, and I cry.

Urien knows he's not the first to bed me; nevertheless, he is kind. He consoles me with promises of his love and loyalty, and expresses his dedication to making me happy in our new life together. He follows this with an assurance that he will be as a father to my child.

I am so alarmed that my tears cease immediately, until I realize that he speaks of Mordred and not my unborn babe. Most important of all, he promises me that he will speak to Arthur at once so that our union can be blessed by God. And for all of these promises, I am more grateful than I can say.

CHAPTER 8

At Urien's request, Arthur receives us both. He expresses his pleasure at the news and, of course, gives his permission for the marriage, going even further with the offer of a lavish celebration "as befits the sister of the king marrying one of his most loyal subjects."

Guenevere smirks, and wishes us a long and happy life together, adding that she hopes our union will be blessed with children. I wonder if she has guessed that I am already with child, and I search her face carefully. But there is no hint of jealousy or bitterness, only triumph at satisfactorily settling my future far away from Camelot, along with a certain wistfulness that I translate as a wish for a child of her own.

Having secured Arthur's blessing on our nuptials, I announce my intention of leaving the court for just a few days, citing the need to arrange my affairs at the priory, my old home, before leaving for Rheged. Arthur graciously agrees to my request, while Urien offers to accompany me. I hasten to dissuade him; there are the beginnings of a plan in my mind, hatched in haste and out of necessity, but urgent for all that, for Mordred will come soon to court and I must return in time for his coming. I am desperate to protect him from Arthur.

"I hate to leave you," I reassure Urien, "but the priory houses only women. Your presence will cause consternation, and besides, there will be nowhere for you to stay." It's not quite true, but it is enough to quieten him.

I kiss his cheek, and he puts his arms around me and holds me tight. I sense his need and it takes all my courage not to pull away from his embrace. It is becoming increasingly obvious to me that I cannot go through with this marriage. I will not be banished from court, not again. Nor do I intend to make my home in far away Rheged. The realities of married life are also beginning to dawn on me: that Urien will be a presence in my life day after day, and in my bed night after night. I already know that I won't be able to endure it. It is enough protection that our union has Arthur's blessing and my unborn child a father, for even if our marriage does not take place, as I desperately hope it will not, I shall make sure that everyone knows that Urien and I anticipated our vows and that the child is most definitely his. Everything, and most especially my future happiness, rests on what I may achieve while I am away from court.

"I'll return soon," I whisper in Urien's ear. "I'll return just as soon as I can, I promise you."

"And in your absence, my dear, I shall hasten to Rheged to ensure that my castle and my people are ready and prepared to welcome you when you come to make your home there as my bride." Urien grasps my hand and draws me close to kiss me farewell.

As I set off toward the priory, I mull over my ideas, so hastily stitched together. I believe my plan has every chance of success; that it will ensure the death of Arthur while attaching no possible blame to me, for I shall be at the priory making sure that my ignorance of the affair—and my innocence—cannot be called into question.

At my insistence I ride alone, and I recognize soon enough the danger of having nothing to distract me. The anguish I have suppressed for so long surges to the fore and in such a wave that I am in danger of drowning. Memories of Launcelot and all that I have lost haunt me, leaving no room in my mind for anything else. I recall the moment when Launcelot and Guenevere discovered their love for each other, and a wailing grief arises in me that nothing can assuage. I try to seek comfort from the memory of what we once shared together—a love that I still believe was true, no matter how shaky its foundation proved to be. But I am left trembling with a desire that can have no fulfilment, and I find that a hundred times worse than my howling despair. My ride to the priory becomes a nightmare journey through a desert plain of thorns, pricked with desire, and pain, and loss, and with no relief in sight. When I finally arrive at my destination, it takes all my self-control to compose myself to greet the prioress and beg her to give me refuge once again.

Perhaps she sees and understands something of my inner torment for she is all kindness, and assures me that I may stay at the priory for as long as I wish. And so I am able to flee to my garden, to mourn in private within the secret heart of it. There I abandon myself to a sorrow that seems without end. I cry; I wring my hands and tear at my hair; I scratch my skin, and pinch and hurt myself in an effort to block the misery in my heart and gain relief. Nothing helps, but at least I am left alone.

It is the thought of Mordred that saves me; my son who even now may be approaching Camelot, unaware of the danger that faces him. It is time to put aside my anguish, and act—both to save him and also to save myself. I have no compunction about putting my plan into action. I blame Arthur and Merlin for all the hurt I have suffered and all the pain I now feel. But for their meddling, the kingdom would have been mine, and Launcelot too, along with a life of great happiness and fulfilment. As it is, I have rewarded Merlin for his treatment of me, and now it is Arthur's turn.

And so, using all the magical skills at my disposal, I fashion a beautiful cloak as a gift for Arthur. I weave it through with golden and scarlet thread, each thread steeped in a deadly substance designed to ignite and kill him as soon as he puts it on. Once it is done, I change my appearance into that of an elderly crone. I view myself in the scrying pool and hastily change my mind. Above all, I need to look respectable—and also as unmemorable as possible. I become a plump woman in early middle age with a cheerful expression and dressed unremarkably as the wife of a well-to-do merchant. I gaze again, and nod in satisfaction. To complete the illusion, I sally forth into the village through my secret way, complete with a shopping basket in which the cloak is carefully hidden underneath several hanks of wool.

I walk the high street looking at all the passers-by, and finally I make my choice: a young girl, fresh faced and innocent, but poorly clad and looking in want of a good meal, is coming my way. I greet her, and she stops. I ask her if she will undertake an errand for me, and press a few coins into her hand so that she understands it will be worth her while.

"I shall oblige you, of course, madame," she assures me.

"This is a gift for the king," I say, reaching beneath the hanks of wool to draw the cloak out of the basket. The girl gasps at its magnificence and I am momentarily assailed by doubt. What if she should undertake my task, but sell the cloak instead to a local merchant? The price it would fetch would be enough to keep the child in comfort for many years to come. I hesitate, and the girl looks up at me.

"Is it your wish that I take it to the king at Camelot, madame?" she queries.

"Yes, indeed." After a moment's thought, I produce a few more coins, which I hold in front of her. "The court is some distance from here and I have not the time to make the journey myself. But these coins will be sufficient to hire a fine mount to take you there and back. And there will be a silver penny on your return as a reward for your diligence. May I entrust you with this?"

"Oh yes, madame," she breathes. "On my honor, I shall do whatever you instruct me to do." She quivers with the need to snatch the extra coins from my grasp, but has enough self-control to keep her hands by her side.

I smile then, and reach for her hand to press the coins into it. "Please leave as soon as you may," I tell her. "The king is expecting my gift and I am anxious that he receive it without delay." As well for her to believe that a gift is known and expected by the king, I think.

"I'll go at once, madame." The girl pauses. "As soon as I can find a horse to take me."

I raise my hand in acknowledgment, and she scurries away. I hope she knows how to ride such an animal. It is fortunate she has not thought to ask for my name; perhaps she believes the king already knows it as he is expecting my gift. I mentally congratulate myself on the quick-thinking that has smoothed my path to success. Now, there is nothing else for me to do but return to the priory, and wait impatiently for news.

While I wait, I return to the sacred pool to try to determine my future. This time the still, dark water reflects my image—but shows me nothing else. I am alarmed that I may be losing my magical powers, until I remember that I was able to change my appearance and also weave the cloak for Arthur without any difficulty. Why then, should this be different? I am frustrated by my lack of success, but suspect that my actions have offended the spirits and this is their punishment.

I look into the pool and think of all that I have done since last I saw a vision. I have abandoned my son. The thought of Mordred brings my anxiety and frustration to the fore. He is in danger; he will need me at Camelot to deflect Arthur's questions about his parentage if he arrives before my plan succeeds. But I cannot return, not yet, not until I have news that Arthur is dead. I try to calm my fear as I continue to itemize what else I have done since leaving the priory. I have met and lain with Launcelot. I have tricked Accolon, a trick that brought about his death. I have tried to kill Arthur once, and this time I will succeed. In addition, I have tricked his wife into barrenness and into an ill-advised liaison with Arthur's most trusted knight. I have also imprisoned and maybe killed Merlin, the man who acted as a father to both Arthur and me. I have told so many lies I can scarce remember every one of them. It is a litany of black deeds and, as I gaze into the water, I feel intense shame—until I remind myself that whatever I have done was only because of what was done to me when I was but an innocent child. Nevertheless, I humble myself and ask pardon of the spirits of the pool if I have offended them. But the waters reflect nothing other than my image back at me. Perhaps the spirits are telling me I am the true ruler of the realm, not Arthur. I try to summon his face, but the water stays dark as blood.

I wait for news, and I wait. And finally word comes from a traveler seeking refuge at the priory for the night. "There has been another attempt on the king's life, with a death beyond explanation," he tells the gate-keeper. Unfortunately she has neither the wit nor the good sense to ask anything further, but passes on the news to others until, inevitably, it filters down to me.

It is the sign for which I have been waiting. At once I take my leave of the prioress and, with a confident heart, set off toward Camelot. As I go, I make plans and dream of the future. With the baby's birth still some months away, I shall start with a progress around the country to win the hearts and minds of my subjects, so that they will accept me in Arthur's stead. I must also ensure that they will acknowledge my son's right to rule after I am gone, but I foresee no obstacle to this for once they meet him, they will surely love my son as I do.

Although I am so close to realizing my dream, the thought of Guenevere and Launcelot is a constant shadow. I want them out of my sight and out of my life and yet, when I pass the guards and enter the gate, I cannot help looking up at the ramparts of the castle, seeking the one man above all that I long to see. But the rampart is bare, although the courtyard is busy with traders, with dogs and children, with knights and squires and visitors, all in a bustle about their business. I hand my mount over to the groom, and stand for a moment to look about me, enjoying the noise and movement after the silence of the priory. It occurs to me that they all look far too cheerful when, by rights, they should be mourning the death of their king. Have I misunderstood the traveler's message? I am suddenly assailed by doubt.

A group of women comes out onto the ramparts then, and I squint up my eyes to see more clearly. The focus of the group is Guenevere; she is easy enough to identify with her golden locks, her youth and beauty. If she is grieving over her dead husband there are no obvious signs of it. In fact, I have never seen her so animated. She gestures as she speaks, and the ladies lean closer, shaking their heads as they listen. It appears to be her usual entourage, but without Launcelot. I wonder where he is and whether they are already planning their nuptials. My heart turns over within my breast. But there are more pressing issues for me to take care of right now: the arrangements for Arthur's funeral and the court's acknowledgment of my succession to the crown.

I lower my head to avoid recognition and continue through the great door of the castle, only to find the same commotion going on inside. I make my way to the Great Hall, ready to take my place at the Round Table, albeit briefly. I've already determined that the Round Table will go once the knights have accepted my right to rule in Arthur's stead, and I shall preside over future discussions of state business.

I give my name to the guard who pushes open the great oaken door. I rush inside before he can prevent me and gaze quickly around the room, looking for the man I love.

I stop dead, feeling as if I have turned to stone. The hum of conversation quietens; all swivel in their seats to stare at me.

"It is my pleasure to see you returned to court once more, Morgana," my brother says quietly. "I ask your pardon to excuse us; as you see we are busy here with affairs of state and there is much to discuss."

"Arthur." It takes all my courage to say his name, to bow my head in obeisance, and to exit the Great Hall without falling over. Once outside, I lean against the stone wall and mop the perspiration from my brow. My heart shudders with remembered fright and the realization that I had allowed wishful thinking to triumph over caution. What has gone wrong with my plan? How have I managed to so mistake the situation?

I prop myself against the wall for several long moments, relishing its cooling touch for my whole body feels as though it burns with a wild fever. Only when I can trust my shaking legs to carry me do I move. I flee to the garden, and there try to order my scattered thoughts while I wait until such time as the knights may have finished their discussion. Finally, when I judge it safe to do so, I go in search of the Orkney brothers to seek answers to the questions that torment me. But first, I ask after Mordred—and the news I hear is so shocking that it puts everything else out of my mind.

"Our mother is dead, and Gaheris has been banished from the court." Agravaine's tone is unusually grave.

"My sister dead? How? And where is Mordred?"

"Don't worry, Morgana, he is safe." Agravaine puts his hand on my arm to calm me. "He and Gareth have come to court. But Gaheris …" He turns his face away. I look to Gawain for an answer.

"Gaheris slew our mother," Gawain says abruptly.

"*What?*" I recall how fond Gaheris was of Morgause, and she of him. There must surely be some mistake.

"Our mother was in bed with Lamorak when Gaheris arrived to fetch Mordred. He was so incensed to see them together that he … he cut off her head."

It's an appalling image. I put my hands over my eyes to try to block it, but Agravaine's words are now etched on my brain. I am finding it difficult to breathe.

"It was Lamorak's father, Pellinore, who murdered our father," Gawain reminds me. "We swore then to take our revenge."

I try to collect my scattered thoughts, to make sense of this shocking affair. "But why slay your mother in so brutal a fashion? Why not rather put an end to Lamorak's life, if you think such a bloody retaliation is warranted?"

"That was Gaheris's intention, but Lamorak escaped. But he will be found, and when he is, he will be slain."

"I always suspected Gaheris was wild but this …" My voice is shaking. Morgause and I were never close, but tears are coursing down my cheeks at the thought of her dreadful end. "This is an act of madness," I finish in a whisper.

Agravaine puts his hand on my arm. "It's a bad business," he says soberly, "but, Morgana, you must be strong for Mordred. He has taken our mother's death to heart, for in your absence she became his mother too. He is inconsolable."

"Where is he?" It is inconceivable that my son should love my sister more than me. This thought is followed by another: that Morgause's death will make it easier for me to regain Mordred's love and trust. The thought shames me, even while I acknowledge its truth.

"He is in the kitchen, with Gareth. We think it best that the king should not associate Gareth with Gaheris until he's had time to get over his anger, for he is outraged to hear that his sister has been slain."

I nod, accepting that Agravaine's words make sense. But I am puzzled too. "What is Gareth doing in the kitchen?"

For the first time, Agravaine smiles. "He has become a lowly kitchen hand. And he has been christened *Beaumains* by Sir Kay, who thought him ill-suited even to that task."

Fair hands. Well named. A knight's hands may become scarred and disfigured in battle, but Gareth is not yet old enough for that. But even from a young age a kitchen churl's hands will be marked by clumsy knife cuts and burns from turning and handling a hot spit. I wonder if Gareth's fair hands already bear the brand of his new trade, and I hurry to the kitchen to find him and my son, wiping tears from my eyes as I go.

There, Gareth greets me soberly, while warning me in an undertone not to seem too friendly, nor to betray his true identity. But I cannot restrain my joy on seeing Mordred again. I find him standing close to a barrel of apples, practicing his juggling. He drops several apples when he notices me. He makes no effort to pick them up, but folds his arms and stands staring at me.

"Mordred." I gather him up and smother him with kisses but he remains rigid. Finally, I release him, marveling at the changes time has wrought. He is no longer a child, a little boy; he is fast taking on the appearance of the handsome man he will become.

"Don't you remember me? I'm your mother."

He takes a few steps away from me, but otherwise makes no acknowledgment that he's heard or understood my words. I rush to reassure him.

"I'm so sorry I've been away from you for such a long time. But you have been ever in my heart, my darling. I've missed you so much."

He regards me gravely. "You left me," he says, "and I forgot all about you. Morgause is my mother now. *Was* my mother." The desolation in his voice brings the sting of tears to my eyes once more. I am appalled to think he may have witnessed Gaheris's attack. My imagination has produced images that are shocking enough. How much worse for Mordred if he actually saw Morgause die.

"I am here, Mordred, and I'll take care of you. I swear I'll never leave you again." My voice shakes as I put my hand on my heart to solemnize my oath. How bitterly I regret that my scheming has come to naught. Instead of being able to promise Mordred a kingdom as an inheritance, I must make other plans, both for Mordred and my unborn child. Marriage to Urien is the obvious solution but, looking at Mordred, I wonder if he will agree to accompany me to Rheged. I know that I cannot bear to be parted from him again and besides, I have made him a vow.

"If you wish, we can go back to the priory and live quietly there. I shall be a mother to you once more. We won't be parted again, I swear it." Even as I say the words, I yearn to be back there, free of the affairs of court and alone with my son once more.

He regards me with a scornful expression. "I cannot go back to the priory with you," he says. "I will not. My place is here at Camelot, with my brothers."

Stricken, I stare at him. He lifts his chin and stares back at me. In that gesture he looks exactly like his father—who is alive and well, and still a threat to my son. The priory will be a place of safety for him. I must convince him to accompany me there. It suddenly comes to me that no one has mentioned the attempt on Arthur's life, and I wonder at it. Even though I'd misunderstood the words used by the traveler, an attempt had certainly been made for he'd said that a death had occurred, and there must be repercussions from that. It is essential that I remove both Mordred and myself from danger.

"When did you arrive at Camelot? How long have you been here?" I look to Gareth for answers.

He considers for a few long moments. "We arrived just after the moon was full. It is now a small crescent, but it is beginning to wax again."

At least two weeks then. "And have you and Mordred met with the king in that time?" I ask carefully.

"No. The king is extremely angry over his sister's death. He is also distracted by the recent attempt on his life. The court has been in uproar over it all. We thought it well to pretend we are merely the new kitchen staff and as such, he has not noticed us. But Gawain will make sure to win his favor again, and then he will take us to the king and all will be well. It is only a matter of waiting for the proper time."

"Camelot is a much finer court than we kept at Lothian," Mordred says eagerly. "I will not leave here, not for anything." He folds his arms against me once more. "And you can't make me go."

"There's no need to make any decisions now," I say hastily, trying to keep my tears in check as I look at his indignant, rebellious face. "We'll talk of this again … when you're not so upset." As I walk away, the thought occurs to me that I handled our meeting very badly. I didn't tell him how sad I was to hear of my sister's death, nor did I commiserate with him on losing his foster mother. Instead I barreled straight in and demanded that he accept me back into his heart.

Merlin was right in one thing, I think, continuing to berate myself as I join the members of the court now assembling for dinner in the great hall. I lack judgment and am ever too quick to act. I can only hope that I have not alienated Mordred for all time.

It is clear, from the way that Guenevere has arranged the seating at table, that the Orkney brothers are far from her favor, and I am dumped in with them. While she has not dared to demote Gawain to a lesser table, Agravaine and I have been banished to sit at a separate table among the scribes and other minor dignitaries at court. If Agravaine resents such treatment, he doesn't show it. I seethe with rage but Agravaine is his usual cocky self. I look about for Launcelot, expecting to find him in his customary place on the queen's left, but there is no sign of him. I scan the seated guests and servants, looking for the young girl to whom I entrusted the cloak—but there is no sign of her either.

It is Agravaine who unwittingly answers my unspoken questions.

"I don't suppose you've heard about the latest attempt on the king's life," he says. "A young lass came with a beautiful cloak that she said was a gift for the king from a well-to-do lady. She said that the king was expecting the gift, although he claimed to have no knowledge of it. However, he was greatly pleased with the cloak, and was about to put it on when the Lady of Avalon stopped him."

Viviane again! I clench my hands into fists under the table at the thought of that meddling witch.

"Lady Viviane asked the young girl to put it on first, 'so that the king can see its true beauty,' she said, although I think she suspected even then that there was something amiss with it."

"Something amiss? Whatever can you mean?"

"As soon as the girl put it on, it burst into flames and killed her." Agravaine's eyes widen with remembered fear as he concludes, "There was great magic, dark magic, involved in the making of the cloak, the king is sure of it. He believes in the girl's innocence, that she was someone's dupe, but unfortunately no one thought to ask where she came from, or interrogated her about the lady who gave her the cloak. We were unsure where to start making enquiries until a trader arrived yesterday searching for his horse. He told us that it had been hired by a young girl to make the journey here and back to Glastonbury, but that she had not returned it within the stipulated period of hire. So now we know where the girl came from, and the king has sent Sir Launcelot to make enquiries."

Agravaine sits back in his chair, and his lips quirk in amusement. "I don't suppose you'd know anything about all this, would you, Aunt? You've just come from there, haven't you?"

"Of course I know nothing about it!" I snap. "This is the first I've heard of it." I stare him down, determined to establish my innocence in the whole affair. Yet I feel a lump of dread in my chest; sorrow and regret over the death of an innocent young girl, overlaid with anger at being thwarted by the Lady Viviane. I steal a glance in her direction. She is gazing at me, looking thoughtful. The lump of dread grows so large, it threatens to choke me. I would like to drink myself into oblivion; to put an end to this dreadful day with all its shocks and surprises, but I am afraid that I might betray myself if I loosen my wits.

The meal drags on. I long for it to be over—until something happens that sweeps everything else from my mind.

A platter of fruit is brought out and placed on the Round Table. I look at it with envy; my mouth waters as I survey the colorful cornucopia of assorted fruits. I lick my lips, wishing I could choose a sweet, juicy orange from far-off climes to wash the taste of defeat from my mouth. I watch as the platter is offered to Sir Patrise, hoping that any fruit left may be brought to our table, for the meals are plentiful and for the most part platters of fruit are usually ignored. Sir Patrise takes an apple, the largest of them all. Gawain, sitting close by, also chooses an apple, that fruit being ever his favorite. He bites into its crisp, sweet flesh.

Platters of fruit are now being placed on other tables, including our own. I select an orange, and am handed a small silver knife with which to peel it. The talk and laughter continue until the sound of a choking rattle draws everyone's gaze to Sir Patrise. The knight's face is red and swollen, and he clutches his throat as he staggers to his feet.

"I ... I ..." He pitches forward onto the floor; his body jerks in the death agony while a white froth spews from his mouth.

A deep silence falls as the court looks on, stricken with horror at this unexpected disaster. I am the first to move. I have knowledge of healing—and of poisons, for I am convinced that this is no ordinary choking. I kneel beside the knight and check his mouth for any obstruction. There is none. Thereafter I do all in my power to revive him, knowing all the while that my efforts are in vain—he is already dead and gone beyond us all.

A priest hurries over, crosses himself, and kneels beside the knight to mutter a prayer for the dead. Gawain leaps to his feet and points a shaking hand at the queen.

"This is your doing, my lady," he says, "for you have overseen this feast and you know well my custom of taking an apple at the end of a meal."

"No!" Guenevere cries, clutching her hand to her breast. "I swear I know nothing of what has happened here. You are mistaken, Sir Gawain."

But Sir Mador is also on his feet now, accusing the queen of deliberately poisoning his cousin, Sir Patrise, and crying treason on her.

"I know nothing of this, my lord, I swear it." Weeping, Guenevere turns to Arthur for help.

But he holds up his hand to prevent her from casting herself into his arms. "I believe you," he says, his voice ringing out over the sudden hubbub that has now erupted. "But I must be seen to be fair in this matter. Find yourself a champion, my lady, and you," he gestures toward Gawain and Sir Mador, "shall do battle against him. Whoever wins shall signal the truth behind this affair."

The court falls into a stunned silence as the weeping queen is led away. I cannot help but feel pity for her plight, and grave annoyance with Arthur. If only he loved his queen more, and showed his love, she would not have had to seek recourse to Launcelot right from the start. Truly he is an indifferent lover, and now he has shown himself as an indifferent husband.

*

I say none of this when I am summoned to an audience with my brother.

"My liege and dearest brother." I sweep into a deep curtsy and kiss his hand. "I am truly sorry to hear that you have all these troubles to bear." I look up at Viviane who, as usual, is standing guard behind Arthur.

"Morgana!"

I hear the relief in Arthur's voice as he raises me and holds me in a close embrace. It seems that his gratitude over my impending marriage to Urien has softened his feelings toward me. It seems also that my brother looks upon me as an ally in an increasingly troubled court.

"I am more than pleased to see you, sister. You know that Sir Patrise has died after taking a bite from a poisoned apple. Now there is talk that the apple was meant for me. And that

Guenevere is to blame, for it is said ..." His voice dies to a mutter so I have to lean close to hear his last words, and then I can hardly believe them. "It is said that she wishes me dead."

There are always rumors flying around Camelot, but this one I haven't heard before. Has the love between Launcelot and Guenevere grown so irresistible they are now trying to get Arthur out of their way? An unexpected gust of fury shakes me at the thought. I had almost convinced myself that I was indifferent to their love, but this is a step beyond my expectation. My plan was to make them suffer the pangs of unrequited love, not lead them to murder—with ecstacy as a reward for their wrongdoing.

"Perhaps you've mistaken what you've heard, sire?" I ask hopefully.

"I think not, for the story has come to me from more than one source: that she longs to have a child and she blames me for her failure to conceive an heir for Camelot. I have seen how men look at her, and it may be she is tempted to consider another ..."

Arthur looks so miserable I am moved to take him into my arms and give him a comforting hug, just as I used to do when he was small. And yet I cannot gainsay his imaginings for the evidence is right there in front of him, if only he is prepared to face it.

"The problem I have now," Arthur continues, "is that any attempt on my life is treason, punishable by death. So unless I can prove the queen's innocence, Guenevere will burn." He squeezes his eyes shut, perhaps imagining the horror of such a death.

Trying to put my own feelings aside, I consider the matter. "Gawain claimed that the queen arranged the feast. Is that true?"

Arthur hesitates, opens his eyes. "Yes, it is."

"And Gawain was seated at the Round Table—whereas Agravaine and I were not." There is a sting in the last words;

my demotion still rankles. "So perhaps the queen wanted Gawain under her eye, in which case he may be right in claiming that he was indeed the intended victim and not you, Arthur."

A succession of emotions flit across Arthur's face: relief, followed by regret, anger, suspicion. "Does this mean that you believe in her intention, and her hand in the matter, Morgana?"

I give a reluctant nod.

"But why would she want Gawain dead?"

I have no answer, for I am almost convinced that Guenevere is responsible for poisoning the apple, but that Gawain was not the intended victim. I believe the rumors may well be true: Guenevere and Launcelot are so infatuated with each other they will let nothing and no one stand in their way.

Arthur turns away and lightly drums his fingers on the table as he ponders the problem. "I have proclaimed that Guenevere's guilt—or innocence—is to be decided by battle. I cannot take any part in it, but unless I can find a knight to fight for her honor, she will die. I have asked for a volunteer, but no one is prepared to come forward on her behalf."

It is a mark of how far the queen's fortunes have fallen within the court that no one, now, is prepared to defend her. The knights have seen what Arthur will not admit: the infatuation between Guenevere and Launcelot that strikes at the heart of their love and loyalty toward husband, friend and king.

"What about her champion, Sir Launcelot?" It almost kills me to suggest it.

Arthur shakes his head. "He is away from court, seeking to find the enchantress who fashioned a magical cloak that was almost certainly meant for my destruction." He presses his lips together. It seems his suspicions now rest on Guenevere for that as well.

"Is there no one else who will fight for her?" None of the Orkney brothers will, not after Gawain's accusation. "What about Sir Kay? Or Sir Bors?" I can't think why I'm making these suggestions. Guenevere can burn for all I care. Perhaps it's because Arthur looks so wretched. In spite of my thwarted intentions, my heart is wrung to see him so.

"One of the other knights might agree, if I ask it as a special favor." Arthur brightens slightly. "I could even offer a reward. Viviane?" He turns to the Lady of Avalon. "Will you petition the knights on my behalf? I cannot be seen to involve myself in proving the queen's innocence, but I will do all in my power to save her if I can."

With a sour glance in my direction, Viviane agrees.

"Search high and low, if you will," Arthur tells her. "I shall wait a week, and I shall pray for your success."

"I shall make all haste to find a willing knight to bring to your court, sire." Viviane does not look happy as she takes her leave. I wonder if she, too, is convinced of the queen's guilt.

Arthur gazes at me, looking thoughtful. "I mourn our sister's death, as I'm sure you do too, Morgana. I have sent an armed guard to Lothian to make further enquiries regarding her death, and the death of Lamorak, for word has now come to me that he has also been slain. I have ordered the guards to return with your son. Be assured I have not forgotten him, nor have I forgotten what once transpired between us."

There is dread in my heart as I take leave of Arthur. I must persuade Mordred to come away with me at once, for I fear Arthur's revenge once the truth of our son's birth is known. An even greater fear is that Launcelot's investigation may uncover the truth behind the poisoned cloak, for then I shall suffer the same judgment as Guenevere. And while she may yet find a champion to defend her honor, I know that I will not.

*

In the days that follow, while Viviane tries to bribe a knight to fight for the queen, I do my best to re-establish the love that once existed between me and Mordred. It works in my favor that Urien is still absent from court; that is one less worry on my mind. I know Mordred will refuse to accompany me to Rheged, but a solution to my predicament is becoming more urgent as my stomach swells to accommodate the child growing within. I must find somewhere that Mordred will agree to go, and soon.

I take to waiting around the kitchen so that I can see him and talk to him, earning suspicious glances from the kitchen staff although they do not say anything to my face. But our snatched conversations are never satisfactory. While I try to coddle him as the child I knew, Mordred resists any signs of affection, taking great care to prove at every opportunity that he has grown beyond me in more ways than one. And always when we talk, I am conscious that there are people about and that anything we say might be overheard by others.

"We don't have to go back to the priory," I tell him eagerly, on the one occasion when I persuade him to walk out in the meadows with me. We are walking side by side, with Mordred using the stick he's brought with him to decapitate the plants and flowers that we pass along the way. I am surprised at the ferocity of his blows, but tell myself it is to compensate for the loss of his foster mother. I do not remonstrate with him about the destruction of plants that might well have provided food or healing treatments for the poor. To get my own way, I need to keep my son on side, and I hasten to put my new proposal before him.

"I have another suggestion, one I think you'll like."

"I know that you are promised to Urien of Rheged." Mordred's tone is savage. "Do not try to pretend you wish to make a home with me. And do not, for one moment, expect me to come to Rheged with you either."

Of course he would have heard the news of our betrothal. I should have anticipated it so that I could prepare an answer.

"The king, your uncle, is anxious to make an alliance with Urien," I say quickly. "In a moment of weakness, I agreed to it. But what is not yet done can be easily put aside. No, Mordred, I was thinking instead of taking you to Castle Perilous, the castle given to me by the king for my very own. There, I shall make you king of your own demesne, and you will have your own subjects at your command. We can leave at once, if you wish, for there is nothing to keep us here."

I wait, hoping and praying that he will agree to my request. If he does, I make a private vow that I shall have no more to do with Urien, not even to let him claim this baby as his own. It will be enough for me to live in seclusion at the castle with Mordred. There I can have Launcelot's child, after inventing yet another story of a tumble in the bushes with an ignorant churl. There we shall be safe from Arthur and every other threat, for I shall make sure a watch is kept and that the castle is guarded at all times.

"You must be out of your wits to think I'd live in a priory, or a castle, or anywhere else with you!" Mordred snaps. "My place is here, at Camelot. If the queen stays barren there'll be no child to follow Arthur. As I am one of the king's nephews, I intend to make sure that when he names his heir, he will realize I am far more worthy than my Orkney cousins, who are already off-side with him in the matter of my mother."

He pauses, perhaps arrested by my expression. I cannot conceal my shock, my desolation to hear him call Morgause "mother." But there is no vestige of remorse in his tone as he continues. "I am determined that Camelot must come to me, for I am a worthy and just heir to the throne. And I intend to stay here to claim the kingdom as soon as the opportunity presents itself."

He raises his stick and, before I can say anything, he smashes it down on a tiny rabbit that has strayed a little too far from its mother. Blood and brains spill from the broken skull, spraying Mordred with droplets of gore. He strides on, whistling softly under his breath.

Horror struck, I gaze after my son, this boy who is fast growing into a man and who has become a stranger to me. Where has he learned such cruelty? From witnessing the attack on Morgause? I long to comfort him but dare not touch him, for it is clear as water that he will never forgive me for deserting him.

But I wonder who has stirred such vaulting ambition. Not Morgause; she was ignorant of his true siring and would certainly have put her ambition for her own brood far above any claim coming from Mordred. In truth I am quite proud that Mordred has seen for himself the possibilities of his inheritance. But I also wonder when he started plotting to inherit the throne from Arthur. That he will not hesitate to seize it I have no doubt; the determination on his face, so like his father's, shows me that he means every word he said. But how far is he prepared to go to secure his future? I think of the baby rabbit. I look at my son, and feel a frisson of fear.

Once upon a time I determined to teach Mordred all the magical arts that I know. Now, I am no longer so sure. Mordred has the capacity to be ruthless, he has just proved that. With my magical arts at his disposal, what damage might he wreak, what ruin might he bring on us all, including himself? There is disappointment in the thought, for I'd been looking forward to sharing my skill and knowledge with him. I'd even hoped it might bring us close together again. Now, it seems too great a risk. Instead of thinking about my own future, I need to consider what to do with him.

Before making a decision about it, I corner Gareth on his own and question him about Gaheris's attack on his mother, and whether he and Mordred were witness to it.

"It was early morning, and Gaheris was into the castle and up the stairs shouting out greetings before anyone could warn my mother that he'd arrived." Gareth has grown pale; his eyes are haunted. "Mordred and I came out of our room to welcome him just as he reached our mother's bedchamber. Knowing what he would find, we tried to stop him from going in. But he pushed past us. Both of us were witness to the killing. It was …" His voice starts to shake. "It was beyond anything you can imagine. My mother, stricken and helpless as Gaheris drew his sword and shouted his accusation. Lamorak, naked in my mother's bed and unable to reach his sword in time to defend her. The blood … the horror of it all …" He buries his face in his hands.

"But Lamorak managed to escape on that occasion?"

Gareth nods. "He was out of my mother's bed and through the window in the blink of an eye. Stark naked but that didn't stop him. He knew his fate should he linger to clothe himself."

"And Mordred saw it all?"

"Yes. I'm sorry, Morgana, but yes, he did. There was no time to shield his eyes or send him away. No time for anything. It all happened so fast and … and I couldn't move, not even to defend my mother. I couldn't believe what was happening. I am so sorry."

"It's not your fault, Gareth," I say. "At least you were there to comfort Mordred after the event." There is still something I must ask, something I need to know in order to see my way forward. "Mordred seems very troubled, and now I can understand why. But I've also witnessed that he can be cruel, sometimes even quite vicious." It pains me to say such things about my son, but I must find out the truth. "You've spent more time with him than anyone else, so I need to ask you this. Have you noticed this trait in his behavior at all, even before the slaughter of your mother?"

Gareth winces and I'm sorry that I haven't phrased my question a little more delicately. He looks at me as if deliberating what to say.

"Please, tell me the truth. I'm trying to find a way to reach Mordred, to understand him. We have grown so far apart in the time I've been away that I feel I hardly know him any more."

"I once saw him tormenting some newborn kittens in a barn," Gareth admits. "He held the first one high and dropped it, I think to see if it would land on its feet as we had been told cats were wont to do. But one of the hounds jumped on it and ate it, and thereafter he fed the rest of the kittens to the hounds. He was quite young at the time, maybe seven or eight, but he wouldn't listen when I begged him to stop. He knew what he was doing all right."

I listen, sickened by the story, and also by what Gareth isn't telling me: that he is afraid of Mordred. He was too afraid to fight him and make him stop then, and he is probably still afraid of him now.

But Gareth hasn't finished yet. "That wasn't the only thing I witnessed," he tells me. "I have seen Mordred ride a horse almost to death, flogging it until blood ran down its sides and for no apparent reason. I think he likes to see how far he can push a situation—and how much he can get away with when he does."

"With no father to check him, you mean?"

"Certainly my mother made no effort to curb his wildest excesses. Mordred could do nothing wrong in her eyes." The bitterness in Gareth's voice reveals much about the relationship between the cousins, and their relationship with Morgause. How I regret my long absence, now more than ever. Morgause and I have damaged my son, by overindulgence and by neglect, so that it seems he has now become a danger both to himself and to others.

Gareth's words are enough to make up my mind. I shall not teach Mordred any of my magical arts, for to do so would put power into the hands of a bully with no conscience, and give him the means to harm us all.

*

The week draws to a close with no sign of Viviane or any knight to act as Guenevere's champion. Arthur can delay her trial no longer. The knights and their consorts adjourn to the meadow where the tourney for the lady's honor is to be held—or alternatively, where Guenevere's death will be decided upon. I accompany Arthur, who looks pale and sick with misery.

Guenevere is led out into the throng. She has been held in custody until now, but is released to watch her champion fight for her honor. She holds up her hands in entreaty to Arthur, but he ignores her. I can see the strain she is under as she tugs and tears at her kerchief, while her lips move constantly in a silent prayer.

Sir Mador takes the field, clad in black armor and with his shield at the ready, to the encouraging hoots and applause from the crowd. Everyone twists and turns then, trying to catch sight of who the queen's champion might be. I suspect their wait will be in vain, but then I spy Bors. He, too, is clad in armor and presumably is ready to fight. Beside me, Arthur exhales a deep breath of relief. Sir Mador is already mounted, but Bors lingers beside his mount until the hoots turned to loud jeers and whistles. Finally, and with apparent reluctance, he calls for a mounting block and steps upon it.

Before he can mount, Launcelot gallops onto the field to take his place. Arthur whispers to me that it was Viviane who persuaded him to abandon his search for the mysterious matron at Glastonbury and return to court, but that Bors agreed to stand in for him if he did not come in time. And so we watch as Launcelot fights for the life of his love, ferociously and with honor.

I am filled with bitterness that he can so openly champion the queen, despite her guilt, and the guilt of their illicit love, when he would not do the same for me even after the life we shared, and the love that has resulted in the child growing in my womb. I place a comforting hand on my stomach and mourn silently.

The knights ride hard at each other, lances at the ready. I hear the thunder of the horses' hooves, the clash as lance deflects lance as they wheel and strike, and strike again. Dust rises, thick and choking. There are groans and grunts as weapons find their mark, but still both knights manage to stay on their mounts. The courtiers cheer on their favorites. I realize that the cheers are not evenly matched in volume. The queen and her knight are no longer the favorites of the court.

A final clash together; this time Launcelot manages to unhorse Sir Mador, who tumbles to the ground and lies prone, begging mercy. He is carried from the field, and Gawain takes his place. Once again Launcelot charges, and the two knights buffet each other until it is Gawain's turn to be unhorsed and fall to the ground. He declines to fight on, and holds up his hands in surrender. Thus the queen's innocence is supposedly proven in the matter of the poisoned apple, but still there are mutters among some in the crowd.

Launcelot dismounts, and hands his steed over to his squire. Rather than coming straight to Arthur, he approaches Guenevere, who flings her arms around him and embraces him in gratitude. I marvel at my brother's seeming indifference to their brazen behavior. Looking around at the discomforted members of his court, I see they share my sentiments. I begin to wonder if perhaps the poisoned apple was a ruse to end the scandal of this illicit love affair, and if it was, in fact, intended for Guenevere herself. And it occurs to me that, with Guenevere out of the way, the love spell would be broken and Launcelot might then remember he loved me first.

I remind myself of his faithless abandonment of me at the time of my greatest need, but already my heartbeat has quickened at the thought of being with him once more. My body aches with wanting him. I stumble, and Arthur takes my hand. He holds it fast, and we cling to each other, both of us needing support.

The Lady of Avalon, interfering witch that she is, tells Arthur that she intends to walk around the assembled multitude, for she has the power, she says, to look into men's hearts and find the truth of who really poisoned the apple. I am sure Viviane is lying, otherwise she could have done this right at the start. It would have saved us all a lot of trouble and heartache—unless she truly believed that Guenevere was indeed behind the plot. I stifle a smile, thinking this must be a pretense, for she certainly hasn't succeeded in looking into *my* heart!

But I no longer feel like smiling when she pauses beside me and whispers softly, "I know you for what you are, Lady Morgana, and I would stop your mischief if I could. But I have not the power, and so I give you fair warning instead: take care that in your desire for revenge, your schemes do not lead us all to doom."

"I don't know what you mean." I stare over her head toward Launcelot, willing him to look my way. Viviane's eyes follow my gaze.

"Your desire for revenge will also break your heart."

The lady moves on. I look after her, for she is correct in one thing at least: my heart is broken. But that was not of my doing. Merlin, Arthur, Launcelot—and yes, even Mordred, my beloved son—all of them have played their part in causing the desolation I feel now. Everything I have tried in order to follow my destiny has turned to ashes.

Viviane has continued her progress through the crowd, scrutinizing each face as she goes, and now she stops abruptly in front of Sir Pinel. "This is the man responsible for poisoning the apple," she says, and places her hand upon his chest.

His cry of rage is lost in the scuffle that follows Viviane's words. But once Sir Pinel is seized and held fast, Arthur strides down to confront him and finally the truth emerges. The apple was indeed intended for Gawain—or any other of the Orkney brothers for that matter—for Sir Pinel blames them all together for the killing of his cousin Lamorak.

I am greatly relieved to hear that my meddling between Launcelot and Guenevere has not been behind this affair. But I have also noticed the growing rift among the knights that has its origins in the flaunting of the queen's desire for Launcelot and his for her. It seems that while most remain loyal to Arthur there are others who mutter that he must surely realize the strength of the affection between the two, so why is he not man—and king—enough to put a stop to it?

CHAPTER 9

Now that the danger to Guenevere has passed, it seems that Arthur is able to turn his mind to other problems that beset him. Most notably, my son and me.

The first intimation I have of danger is when Arthur summons me to attend him in his private solar. To my horror, Mordred is already there when I arrive. He and Arthur are not talking. They stand at opposite ends of the room, utterly ill at ease. Looking at them, I can see how closely my son resembles his father. I wonder if Arthur has noticed it for himself or if the interfering Viviane has pointed it out. She is standing behind him in her usual position. I am quite sure she has either intuited or guessed the truth. Guenevere is nowhere to be seen. I move to Mordred's side, understanding that whatever happens next, he will need my protection.

"I have discovered that Mordred is your son, Morgana," Arthur states with cold precision. He looks pale; his mouth turns down as if he's tasted sour wine.

"Yes, sire." I shall not venture any information until I find out how much he knows. Or guesses.

"How old is he?"

"Nine summers."

"Eleven summers," Mordred corrects me. "You've been absent for many years of my life, Morgana, but you should still remember the time of my birth."

I cannot explain to him that my lie was a feeble effort to protect him. Now, in despair, I wait for Arthur to work out the truth.

"His father, I have been told, was a shepherd boy with whom you tumbled under a bush. What is his name, Morgana? Who is the father of your child?" Arthur watches me like a snake preparing to strike.

My mouth is dry. I swallow hard to bring saliva into my mouth, but still I cannot speak. Viviane steps forward and rests her palm on Mordred's chest. She bends, listening intently as if his heartbeat will confirm what I'm sure she's already guessed. She straightens, and resumes her place behind Arthur.

"He is your son, sire."

Briefly, fiercely, I wish I had the art to strike her dead with a bolt of lightning, for I would have done so when first we met. So much trouble could have been avoided had I been able to remove her from the court. All I can do now is try to talk my way out of the situation. I turn on her.

"You weren't there when Mordred was conceived, lady. Do not presume to answer for my actions."

"Stop lying to me, Morgana." Arthur sounds weary to death. "You tricked me into lying with you after our win on the battlefield, and you've been lying to me ever since."

I glance at Viviane. Her expression is somber. It seems she's taking as little joy in the proceedings as I am. And then I notice something else. Beyond her, Guenevere stands in the doorway, paused as if turned into stone. Judging from her stricken face, I suspect she's heard everything. Despite the perilous situation I'm in, I feel a twinge of remorse on her behalf.

It seems the only person gladdened by the news is Mordred. Joy has transformed his face. "Are you really my father?" he whispers.

Arthur turns on him. "It would seem so. But I take no pleasure from the knowledge, for you are ill bred and bastard born."

I watch the joy leach out of Mordred's face, and wonder at Arthur's cruelty. And his stupidity. Because I notice, even if Arthur does not, the calculating gleam that now begins to shine in Mordred's eyes. I know what it means. His claim to the throne is secure now. Furthermore, his father's rejection has severed all ties and any lingering notion of love or loyalty to his king.

"Mordred!" I put my hand on his arm. In warning? To protect him? To show affection? None of it matters because he shrugs me off, straightens his shoulders and faces his father.

"Ill bred I may be, but I am your son and you *will* acknowledge me."

A pitiful moaning from the doorway draws our eyes to Guenevere. Her fists are crammed to her mouth as if to silence her distress, but tears stream down her face and her body sways as though in a high wind.

"Guenevere!" For once Arthur does the right thing. He hurries to her side and takes her hand. "You have nothing to fear from Mordred—or his mother," he reassures her. "We shall make a fine son of our own, Guenevere, a legitimate heir to rule over Camelot after I am gone. This I swear to you."

He pats her shoulder while I reflect that Launcelot would have encircled Guenevere within his arms and kissed her tears away. As it is, she shrugs away from Arthur while her high, wild keening continues. Mordred stares on with a stony face and the glint of triumph in his eyes.

And I am more fearful than ever: for Arthur, for Mordred, and most of all, for my unborn child and the future I have in mind for him. Or her.

It is clear that my presence is no longer welcome in Camelot. Arthur tells me that he has sent a message to Urien advising him that I am about to leave for Rheged so that our marriage may be celebrated there instead of at Camelot. "I will send an escort with you," he adds.

I open my mouth to protest. We both know that by "escort" he means "guard." But he silences me with an upraised hand.

"It is for the best that you leave here as soon as possible," he tells me sternly.

I am forced to agree, although I beg a few days' grace in which to pack my belongings and make myself ready. Once more I plead with Mordred to accompany me, but he laughs in my face.

"My father may not want me here," he says, "but I am his heir and I will stay to remind him—and the court—that I have a claim to his crown."

I have to admit, albeit grudgingly, that in his place I would have done the same thing. It's already becoming apparent, as news of his parentage spreads through the court, that Arthur's reputation has also been tarnished. Indeed, some of the younger knights have already promised their future allegiance to Mordred, who ignores his father's displeasure and instead crows his right to the throne at every opportunity and with all the enthusiasm of a rooster welcoming the dawn.

To my sorrow, Mordred will have nothing further to do with me, nor will anyone else at court, for I am now shunned by everyone. It is no comfort to me that as I watch my plans come to fruition, I am more afraid of the future than I have ever been. Instead of following Arthur's instructions to join Urien at Rheged, I decide instead to escape, if I can, to the priory.

Before I leave, and against my better judgment, I seek out a last meeting with Launcelot. I know I cannot count on comfort or support from him—I have seen in his eyes the contempt he holds for me—but I am desperate to put a gloss on my behavior so that he will think more kindly of me, and of our time together. But he will not listen, nor will he make any effort to understand.

"I wish to God we had never met, Morgana." I try to tell myself that his regret is because he's so deep in love with Guenevere, but he's quick to disabuse me. "What the queen has said about you is true. You are an enchantress who will snare any man with your wiles if it suits you to do so, be he low-born shepherd or High King, or any man in between. My deepest regret is that I could not see your wickedness but instead fell under your spell."

"It was no spell, Launcelot! I loved you, and I love you still!" The words erupt from my heart and burst from my lips before my mind has time to urge caution. Yet every word is true. I look into his eyes, and mutely beg him to understand how deeply I care about him. But he flinches and looks away.

"And I loved you too, Morgana, more than you will ever know. After you left Joyous Garde I scoured the kingdom, seeking to find out the truth of the matter, any evidence to counteract the accusation and to bring down those who would witness against you. For your own sake, I needed to appear impartial, and for your sake I did all in my power to clear your good name before I came to court. I even questioned the king, who confirmed your knowledge of magic and your ill use of it in the past, although I could not find the mage who schooled you in these dangerous arts. I could find no one who would speak for you, Morgana, no one at all.

"Now, at last, I know your true worth, and I wish you gone from my sight. My only desire is that I never see you again."

Launcelot's words stab sharp as a dagger. I am speechless, unable to defend myself against his fury and his loathing. I hasten away from him before my tears can spill. I shall not give him the satisfaction of witnessing my absolute desolation. How badly I misjudged him and how misguided I was in seeking revenge! Now, more than ever, I wish I'd heeded Merlin's warnings to use my magical powers wisely, and not to be so thoughtless of the consequences of my actions.

Arthur is becoming impatient with my delay, but I stall while I search for a way to evade him and avoid my fate. I'm unwilling to change my form in order to escape, for the babe is six months developed now, and I cannot risk any harm coming to it. I'm almost resigned to having to go to Rheged under guard when I receive a message from Urien to say that he has been taken ill and is unable to travel to Camelot for our marriage. I'm about to dismiss the messenger before Arthur comes to hear of the news and sends me back to Rheged with him, when he tells me further that Urien does not wish me to see him so indisposed, and has asked if I'll wait for him at Camelot until he is well enough to travel.

A new plan begins to unfold in my mind; a way to avoid Arthur's grasp and, at the same time, give me what I most want.

"Please tell King Urien that I am greatly distressed by his news, but rather than stay on at Camelot I prefer to return to the priory close to the great abbey at Glastonbury," I say. "You will find me there when King Urien is ready to send for me. In fact, I was preparing to leave within the hour, so you would be doing me a great service if you would escort me there before returning to Rheged."

The messenger agrees to my request. I bid him wait for me at the gatehouse with my palfrey, after which I quickly throw my belongings into a bag. I then take leave of Arthur.

"Urien has sent for me so there is no need for you to provide an escort," I tell him. "I know you are anxious for me to be gone, and so I bid you farewell."

"I shall come with you to the gatehouse."

"That is not necessary, Arthur."

He doesn't bother to reply, but stalks after me. The messenger is waiting for me, as I requested, and bows low when he sees Arthur.

"You come from Rheged? You are Urien's man?" Arthur asks.

"Yes, sire." The messenger bows again.

"It's getting late. We must go," I intervene, not wanting to risk any further conversation between the two men.

Arthur nods, and turns away. He does not bother to say farewell, or wish me God's speed on my journey. And so I say nothing either, but I am conscious that the rift between us has now widened to an insurmountable chasm. If the messenger is surprised by the lack of fond farewells, he does not comment. I am grateful for his reticence although I suspect my chilly relationship with the king will be duly reported to Urien. But the man is pleasant and courteous, and our journey to the priory passes without incident.

"I hope to see you before too long, mistress," he tells me as he bids me farewell.

In return, I send with him a fond message to Urien and I bid him a safe journey. But I cannot echo his sentiments for I'm hoping he'll stay away for quite some time—at least long enough for my baby to be born. By then I will have thought of some way to thwart Arthur's wishes and avoid this marriage altogether.

*

Once I am settled back at the priory among my own possessions, I recall Merlin's words and take from their hiding place what I have stolen from him. I am determined this time to understand and harness the powers I had not even guessed at before I confronted him. I cannot think of going back to Camelot until the scandal of Mordred's birth is forgotten and the court has found some new wonder or disaster as a diversion. And I certainly can't show myself outside the priory gates until after the birth of my babe. The prioress has already guessed at it, and tut-tutted over my explanation of another ill-judged liaison. Whether I go to Urien or not, I have decided that my child shall stay here among these good women, safe from the devious machinations of the court.

Of more concern is the need to keep the child safe also from Mordred. I try to calm my fears with the thought that, as firstborn and son of the High King, albeit illegitimate, he is the obvious successor to the throne. This baby poses no threat to him at all. Unbidden, a vision of the shattered skull of the baby rabbit comes into my mind. I shudder and push it into the deepest recesses of my memory.

To take my mind off the dark imaginings that come in the blackest hours of the night, I spend my time refining and perfecting my magical arts while attempting also to uncover the secrets of the mysterious wooden tablets with their elaborately etched pictures. In the privacy of my room, I fan them out and study them closely.

Try as I might, I can see no apparent order or meaning to them. There are symbols in common: a cup, a wand, a sword and a pentacle that looks rather like the rock crystal I stole from Merlin's cave. Some tablets bear the representation of one or other of the symbols and depict various scenes. There are representations of death and destruction, of trial and terror, but also of joy and celebration. Other tablets depict only one figure or some sort of object. Two lovers stand close together: Launcelot and Guenevere? I scrutinize them more closely, and think that perhaps there's more of a resemblance to Launcelot and to me. But there is also a tablet showing a heart pierced by three swords—my heart pierced by the love between Launcelot and Guenevere, a love that I helped to create? Or do the swords represent the triangle between Arthur, Launcelot and Guenevere? There is a man with a gray beard carrying a wand. The other symbols are spread on a table before him. Merlin with his magical objects? An overlapping tablet, showing a sly-looking man creeping away with a sword puts me in mind of Merlin's trickery with Excalibur.

I shudder as I note some of the other tablets: a devil, a burning tower, a skeleton upon a horse trampling over dead people—and dead people rising from their tombs as an angel sounds a trumpet. I don't need the nuns to tell me that I'm looking here at the Day of Judgment. Yet death comes to us all, so what is this card's significance other than to serve perhaps as a reminder—or a warning?

More to the point, how am I meant to use these tablets? If it's to tell the future, then I need to understand more of their meaning. I stare at them fanned out in front of me, and hammer my fists against the table top in frustration.

Grasping for enlightenment, I think back to what Merlin said. *I doubt she has the wisdom to see what should be plain in front of her. If she can but find the key she could read the future and, perhaps, even change it—if it's not too late.*

What should be plain in front of me? I study them again. What do the symbols represent? The sword? Excalibur, of course! I feel a frisson of excitement. The wand? I have three of them! The pentacle? Surely it represents the crystal I stole from Merlin. And the cup, what is that? I cast about for inspiration but cannot think of any cup of note, unless it's as a receptacle for the water that is so necessary to sustain life.

I group the tablets according to their symbols. I try to empty my mind of everything as I contemplate them. I notice that there are similarities between them. Each group has a hand holding one of the symbols; the other tablets show two, three and upward to ten of each symbol. There are also four figures, rising in status from a serving page on bended knee to a mounted knight, a crowned queen and a king. I wonder if these tablets are meant to symbolize a progression of sorts, a journey through life, and through fortune. Of course! That is what Merlin meant when suggesting that by finding the key I would be able to read the future!

I stare at the tablets in triumph, which is quickly trimmed as I realize I still do not understand the meaning behind each tablet.

I study the second set of tablets more carefully. If I'm right, I've already sensed what and who some of them represent. There are two more crowned figures, both seated on elaborate thrones. They bear some resemblance to Guenevere and Arthur, but are far older in years. Lines of experience—and regret, perhaps—crease their faces. What of the lovers? And death? That comes to us all—or does it signify the death of ambition? The devil? And judgment? Cold shivers crawl like spiders across my spine as I contemplate the possibilities. Quickly, I push those thoughts away, focusing instead on a child with an innocent expression about to step out into the void. There is something about the figure that reminds me of myself, when I thought that I would inherit the world—and instead fell into the abyss. There is also a star with its promise for the future—and a woman holding a crystal pentacle.

I sort through the tablets and let my mind wander, hoping for illumination. I sense glimmers of ideas that seem to make sense, but I cannot catch hold of them to make them whole enough to weave into a pattern.

Exasperated, I seize up the tablets and mix them all around. I lay them all out again, but they still leave me with only a jumble of impressions. I remove a few, and then whole handfuls, but no clear message comes to me. I sweep them up once more. After a moment's thought I give them a thorough mix and lay them out, this time with their designs hidden so that I am choosing at random. I pick up seven and turn them over. They make no sense, and so I add another seven. This time, no matter what, I am determined to read and understand their message.

The same tablets that have previously caught my eye are now revealed: the innocent child stepping into the abyss, the magician with his wand and other implements, and the sly man creeping about with his sword. The lovers, cup raised and drinking a toast to each other. My heart aches with loss. The crowned figures, looking as if they bear the cares of the world upon their shoulders, along with a knight, the queen, the pierced heart—all are there as well as the devil, death, judgment and several others. I arrange them in the order in which I have chosen them; they have fallen into the pattern I was looking at before.

I shiver with a dreadful premonition, but try as I might, I am still unable to say for certain what each tablet signifies, either on its own or when looked at as a whole.

While the secrets of the tablets remain tantalizingly out of my reach, I prepare for the birth of my babe. My feelings toward the child are ambivalent. I mourn the absence of Launcelot; shame runs hot through my body as I recall his distaste, the cruelty of his last words to me. And yet it is true that I loved him, and that I love him still. This child is the embodiment of that love, but it serves as a bitter reminder of all that I have lost. Perhaps the baby senses this for it seems to take a malicious pleasure in disturbing my rest, being peaceful while I wake but squirming about and kicking endlessly as soon as I lie down.

To refresh my spirits, I spend long hours walking in my garden, both in the open where all may see me, but also in the secret places where only I can go. I try again to see the future in my scrying pool, for I feel ever anxious, afraid of the consequences of all that I have set in place. Mostly I see only my reflection, but occasionally I catch a glimpse of another face, the girl who looks like me but who is not. My daughter grown? Is this a girl child I am carrying?

Whispers come to me, questions from this young woman whose name so closely resembles mine. "Where are you?" she asks, but does not answer when I ask her the same question. It is my impression that she comes from a time in the future, a boundary I have tried to cross although I have never succeeded. I send her my strongest thoughts; I beg her to talk to me, but the vision always fades before she can tell me what she knows.

On one glorious occasion I feel the presence of Launcelot, and I am suffused with warmth and joy. Is this a message from the future—that he thinks of me and that in time he will return to be a father to his daughter and a husband to me?

This thought sustains me through a long and agonizing labor. I suspect that the child is not positioned as it should be because it seems to be taking its time to move down through the birth canal. The young midwife, summoned for the occasion, gives me a drink containing mugwort and mint, and perhaps some other herbs, which she says will help with the birth. She also gives me pepper to inhale and bids me "sneeze the child out." If only it could be that easy!

"Do you have a saint's relic to help you, madame?"

I shake my head.

"A piece of coral or a precious stone to hold?" She looks about the room with a hopeful expression.

I know from my own experience that these things do not help in cases such as mine. "No," I say shortly. "You are better off to massage my belly and see if you can persuade this baby to come." I gesture toward a vial containing oil of roses, which I've made up in preparation for the birth.

She tips some drops into her hand, and sets to work. Her touch is light as a butterfly's kiss and I cannot think it will achieve anything. But I assume she knows what she is doing, and so I keep quiet.

Still the baby won't shift, and finally she wrings her hands and says she knows not what to do other than cut my belly open once I am dead in order to save the child. "And you'll have to ask someone else to do that," she adds, "because I cannot."

This I will not tolerate, at least not without a fight. This baby has caused me more than enough grief already. Besides, I know something of childbirth, having borne one of my own and helped with other births at Joyous Garde and elsewhere. "You must try harder," I tell her. "Try massaging my belly in this way." I move my hands across my bloated stomach in opposite directions, to show her what I mean. "See if you can turn the baby around and position it so that it can come down head first through the birth canal. You should already know how to do this!"

"Forgive me, madame." The young woman looks fearful as she explains. "It is my mother who is the midwife, but she is away yonder delivering a baby elsewhere. Being unsure of when she would return, I came in her place to do what I may and in the hope and expectation of an easy birth." She tips more oil into her hand, and begins to pat and rub once more.

"Not like that!" Now I am thoroughly irritated. I seize her arm in a hard grasp. "Like this." I massage my hands around her arm, and she squawks with the pain of it. But when I release her and she tries again, the pressure is firm and I begin to hope that it is not too late for the baby to be turned.

"If this fails, then you must grease your hands and see if you can pull the baby out."

The young woman looks so horrified at the notion that she sets to work with a will. Sweat stands out on her brow; she grunts with the effort. I lie beneath her hands, and know despair. Only now, when it is too late, do I realize how very badly I want this child to be born, and for me to live long enough to be its mother, guardian and protector.

The child has squirmed in my belly, keeping me sleepless night after night. Now, when I most want it to shift, it stays stubbornly still. I have the sudden horrible notion that it might have strangled on the cord that binds a child to its mother, and that it might already be dead. I have seen such things before, and witnessed the grief of the mother when she holds the dead baby in her arms. Tears spring into my eyes, and course down my cheeks.

Turn, you little bastard, I think. *Turn!*

As if in response, I feel the baby stir into life and begin its familiar squirming. I draw in a sobbing breath of relief and smile through my tears at the midwife's daughter.

"It's beginning to move. Please, please keep on doing what you're doing." And the young girl responds with doubled effort, and the baby starts to squirm in earnest.

I feel a sudden shift, and know that the head has locked into the birth canal. Without waiting for instruction, I bat the young woman's hands away and begin to push. The pain is agonizing. I feel as if I'm giving birth to a horse. I pant, I take deep breaths, I push again. And pant. And push. And push. And all of a rush, my daughter is born.

CHAPTER 10

She is an ugly baby, my daughter. In this she resembles me rather than her father, for I recall overhearing a slighting comment from my mother regarding my appearance when I was born. She was comparing me unfavorably with the newborn Arthur: a beautiful baby who subsequently grew into an appealing toddler and finally a handsome man.

"Morgana looked just like a little frog when she was a baby," my mother said. Uther had laughed, and so did my mother. It only served to make me hate them more, although I couldn't hate Arthur, not then while he was still so small. Now I understand my mother's words, for so does my daughter look like a little frog with her wide apart eyes and wider mouth. It only serves to make me feel more tender toward her. I can't resist rubbing my cheek against the fuzz of soft brown down that covers her head, and inhaling her sweet baby smell. I have called her Marie, and I love her with a passion equal to the love I felt for Mordred after he was born.

She was fussy in my womb, and she is fussy now, quick to cry and always eager to suckle. I walk her endlessly around my small room at the priory, trying to quieten her so that she will not disturb the other guests or the nuns, for the guest house is in close proximity to the priory itself. She closes my fingers in her tiny hands in a grasp so strong that it is difficult to persuade her to let go. She is a fighter, this one, and greedy for life—and in this she is most definitely my child.

I gaze and gaze at her, seeking signs of her father, but can see none. I don't know whether to be glad or sorry for it, but in the end I give up worrying for she becomes who she is: Marie, a child in her own right. I make a solemn vow to myself that this child will be different from Mordred. I shall be with her always; I shall educate her in the ways of our world and in the magical ways of the Otherworld. I acknowledge, but only in my most private thoughts, that I believe she'll need all the powers at her disposal to counteract the damage that her half-brother may inflict on us all, and on the kingdom. I am determined to keep Marie's birth a secret from Mordred for as long as I am able, for I have seen his ambition and his cruelty, and I fear for her safety. Marie is no threat to him, but I suspect he may not see it that way.

I am determined also to keep her birth a secret from Launcelot, for I am afraid he will come for her if he learns that we have made a child together. My resolution does not stop me thinking about him, longing for him, wishing he was by my side. My longing grows deeper when I learn that he and Guenevere have had a falling out and that he has left the court. In spite of his harsh words, I cannot help hoping that he will come to me. Instead I hear a most worrying tale: his arm was wounded in a skirmish and he fled into the forest where he was taken in by the family of Bernard of Astolat.

I have heard of the beauty of Elaine the Fair, Bernard's daughter, and I am gripped by jealousy. Unbidden come intimations of her ministrations to Launcelot while she nurses him back to health: her intimacy with his body as she bathes him and tends his wounds; her soft voice; her healing touch. None of this I know for certain, but my imaginings are so vivid and so painful that I determine to find him and see the situation for myself.

I have not attempted any transmutation since my return to the priory, and I wonder if my ability to shape-shift has left me along with my skill at scrying. Marie is asleep. I call for a lay sister to keep watch over her, and then go out into the garden. I look up into the sky where ravens wheel around a field of ripening wheat. Their hoarse caws shatter the air, calling me upward into freedom. I gaze at them and, as I did so many years ago under Merlin's watchful eye, I focus on thinking like a raven, *being* a raven. And within a heartbeat I am flying up there with them and looking down as they do for signs of field mice or other tasty things to eat.

I shudder, and veer away, making for the forest of Astolat where I hope—or dread—to find Launcelot. I fly for some distance, until movement in a forest glade below draws my attention. I come closer in order to inspect the scene, and I see Launcelot. He is mounted, but not on his usual steed. Apparently he is healed and ready to depart. I am about to rejoice when I see who is with him—Elaine the Fair has lingered to bid him farewell. She tries to steal a kiss, and he turns his cheek to her. I smile to myself, but not for long. She has unpinned one of her sleeves and now she hands it to him.

It is the fashion at Camelot for knights to wear the favors of their ladies when going into battle, or when taking parts in jousts or melees. Launcelot, to my certain knowledge, has never worn a lady's favor: in the first instance because our relationship was a secret, and in the second because his love for Guenevere is also supposed to be a secret. And yet he takes the sleeve from Elaine and fastens it to his helm where it unfurls in a bright red ribbon.

I notice that he is armed, and frown, for he appears to be wearing someone else's armor. It would appear that he is going into battle in disguise.

Elaine lifts her hand to her mouth and blows him a fluttering kiss. "God's speed, my lord, and good luck in the tournament."

"If I should win the prize, it shall be yours."

Elaine gives a girlish giggle; a blush colors her pale skin. She is truly beautiful—and I hate her.

I am also confused. How has the spell binding him to Guenevere come so undone that he makes promises to this girl and even wears her favor? I wish I could look into his heart for the truth of the affair, for their leave-taking is anything but a loving farewell. My body stirs as I recall how ardent Launcelot was when he was with me. But not with Elaine. Perhaps I should be glad of it; perhaps, I think, I should also follow him to Camelot to see for myself what this is all about.

I become aware that Elaine is staring up at me. I've been so caught up in watching them that I have flown close to hover over their heads when I should rather have settled on a branch some distance away.

"Get you gone, you black devil!" she cries, and I hear the fear and loathing in her voice. She bends, picks up a stone and, before I can put a safe distance between us, she throws it at me with all her might. The stone slams against my body, a stinging blow that weakens me so that I lose height and the power to fly. I struggle to keep myself aloft, for I know that she will show no mercy if I fall at her feet. She shouts after me, and beats the air with her fist. Fortunately, she does not throw another stone. Nevertheless I am hurt and, once I have flown out of her sight, I alight in a tree to groom my feathers and inspect my wound.

There is no blood, nor do my wings appear to be damaged in any way; for this I am deeply thankful. I can keep going if I am only bruised. And so I fly on, this time following the path that Launcelot took. He is attending the joust for the ninth crystal, I understand that much, for there have been similar jousts before, each time with a beautiful crystal as a reward. The prizes are offered by the king, but they are always won by Launcelot who, ever the queen's champion, presents them to Guenevere.

I remind myself that he and the queen have fallen out; he is at liberty now to give the crystal to whomsoever he chooses. And I smile to myself as I picture the queen's fury when it is not given to her. At odds with Launcelot or not, she will not forgive such a slight in a hurry.

I fly on and, as I suspected, the tournament is taking place in the field near Camelot where it is always held. The day is fine, the meadow is a rainbow of wildflowers: pink ragged robin and purple selfheal, scarlet poppies and blue forget-me-nots, yellow buttercups and starry white daisies, their colors matched by the gaiety of the pavilions that have been set around the tourney field.

The competitors come out in order, one pair after the other, all going through the same motions. I find it a tedious business, watching knights ride hard at their opponents, slamming into each other with lances at the ready in the hope of unhorsing each other, and fighting in close combat if they do not manage to stay mounted. Some are wounded quite grievously, while others cry mercy as soon as they hit the ground. Launcelot fights like a lion, as always, and I am proud of him although ever fearful when he takes a blow, for I see how he favors his left arm and I fear the old wound will open if he does not protect it sufficiently.

I perch on the rigging of the queen's pavilion to watch her. She appears agitated, jumping up to pace about and scan the crowd before sitting down to fiddle with her tasseled sash, or her hair. I know she is looking for Launcelot but does not recognize him with his helm in place, although the scarlet sleeve is like a beacon. I notice that the queen's eyes are drawn more than once to the mysterious knight; each time she blinks and looks away, and I know she is telling herself that it cannot be Launcelot for he would not wear anyone's favors but her own—and that, of course, he is unable to do. I smile to myself with malicious satisfaction.

Launcelot wins, and keeps on winning. The queen continues to watch him; I read the confusion on her face, and see in the way she shakes her head that she is still not willing to accept him for who he really is. But I see also her desolation as she seeks him among the crowd.

Arthur meanwhile stands with his knights, laughing and joking with them, and urging them on to victory. Launcelot, I notice, keeps his distance when he is not on the tourney field, and does not remove his visor.

Recognizing his duty as a husband at last, Arthur comes to sit beside Guenevere for a short time. "Where is your champion today, my lady?"

"I know not. I cannot see him anywhere," Guenevere replies in a low voice.

"He must surely come to claim the ninth crystal for you, wife! I know you will not be satisfied unless you have it."

Guenevere gives a small moan. Arthur smiles at her, apparently indifferent to her distress. "Well, it's time someone else has the chance of winning!" he says cheerfully. "That knight with the red favor stands out among all the others who have fought so far. I wonder where he hails from?" He jumps up. "I'll see if I can find out."

Guenevere stares after Arthur as he hastens away, her expression unreadable. I suspect that if things were bad between them before, they have now become worse. I wonder if she recalls my advice about the need for a passionate relationship in order to have a child. And I wonder when she gave up trying.

As expected, the ninth crystal is awarded to Launcelot at the ceremony following the day's activities. By then, I've transformed myself into a fieldmouse in order to enter the pavilion and run up one of the supporting wooden poles to observe Guenevere's reaction when it becomes clear that the coveted crystal will not fall into her hands.

I wonder if I have mistaken the situation for, to my surprise, Launcelot removes his helm as Arthur calls out for the knight with the red favor to claim his reward. A gasp ricochets around the room. Guenevere puts her hand to her mouth; she is so pale I wonder if she is going to collapse.

Launcelot comes forward, bows to the king and then to the queen. He takes the crystal from Arthur, and the queen smiles at him. He seems ready to break his promise to Elaine of Astolat and hand his prize to Guenevere after all—but he does not. He thanks them both courteously, and takes his leave. There is complete silence as he walks out of the pavilion and whistles for his mount. The silence isn't broken until the sound of galloping hooves retreats into the distance.

By then I have scurried down the pole and out of the tent. In the concealing darkness I transform myself into a raven once more. I think to follow Launcelot, but my heart fails me. He will give the crystal to Elaine, I know that now. And then he will probably speak to her father, for having worn her favor he is nigh betrothed to her already. He may even bed her—and that I cannot bear to witness. So I fly back to the priory, and to my Marie who, I am told, has been fretful without me even though the lay sister had the good sense to send for a wet nurse when I did not return in time to feed her.

As I tend the bruises inflicted on my body by Elaine's stone, I listen for news of Launcelot's nuptials to the fair maid of Astolat. I hear instead of her death. Sir Ector has called in to the priory seeking shelter for the night. I cannot show myself to him but, when I hear him talking to the guest mistress at the gate, I creep closer to listen. It is a sad tale and I cannot help feeling sorry for the young woman whom I'd envied so fiercely.

"Elaine was in love with Launcelot and he played her false," Sir Ector says sternly. "His heart was ever unto the queen, but we all hoped that he had seen his error and was preparing to make a new life with a beautiful young woman who loved him. It is said that she told him she would die if she could not have him as a husband."

"And he refused her?" Sister Ursula's tone is incredulous.

"Indeed he did. And she fell into such sadness that she called for a boat and asked her brother Lavaine to sail downriver with her to Camelot. I don't know if she hoped to see Launcelot and change his mind, but she died of grief along the journey. The boat floated beneath the castle walls and Lavaine brought it in to the jetty, where they were greeted with lamentations and prayers for her soul. The queen was furious with Launcelot over the affair of the ninth crystal and other things besides, but there seemed to be some reconciliation between them until this happened. Now she reproaches Launcelot for being an unfeeling cur, although we do wonder if he only took up with Elaine because he was banished from the court by Guenevere."

"The poor lady. She shall have our prayers here, at the priory."

Elaine has my prayers too—I know exactly how she felt. The wound of losing Launcelot sliced so deep that even now it has not healed; I think it never will. I did not die for love, at least not openly. But inside, my heart has shrivelled into something hard and small. I am riven with despair and longing, with love and with hate. At least I have Marie; without her I think I would have lost the will to live. I leave my hiding place and hurry to find her, to hold her in my arms and kiss her; to promise her that I shall never leave her and that we shall be together always.

I make these vows in good faith, while I wait for Urien to send for me. I am determined not to go, nor can anyone make me. But no one comes from Rheged. Instead, just when I'm starting to feel safe and secure, armed men appear at the priory. They tell me that King Arthur was enraged to discover that I have not gone to Rheged as I'd promised, and they have come to escort me there so that I may be married to Urien without delay.

My immediate reaction is a feeling of relief that Marie is asleep in her cradle and out of their sight. I open my mouth to protest, to refuse to go, but the soldier at their head produces a letter for me from Urien, and a written message also from Arthur. I quickly scan the message from Urien; it professes his undying love for me and his hope that I will hasten to be with him. I cast the message aside and unscroll the parchment from Arthur.

> *You have agreed to this marriage, Morgana, and I hold you now to your promise, both for the sake of the realm, for we need Urien's allegiance now more than ever, and also for your own future. After the trouble you have caused, and the trouble now being stirred up by our son, you will never be welcome at Camelot again. Be warned also that should you fail me in this, you will be sent into exile across the sea, under escort but without a retinue or any means with which to support yourself. I urge you therefore to consider your future carefully, and choose wisely.*

There is no salutation, just his signature: *Arthur, High King of Britain.*

I am trapped, and I know it. My thoughts scurry around like moths flittering at a lantern. I am about to fetch Marie when I stop. If I take Marie to Rheged, it could so upset Urien that he might well make trouble for me with Arthur. The whole court could find out about her existence, including Launcelot. And Mordred.

I come to the inescapable conclusion that I shall have to leave her here, in safety and in seclusion, while I journey to Rheged. I feel the painful tug of separation; milk leaks from my breasts and I hastily fold my arms over my chest. I try to comfort myself with the thought that, once I am married to Urien, once he is sure of me, he will not want to hold me captive against my wishes. Surely I shall be able to find excuses to visit Marie, although the thought of leaving her now is almost enough to undo me altogether.

Knowing I have no choice, I agree to go with the guard. But he comes with me to oversee the packing of my belongings, and so I am unable to say farewell to my beloved child or hold her in my arms one last time. It takes all my courage and self-control to hold my tears in check as I say goodbye to the prioress and at the same time, in a low whisper, bid her take care of Marie in my absence.

She is kind, this prioress. Although disapproving of my actions, I have seen her with Marie, seen how her face softens as she gazes on my small frog, how she lapses into the sort of baby talk entirely unfitting for a woman in her high position. She loves Marie, they all do, and I know my baby will be safe here. Nevertheless I am in deep sorrow and despair as we ride away, and I cast longing glances over my shoulder as the priory dwindles and finally disappears altogether.

CHAPTER 11

What to say of my life with Urien? Seasons turn, and turn again, and my mouse-brown hair becomes sprinkled with the snowy signs of age. I am a dutiful wife and a competent chatelaine at Rheged, but I also need to spend time at Castle Perilous, that was given to me by Arthur, for his gift was not so generous as I had first supposed. On my first visit, I found the castle in disrepair and its tenants too poor and too dispirited to do the work necessary for the estate to thrive. I accepted the challenge and, using the experience I'd gained at Joyous Garde to educate and train the castle servants and my tenants, we have turned Castle Perilous into a prosperous demesne. I am now proud of my dowry; nevertheless, I maintain a close watch, knowing that my presence keeps my subjects diligent and in good cheer.

But none of this feels like my real life at all. My real life is at the priory with Marie. Each time I visit her, I marvel at the changes, and mourn that I am not there to watch her as she grows from toddler into a young girl. The nuns are loving and kind to her, and I am grateful. To my surprise she calls me "Mamm," the same word Launcelot used when referring to his own mother.

When I question her, she seems confused. "Is that not what I should call you?"

"You may call me whatever you wish, my darling," I tell her, thinking that perhaps she has somehow intuited her father's origins in Brittany across the water. And so I teach her something of the Breton language, but without saying why. It becomes a game between us, but it also helps to keep Launcelot close to my heart, for this was how we sometimes conversed together in our time at Joyous Garde.

But there is another reason to keep me in Rheged at Urien's side. To my great surprise, we make a child together, a son: Owain. He is a strange child. As he grows older, he ventures further and further afield, always bringing back with him some injured bird or baby animal in want of care. I watch him tend these creatures, and I could swear he communicates with them. I ask him about it, and he frowns at me in puzzlement.

"Of course I can communicate with them. Can't you?"

I shake my head. "How do you do it? Do you talk to them? Do they talk to you?"

"No. I know what they're thinking and they know what I'm thinking. There's no need for words between us." He shakes his head and his frown deepens. "Isn't this what always happens between man and beast?"

"No!" I laugh at him, yet I am touched by his earnest care of the creatures he takes in. "You have a gift, Owain. A special gift all of your own."

He looks pleased by my praise, while I wonder if perhaps this special gift of his might manifest itself in other ways, magical ways, the ways of the Otherworlds. Until now I have shared my gifts and talents with the only person whom I deem worthy enough to succeed me. Mordred has disappointed me in this, and it is Marie who carries my hopes and dreams for the future. She is, after all, the daughter of the true born ruler of the kingdom and also of the bravest knight in all the land.

But she is illegitimate, whereas Owain is not. I make a note to watch him more closely in the future for this is something I must consider more carefully. My wands and the objects I stole from Merlin are all safely hidden at the priory. On that first occasion I had to leave them hidden there, closely watched by Arthur's guard as I was. Thereafter, I deemed it safer to store them where they are at hand when I need them. But the next time I leave the priory I take them back to Rheged with me, thinking to initiate Owain and test his aptitude for the practice of magic. He listens to what I say, but frowns in disapproval when I demonstrate the spell of transformation. I become a raven, imitating his voice, stealing his kerchief, flying in loops and rolls and perching on his head to entertain him.

"I already know about birds," he tells me. "And I don't want to play tricks on people."

Although I am disappointed by Owain's lack of interest, Marie's enthusiasm for all I can teach her more than makes up for it. She is an apt pupil. Merlin would have been as proud of her as he was once proud of me. I remember his wisdom, and his patience, and I acknowledge that he was right to call me wild and headstrong. It is an uncomfortable realization; nevertheless I know that I learn a valuable lesson by remembering it.

As she grows older, Marie proves she is as quick and clever as ever I was. She follows me through the secret way of the garden to the scrying pool. I show her my wands. I instruct her in the ancient alphabet of the Druids and make sure she understands how to read the runes so that I may send her secret messages when I am away from the priory. We have not yet visited any of the Otherworlds together, but gradually she is coming to learn what I know. Everything, except for an understanding of the decorated wooden tablets, for they are still a mystery to me. Sometimes I look into the scrying pool, but it stays as dark and mysterious as always.

"Why do you look into the water so intently, Mamm?" Marie asks one day, coming to stand close behind me. I see her face shimmering in the pool, and something twists in my belly, some intuition perhaps that I may once more be blessed with a vision.

"Shh." I draw her down beside me, and together we sit in silence while I pray to the gods for guidance.

The water ripples. Marie gasps, and quickly puts her hand over her mouth. I know she has seen what I have seen.

A hand holding a golden cup. It looks somehow familiar, and I wonder where I have seen such a thing. And then I remember. It is one of the symbols on Merlin's tablets. I have identified the other three. The sword—Excalibur. The pentacle—Merlin's crystal that enables me to cross into Otherworlds. The wand—Merlin's or mine, symbol of power and magic. And now here is the cup—but I still don't know what it represents.

"What is it?" Marie voices my question.

"I do not know. Let us be quiet in the hope that the answer may come to us."

When the answer comes, we do not find it in the scrying pool. A few days later, there is a commotion at the gate; a small party of knights pushes in, asking for food and shelter for the night. At their head is a young man who seems somehow familiar, although I cannot put a name to him. He is in company with some others whom I do not know. I assume they have all come to Camelot during my absence.

I am drawn, for some reason, to the young man, and so I undertake to bring them their bread and wine in the hope of finding out more about them.

His name is Galahad, he tells me, and introduces me to his companions.

"Galahad has come to court only recently, and he now occupies the Siege Perilous," one of them, Sir Perceval, says proudly.

The Siege Perilous! I am impressed. It is the one seat at the Round Table left unoccupied for as long as the table has been there. None would dare sit on it for it was believed that it was reserved for the truest and most worthy knight of all, and that anyone trespassing there would instantly die. Yet Galahad is very much alive.

"We were all seated at dinner," Perceval says, "when a fair damsel, clad all in white samite, appeared before us. Clasped in her hands was a large golden chalice.

"She called it the Sangreal. Everyone believes this was the chalice used to capture drops of Christ's blood while He hung on the cross, although it was lost—or hidden from view—thereafter. She begged us to bring the Sangreal to King Pelles' court in order to heal him of the grievous wounds that have nigh on killed him, for she says that in healing the king we shall also heal his kingdom, which now lies ruined and laid to waste. We have all taken a vow to follow her bidding, although she warned us only the pure of heart would succeed in this quest."

I have never heard of King Pelles, but I remember Merlin telling me the story of the Sangreal: how a few drops of this elixir are enough to bring even the dying back to life. But he said nothing of its connection to the Christ, only that it was some magical potion that has never existed except in men's imaginations. I wonder if these young men have mistaken dreams and illusions for reality.

"Is that where you travel to now?" I ask.

"Yes, madame, although we know not where King Pelles dwells, nor do we know where the Sangreal is, for having appeared before us, the damsel then vanished, taking the Sangreal with her." Galahad looks somewhat shamefaced as he makes the admission, while I stifle a desire to laugh.

"Are you sure you did not dream this wonder?"

"No, not at all!" It is another of Galahad's companions who answers. "We all saw the Sangreal, even the queen. And the court is in uproar because of it. All the knights are determined to quest after it, but as we do not know where King Pelles resides, we have split up and gone our separate ways in search of his ruined kingdom."

"Even Sir Launcelot?"

Galahad exchanges glances with his companions. "Yes, my lady, even Sir Launcelot. The queen begged him not to go; in fact, she begged all of us to stay and wait on the king. The king himself asked us not to venture forth, for I think he is afraid that our absence from court will leave Camelot open to invasion."

"As it will!" I say, suddenly aware of the dangers of the situation.

"Nevertheless, it is our sworn duty to find the Sangreal and fulfill the maiden's request."

I read the determination on Galahad's face, and suppress a sigh. I understand the futility of further argument or attempts at persuasion. "Then I wish you God's speed in your endeavors," I say quietly, and take my leave.

It is time for me to return to Rheged, but my sleep is haunted by dreams of Launcelot. I think of him setting out on his quest to find the Sangreal, and for some reason Galahad's face comes into my mind. He seems so serious, so thoughtful, it's hard to imagine him being persuaded to go off on a wild chase such as this one. I'd caught a glimpse of his goodness, the pure heart beneath his boyish exuberance, and I suspect that as yet, women are unknown to him. He seems determined to give the quest his all and, if honor and chastity are the key to finding the Sangreal, if such a thing exists, then I believe he'll succeed.

I wonder what chance Launcelot has, going off on such a fool's errand. By no stretch of the imagination can one call him pure of heart, not after how he has treated me, and certainly not when one considers his long infatuation with the queen. Has he risked everything to bed her yet? I shiver at the thought, and put it aside. Surely not even Launcelot would consider himself worthy of questing after the Sangreal if he is familiar with the queen's bedchamber.

I long to see him again. It is an ache that spreads and spreads until I am consumed by it. And so I bid Marie farewell but, instead of going back to Rheged, I go in search of Launcelot, wanting to see him, to look upon his face for a few moments just to ease my aching heart. To hasten my journey, I assume the guise of a raven. But I am unsure where to start looking. Galahad had said that the knights had split up and gone their separate ways, and so they had. I encounter a number along my journey, some in groups and some venturing alone, but all with a grim determination on their faces. I suspect that what may have started with a holy purpose has become a race between men who, while they may profess that the only prize is the healing of King Pelles and his kingdom, yet strive to be first for the honor and glory that success in their quest will bring them.

I fly above a wild forest, the sort where men might lose themselves; where they would be ever at the mercy of wild beasts and the elements; and where they might seek adventure and even a Grail. And there, in its heart, I find Launcelot, on his knees and quite alone. I am almost afraid to fly close, to look into his eyes. I swoop down to him and perch upon a branch above his head. I suspect he has been praying, but he looks up at me, and my heart twists as I note the defeated slump of his shoulders and read the weariness on his face. We are deep within a thick tangle of trees and bushes, and I wonder if he is lost. My suspicion is confirmed when he addresses me directly.

"Can you lead me out of here, bird?" He pushes his long dark hair out of his eyes. He is unshaven, and somewhat grubby from living rough, yet I love him for all that. He sighs deeply. "Shame on me for talking to a raven, but the sound of my voice is a comfort, for I have not spoken to anyone in days. I have walked and walked, but have encountered nobody on my travels. Indeed, I fear I may die here." He smiles at me then, or rather smiles at his folly, and shakes his head before falling into prayer once more.

I wait, and wait, but he continues to pray without looking up. I become impatient with him. Small wonder he can't find his way out of the forest if this is how he spends his time! Finally, I fly away, out of his sight. At the flapping of my wings he raises his head to watch me go. His expression is one of utter desolation. But I am not leaving him alone for long; I have every intention of guiding him through the forest—but not yet. I have other plans for him right now, hatched in a hurry but no less important for that.

I assume my natural mien to go to him but my courage fails me. His harsh, hateful words sound in my ear: *I wish you gone from my sight. My only desire is that I never see you again.* I cannot go to him like this, no matter how loving my heart. Nor, as I remember the fate of Elaine of Astolat, does it seem that I can go to him in any other guise, for he will not take me and love me as I wish to be loved, not while the queen is foremost in his mind and in his heart.

I know what I need to do, but my mind rejects it utterly. Yet I am wild with longing, I ache with the need to be close to him one more time, to lie with him and hear his loving words. And so, hating myself for what I am about to do, I transform myself into a younger woman with golden hair and eyes the color of blue gentians, and I walk toward him.

He is still at prayer. I lay my hand lightly on his shoulder and he jerks upright and swings around.

"Guenevere!"

I see the shock on his face giving way to a slow delight, and I know that my trick is successful. I silently pray that he will not say that name again as I walk into his arms and feel them close around me. I breathe in his dear, familiar smell, overlaid by woodsmoke and sweat it is true, but dear to me nevertheless. And I burrow into his shoulder as I was always wont to do when we were alone together at Joyous Garde.

"My lord," I murmur.

"But ... what brings you here?" He puts me away from him and scans the forest around us, perhaps expecting to see Arthur or one of the knights closing in.

"I am alone, lord," I reassure him, knowing this to be true. "I found you because I could not stay away from you. I long for you, Launcelot, more than I can say. And so I have come to you, to lie with you as should any man and woman who love each other more than life itself."

I close my eyes and raise my mouth for his kiss. It comes to me suddenly that perhaps this is a dreadful mistake. If Launcelot and Guenevere have not yet consummated their love, then I am starting something that Launcelot may well wish to continue; may insist on, in fact, if and when he returns to court. But it is too late now to hold back, and so I surrender myself to Launcelot's kiss, unwilling to spoil our time together with useless regrets.

He groans suddenly and once more thrusts me away from him. I cannot breathe in my distress, thinking that he will yet reject me from some sense of honor and duty to Arthur. But his hands fall on my gown with feverish haste and, without ado, he rips it over my head and begins to undo my undergarments with shaking hands, tearing the delicate fabric in his impatience to see my body naked. I am flooded with warmth as I untie his breeches; he is ready for loving and he falls upon me, taking me to the ground and thrusting into me with a desperate need. But I am already open and ready for him, my need matching his as he thrusts deeper and I push myself against him until, with spiraling joy, we reach a shuddering climax.

Afterwards, we lie quietly together upon the grass, while around us birds sing and butterflies flit and skitter among the flowers. He holds me close, and dusts my face with soft kisses. "My love," he sighs. "I have waited so long for you."

I stay silent; the urge to confess is strong within me. I long to tell him that I love him, that I have always loved him, no matter whatever else I may have done. I long to tell him about the child we made together, our Marie, who has become such a fine young woman, and a beauty too. For Marie has grown into her big eyes and wide mouth and in fact now looks more like Launcelot than me, although still not enough to cause suspicion, thank the gods. I open my mouth to speak the words, but Launcelot's kiss stops me. Once more my body opens to his, but this time our loving is slow, gentle and unbearably sweet.

"We cannot do this again," I say, as we lie, sated, at the end of it. "It is too dangerous. It will cause talk around the court if people realize that we have become intimate." It is the only way I can think of to prevent Launcelot from finding out how I have tricked him.

"You are right, of course. But oh, my dearest one, I wish that we could proclaim our love to all the world, and that we could live openly as man and wife."

"No, Launcelot! We must never speak of this again, not even between ourselves lest someone overhear us!" I am panic-stricken now, wondering what I have unleashed.

"Yes." He takes my hands, and holds them against his heart. "But you are my life, and my love. You know that, don't you?"

"Yes, Launcelot, I do." I feel a deep grief that the words I most long to hear are said to another woman. Nevertheless I lie quietly, savoring the last moments of my time with him as I wait for him to fall asleep.

Once I am sure, I stealthily release my hands from his, pick up my clothes and walk some distance away to dress. I do not want him to see me in my true guise. But he slumbers on while

I, a raven once more, keep watch over him from the branch above his head.

The afternoon wears on, and still Launcelot sleeps. I watch the sun arc lower through the sky, and finally give a hoarse croak to waken him. I need to lead him through the forest to safety before it gets too dark for him to see me.

He wakens with a start and looks about him. "Guenevere!"

There is such love and longing in his voice that my heart aches. I see his desolation as he realizes he is alone. He shakes his head, then spills some water from his flask onto his hands and washes his face. As he dries himself on his sleeve, he catches sight of me.

"Tell me, bird: did this really happen or have I been dreaming?"

I am well pleased if he thinks his lovemaking with Guenevere was but a dream; it is safer that way. But he looks down at his state of undress, and frowns.

"I could swear it was real, and that she was here." He looks up at me, as if in accusation. "Who are you?"

Fear dries my throat; I can manage only a murmuring croak. But he laughs then, and looks about him. "If you know the way out of this forest, I pray you lead on."

I know he is joking; nevertheless, I leave my branch and fly on to another, some distance away, and wait for him.

Launcelot gives me a long, dubious look. "All right then," he says. "I may as well follow you, for 'tis sure I know not where else to go."

And so, in a series of a short flights, I lead him through the wild innermost part of the forest, and out onto the plain beyond. The light is almost gone now; I am a black shape among shadows, but my task is done. Ahead of us stand the silhouettes of small cottages, some with unshuttered windows that show the gleam of lighted candles within. I know that Launcelot will find food and shelter here.

"I thank you, bird." He sketches me a mocking bow, but his face is serious, reflecting his gratitude. I answer with another hoarse croak. As I fly away, I steal one last, loving glance behind me, knowing that it will have to last me a lifetime.

CHAPTER 12

Conscious that I am long overdue at Rheged, I stop for a few moments to change from raven to swift before taking wing once more. As I fly onward over forests, rivers and high peaks I become ever more weary, and wish that I'd thought to commence this journey on horseback. But I tell myself there are several advantages to flight: being able to fly true and without having to avoid any danger or obstacles along my path, and also to see more clearly where I am bound.

I spy several knights along the way and recognize my nephews Gawain, Agravaine and Gareth. It seems they have just met up with Gaheris, who had been banished from court, and also with Mordred.

Despite my haste, the tie that binds mother to child proves too strong to resist—and besides, I am feeling my age; I am exhausted and in need of a rest. Feeling safe in my disguise, I fly closer and perch on a branch, listening to the cheerful banter between the brothers that not even Mordred's sarcasm can dampen.

"So you have finally been knighted, Beaumains," he sneers. "Is it because you cooked up a feast worthy of my father, the king? Are you pleased to be out of the kitchen at last?"

I expect Gareth to fly into a temper at this reminder of his lowly position and his cruel treatment by Sir Kay, but he remains calm as he unties the strings of his breeches to relieve himself, narrowly missing Mordred's mount as he does so. "I had to wait for a chance to prove my true worth to the king, so when Lady Linet asked the king for protection for her mistress, Dame Lyonesse, I seized the opportunity to come forward." He reties his breeches.

"Causing Lady Linet great shame," sneers Mordred. "I heard her say that you stank of the kitchen. She begged the king to find her another champion for her mistress."

"But she still consented to journey along with me, although she served me ill by inciting the Black Knight, the Red Knight and the Green Knight into combat against me."

"But by so doing, you were given the chance to prove your worth as a knight by defeating them all," says Gawain, ever the peace-maker.

"And I am delighted that Lady Linet has now agreed to become my wife," Gaheris boasts.

"Then you can have no complaints about the affair," Gareth replies.

"Neither can you, for Linet tells me you are to wed her mistress, Dame Lyonesse," Gaheris points out.

This is all news to me, and I am pleased that I have interrupted my journey to spend time with them.

"Indeed, our marriage has been planned. As Gawain says: I have proved myself as a knight, and as a worthy companion for Dame Lyonesse." Gareth shoots a hard look at Mordred. There is little friendship evident between them, nor, I think to myself, does Gareth seem quite so afraid of Mordred as he once was.

His next words confirm my opinion.

"That being the situation, none shall dare call me *Beaumains* ever again—not even you, Mordred."

The threat is unmistakable, and is enough to silence Mordred, at least for a time. As dusk falls, Gawain has called a halt to their journey so that they may prepare a safe haven against the creatures of the night. A pile of wood is gathered and lit. I watch their activity while I rest my weary wings. Smoke billows above the leaping golden flames, and I shift position so that it cannot irritate my eyes and throat. The knights remain silent, their eyes drawn to the dancing light, listening to the fire's pop and crackle, and the calls of the wild hunters and their prey.

The sky is black as ebony, pierced with glittering stars that promise light but give none. There is no moon, not yet. It is a night for the telling of secrets and I edge closer along the branch in the hope of hearing them.

Agravaine begins the conversation. "You've been away from court, Mordred, so I don't suppose you've heard the news that most concerns you."

"What news?"

My heart falls anew as I hear Mordred's surly response. I had hoped—what? That my absence from court might encourage his father to treat him more like a son? That my absence might remove the burr that pricks his heart and turns him to violence? Yet it seems he himself has been absent. Has he been gathering support for his cause from disaffected knights across the realm, as I once did? Is that why he travels with Gaheris?

"You have a half-brother by the name of Owain. He is the son of your mother, Morgana, and Urien of Rheged."

"I don't believe you."

Agravaine, being ever one to enjoy passing on news of the court, is not deterred. "Ask my brothers. They know all about him." He glances around the company. "Well, not Gaheris. He's not welcome at Camelot after what he did to our mother and to Lamorak."

"Never mind ancient tales of revenge! Tell me what you know of Owain," Mordred insists.

"He is young; he was only sixteen summers or thereabouts when he first arrived at Camelot. But despite his youth he was knighted almost straight away by the king." Agravaine splutters with laughter as he continues the story. "At the start he scared the court half to death—in fact the queen was so terrified she dropped down in a deathly swoon."

"Why should she be so afraid of a vagabond knight?" Mordred says.

"Because the 'vagabond knight,' as you call him, travels everywhere with a very large and ferocious pet lion."

If I had doubts about Agravaine's story before, they are dispelled by this news that, to anyone else, would seem beyond belief. But I know that if anyone can befriend a lion, it is Owain. I hop down a couple of branches so that I can hear more.

"A lion!" Mordred's jeering laugh cracks through the quiet forest. "There never was a lion for a pet in all of Christendom! Where do you find such stories, Agravaine?"

"He speaks the truth," says Gawain, the oldest and therefore the one for whom they have the most respect. "It is said that, after Owain left Rheged in a bid to be admitted to Arthur's court, he encountered a snake fighting a lion. The snake had the animal tightly bound within its coils and was about to make a fatal strike. But Owain drew his sword and cut the snake's head from its body. He then unwound the lion from the snake's deathly embrace before setting off once more for Camelot. But the lion followed him and, on occasion, protected Owain from errant travelers who wished him harm. So Owain told the king, and the king believed him. And for that deed he knighted Owain and bid him—and his lion—welcome at court, although he did not stay for long."

Owain! I berate myself for my recent absence from Rheged, for not realizing that of course he is now old enough to seek his fortune at court. I remember the child who was always bringing hurt creatures home to nurse back to health, and my eyes fill with fond tears. I wonder if he too has set off on this fool's errand for the Sangreal, and I determine to look out for him. What I hear next chills me to the bone.

"If I find him, I shall kill him."

The silence that follows Mordred's pronouncement is absolute and profound.

"Why would you want to do that?" Gawain asks cautiously.

"Because I mean to inherit Camelot, of course, and I will let no one stand in my way." Mordred's tone reflects his scorn for their dullness in missing the obvious. "The king has no heir by Guenevere. And I am his only son."

"Begotten on his sister," Agravaine points out.

"What of it? To my way of thinking, that makes me twice the legitimate heir. But my mother may well disagree with me. She has long schemed against Arthur to reclaim what she believes was hers by right. If Owain is truly her son, then he stands in line as her legitimate heir—but only while he lives." Again, there is a silence as the brothers ponder his words.

"You have a far lesser claim than I do," Mordred points out, adding, "and even though the king will not anoint me as his heir, he'll never forgive Gaheris for slaying your mother, his sister, either. You are all tainted in his eyes."

"But we are as much in line to succeed Arthur as Owain is," Gawain says quietly. "Are you planning to kill us too?"

Mordred grunts, but does not reply.

"If you are searching for the Sangreal with murder in your heart, you may as well give up the quest right now," Gawain continues, perhaps hoping to change the subject and keep the peace.

"I have as much chance as any of finding it," Mordred boasts. "Besides, who among any of us has a pure heart?"

"Galahad," says Gawain.

"Who is Galahad?" Gaheris asks.

"He is the son of Launcelot and Elaine of Carbonek."

The shock is so great I loosen my hold on the branch, and almost fall. I cannot believe I have heard aright.

"Galahad considers himself so worthy of respect that he has occupied the Siege Perilous at the Round Table. But he comes from tainted stock," Mordred sneers. "You only have to look at how devoted his father is to the queen. Launcelot loves Guenevere beyond anything, and everyone knows it. Only my father, the king, seems blind to their betrayal. But that's not the worst of it. He has betrayed other young women too. Elaine of Astolat died of love for Launcelot after he wore her favor in combat and led her to believe that they would wed. And Galahad's own mother, Elaine of Carbonek, suffered at Launcelot's hands. He says that Elaine seduced him into her bed with the use of a love potion, and he swears that he left her as soon as he found out the truth. He will not accept that he was at fault, nor will he offer the lady his support and protection. It seems she is estranged from her own family, and she kept Galahad hidden away and both her family and Launcelot ignorant of the boy's existence. When Elaine of Carbonek finally brought her son to court to meet Launcelot, I thought the queen would die of rage. In fact, she banished Launcelot from her sight for quite some time."

"I heard that Elaine managed to get him to lie with her and give her a child by assuming the guise of the queen herself," says Agravaine.

I am torn between laughter and fury. Galahad is Launcelot's son! No wonder that, when I met him, I thought of his father. And when I looked on Launcelot, Galahad came into my mind. I, who thought I could read men's hearts and minds; how could I have been so blind! And yet I cannot help but feel a grim amusement over the situation. It seems that I am not the only one to have tricked Launcelot into making love to someone other than the queen! Not that another child is likely to result from our recent coupling; I have gone too far in age to bear any more children.

"Twice the shame for Launcelot then, that he would believe that he was lying with the queen. But however it came about, Galahad is bastard born and therefore unfit to find the Sangreal."

"Should the son be judged by the father?" Gawain's clear, cold sense silences Mordred, particularly when he continues, "For if that is so, you should look to your own heritage, Mordred."

It is a fair comment, and it bites my conscience with the venom of an adder's strike. Mordred's birth, his very existence, was by my hand and through trickery—and that one fatal decision has led me on to all that has happened throughout my life. Would that I could change the present by changing the past, for there is so much that I now regret and would undo if it was possible! I try to seek comfort from the notion that perhaps, one day, I shall learn how to traverse time and, even better, how to reverse it. Until then, however, I must live with the consequences.

The conversation drifts into a drowsy murmur, and thence into sleep. I stay on a little longer, mulling over what I have heard. It grieves me that my son has not seen the danger into which his anger and hurt pride might lead him. But, unwittingly, he has warned his cousins of his vaulting ambition. I could not mistake their shock, their horror, as they heard of Mordred's intention, and I hope that Gawain, at least, will now try to steer him along a wiser path.

For myself, I am more determined than ever to keep Marie's birth a secret from Mordred. And for love of my son

Owain, I know that I must go in search of him, in order to warn him and so protect him from his older brother's jealousy and lust for power.

But what has most upset me is the startling revelation of Galahad's birth. I try to calculate when Launcelot lay with Elaine of Carbonek. It must have been after our time together at Joyous Garde if the girl needed to assume the guise of the queen. This leads me to wonder if their bedding marked the start of a new relationship between Launcelot and the queen, but then I remember his haste with me and I think not. Nevertheless I am haunted by the fear that our coupling might prompt him to steal into Guenevere's bedchamber for another taste of forbidden love, and come to an understanding of how he has been tricked once more. Worse: it would lead to their deaths if they were found out. Not only would I lose the man I love, I would also lose my chance of the crown, for the court would unite in support of Arthur while my kingdom would slip even further from my grasp. Now I most bitterly regret giving way to desire, and can only hope and pray that Launcelot will honor my warning to keep our meeting in the forest a closely guarded secret.

I must have dozed off on the branch, for I wake to the dawn chorus as birds open sleepy eyes, fluff up feathers and warble their greetings to the new day. A quick check reveals the Orkney brothers and my son are also astir and I am gripped with alarm by the thought that I have no idea where Owain might be if he is not at Rheged, and that Mordred could well come across him before I have a chance to warn him. I stretch out my wings, hoping that the sun's early rays will warm my feathers and ease my aching joints. I am not as young as I was, and I am used to sleeping in a bed rather than on a branch.

From my perch high in the treetops I scan the countryside to determine the direction in which I should fly, already dreading the long journey to Rheged. If only I could transform myself into a winged beast, something big and powerful, something that could effortlessly cruise on the currents of the wind without the expense of so much energy!

Unbidden, the image of a silvery white unicorn comes into my mind. "Aleph," I breathe, remembering how I'd once asked him if unicorns could fly. I've never tried to transform into a unicorn before, nor have I visited that Otherworld since Merlin withdrew his patronage from me. Can I do it without revealing my true self?

I close my eyes and feel my way back into that Otherworld and the creatures that inhabited it. I think of Aleph, imagining myself within a smooth silvery coat, with a flowing tail and a silver horn on my brow. I go into myself and breathe deeply, sinking into the soul of a unicorn.

My whole body is falling; I hear the crack of breaking branches, feel the crunch of impact as I hit the ground. My eyes fly open and I realize I have succeeded in my transformation, but that I should have given more thought to the commencement of it. Too late, I understand the danger I have brought upon myself. The Orkney brothers stand frozen mid-gesture, transfixed by my unexpected appearance. But Mordred has already snatched up his bow and is busy nocking an arrow into the string.

"The creature is mine!" he shouts.

Panic-stricken I spin around and race for my life. An arrow flies past my shoulder, and I pick up speed, dodging the trees and brambles that block my path. I feel the pinprick of another shaft, and wonder if it has drawn blood. I hear the thud of running footsteps behind me, and know that Mordred has given chase, probably joined by his cousins. I dare not look back to see how many are in pursuit. The forest is thicker here; it closes us in under a green canopy. Tightly knit branches bar my way and snag my mane so I am forced to duck and weave, tactics that possibly save my life, for arrows are flying everywhere now, shot from more than one bow. If ever there was a time for a unicorn to be able to fly, it is now!

I spy a gap in the trees and aim straight for it, wondering how I might outwit my pursuers. I notice the sparkling drops of dew that ornament the delicate filaments of a spider web, and I crouch low to avoid it as I flash past. In the next instant I know what I must do. A quick chant and I check my speed slightly, praying to the gods that my trap will work.

Shouts and curses tell me that my spell has been successful, and I pause in my headlong flight and turn to watch from behind a sheltering leafy screen. The web has grown into a net of tough, sticky strings that stretches from one side of the gap to the other. The Orkney brothers and Mordred have run straight into it. Their swords flash silver as they try to hack their way through, but the more they flail about trying to extricate themselves, the tighter they become bound within its coils.

I am able to continue my search for Owain in safety, although what has happened has served as a warning that I must change my guise in a hurry rather than risk encountering another hunting party. I say the spell of transformation and after a moment as a mortal, during which I check myself for wounds, I once again fly free, but with reluctance and a great deal of regret. Brief as it was, I enjoyed my time as a unicorn.

*

Before I reach Rheged—and to my relief—I come across Owain traveling toward a secret glade within a dense forest. I circle several times, marveling how, in the time I have been away, my son seems to have come into his own and is now becoming a fine young man. He is wearing full armor, and is accompanied by a sturdy steed. A moving patch of dun yellow close by catches my eye. Curious, I fly closer to identify the creature. It is a lion! Fear slows my wings and I almost drop from the sky, until I remember Owain has tamed this fiercesome creature. It is his pet—and his protector. It comforts me to realize that Owain does not travel alone. I am about to reveal myself as his mother, so that I may give him both the warning about Mordred and also my blessing, when I hear the blast of a horn. A party of knights approaches. They are mounted, and in full armor, just like my son, and I wonder what trouble they are expecting. Concerned for my son's safety, I fly toward them to find out.

One of the knights dismounts. "Show yourself, Esclados!" he shouts. "Be prepared to defend your sacred spring!" There is a stone slab underneath the pine tree in which I've settled. The knight pours water upon it, and at once a wild wind shrieks through the forest, shaking the trees so hard that it takes all my strength to cling onto my branch. A heavy rain begins, teeming straight down like a waterfall so that we are all soaked and shivering. Thunderclaps echo through the forest, loud as the trumpets of doom, while vivid stripes of lightning blast through the air and strike the ground. The knights cry out in fear, while I hang on to my branch and wait for the storm to pass. This is no ordinary storm, and I wonder what trickery has brought it about.

At last weak threads of sunlight filter through the black cover of cloud, the wind dies, and the trees drip with moisture.

"Where is that coward, Owain?" cries one of the knights. "He vowed to defeat the keeper of the sacred spring, having said that he would be first in line to challenge Esclados when he came. More, he promised that he would kill the tyrant and free his subjects."

"Hold your tongue and let Owain speak for himself when he gets here," says their leader. "And if Owain does not come, then it will be to your glory to mount the first challenge."

"Who calls me a coward?" Owain has caught up to the party, and now he bursts through the screen of bushes. His helm is on and his lance is at the ready. The waiting knight reaches for his own lance and readies himself to meet the attack.

Owain charges at him and they clash with such force that both lances split and shatter into pieces. Owain has dealt such a mighty blow that the knight loses his balance and falls from his horse. There, on the ground, he cries mercy. And my son takes off his helm to reveal his true identity. In turn, the vanquished knight takes off his own helm, revealing himself as a somewhat chastened Sir Kay. I am proud of my son, who has proved himself a true warrior, and pleased to see Sir Kay taken down after his sneering words. The other knights also reveal themselves, and led by their leader, the king, they applaud and congratulate him. Even a grudging tribute is paid by Kay. But they clamor with questions about Esclados, and won't be quietened until Owain tells them that he has already defeated Esclados in battle, and that the much-feared tyrant is dead.

"I came on ahead, and managed to defeat Esclados on my own," Owain tells them, with no hint of boastfulness. "In return, I have won the gratitude of all his subjects, along with a lady's hand in marriage. Her name is Laudine, who was once the wife of Esclados."

"You killed the husband and then married his wife?" Arthur's tone is incredulous.

Owain gives a small smile. "Not yet, for she calls me still too young. But I fell in love with the lady, and would not depart from her. With the aid of her serving maid, Lunete, I persuaded her that I was the only knight capable of protecting her sacred spring from intruders, while those others in her court who might have taken my place had they the courage to do so, joined in urging her to accept me as her husband and protector. Once we are wed, I mean to do all in my power to live up to the honor she has bestowed on me."

"In the absence of anyone else from King Arthur's court," Kay sneers.

"That's enough, Kay!" Arthur's tone leaves no room for argument. "You were bested by a man you called a 'coward', and don't you forget it."

After the knights have congratulated Owain on his coming nuptials, he invites them to ride to his castle for a feast. Intrigued, I fly some little way behind them, for it is news to me that my son now possesses a castle, and I long to know more. But I am tired of my feathery appearance now, and I need to resume a mortal's shape so that I may issue my warning and depart. I dare not reveal myself while Arthur and his men keep company with Owain, and so I wait outside in the courtyard, fuming impatiently, hoping to catch him on his own.

Finally, tiring of the pretense, I retreat into a barn and once more become myself. As Morgana, I beg parchment and sharpened quill from the porter and write a message to my son, requesting he come out to meet me in a place where we shall be safe from prying eyes.

"Why are you here, Mother?" he greets me when at last he comes. His tone is cool, distant, and I hear the echoes of a child abandoned and ignored. I am full of remorse, and take him in my arms in an effort to reassure him that he is loved.

I hear a low growl. It is Owain's lion, there to protect him from his enemies—and seemingly even from his mother! Owain stands still within my embrace, making no effort to return it. I release him and he steps back and, with arms folded, surveys me gravely.

"I am here to see you. I have missed you." How can I explain to Owain that I do love him, but that I love Marie more; that I have found it increasingly difficult to spend time away from that child of my heart, living proof of the love between her father and me? I read the disbelief on Owain's face as he listens to my words, and understand that he has grown beyond the soft words, the sweetmeats and treats that have won him over in the past. He is a young man now, able to make up his own mind and judge me accordingly. The lion has come to his side; he fondles its ears in a gesture that speaks poignantly of his capacity for affection, while marking how wide and deep the chasm between us has become.

"I have not been a good mother to you," I say quietly. "I know that, and I regret it. But you are still my son, Owain. And I love you dearly."

"That may be. But you did not love my father, nor have you been a good wife to him."

Unable to deny it, I bow my head. What he says next bites at my conscience, and saddens me.

"Urien is dead." His face twists in misery, but his gaze is flint hard as it rests on me. "I sent word to Camelot begging you to come, for he was asking for you toward the end, but no one knew where to find you."

I can see that Owain is grief-stricken, and I try to find words to excuse my absence. And my negligence. I cannot tell him about Marie, so instead tell him that I've been at my Castle Perilous, and that no one has known of my whereabouts.

"You should have been at Rheged, with us."

"I know that now, and I am more sorry than I can say that I was not there at your father's passing. It is true I did not love him, but he was a good man and a good husband." My words are heartfelt, and the tears of remorse I shed are genuine. After some hesitation, Owain puts his arms around me to comfort me. I am surprised that he is touched by my distress, and determine that I shall do all in my power to win back his love and respect.

"I was on my way to Rheged to find you because I have reason to believe that your life is in danger," I tell him.

"Who threatens me? And why?"

"The threat comes from Sir Mordred, one of the knights at King Arthur's court." I wonder if Owain has heard about Mordred's parentage. He already holds me in contempt and I am reluctant to earn his further scorn by spelling out all the details. No doubt he will make enquiries, and will find out soon enough without my having to tell him about it now.

"He is the king's illegitimate son from a previous liaison, and therefore has ambitions to succeed him," I continue, understanding from the puzzled frown on Owain's face that as yet he knows nothing. "But I am the king's sister, and was always the chosen heir to the throne until Arthur usurped my crown. So Mordred now fears that you, as my son, will challenge him for the right to rule."

"But I wouldn't think of it." Owain still looks bewildered. I reflect that for all his prowess as a warrior, Owain is too innocent for his own good.

"It might help if you make that fact as widely known as you can, but please do not tell anyone who warned you against Mordred. Be ever on your guard, for no matter how hard or how often you protest, it may still not be enough to keep you safe. I have already heard Mordred say that he wishes you dead, and it is quite clear that he means what he says." It grieves me to speak of my firstborn thus, but I know that my caution is necessary. It is a sad indictment on Mordred—and also on me as his mother, and Morgause as his guardian—that he should be judged thus. "Promise me that you will not trust him should you ever encounter him," I insist. "And keep your lion with you always."

Owain makes the promise. To my surprise, he also asks for my blessing. I discover, to my woe, that the knights have been telling him about this quest for the Grail and now he is on fire to join them.

"It is a fool's errand," I tell him.

He is quick to disagree. "The king has told me that this is the cup that once caught drops of blood from Christ as He died upon the Cross. His uncle, Joseph of Arimathea, brought it to Britain afterwards, and it then disappeared. But Mother …" Owain's face is alight with eagerness. "It has now been seen! Joseph of Arimathea's own descendants are also searching for it."

This is something new! I raise a questioning eyebrow.

"In the past, Sir Launcelot has never spoken of his childhood, or of his parentage, save that he was born in Brittany. All we know of him are his deeds since he came to the king's court at Camelot," Owain explains breathlessly. "But the king has discovered that Launcelot himself is a descendant of Joseph of Arimathea, as is his son, Galahad."

And therefore, so is my daughter, Marie. I blink, hardly able to credit what I'm hearing. I cannot believe in this so-called Sangreal, nor can I believe that Joseph of Arimathea was present at the death of the man they call Christ. As for Launcelot being his descendant—that seems much too far a stretch! And yet it is true that Launcelot never told me of his childhood or anything of his family save that he is the son of King Ban. I marvel now that I never thought to question him further.

Does Owain speak the truth? I cannot tell, but what I have already heard is almost too much to comprehend. I need to think on it further, and ponder what it means for Marie. In the meantime, I bid my son farewell. I tell him that I love him, that I am proud of him, and I give him my blessing.

"May God go with you," I add, for I know that this is what he would want me to say. And perhaps it is true, at least for this world we inhabit. "And remember: beware of Mordred."

"But I still don't understand why he considers me a threat to his claim. After all, the king may yet have a child with Guenevere."

"No, he won't."

"You sound very sure of that."

I'd spoken without thinking, and now I regret it. "The queen is past the age for bearing a child," I say hastily. I'm not sure how true this is, but I doubt Owain would know of such things anyway.

And indeed it proves to be so, for he laughs and, forgiving son that he is, gives me a warm hug. "I'll be careful," he says. "But Mordred has little to fear from me, for his bloodlines are purer than mine."

"But tainted." It is true, as Owain will find out soon enough. At the same time, Mordred's comment regarding the tainted bloodlines of Launcelot and Galahad come into my mind. I reflect how mortified Mordred will be once he hears of their illustrious ancestor, and I can't help laughing out loud at the thought.

Owain looks somewhat alarmed. "Come in and rest, Mother," he says kindly. "I should like you to meet Laudine, who has consented to become my wife."

It is a temptation, for I am so tired. But the last person I want to see is Arthur.

"I thank you for your invitation, but I was on my way to Rheged and after your news, I am even more anxious to get there."

Owain looks somewhat skeptical, and I can't blame him. To his credit, he tries once more to change my mind. "I have left Rheged in the trustworthy hands of a good steward. There is no need to rush back. You must be tired and hungry after your long ride." He looks about for my horse, and sees none. His brow furrows in thought.

"My mount is in the stable," I say hastily. "And no, I must set off at once, although I am sorry not to meet Laudine."

"Are you sure you can't stay for the night at least?"

I shake my head and Owain does not press me further. I wonder if he knows that I am not welcome in Arthur's sight. Instead he escorts me to the stable to fetch my so-called mount, which means that I am forced to steal a horse and claim it as my own.

I wave farewell, and ride some way from the castle. I am cast down by the news of Urien's death, and regret that I was not there to ease his passing. I also feel some responsibility, for, although Owain claims to have left the realm in good hands, he is Urien's heir and the kingdom depends on him for good governance. If he follows this quest for the Sangreal he may well be gone for quite some time; I should be there in his stead to ensure that Rheged does not suffer in his absence.

With Owain soon to be wed, I realize that I should be giving some thought also to a suitable match for Marie, especially in the light of what I have just learned about her father! My conscience troubles me. My thoughts turn around and about as I am tugged between duty to Urien and Rheged, and my desire to speak with Marie about her future.

Marriage to Urien was not as hard as I'd supposed. After the first joy of having me in his bed, his ardor had waned and we had settled into a relationship more akin to that of brother and sister—better than that, in fact, for he was a kind man, with a wry sense of humor that more than once lifted me from black despair into laughter. If I could not wed Launcelot then I did well to marry Urien; I acknowledge that now. And I owe him a great deal for giving me shelter and status as his wife despite my tarnished reputation. I knew he was unwell when I last left him. Now I know I should have stayed and taken care of him until the end.

Making up my mind, I continue on to Rheged. I know that I owe Urien's faithful retainers a debt of gratitude for their care of my husband and his demesne, and in turn I too have a duty of care. I need to ensure that the man Owain left in charge can be entrusted with managing the estate in our absence.

On my arrival I am greeted warmly, and all looks well. Nevertheless, I stay at Rheged long enough to reassure myself that both the steward and the reeve are more than capable, and that I can leave Rheged in their good hands for the time being. Only when I have settled my concerns do I finally take the road that will lead me back to the priory. I promise myself that, as soon as I have spoken with Marie, and assured her future, I shall return to Rheged to assume my role as regent until Owain recalls his duty to his father and to his heritage.

CHAPTER 13

Just as Owain is becoming a man, so Marie has reached an age to wed and bear a child. Now that I'm looking at her, not as a daughter but as a grown woman, I am somewhat alarmed by what I perceive. The nuns have given her a good education, as I had requested, but they have also worked their influence on my child. She has become quiet and thoughtful. She attends Mass regularly, and I see her cross herself when she thinks I am not looking. I draw out Merlin's tablets, for I remember that her presence at the scrying pool helped both of us to see a vision. Now that I know of the Sangreal and its significance, I hope that between us we may bring new insight into what the tablets are telling us. But she draws back at the sight of them.

"Is this another part of your magic, Mamm?" she asks.

I nod, and fan them out in front of her.

"I want to talk about your future, Marie, and what lies ahead for you." I give the tablets a light tap. "I have already taught you much of what I know about the craft of magic, but now I need your help to decipher these, for I confess I find it difficult to understand their true meaning. You have inherited my gifts and may well see more than I can, for I hope that these tablets will help us find a way to tell the future; that they may even help us solve all the secrets of our world and those Otherworlds around us!"

"No!" She springs up and puts her hands behind her back. "No, Mamm, I don't want to practice magic any longer. I don't want to learn any more about it."

I stare at her, speechless with disappointment. When I neglected Mordred, he turned to darkness and evil. In my frequent absences from Marie, it seems she has turned toward the light and sanctity of Christ. But I shall fight for her; I shall not let her go! I quickly gather up the tablets.

"Of course, Marie. Whatever you think is best for you," I say lightly. "You are old enough now to choose your own path. But at least let me tell you what I have discovered about this one tablet, for I know it will interest you." I show her the hand holding the golden cup. "I believe this tablet represents the Grail, the Holy Cup of Christ."

She has already heard from visitors to the priory that the knights of Camelot have gone in search of the Sangreal, and her interest sparks as I relate what I have learned of its origins. I touch briefly on the subject of Launcelot and then go on to tell her about Galahad and their lineage that dates back to the time of Joseph of Arimathea.

Marie regards me thoughtfully. "You have never told me anything of my own father," she says wistfully. "It must be such a joy to Galahad to have found his father after all this time. Will you tell me something about my own father? I care not how low born he was, I would just like to know."

It is the question I had always dreaded she would ask. I had rehearsed a hundred different replies but, in the face of her earnest gaze, I know that only the truth will suffice. Besides, there is a difference now, for her father is descended from someone of whom she can be proud. If she believes in the Christ, then this will mean everything in the world to her.

"You are of the same lineage, my dearest daughter," I tell her tenderly. "You are half-sister to Galahad, although he doesn't yet know of your existence. Neither does your father."

There is a dawning horror in Marie's eyes as she comes to understand what I have just told her. "You lay with Launcelot?" It is more an accusation than a question.

"Yes. I did so because I loved him more than I can say. I love him still."

If I hope this will make Marie think better of me, I am wrong. "But you were never wed, at least not to him."

"No. It was only after I realized there was a child growing in my womb that I wed King Urien."

"Surely you did not pretend that I was Urien's child?"

"No." I tell her the truth, although I know it probably won't redeem her good opinion of me. "I had thought to do so. I was tempted, but at the end I found that I could not. And so I came to the priory instead, knowing it would be safe for me to give birth to you here." Pray to the gods that she never finds out about Mordred, or worse—that he finds out about her!

"So you've kept your shameful behavior a secret! Does anyone outside the priory know about me, that you even have a daughter?"

Faced with Marie's anger, there is nothing I can say. I shake my head.

"So I may as well not exist at all!" Marie turns and runs away from me.

My heart aches as I watch her go. The bells for Mass are ringing, and I know that she answers their summons. If she confesses what she's learned to the priest, I can only hope that her confessor will honor the silence of confession, and that his discretion is absolute.

I retire to my bedchamber and spread out the tablets, hoping that I might be able to decipher their meaning even without Marie's help. As I did once before, I lay them face down and jumble them up. This time, I hold Merlin's crystal in my hand, praying that it will help me find enlightenment. Again I choose fourteen, and turn them over. I gasp in amazement as I notice that in spite of my care to choose blind, I have turned up exactly the same tablets as I did before, but the crystal in my hand enables me to see more clearly. The two crowned figures on their elaborate thrones are an aging Arthur and Guenevere, scarred by life and by experience. The knight bearing the cup is definitely Launcelot, and I am the woman beside him. I recognize Merlin with his collection of magical objects. The knight bearing a sword and galloping through storm clouds is Mordred as he is now: a grown man. The burning tower deepens my unease as I notice its resemblance to Camelot.

Once more I try to empty my mind of my thoughts and fears. I study the tablets in order, beginning with the first one I turned over, and finally I am able to understand their message. I, the innocent, step into the abyss, gulled by Merlin who, through his trickery with the sword Excalibur, ensures that Arthur inherits the kingdom in my place. The responsibility has taken its toll; I see it on the faces of Arthur and Guenevere. Beside Guenevere is Launcelot, and I am seated on his other side, with my wand in my hand. We are lovers, but a sword pierces my heart. Here is the hand with the cup, offering what I now know is the Sangreal. And Mordred rides toward it, with crown in one hand and sword upraised in the other, hell bent on destruction. The devil looms over the lovers, who are chained and powerless—and I know that I must take responsibility for their fate. The tower burns and people leap into the air. Death follows, trampling over all that has gone before. Finally an angel calls the dead souls to judgment—and I know I shall be judged most harshly of all, for I have caused this and I am doomed, as are we all if the fate of Camelot cannot be overturned.

My hands clench in fear and in sorrow. A cry bursts from my throat: a prayer for the knowledge to turn back time, to change things around, to have the chance to make everything anew.

With shaking hands I scoop up the tablets, ready to pack them away with the rest of the pile. How bitterly I regret learning this skill. I would rather have died in ignorance than know the fate that will befall us all.

But it seems that I have inadvertently picked up an extra tablet, which lies close to my hand. A young child carrying a pentacle, the magical crystal. The world spreads out beneath its feet, ready for exploration. This child has an eager, innocent expression. I have seen this tablet before, and now I recognize who it represents. The child is Marie, inheritor of my knowledge of magic whether or not she is prepared to accept it.

I take in a deep, quivering breath, striving for calm. What can this mean? That, after all, there is hope for the future, that Marie holds the future in her hands? My gaze strays to the turned-down tablets. I long to know more. I stretch out a tentative hand, and choose one. An older woman, with a crown on her head, is seated on a throne with a crystal pentacle on her lap. Eagerly, I study her face. She is not Marie, nor me. So who is she, and what does this mean? My heart hammers in my breast.

I reach out for another tablet, promising myself that this will be the last. It seems to me that I have unlocked the past and the present, and have now been granted a glimpse of the future. But I still don't understand what it means, nor what I need to do, or even if I have a role in determining how the future will play out. My hope is that this last tablet will tell me.

It depicts a great shining star set among a host of others. Below, a woman kneels by a pool, scooping water into a pitcher with one hand and emptying another pitcher of water onto the land with her other. I have noticed it before, but have not deciphered its meaning. Now I allow myself a moment of hope; perhaps all is not yet lost after all? There is a feeling of serenity and joy in this depiction of the water of life that nurtures us and flows on into eternity, while the stars smile down on our earthly endeavors. It seems to me a promise that all will be well.

I pack the tablets away as I ponder the future. Beyond doubt, they had spelled out our doom, yet I recall Merlin saying that if I could only learn to read the future, I could change it—if it's not too late. These last three tablets seem to promise hope. But I must act now, for there is no time to lose. My first thought is to make all speed to Camelot, to warn Arthur of what is about to befall the kingdom, and of his fate should he continue to ignore the treasonous love between Launcelot and Guenevere, and deny the connection between himself and his son. I pray that it is not too late to put my magical powers to good use so that I may yet save the kingdom from destruction.

My momentary pride in my ability gives way to amazement. Not so long ago I would have retreated to Rheged and lived there quietly, content that in time the court at Camelot would be so divided in loyalty that it would result in civil war, the situation exacerbated by the scandalous behavior of Guenevere and Launcelot, and the overweening pride and ambition of our son. I would have waited, knowing that with the doom of Camelot would come the need for a new ruler, for the one groomed from childhood to lead our people, but who was cast aside on the whim of an old man.

And yet, and this is a grudging admission I grant, I have seen how Arthur has united the tribes and has brought peace to our land, even if I have not openly acknowledged it. I have also seen how his men love and honor him—that is, how they used to love and honor him before my meddling brought Launcelot and Guenevere together, with Arthur positioned as cuckold.

I know I could have united the kingdom as Arthur has done. I am equal to the task. But my rage has almost burnt itself out now. More than ever, I am mindful of Arthur as a small child, and how greatly I loved him then. My instinct now is to protect him from his foes, all of them, including his queen and his illegitimate son. I feel I owe it to the loving child that he was, and I acknowledge at last the part I have played in the unfolding tragedy foretold by the tablets. It is a bitter admission, and a shameful one. If Mordred is a danger now, it is because he has inherited my own pride and ambition, while my desire for revenge on those I perceived as my enemies caused me to take that first fatal step to lie with Arthur. Everything has flowed from that: the lies, the deaths, the loss of Launcelot, all leading now to the looming peril that threatens the kingdom.

Marie was right to berate me. She is a good person, my daughter. Her purity stands as a sickening indictment on the blackness of my own heart. It is a shameful legacy she has inherited from me, one that I would give all in my power to change—if only I could turn back time.

My thoughts go to where it all started. Merlin understood more of human nature than I'd given him credit for; he'd understood my blind ambition, my furious need for revenge, and my tendency to act without thinking through the consequences. No wonder he questioned my ability to rule a kingdom! If only I had accepted Merlin's decision and done my best to smooth Arthur's path to leadership, what a powerful kingdom we might have forged together! With Arthur's skill on the battlefield and his ability to lead his men, matched with my quick wits and knowledge of magic, we would have made a formidable team. Unbeatable. And I would be happy, because I would be wed to Launcelot. We might have made other children after Marie, a whole tribe of them to brighten our days and keep us young at heart. With Launcelot out of the queen's reach, and no Mordred, Camelot would not be divided nor would it be as vulnerable as it is now.

If I hadn't meddled and Guenevere had kept faithful to Arthur, she might well have borne a child and secured the kingdom for Arthur's line, not mine. Anger flares at the thought, but it is quickly checked. A lost kingdom in return for a long and happy life with the man I love, and the safety of the kingdom? Yes, I would consider that a good trade, especially when it seems that sacrificing my happiness has counted for naught now that our kingdom faces almost certain annihilation—if the tablets are to be believed.

I cannot change the past, I know that. But it may yet be possible to change the future, if only I am able to change what is happening in the present, for this is a foretelling only. And so I swear a silent oath to make this my mission.

*

Marie expresses her surprise to see me depart so soon after my arrival. Apparently she feels some guilt over her accusations, however well-founded I know them to be.

"I am truly sorry, Mamm, if I have hurt your feelings," she tells me. "But your revelations were such a shock and I need time to come to terms with my heritage, to contemplate my future, and to pray." She hesitates. "There is something else I must say. I know the way of God and Christ is not your way, but it has become important to me. And while I wish to obey you in all things, I know that what you have taught me about the practice of magic is against the word of God, and I want nothing further to do with it. Especially when I see the unhappiness it has brought you." She takes my hand, and presses it gently.

Her words pierce my heart, as does the truth of what she says. I hear the determination in her voice, and recognize the finality of her decision. Nevertheless, having embarked on this path, I must see it through. I cannot give up my skills in the magical arts for I know that I shall have need of them. But I cannot tell her that, so instead I try to comfort her.

"I have seen that trouble is brewing in Camelot, Marie. I believe that the king is in danger, and so I must go there at once to warn him." True, the warning may have to wait if he is still in pursuit of the Grail, but Guenevere will be at Camelot, and if necessary I shall deal directly with her. My hope is that I may be able to undo what I began with Launcelot so that the knights will regain their respect for Arthur and unite behind him to resist Mordred's ambition to rule. I have not attempted to undo a love potion before; it was a strong and binding one that I brewed, with the purpose of forging ties so strong that only death would sever them. In the first instance, this is what I must try to undo, although I have found no remedy for this in Merlin's old book.

If I don't succeed? Should I try to remove the spell of barrenness on Guenevere instead, so that an heir might be born? But would Arthur be the father? Now that Launcelot believes he's already lain with the queen, my greatest fear is that he might steal into her bed once more, and this time they might make a child together.

Is the death of one of them the answer? If so, who should it be? Not Launcelot! I squeeze my eyes tight shut, trying to block out the bleakness of a world without him in it. No. If anyone should die, it must be Guenevere.

"Mamm?" Marie touches my hand. I open my eyes to look at her. "Will you take me with you to Camelot?"

"No, Marie!" I am horrified at the very thought of it. "It is not safe for you to go there, not while there is so much unrest at court."

She straightens her back and tilts her chin. I can see what this defiance is costing her, and I silently applaud her bravery.

Nevertheless, what she says renders me speechless for a few moments.

"I wish to meet my father. I have a right to know him, just as he has a right to know about me."

Her eyes are wide and troubled as she surveys me. I must think of something to say. I know I must refuse her; her presence would add an unwanted complication to what I must achieve there. Worse, if Mordred comes to hear of her, he will perceive her as another threat to his ambition. At all costs, I need to keep Marie safe—and her safety lies in the secret of her birth. "I am mindful that we need to discuss your future, Marie, and I beg you to wait here and make no decisions until things are settled in Camelot and I am able to return to you. In the meantime, I shall think about your request, and whether or not you should come to Camelot to meet your father."

"Very well, Mamm." She bows her head in submission. I cannot see her expression, and that concerns me. But at least she has given me her consent. I know that I can trust her to obey me.

"I'll return as soon as I may. I promise you we'll talk again." I kiss her on both cheeks, and she suddenly clings to me as she used to when she was a small child and I had to leave her to go back to Urien.

"I will not change my mind about practicing magic, Mamm," she whispers. "Nothing you can say will change my belief that what you are doing is dangerous meddling. And unnecessary. We should rather let God's plan unfold as He wills it, for none then can hold us responsible for causing harm and unhappiness, either to ourselves or to others."

I catch my breath in fright, wondering if she has read my mind, if she knows what I plan to do—and if she has any inkling of the harm I have already done. But her face bears only an innocent determination that I should heed her words.

I nod, feeling infinitely saddened by her decision. Yet I will not deny her my blessing. "Your path through life is for you to decide, Marie," I tell her. "Stay well, and may your God be with you."

"And with you also, Mamm." She lets go of me and I walk away. I cannot resist looking back for a last glance; she is still watching me. There is a glint of tears in her eyes, which I know is matched in mine. I sniff loudly, and walk on to the stable to find my mount. I ride away with a last cheerful wave, but with a troubled heart and a mind seething in agitation.

As I come closer to Camelot, I prepare the speech I shall make to Arthur once he returns; a speech that I hope will convince him that I have truly repented of my past wrongdoings—at least, all those of which he already knows. It is important to win his trust otherwise he will not heed my warning. And heed it he must, if he is to save himself and save Camelot. I have accepted now that he will rule as king until he dies—but there is still the matter of his successor. Somehow, Mordred must be stopped so that someone more worthy can take his place. His cousin Gawain perhaps, or Galahad? But I would rather see my own kin take power in the kingdom that I still believe is rightfully mine. Owain, or even my Marie. Both are good and kind, I am sure of that, and I know that Owain is brave, while Marie has wisdom beyond her years. Although Marie is not a man, she has courage too. This I acknowledge, for despite her love for me, she has defied me. She has fought for her future with words, not arms, but either requires courage and determination, along with a clear vision of what the future might hold. Perhaps I can persuade Arthur to name both of them as his heirs so that they might rule the kingdom together?

And if Arthur is not at court? I think of all the harm I've already caused: the deaths of Accolon and an innocent young girl, and the imprisonment and probable death of Merlin. I would scrub my hands free of their blood if only I could.

I make a vow that I must not be responsible for any more deaths—at least, not if I can help it. But I acknowledge that I may not have any choice in the matter.

Having left the priory in a great hurry to warn Arthur, now I dally along the road while I wrestle with my thoughts and with my conscience. I suppose, in my secret heart, I am hoping to give Arthur enough time to return so that I shall not have to face Guenevere, although it might be easier if she is there on her own, for that will give me the freedom to do what I may and, if need be, even act against her.

To my surprise, the courtyard is in turmoil when I arrive, wounded knights crying out for treatment, staggering away from dusty, sweating horses that tell much of their hard flight from danger. In the prevailing chaos I cannot find anyone who can give me a coherent account of what has transpired to bring this about. Finally, I shrug and go inside, wondering what sort of reception I'll receive from Guenevere, or even Arthur, if he has returned.

When Guenevere sees me, she gives a little cry and, to my surprise, hurries to my side to tell me how welcome I am to Camelot.

"I know we parted on bad terms, Morgana," she says, "but I am delighted to see you now. So many knights are returning from this quest for the Sangreal in need of care. All bear the wounds to prove how difficult and dangerous their journey has been. But despite their best endeavors, it seems that it was all for nothing!"

"The quest was unsuccessful?" I can hardly hide my surprise, for having seen the determination on the faces of the knights I encountered, I would have sworn on my life that they would not return until one or other of them had found the Sangreal and taken it to King Pelles.

"Successful for some." Guenevere's voice is bitter. "Sir Galahad, in the company of Sir Perceval and Sir Bors, came to Carbonek Castle and there found the Sangreal—at least, that is what we are told, although their journey sounds too magical to be believed. The other knights are all disillusioned and angry, and have returned to Camelot thinking of themselves as failures. But of course many knights will never return, for they have died in search of this will-o'-the-wisp fairy tale!"

It surprises me that Guenevere and I are in agreement on at least one thing. "Has Arthur returned yet?" I ask cautiously, and at once her eyes narrow in suspicion.

"How did you know he was away? Have you been spying on us, Morgana?"

"No, not at all!" I wave a hand in the air in dismissal of such a notion. "I merely assumed that everyone had gone, including the king. I trust he is safely returned?"

"Yes."

"And Sir Launcelot?"

"He is also safe, thank God." Guenevere crosses herself. "But many of the knights need urgent treatment, and I know not what to do. You have the skill of healing, Morgana. Will you help me, please?"

I nod in agreement. Guenevere takes me by the hand and draws me across the hall and down a passage to a smaller hall where the sick are usually housed. It bears some resemblance to the infirmarium at Glastonbury Priory, although there are not the same facilities or remedies at hand. I quickly issue instructions for boiling water to be brought, along with soapwort and other herbs that I know will help to ease the pain and heal the wounds of those poor wretches now lying on beds and pallets around the room, sighing and groaning their agony. At my bidding, Guenevere hurries off to find clean linen to tear into strips to bind their wounds, although I suspect her first call will be on her ladies-in-waiting to ask them to carry out my orders.

There are several new knights at Camelot, younger knights unknown to me, and as I minister to their wounds I listen avidly to their talk, although it pains me to hear it. Mordred's name is mentioned more than once. He is now actively making mischief against Arthur, using the affair between Launcelot and Guenevere as a fulcrum.

"A king so blind to the lack of loyalty shown him by his wife and his most trusted knight is hardly worthy of ruling a kingdom," one of them says. I feel sure he is quoting directly from Mordred, and my suspicions are confirmed when his companion replies.

"The old king has worn out his usefulness. We need a younger man now; someone with the right bloodlines, as well as someone who is in tune with the times."

He glances around the room; I wonder if he is looking for Mordred. I have already checked and know that he is not present. I am not sure whether to feel glad or sorry that he is not among the wounded.

"'The old king,' as you call him, reunited the tribes and brought the peace and prosperity to our kingdom that you now enjoy and take for granted!" My tone cuts like a knife, although I smile inwardly at the irony of my defending Arthur when most of my life has been spent in trying to achieve exactly what these young fools are talking about. "He has the wisdom of age, the experience of past battles, and he knows more about statecraft than puppies like you can begin to imagine!"

I pick up my medicaments and walk away, ignoring the sullen whispers that break out behind my back. My attention is drawn by the sound of a slow clapping. I look to its source, and see Gawain applauding me. He is sitting on a pallet on the floor looking pale and haggard. A bloody bandage is wrapped around his thigh. It is filthy, and I hurry to remove it.

"Well said, Aunt!" he greets me, then winces as I try to unwrap the bandage. The linen fabric has stuck to a patch of dried blood and as I pull it, the wound opens and bright new blood begins to seep out. I beckon for a basin of warm water and begin to sponge his leg, hoping to ease the bandage off less painfully once it is wet.

"What I said is true. And I have no doubt they wish to usurp your uncle with your cousin." I find I can't bring myself to own Mordred as my son, but Gawain has no such qualms.

"Your son. Yes, they do," he says.

I close my eyes. "You must put a stop to Mordred's trouble-making, Gawain. Please." In my urgency, I clutch his arm. "I would rather you, or Owain —or someone else—take Arthur's place when it is time. God knows, I've had my hopes for Mordred, but I fear what he has become, and what he might do to us all in his ambition to rule Camelot."

"I fear it too, Morgana." Gawain is serious now. "He has set himself to charm the younger knights, most of whom haven't a grain of sense in their heads beyond dreams of chivalry and winning the hands of fair maidens—and attaining the Sangreal, of course, although that is now over."

"Is it true that Galahad, Perceval and Bors achieved that honor?"

"Yes—but at great cost." Gawain's voice is somber as he begins to recount the story of their quest.

"Only Bors has returned to tell the tale of their search for the Sangreal and their many wondrous adventures along their journey: hazardous exploits in strange lands against magical beasts, and encounters with beautiful maidens who tempted them and who turned into devils when they would not break their vows of chastity. Things were never as they seemed. Bors says he even fought his brother, Lionel, without knowing him for who he was. By all accounts, strange dreams and voices led all of the knights astray—even me. Only Bors, Galahad and Perceval prevailed for, after traversing the country, they found a mysterious ship that, with no help from them or from the wind, bore them to Carbonek. There they found the Maimed King lying abed, grievously hurt and with a broken sword by his side. He told them that his wounds would not heal until this sword, that had shattered when it pierced his side, was made whole again. Bors said he tried to repair it, as did Perceval, but it was only when Galahad took up the sword that it became straight and whole again, with no chip or crack to show that it was ever broken.

"That was when the Sangreal appeared once more. And oh, how I wish I'd been blessed to see such a sight! Bors said that King Pelles bade them drink from the cup, and that he had never tasted anything so fine. Once their thirst was sated, Galahad asked the Maimed King how they might serve him further. And the king called Galahad to his side and gave him his blessing, and in front of them all, he recognized Galahad as his own grandson. And he asked Galahad to pick up the mended sword and lay it on him for healing."

Gawain gives me a faint smile. "It seems that Galahad did not know his identity until then, for his mother, Elaine of Carbonek, had been estranged from her father. And so there was a great reconciliation between the two of them." His smile is replaced by sadness as he continues his story.

"According to Bors, Galahad did as King Pelles asked. And the king arose from his bed as if he was a healthy young man once more, as if he hadn't spent years in pain and misery, confined to his bed and wishing to die. Bors said that they all praised Galahad then, and asked for his blessing."

"Surely that would be a further occasion for rejoicing, so why do you sound so miserable?"

"Because the mysterious ship came and bore them away once more. And Galahad died."

"Died?" I put my hand to my heart, unable to conceal my shock. "But ... why?"

"He said that he had achieved his heart's desire on earth, and that heaven awaited him. And he asked God to grant his wish. And so God did."

The young fool! The words are on the tip of my tongue but I dare not utter them for I can understand now why Gawain is so distressed. Galahad had impressed me when we met; I can see that he would have been a favorite among the knights.

"Does Launcelot know?"

Gawain nods sadly. "He is distraught. But the queen will comfort him, no doubt." There is a touch of acid on his tongue. "Perceval has not returned either. He decided to enter holy orders at Sarras, the place where they left the ship, but it seems that he, too, has died. Only Bors has returned to tell us what transpired."

Merlin's words, from so long ago and long forgotten, come into my mind. He was talking of alchemy, I recall: the search that continues even now in Camelot for the lodestone that will turn base metal into gold.

To some, those who value riches above all else, this knowledge is the Grail. I wanted you to try, Morgana, so that you would know it cannot be done. Nor is it possible to find the elixir of everlasting life, which is another Grail that others may seek. Some people search all their lives for this Grail, the Sangreal they call it. But none has ever found it, and they still die when their time has been spent. No one has ever managed to turn base metal into gold, or create such an elixir.

The quest for the Sangreal! Did Merlin foresee this search that, apparently, has healed the Maimed King but has caused the death of so many knights, Galahad and Perceval among them? Did he know about the cup even before it appeared to the knights; did he understand its significance from the wooden tablets, the ones I stole from him? I stop unwinding the bandage and instead drum my fingers in frustration as I try to fathom the mystery of what it all means.

"Casting a spell, Morgana?" Gawain asks, with a smile.

"Praying for your continued good health, Gawain," I say, and continue to unwrap the filthy linen. Mercifully, he stays quiet, for my mind is now wholly taken up with a new thought.

Galahad is dead. That leaves Marie as the sole descendant of a bloodline that traces through the fairest and best knight in the realm right back in time to Joseph of Arimathea, uncle of the Lord Jesus Christ Himself! Truly, Marie should be proud of her Christian heritage. More important, to my way of thinking, she is also the daughter of the rightful heir to this realm. With Owain at her side, I am sure she would have both the wisdom and the courage to rule Camelot after Arthur; sure, too, that if she will allow it I can teach her all the magic she will need to keep the kingdom united and safeguard it from the enemies beyond our shores. I recall what the tablets seemed to be telling me, and shiver. If I am correct, there is much to be achieved—and much to be averted—before the kingdom can be kept safe for my son and daughter.

"I was sorry to hear of the death of Urien," Gawain says. "I know it was not a love match for you, Morgana, but he was a good man. The king will miss him; we all will."

"As will I." My words are true enough. Since hearing Owain's news I've been conscious that the security inherent in my marriage to Urien has now been removed. I can no longer rely on his name and reputation to protect me. A shiver blows through me like a chill wind.

"Is Owain safe? Did he accompany the king on his return to Camelot?" I ask Gawain in sudden concern.

His lips twitch into a smile. "Your son is well, but he did not come back with us, to Sir Kay's great relief, so I am told." I cannot tell Gawain I already know the story of Kay's discomfiture, and so I listen as Gawain retells it, with praise for my son as he does so. But Gawain has other news that also brings comfort to me.

"The king asked Owain to return to Camelot with him, but I'm told he declined. Instead, he has taken his new wife, and his lion, to Rheged, to fulfill his role as his father's heir, for Urien's death has left his kingdom without a ruler and his people without a shepherd." He gives me a long, measuring glance, and I know he is thinking that I should have been there all along, fulfilling my duty as Urien's wife. And so I should, but I believe I am more needed here and so I merely nod my thanks, and move on. I rejoice to know that Owain is safely out of reach of Mordred's influence and malice.

The young man next in line seems to bear some resemblance to Gawain. I look between them to check the likeness.

"Guinglain. He is my son." I hear the pride in Gawain's voice. Indeed, it is not misplaced, for the youth is built like his warrior father but he has the dark beauty of his mother, Dame Ragnell. "He is a voice of reason among the younger knights. Would that there were more of them to temper Mordred's mischief."

I nod as I tend the gash along Guinglain's arm. It is a surface wound only; nothing of great concern and I soothe it with a healing lotion, and tell him it must be kept clean.

Gawain introduces me. "This is your great aunt, Morgana." Great aunt! How ancient that makes me feel! The youth is staring at me with much curiosity, and I wonder what he has been told about me, and whether he believes it all. But his smile is sweet and he tells me how glad he is to meet me at last, seemingly without irony.

From Guinglain I move on to Lionel, brother of Bors, and thence on to the other wounded knights. They are all wary at first—I can just imagine the stories that have circulated about the court in my absence—but as they relax under my healing touch, they begin to regale me with stories of their own quest for the Sangreal, most of which strike me as foolhardy in the extreme, although I do not say so. Instead, I give praise where it's due ("such courage, such honor") and commiserate when it seems appropriate ("I give thanks that you managed to survive such a deadly ambush/so fearful a creature/so perilous an undertaking, my lord"). I know I shall need their good will in the future, and I am glad to have this opportunity to soften their opinion of me. They are grateful for my ministrations and for the relief I bring them. At the same time, I become conscious of how many knights have not returned to Camelot. They will be greatly missed.

Once I have done what I can for the men, my thoughts turn to Guenevere. And Launcelot. An anxious consultation of Merlin's book before leaving the priory had given me no hints as to how I might undo the spell I cast to make them fall in love. Now, I have resolved to use the same potion but with a different purpose in mind. And so I go walking in the water meadows on the pretext of taking the air. There I pick the herbs and flowers I need, and I brew them in secret.

My chance comes when I am seated beside Arthur at dinner. In gratitude for my healing of the knights, it seems I have risen in honor and am thus restored to a high position. As we dine, a page comes to the table, advising Arthur a party of travelers has arrived at court. He in turn bids Guenevere accompany him to welcome them. Launcelot and I are left with empty spaces between us for, as usual, he is seated on Guenevere's other side. It is the first time I have had a chance to study him closely since my return to Camelot, and I am shocked by what I see. He is gaunt, haggard with misery. I long to take him in my arms, to comfort him for the loss of his son, but I dare not. He gives me a baleful glare and turns pointedly to the dame beside him. I cannot help but smile as I note that she is large and somewhat plain, with an unsightly wart on the side of her nose. In spite of Launcelot's obvious devotion to the queen, it seems that Guenevere is still taking no chances with his fidelity.

I cast a quick glance around the table to see if anyone is watching me. Viviane is not present, and I am grateful for that. With Launcelot's attention elsewhere, and both Guenevere and Arthur absent, it is the work of a moment to uncork my flask and tip its contents into the cup shared by Guenevere and Arthur. With the deed done, I cast another quick glance around the table.

Mordred is gazing at me; there is an unpleasant twist to his smile. I recall that I have not sought him out since my return to Camelot. I try to make up for it with a wave and a false smile, but he narrows his eyes and turns pointedly away.

I am not sure how the potion will work, and I wait and watch as Guenevere returns to the table while Arthur directs his steward to find seats for the travelers and ensure their comfort. Guenevere picks up the goblet and takes a heady draught. I'm expecting her to wait and offer the cup to Arthur, but she does not. Instead, she turns to Launcelot with sparkling eyes and moistly parted lips, and hands it to him. My cry dies in my throat; I cannot sound a warning. Nor can I dash the cup from Launcelot's hand, for he has already taken a sip. Blind to all those around them, they gaze at each other in rapture.

I despair all over again, for my plan has failed. Worse, it would appear that I have managed instead to reinforce the deadly love that binds them, and that only death will part.

The thought sickens me. Is this the path I must take? I have enough blood on my hands and on my conscience; I cannot think of shedding more.

I turn to Arthur as he resumes his seat beside me. "May I have a private word with you after dinner, my lord?"

He looks instantly suspicious. "Guenevere tells me you have done good work among the knights since your return,

Morgana, and I am grateful to you. But do not for one moment believe that I am ready to trust you again, or love you as a brother should. Guenevere may have a more forgiving heart than I, but I have learned that trust is not a luxury that kings may enjoy."

"But you trust Guenevere. And Launcelot?"

"Who else should I trust other than my wife and my dearest friend?"

"You should trust them least of all."

Arthur's expression hardens into bitterness. "You always resented me, didn't you, Morgana? My kingdom, my happy marriage, my friends—all denied to you because of your ambition, your jealousy, your spite and your determination to manipulate events to give you what you cannot have, using the magic that you learned from Merlin and which has brought you nothing but unhappiness."

Arthur's words flay me to the bone. I open my mouth to deny them, to say that he, too, played his part in my downfall, as did Merlin. But in essence he speaks the truth, and it is a truth too dreadful to bear. I sit beside him, speechless, praying only that no one else has heard his accusation. I am mortified that he has had the wit to see what I have been so blind to all these years; a truth that even my own daughter seems to understand: every unhappiness I have known has been caused by my own hand. I berate myself once again as I imagine how different my life could have been if I had accepted Merlin's words of caution, and learned from them. Camelot would have prospered if I hadn't interfered—with or without my rule. I could have been happily wed to Launcelot. Marie would be legitimate, and there would be no Mordred to threaten the crown. Perhaps even Guenevere and Arthur might have found comfort and ease together, especially if Guenevere had borne him a child.

I close my eyes in anguish, wanting to hide from the knowledge of how I have ruined my life along with the lives of so many others. But I cannot. It takes all my courage to open my eyes and look at Arthur.

He is regarding me as a king might regard a lowly and unfavored subject. There is no mercy in his eyes, only coldness.

"I am ... so sorry for the harm I have caused you, Arthur," I whisper. "If I could, I would turn back time and live my life differently. Unfortunately, Merlin didn't show me how to master that particular trick." I attempt a smile, but Arthur's expression remains stony.

It seems obvious he won't hear anything against Launcelot and the queen, but I can still warn him against his son. "It is true that I thought to use Mordred against you, Arthur." No one will ever know how much it costs me to admit it. "You should know that I abandoned that plan when he was but a child, for I loved him and could never have used him as a means to usurp your throne. But I've come to realize that there is a darkness in him; a wild ambition that burns like a raging fire and that is out of control. By not acknowledging him as your heir, or showing him any regard as your son, you have given him permission to act against you without conscience or thought for the consequences. I regret his birth more than I can say, but he is here in your court and it is you who must deal with him now. You must fear him as I have learned to fear him, for I know that he is encouraging the knights to believe that it is time for a younger king, and that you, Arthur, are no longer worthy of the crown."

Fire kindles in Arthur's eyes; I am pleased that he has been provoked to anger by my words and that he has taken my warning seriously.

"I have already taken Mordred's measure, Morgana. I know him for what he is: ambitious, dangerous and utterly ruthless—just like you. He is, after all, your son. What else should I expect?"

I open my mouth to protest. And close it again. How can I defend myself against the truth? But I must still say what needs to be said. "Please, Arthur, heed my warning. Send him away from here before it's too late, before he undoes all that you have achieved. Put an end to the court's uncertainty by naming your successor—my son Owain, if Guenevere proves unable to give you a child. And I beg you also to consider sending Launcelot into exile at Joyous Garde, out of reach of the queen." My heart is breaking. But I will not give Arthur the satisfaction of seeing how his words have wounded me, and so I hastily excuse myself and flee the table.

Utterly cast down, I fling myself onto my bed. I am shaking with grief and remorse for the past, for the present and for the future, but no tears will come. I have gone beyond weeping. My shattered heart is dry, as arid as a desert; there are no tears left to shed.

CHAPTER 14

I wait and I watch, but Arthur shows no signs of heeding my advice. It seems only action is left if I am to undo the harm I have caused and so save the kingdom. My chance comes one morning when Guenevere appears at table to break her fast. She is attired entirely in green, as are all her ladies, while the knights who escort them have green kerchiefs tucked into their helmets. Kay and Agravaine are among the crowd, and also Pelleas, who had once thought to woo me when I was at court in the guise of Nimue. I am pleased that, recognizing me as Morgana, he will keep his distance now. I look about for Launcelot, but he is not among the group. It is just as well, for his grief would have cast a pall on the proceedings. As it is, the ladies are buzzing around like a swarm of bees, their voices high with excitement and their laughter shrill. I wonder what is afoot.

It is a beautiful day, but my heart is heavy. I plan to go out to the water meadows to search for deadly hemlock or some other such herb that will bring swift death when swallowed. I have a flask of honey mead handy to disguise the taste, and I pray I have the courage to see my plan through.

But my intention is foiled when Guenevere catches my arm and tells me, "My ladies and I are going a-maying today,

Morgana, to raise our spirits and forget, just for a while, the unhappy toll that the quest for the Sangreal has taken on us all. Would you like to come with us?"

I suspect it is duty that prompts her invitation rather than a readiness to forgive me and forget my misdeeds; nevertheless her generosity of spirit is a stinging reproach to my conscience and my heart, and I stammer my agreement while quickly revising my plans.

And so we set forth into the forest. The trees are lush with late spring growth, the leaves already turning a dark green so that the forest glades are cast into deep shade. I ride on ahead, on the lookout for a shadowy spot where I may catch Guenevere alone; I have some thought to become a snake, to make her horse rear in fright and throw her. It sickens me to admit it, but I am hoping she will break her pretty neck, with no blame attached to me. It helps my cause that the queen has forbidden our guard to ride with us, but has told them to stay some distance behind, "so that we may enjoy our silliness with no one to witness and disapprove of us."

There are many possibilities for ambush in the dark glades and I find more than one likely spot. But Guenevere stays always amid her ladies, enjoying the ride, the fun and the freedom. I am almost resigned to giving up my quest, on this day at least, when I hear a shriek of alarm. I wheel my horse around and canter back to find armed knights fighting for their lives. I recognize the green kerchiefs and shield symbols of the men from our own guard, but there is also a group in unmarked armor. Steel clashes against steel, there are shouts and oaths, and it is difficult to know who is besting whom. I look about for the queen and her ladies, but cannot see them. Frightened, I try to find a hiding place but I am too late; my arm is seized and I am dragged away by one of the unknown warriors. It would seem that he enjoys his position of power over me, for his grip is too tight and his expression overfamiliar as he hauls me along. Anger takes the place of fear.

"Who are you?" I demand.

He leers at me. His teeth are blackened and filthy, and his breath stinks. "Sir Meliagrance's man at your service, my lady."

"Unhand me at once!"

He grins. His grip tightens on my arm.

"What do you want?"

"I'm taking you to my lord's castle. Netting the queen was his intention, but netting the king's sister along with the queen will no doubt earn me a bonus."

I struggle and try to kick him as he drags me along, but he is so tall and strong I feel like a gnat attempting to bring down a donkey. And so I cease and instead think how else I might outwit him. I could become a bird, a beetle, maybe a rat and bite his hand? A snake would be more deadly. But if these ruffians plan on holding the queen captive, then I would do well to go with my captor and find out where we are to be held, for I'm not sure if anyone knows where Meliagrance's castle is, as he is something of an outcast from Camelot. There will be time enough for magic later, if magic becomes necessary.

We quickly catch up to Guenevere and her ladies, and we are all marched through the forest to a castle I have never seen before. We are taken into the Great Hall where a tall knight soon joins us. His dark hair and beard are threaded with silver, but he is manly in his bearing for all that. He wears a costly embroidered tunic of gold and green with flowing sleeves. Tight-fitting hose and pointed shoes complete the ensemble, all of which speak of wealth and prestige. He walks forward and takes firm hold of Guenevere's hand. She tries to snatch it away, but cannot. He raises her hand to his lips for a lingering kiss.

"Meliagrance!" Guenevere's voice drips with disgust. "I might have known you were behind this."

"My queen, I have longed to welcome you to my castle. You and your ladies will stay with me as my guests."

"Guests? Captives, you mean!"

"As you will." He smiles. "But you will find me a good host, I assure you. Every comfort will be at your disposal."

"Except the comfort of going home to my husband!"

"You do not need him, Guenevere. Not here. I shall provide comfort enough, I assure you."

His meaning is clear. To her credit, Guenevere stares him down. "Is this the only way you can get a woman into your bed, Meliagrance? By capturing her and holding her here by force?"

"Not any woman, Guenevere; only you. And not by force, either, I assure you. I am a skilled and considerate lover, as you will soon find out, to your great enjoyment."

Guenevere closes her eyes for a moment. I wonder if, after years of enduring Arthur's fumbling, she might be tempted by Meliagrance's proposition. But her eyes flash fire when she opens them again.

"You've long wanted me in your bed, Meliagrance. Before God, you've been trying for years to woo and bed me. But I am not interested in being your paramour, and I demand that you let me go!"

"Demand, Guenevere?" he says softly. His grip tightens momentarily before he releases her. "I shall show you to your room. You and your ladies may rest until it is time for us to dine. I shall send for you after that." He leads the way out and up the stone stairs, while the rest of us are herded in his wake by his attendants.

The chamber into which we are shown is large and airy but there are bars across the windows. I walk over to one of them, and look out. The scent of roses assails my senses. A sturdy briar, heavy with blossom, crawls across the wall, sending its sweetness into the air. It is a long way to the ground.

The heavy door closes with a thud as Meliagrance and his men depart; there is the sound of a key turning in the lock.

Guenevere's bravery collapses once we are alone. She is almost swooning with fear. Her attendants help her toward the bed that stands close to the window, shrouded from view by heavy curtains. They sweep the hangings aside and she lies down while they all fuss around her. Unexpectedly, I feel pity, for I know the fate that awaits her once Meliagrance sends for her. And yet, I know that if he ravishes her, it will change how she is perceived at court—that is, if she is allowed to return to Camelot. And isn't this exactly what I want, to drive a wedge between her and Arthur—and Launcelot? To drive her away? It seems that all my prayers have been answered without my having to do anything.

I walk across and look down at her lying on the bed. She grasps my hand, and holds it tight. "Help me, Morgana," she whispers. "For the love of our Lord, please help me!"

I shake my head. Her grip tightens. "I have heard from Arthur that you were schooled in the magical arts by Merlin. If you can think of any way out of this coil, I beg you to bring it about." Her eyes are wide with terror; her face pale as curd. In spite of myself, my pity for her intensifies. I suspect that she will not go quietly to Meliagrance's bed, and that it will be to her cost if she does not make his ravishing easy.

I am reluctant to practice magic in front of them all, for I know that Camelot is a Christian court and that the magical arts are frowned on; my own daughter has made me well aware of that. And yet it seems that I have no choice if I am to prevent her defilement by Meliagrance and her subsequent disgrace. I tell myself I should be cheering on these events but to my surprise, I find that I am not, perhaps because I know how I would feel if I were in Guenevere's place. I release her hand and walk over to the window. There is no escape down there; not by earthly means. I look behind, into the room.

The ladies are all fussing around Guenevere and only she is watching me, her desperation plain upon her face. I nod and, in the blink of an eye, I am gone; a kestrel flying swift and true toward Camelot for help.

As I fly, I see below the remains of our guard, beaten and bloody, walking slowly toward the castle under the watchful eyes of Meliagrance's men. I realize there's no chance of anyone else taking word to Camelot of our capture; it is as well that I have chosen this way out. As I pass over their heads, Agravaine glances up at me with a thoughtful expression. I feel uneasy, even as I reassure myself that he can have no way of knowing that I am anything other than a bird.

As soon as I am close to Camelot, I alight on the ground and become myself once more. I hurry into the castle and ask for an urgent audience with the king. I am told that he is in conference with Launcelot and Viviane, and cannot be disturbed, but I burst in on them anyway, believing the situation too dangerous to brook any delay whatsoever. It seems they have been discussing the quest for the Sangreal and Galahad's death, for Launcelot is visibly distressed and turns aside at my entrance. He knuckles his fingers to his eyes, and it is only when he has mastered himself that he faces me once more.

I begin to spill out my story. Arthur and Launcelot both listen in silence, as does Viviane, but as soon as I've finished my account, Launcelot offers to lead a party of warriors to release the queen.

"No!" The possible consequences of such an expedition horrify me.

Launcelot ignores my protest. "I passed that villain's castle while questing for the Sangreal," he says. "In fact, he offered his hospitality, and questioned me regarding the queen. I thought at the time he seemed overly anxious to have news of her. Now I know why!" His expression hardens as he rises to his feet and reaches for his sword.

I look at Arthur, willing him to remember my warning and recognize the danger. But he does not. Instead he gladly accepts Launcelot's offer.

"Should you not go with Launcelot, Arthur?" In my desperation I forget to honor him with the respectful title I usually employ in public. My brother frowns in displeasure.

"I am needed here, at Camelot, to deal with affairs of state," he says. "I trust Launcelot in all things, Morgana, and I can think of no one better able to rescue the queen than her own champion."

It is clear that he will brook no interference from me; I can say no more. To my surprise, Viviane takes up the argument.

"Surely there is no more important task in your kingdom than the rescue of your queen, my liege?"

Arthur flushes with temper. "And that is why I have entrusted the task to my best and bravest knight," he snaps.

"But Sir Meliagrance may—"

"There is no time for argument, Viviane." Arthur has risen and now he pushes Launcelot toward the door. "Pray, find a party of good men and ride to Meliagrance's castle at all speed," he instructs. "Make sure you bring him to Camelot in chains, for I shall ensure he suffers sorely for his deeds this day. We await your return with every expectation of your success." He raises his hand in a gesture of farewell.

Viviane and I exchange a glance; for the first time it appears we are in agreement. My suspicion is confirmed as she walks out of the hall with me, and guides me toward Guenevere's private garden.

"The king will regret his actions this day. He should have sent anyone but Launcelot to rescue the queen," she says quietly.

"I agree." In fact, I am filled with fear. "Being away from Camelot will give them an opportunity they will not be able to resist, and I dread the consequences," I say. "There is already far too much affection between them. Even if Arthur isn't aware of it, the situation is causing division among the knights. I'm afraid Mordred is behind much of their disquiet; he is stirring up trouble by saying that it is a weak king who cannot control his own wife, and that Arthur has grown too old to rule Camelot. Mordred's aim is to gain their allegiance as the son and only heir of the king."

Viviane shoots a quick glance at me. "But isn't that your intention, Morgana? Or should I call you Nimue?"

I blink as she utters the name of my disguise. I had often wondered just how much she could see and how much she knew, but had reassured myself with the thought that most of what she said seemed to be merely guesswork. But perhaps I was the one who was deluded? I can't think of anything to say now, so I keep silent.

"And what happens next will help to bring about the doom of Camelot," Viviane mutters, as if to herself.

I am instantly alarmed, both on my own behalf and for the sake of my children. "Not if Arthur names someone else as his heir, as I have already asked him to do." I cannot accept, as Viviane seems to, that our fate cannot be changed and consequences avoided. I would not be here if I thought that.

Viviane shakes her head and does not reply. Instead, she asks a question of her own. "How do you know of this, Morgana? Were you with the queen when she was abducted?" Her clear gray eyes seem to see right through me and I realize that she probably already knows the answer.

"Yes, I was there."

"How did you manage to get away and come back to Camelot so quickly?"

I think of several answers, but suspect that she will believe none of them. I sigh. "Through magic." I will not tell her what I have done, or how I managed to achieve it. Fortunately, she does not ask.

"Perhaps you'd better get back there and keep an eye on proceedings," she says instead, adding as an afterthought, "And if you can keep Launcelot away from the queen, so much the better."

She is speaking my mind. I retreat behind a high hedge, for I don't wish to be observed, particularly by Viviane. But she watches me as I soar above her head in the direction of Meliagrance's castle. The thought of Launcelot spurring forward to rescue the queen adds speed to my wings, so I am quite breathless by the time I alight on the windowsill of Guenevere's prison.

I am relieved to see that nothing of great event seems to have happened in my absence. The queen is still prostrate upon the bed; her ladies are still fluttering about her. The wounded knights of her party are also present; those who are less badly hurt are trying to take care of the more grievously wounded among them. I hop down and quietly transform myself. My sudden presence among the company merits no more than a half-glance.

Guenevere sees me, and waves her ladies away. "Do you have news?" she asks urgently.

I hesitate. I have flown in advance of Launcelot and his companions, but have no doubt they are flogging their steeds to get here as fast as possible. I decide to keep the details of Guenevere's rescue attempt as vague as I can.

"The king has sent a large party of knights," I reassure her. "It is up to you, my lady, to stall Meliagrance for as long as possible."

"Is the king among them?"

"No, my lady."

Guenevere sighs. I suspect she shares my opinion of Arthur's apparent reluctance to involve himself in affairs of the heart.

"What about Launcelot? Is he among them?"

Reluctantly, I nod.

"I warrant Meliagrance only dared lay his filthy hands on me because Launcelot was absent from our riding party," the queen says angrily. "He will soon change his mind about keeping us when he knows who comes to my rescue." Her face is all sunshine now that she knows her beloved is on his way.

"It would be best not to threaten Meliagrance, my lady. For now, he thinks he has you secure, and that no one knows where you are. Do not warn him; do not give him time to prepare a counter-attack."

The queen tips her head to one side as she considers my words. "You are right, Morgana. And I thank you for undertaking this task on my behalf."

It occurs to me that perhaps my actions this day will take me some way further toward my rehabilitation at court, and for this I am grateful. I leave her then, and go to tend the wounded knights as best I may, given the lack of medicaments at my disposal. But a bath has been brought and filled with water and rose petals, presumably for the queen to bathe in before giving herself to Meliagrance, although she has obviously not yet availed herself of this convenience. So there is clean water to bathe the wounds of the knights, while the hems of the ladies' undergarments may be torn into bandages. Although they protest somewhat, Guenevere orders them to do as I ask, and my ministrations bring some relief to the men.

We are summoned to dinner in the Great Hall. A feast is laid out on a snowy white cloth, but none of us has the appetite to do it justice. Meliagrance and his men set about gorging themselves, working their way through salmon and duck, wild boar and a baron of beef, all accompanied by huge quantities of wine and ale. I am hoping they will drink themselves into a state of insensibility, but Meliagrance is too canny for that. He is seated between the queen and me, and as the honey wafers and fruits preserved in syrup are passed around, I am well able to hear when he leans over to Guenevere and tells her that she is to come to his chamber at the conclusion of the meal.

"No," she says, in a voice that quavers slightly. "My lord, I cannot."

"My queen, you will." The menace is apparent in his eyes, and in the way he takes hold of her arm in an iron grip.

I struggle to find something to say to put off the evil moment, for Launcelot and his men, riding as hard as their horses will bear them, must surely come soon.

"The queen has been quite overcome with the shock of what has happened to her and her knights," I say. "She has been too faint and unwell to bathe as yet, but would like to do so before ever she comes to your bedchamber, lord."

Meliagrance scowls, but I can see gratitude in Guenevere's eyes.

"Very well," he says curtly. "But do not tarry. I have waited long enough for you, and my patience is growing very thin indeed."

"Shall I bathe?" Guenevere asks me, when once we are back in our chamber.

"No. You must keep yourself ready to leave, for help must come soon." I wonder if she is always so helpless in times of trial. But I hide my irritation and go to stand beside the window, watching for signs of Launcelot and his men.

The afternoon wears on; the rays of the setting sun slant across the courtyard bathing it in a rosy glow that belies the chill of desperation permeating the room in which we are incarcerated. Meliagrance's patience will not last forever. The chatter has died away; everyone sits silently. Guenevere's face is gray, haunted. I feel sorry for her, and wonder now that I could ever have wished her dead.

Perhaps it is Launcelot who will die instead, cut down in battle by Meliagrance or one of his men? I put my hand to my heart at the shock of the idea, although I know it would solve a good many problems if it came about. But the very thought of it so grieves me that I cannot prevent despairing tears flooding into my eyes. I try to force my mind on to more cheerful thoughts, but the possibility of Launcelot's death lurks like a black shadow.

I feel excitement mingled with dread when, finally, I hear a warning cry from below. I look down from my seat at the window. The courtyard is swarming with armed knights. Launcelot has come at last and he and his party are wasting no time in hacking their way toward their queen.

"Help has arrived! The king has sent a party to free us," I call out.

At once there is a pushing and jostling as everyone tries to get to the windows to see what's happening. I am shoved aside by the queen herself. With flashing eyes and gasping breaths, she gazes down at her beloved, and I remember all over again why I hate her. But there is no time to reflect on this for there is the sound of cheering, followed by the thunder of feet coming toward us.

The door swings open and hits the wall with a thud. Launcelot is already halfway across the room, his arms held out. The queen rushes into his embrace and, in front of all assembled, they kiss.

Excited cheering has given way to a deep hush as we all witness the intensity of their devotion and the passion of their kiss. Becoming conscious of his surroundings, Launcelot thrusts the queen away from him and sinks onto his knees.

"I am at your service, my lady."

But the damage is done. No one present can doubt that the rumors swirling around the pair must be true. Guenevere knows it too, for a deep blush stains her fair complexion as she gives Launcelot her hand and bids him rise.

"I beg your pardon, my lady," he stammers. "I was overcome by my fear for your safety."

"And I thank you for your concern, Sir Launcelot." Is there a tinge of self-satisfaction in her voice? "Fortunately, I shall be able to reassure the king that no one has had knowledge of me to which he is not entitled."

Perhaps this is meant as a reproof to all present for what they must now be thinking, but I am fearful. Having impersonated the queen when I lay with Launcelot, I know that he now believes that he does, in fact, have intimate knowledge of Guenevere. I cross my fingers behind my back, and pray that he will not betray the secret.

"It is a great relief to me to hear you say that you are unharmed, my lady," Launcelot assures her gravely.

The queen is still flushed; her breath has slowed, but her eyes are bright as fire. It seems that all her fear has flown now that Launcelot is present. More, his embrace has kindled a desire that burns across her face for all to see.

"Where is Meliagrance?" she asks.

"In chains and locked up." Launcelot surveys her with a smile. "You have no more to fear." The queen exhales, visibly relieved. Their eyes lock, and hold; the connection between them is plain.

I am becoming increasingly anxious. "It is growing dark, my lady. We really should set out for Camelot without delay." The courtyard is already in deep shadow, but even if it means riding at night I would rather take that risk than stay here.

"Nonsense. We are quite safe now; we have Sir Launcelot's assurance on that." The queen flashes a quick smile in his direction. "I am completely worn out and undone by the travails of the day, as I am sure are all of you. We shall abide here for the night, and take our rest. Tomorrow will be soon enough to return to Camelot."

I can see the queen's suggestion is welcome to all; indeed, I am also weary beyond measure. It is only my concern that drives me to make one last protest.

"The king will be worried about you, my lady. I am sure he will fear the worst if you do not return this evening."

Guenevere does not deign to reply. Launcelot gives me a quizzical look, and I realize that he now has proof, if proof were needed, that I do indeed possess magical powers.

"The king knows that the queen is in good hands. He would not want her to tire herself unnecessarily," he says.

I am defeated, and I know it.

Several knights have gone scavenging, and now they return with armfuls of pallets, some of which they scatter around the room, while the rest are reserved for the knights who will sleep in the room across the passage. Launcelot and Guenevere are huddled in the corner. I long to know what they are saying, for my fear increases moment by moment. But the knights gravely give the ladies good wishes for the night, and take their leave. I am relieved to see Launcelot is among them.

With as good a grace as I can muster, I prepare myself for bed, as do Guenevere's ladies. After some thought, I position my pallet as close to the queen as I dare, perhaps with some thought of warding off danger, although I am unsure who or what I most fear.

I cannot sleep. The night is awash with moonlight and starshine. The scent of the briar roses perfumes the air. It is a night for lovers, and I ache with loneliness. I do not mean to keep vigil, but the hours pass and the darkness deepens, and still I cannot sleep. And then I become aware of small sounds outside: the rustle of leaves, a grunt, a quiet curse. A face appears at the window. Only with difficulty do I suppress a small squeak of alarm—until I recognize our night visitor. It is Launcelot.

His hands are on the bars and he heaves and strains, and I pray that he will be defeated. But he is not. One of the bars gives way, and he turns his attention to the one beside it. Once he has made enough space, he wriggles through and quietly steps down from the windowsill into the room.

I realize then that I am not the only one who has kept vigil. Guenevere props herself up on one arm, and beckons him across to her bed. I'm about to shout a warning, but realize that they would be fatally compromised in the eyes of the court if I did so. Instead, I leap up and stand in Launcelot's path. But he sweeps me aside and disappears behind the bed hangings that Guenevere closes to screen what will happen next.

But the fabric cannot stifle the sounds they make, and even though I put my fingers in my ears, I hear every soft cry of pleasure, every sigh of delight. It is as if a thousand knives are cutting into me, so great is my pain, my grief—and my envy. I reflect that unknowingly, they have taken their revenge on me this night for all the harm I have done to them in the past. And I wish, more than anything, that I had positioned my pallet as far from the queen as was possible.

An even greater alarm presents itself for my inspection. The potion I had brewed for Guenevere ensured that she would never bear a child to Arthur. Would it also hold true for Launcelot? I close my eyes, thinking I shall surely die if a child results from their union this night.

Sighs of delight have given way to a soft murmuring, which gradually changes to muffled cries and moans as they come together once more. The thought of the pleasure they are taking with each other awakens my own desire, which nothing can assuage. I ache with wanting; I am hollow with loss. Every moment lasts an hour, and I believe that this night will never be over.

Fortunately Launcelot has the good sense to creep out of our chamber before daybreak. I watch his dark form squeeze between the bars, and hear once more the grunts and soft curses as he works his thorny way down to the ground. But his passage is clear for all to see when the ladies awake. Guenevere is still asleep, with a smile curving her lips, but it vanishes as she wakes and hears the squeaks and exclamations of alarm.

"Someone has come into our room in the night!" One of her ladies gestures toward the broken bars and the drops of bright red blood that lead a telltale trail to Guenevere's bed. Launcelot must have injured himself in his desperation to get to the queen.

Guenevere slowly draws herself up, no doubt giving herself time to think. "It must have been one of the wounded knights," she declares, looking around. Her gaze alights on me and on my pallet, the closest to her bed. "Morgana, have you had a visitor in the night?"

I read the appeal in her eyes, but I am too furious to respond to it. She was the one who had branded me a whore at Camelot; she will not have the chance to do so again.

"No, my lady," I say. "I slept single all night."

"Then who could it be?" She throws out an arm in appeal to her ladies. They exchange uneasy glances before turning to stare at me.

"No!" But my cry in my own defense stands for nothing as they recall the gossip and innuendo that has circulated around the court in the past. Their hostile faces tell me that I stand condemned, with no way of proving otherwise.

The knights knock and enter at the queen's bidding. The ladies break into small groups; they huddle together, surveying each of the knights and with covert looks in my direction. I don't need to hear their whispers to know what they're saying, and my anger intensifies.

Launcelot approaches the queen. Now that the danger is past, she has a new air of serenity, the small lines of frustration are smoothed from her face. She is truly happy. Launcelot makes his obeisance and smiles at her with deep tenderness.

She touches his arm; he puts his hand over hers, and quickly withdraws it. I sense how difficult their restraint must be after their night of love. They stand close together, as close as they dare. And I feel faint with jealousy, and silently curse the knowledge of magic that has brought about my doom.

The ladies do not even look their way. Nor do the knights, for by now everyone knows what has happened and is busy looking everywhere but at Launcelot for the man who has shared my bed.

I can't stand it any longer. I leave the room.

CHAPTER 15

Once out in the courtyard I pace around, breathing in great gulps of cool morning air as I try to calm down. I am seething over the fact that Launcelot and Guenevere will happily let me take the blame for their misdeeds and that my name will once more be blackened throughout the kingdom. But I am also sick with worry. It seems to me that their actions have brought the prophecy of the tablets several steps closer to fulfilment, while the prospect of Guenevere bearing a child to Launcelot fills me with absolute horror. And so I pace, and pace, and mutter to myself, but without coming to any conclusion as to a way forward that will help to turn things around, let alone clear my name.

"Would it help if I said that I found it difficult to sleep last night; that I saw Launcelot leave our room and that he was absent for quite a few hours?"

I haven't heard Agravaine approach. Now he surveys me with bright, questioning eyes as he falls into step beside me.

"Really?"

He nods. "But you make a convenient scapegoat, of course."

"Of course." I cannot keep the rancor from my voice.

"The question is: was this the first time? How long has Arthur been a cuckold?"

I remember Agravaine's disposition to spread rumors, and keep silent. The knowledge that he holds endangers us all, yet I feel comforted to think that at least someone knows the truth.

"Shall I tell the king of my observations?" Agravaine muses. "It's about time someone did."

"He should have come to rescue Guenevere himself."

"What I can't help wondering, Aunt, is how the king came to find out our whereabouts quite as soon as he did?" Agravaine tilts his head on the side, rather like a bird watching for worms.

I shrug in a non-committal fashion. I'm certainly not going to confirm what he obviously suspects.

"So where did you disappear to, Aunt, for I know you were absent when first we arrived under guard and yet you appeared quite out of the blue sky later?"

"I have been nowhere of note." I curse his sharp eyes, and fear his busy tongue. Soon enough, Camelot will have plenty to talk about without also being awash with rumors of sorcery.

Agravaine sighs. "We all know that you were schooled in magic by Merlin, Morgana. Arthur admitted as much to the whole court during the affair of the false scabbard that implicated Accolon. Of course, the deadly cloak only reinforced everyone's opinion of you as a sorceress." He smiles at me. "But have no fear; I rather admire you. In fact I wish I had some magical abilities of my own." His tone becomes wholly serious as he continues. "If you can use your magic to put an end to this affair between Launcelot and the queen, I suggest you do so. The knights are fast losing respect for Arthur, and this will only reinforce their belief that he is no longer fit to rule."

"Leaving the way free for Mordred."

"Who would be a disaster."

I shrug again. "I don't know what to do," I admit.

"Tell Arthur. And I'll back you up."

"I've already tried to warn him—and was given a tongue-lashing for my pains."

Agravaine looks thoughtful. "Be of good cheer, Morgana," he says at last. "Maybe there's a way to make Arthur face the truth—and clear your good name at the same time."

I press him for details, but he will say nothing further. He leaves me in the courtyard and disappears inside once more. I wonder what he has in mind, and suspect that whatever it is will count for nothing against Arthur's refusal to believe the worst of his queen and her champion.

I have not yet broken my fast, but am too angry and too ill to eat. I am keen to be gone. I wonder if it might be possible to persuade Viviane to help me convince Arthur that Launcelot should leave the court. Would she be prepared to put aside her suspicion of me and prove a worthy ally?

My thoughts move on. If Launcelot left the court, where would he go? To Joyous Garde? I close my eyes, remembering our time there and how happy we once were. And I wonder if it might be possible to follow him there. Could we make a life together once more? True, he has much to forgive, but his character is no longer without blemish; he cannot be too proud. And he now depends on my silence.

I am still lost in thought as our party finally assembles in the courtyard, with Meliagrance in chains and under guard. Grooms are ordered to saddle our mounts, and we start the journey back to Camelot. I am conscious of the stares and sneers of the rest of the party. One of the grooms, with a sidelong peek in my direction, circles his thumb and forefinger around his nose in an unmistakably crude image of the sexual act. To chastise him would only add fuel to an already blazing fire, but for my own peace of mind I cannot stand to witness any further evidence of the court's contempt. And so I ride to the front of the party, and thereafter keep close to Guenevere and Launcelot, hoping my presence will act as a silent reproach and a prickle to their consciences.

But the reckoning cannot be put off indefinitely. Arthur greets Guenevere with a chaste kiss on each cheek and then turns his attention to Meliagrance. He abuses the knight in front of all the court, but Meliagrance unexpectedly defends himself with an attack on Guenevere.

"You should know, noble king, that although I had intentions to bed your queen, I failed in my quest—unlike your most trusted knight and greatest friend, who went to your queen's bed last night and had unlawful knowledge of her."

The court falls silent, stunned by his words. I glance at Guenevere; she is deathly pale. But Launcelot stands up to Meliagrance. "You lying hound," he shouts. "It was the Lady Morgana who entertained a man in her bed last night."

I close my eyes, shattered to the core by Launcelot's betrayal.

"I was kept in chains in the same room as your knights. I saw you creep out under cover of darkness, and I've been told you left a trail of blood from the window to the queen's bed." Meliagrance points at the bandage on Launcelot's hand. "Where did you cut yourself if not when you broke through the bars to get to the queen?"

"I injured my hand during the melee against your men. It was too painful for me to sleep, and so I rose from my bed and went walking out into the forest. You must look elsewhere rather than make accusations against me."

I've had enough of their lies. I will not let my name be maligned further. "Let me assure you, Arthur, neither Sir Launcelot nor anyone else came to *my* bed in the night."

There is a deathly hush as everyone waits for the king to say something. But Guenevere speaks first. "And let me assure everyone here today that my honor remains intact! You must look elsewhere for an explanation of this so-called midnight intruder."

I had thought Agravaine might speak up in support of Meliagrance's accusation. I realize that it would be futile for him to try when Arthur places his arm around his wife and glares at Meliagrance. "You shall pay dearly for your deeds, and for maligning the queen in this manner, and before the court." And I know that Guenevere and Launcelot have won at my expense when Launcelot challenges Meliagrance to combat, which, he says, will end only when Meliagrance is dead.

And so the time of their battle is arranged. I do not expect any good to come of it, for I know Launcelot will easily best Meliagrance, which will further endear him to the queen, and further undermine my good name. I am half expecting Arthur to banish me once more, but he does not. I wonder if, in his heart, he knows the pair are lying, but thinks to divert attention from them by keeping me the focus of the court's malicious rumors. I debate leaving anyway, but in the end I do not and so I continue to endure the sneers and whispers until the time comes for us to assemble at the tourney field to witness the combat.

The two knights are dressed for battle. Lances at the ready, they gallop toward each other. A thunderous roar erupts from the crowd as Launcelot easily unhorses Meliagrance. He springs from the saddle, ready to meet Meliagrance with drawn sword as the knight slowly rises, takes up his sword and comes at him. They slash and clash together with a ringing of steel, with grunts and with muttered oaths, neither of them yielding until Launcelot momentarily breaks free. He raises his sword and brings it down on Meliagrance's head, cleaving his helmet in two and giving him the death stroke.

More cheering rewards Launcelot for his victory. I watch, stony faced, as Guenevere decorously extends her hand for him to kiss, and congratulates him on his prowess. Arthur, meanwhile, seems overcome with joy, apparently taking this as proof of Meliagrance's lies.

"We shall have a feast this night," he declares, as the knight's body is removed from the field, and everyone lines up behind the royal party, and the victor, to escort them off the field.

"Take heart, Morgana." Agravaine is by my side once more. "The truth will out; my brothers and I shall see to it."

"But how?"

Agravaine taps the side of his nose. "When the time is right."

"For what?"

He smiles, but will say nothing further.

*

We are seated at dinner later when a messenger appears and asks for me. Puzzled, I follow him to an antechamber, and am stunned to find my daughter waiting for me.

"Marie!" Delighted as I am to see her, I am furious that she has disobeyed my order to stay at the priory. I cannot keep the displeasure from my voice. "What brings you here?"

"A thousand pardons, Mamm, for breaking my word to you, but I had to come. I need to ask for your blessing." She raises her face to mine, and I see how pale and strained she looks. I am so moved I cannot help but put my arms around her in a close embrace.

"Why do you seek my blessing?"

"I have decided to take my vows and give my life to Christ." Her voice quavers slightly. I marvel at her courage; she knows well how I must feel, hearing her request. Indeed, shock and rage chase through my mind, but in the end I decide it best not to reject her outright.

"What has led you to this decision?"

"It is the only life I know. And I am comfortable at the priory."

I snort with laughter, I cannot help myself. "We should ask more of our lives than comfort and safety, Marie!"

"But it is the life you have made for me," she says, with a mischievous glance in my direction.

She is sharp, my daughter! I try another tack. "And is it really your desire to give your life to Christ, without knowing anything of the world beyond the priory?"

"How can I know for sure, unless you let me stay here for a time, Mamm?"

She has outwitted me, the little fox! Whether her desire to become a nun is true or not, I suspect that her real intention in coming here is to find her father and at the same time experience what life is like at court.

"Very well. You are here now, and so we must make the best of it." My mind spins as I question how I should introduce Marie to my brother and Guenevere. In the present circumstances, Marie's presence can only reinforce their opinion of me as the court's whore if I call Launcelot as her father. And if I speak of Urien instead, Marie will contradict me, for she knows the truth and will let no one say different. A shudder of foreboding runs through me as I consider how Launcelot—and also Mordred—will react.

She looks around, her eyes widening as she notices the hall beyond the antechamber, with its round table arrayed with multiple dishes of food, and the diners seated around it in their costly attire. I can well imagine her awe after knowing only the confines of the priory.

"We are feasting tonight. You must join us." In my distraction, I hardly know what I'm saying.

"A feast!" She claps her hands together. "What are you celebrating?"

"Sir Launcelot fought a duel against another knight today, and killed him." If I'd thought the news would upset my pious daughter, I was wrong. Her face glows with pride.

I take her hand and lead her into the hall, though I dread to think the stories she will be told about me. All fall silent as they watch me approach Arthur and Guenevere with my daughter in tow.

"My liege and my queen, may I present to you my daughter, Marie."

Marie makes her obeisance, while I wait for Arthur's inevitable question.

To my relief, he says instead, "You are most welcome to Camelot, Marie."

"No wonder you kept her birth a secret, for she doesn't look anything like Urien," Guenevere observes, with some glee. I wonder if she has the wit to tell who Marie does resemble. "Perhaps it is time we arranged a new husband for you, Morgana," the queen continues.

I check my anger with difficulty, and hasten Marie away before anyone can question us further. But I am conscious of the whispers behind hands as we pass. My anger returns anew as I realize it's only a matter of time before someone feels it their duty to enlighten Marie regarding the reason for the celebration and the rumors behind it.

"Which one is Launcelot?" Marie whispers, once we are seated.

I point him out. He is seated beside Guenevere and Marie watches him in silence for a time. Then she turns to me.

"My father is now besotted with the queen, is he not? And she loves him. Is that why she was so lacking in courtesy toward you?"

What can I say? I shrug.

"You say you still love him, Mamm. But he no longer loves you?"

"No. Not any more." How it pains me to say that.

Marie lapses into silence, still keeping the pair under observation. I notice, however, that this does not impede her appetite. My little sparrow is eating like a bull. I can hardly blame her, after the austerity of the fare at the priory. Now she is stuffing her mouth with snatches of this and bites of that, tasting everything and coming back for more. The pages are kept busy with her demands, but I notice that although her cup is kept full of wine, she takes only a frugal sip every so often.

Musicians have been playing softly to entertain us as we eat. Now, as trenchers are cleared to make way for fruit and pastries, a group of tumblers and jugglers appear. Quick of wit and sleight of hand, they keep us entertained—and Marie in fits of laughter—with their antics. I realize, with a slight shock, that I have never seen my daughter in such transports of delight.

Next, a young man with a lute appears. I recognize him from one of Guenevere's entourage, a rather tiresome young lad and an inferior poet, although his voice is pleasant enough as he serenades his queen and all in attendance. Guenevere favors him with a smile, but most of her attention is reserved for Launcelot.

I sense my daughter's growing disapproval, although she doesn't voice it. She settles back and gazes around the company. I hear a stifled gasp and feel her stiffen beside me. Alarmed, I turn to her. She is staring across the room. Following her gaze, I discover that she is being stared at in return. Indeed, the young man's eyes are almost starting out of his head, his expression is so intent.

Guinglain. His father has also become aware of the intensity of this first sighting between our offspring, and we exchange smiles. I am overcome with relief. All I can think of at this moment is that Marie may yet be saved from a life in the priory!

"Who is that handsome young man, Mamm?" she whispers, tearing her gaze away from Guinglain for a few moments.

"He is Guinglain, son of Gawain and grandson of my sister, Morgause."

"We are related?" There is such great disappointment in her tone that I rejoice anew.

"Not too close that a marriage would be prevented." I hope I am right in saying this, but I also know that there are ways and means around it, if necessary.

She laughs in protest. "I haven't yet met him, and already you are thinking marriage? For shame, Mamm!" But there is a slight smile on her face as she feasts her eyes on the young man once more.

Her preoccupation frees me to wrestle with the problems she presents by appearing so unexpectedly at court. I cannot see any way out of this coil that won't put her in danger, while further blackening my name. But I console myself with the thought that Marie already knows the worst: that Launcelot and I were not wed when she was conceived. Her opinion is the only one I truly care about.

I steal a glance at Mordred. He, too, is looking our way, and with a face as forbidding as thunder. He must not have any chance to be alone with Marie. I make a silent vow that if he tries to harm her, he will have to kill me first.

The meal finally comes to an end; it is time for judgment. I am wondering how best to approach Launcelot when, to my surprise, he hurries toward us.

"Marie." He takes her hand and raises it to his lips, all the while subjecting her to a close inspection. I wonder if she will say anything to him but she is blushing, and seems too shy to speak.

"How many years are you, Marie?" he asks, still keeping hold of her hand. Now that they are standing together like this, side by side, I am conscious of the similarities in their features rather than the differences I'd thought were there before. It seems to me, from Launcelot's question, that he too has understood their significance.

"Twenty summers, sire."

There is a slight frown on Launcelot's face as he does a swift calculation. Then he looks at me, and I know that he knows, and that I can dissemble no longer.

"Meet your daughter, Launcelot," I say softly.

Shock keeps him motionless as he grapples with the truth. Although he must have expected it, I can see that he is overcome. He keeps holding Marie's hand as if it were a lifeline.

"Why did you not tell me?" he asks at last.

I shrug. The misery of our parting cut so deep that the wound is still festering, kept toxic by all that has passed between us since that time. All, that is, except for when he lay with me thinking I was Guenevere. But I shall never, ever, confess to that!

"I owe you an apology," he says.

"You owe me more than one!"

"Yes." He inclines his head. He seems about to say something else but, perhaps because of Marie, he hesitates, then says, "You have been much maligned in court, Morgana, and I greatly regret it, especially as I know there is no truth in the accusation." He turns to his daughter. "Please remember my words, Marie, no matter what anyone else might tell you."

"I know that you were not wed when I was conceived, if that is what is worrying you. But I am so glad to meet you at last," she says, her face radiant with wonder.

"As I am delighted to meet you." Launcelot swallows hard, and makes a visible effort to collect himself. "I had a son, Galahad, who died shortly after finding the Sangreal. When I heard the news, I thought I might die too." He presses her hand. "You have given me good reason to live, child, and I thank you for it."

"More reason than the love of our queen?"

Launcelot gasps at Marie's presumption. Even I am taken aback.

"Our daughter has been raised in a priory," I say quickly. "She knows little of court etiquette. You must forgive her naivety, Launcelot."

Marie frowns as she looks from her father to me. "You lay with Launcelot when you were not wed; you told me that yourself. You also said that you loved him, and that you love him still. But it is clear that my father dotes on the queen."

"Marie!" I grab her arm, ready to drag her away.

Unexpectedly, Launcelot gives a gruff laugh. "The queen has my loyalty and allegiance, and yes, I am fond of her, Marie. But it would be high treason to love her or lie with her, so you must not ever say such things again." I read the appeal in his eyes as he glances at me, and I give a slight nod. For his sake, I shall say no more.

"I hope you will stay here at Camelot for some time, Marie, and give me a chance to come to know you?" I detect a slight nervousness in Launcelot's tone. I suspect he has already taken Marie's measure and understands that her keen scrutiny and quick mind will not leave much room for hiding and deception. Nevertheless, it seems he truly cares for her and is grateful to have a daughter, for he bends to kiss her on the forehead.

I hear a low moan from behind us, and turn just in time to see Guenevere vanishing through the door. I feel a moment of fierce triumph and joy. Launcelot has also marked the queen's retreat. He looks devastated, and is about to hurry after her when Gawain arrives, with Guinglain in tow.

"I will be given no peace until I present my son to Marie, Morgana." He frowns at Launcelot, no doubt curious about his presence by my side.

"Marie, this is Guinglain, and his father, Gawain." I put my hand on Launcelot's arm, thinking I might as well get it over with, for it will be all around the court soon enough. "And this is Marie's father."

I read the shock on their faces, and smile grimly to myself. Their shock is as nothing compared to Guenevere's. I wonder if she'll ever forgive Launcelot.

Marie and Guinglan retreat a little way. Their heads come together in deep conversation, while Gawain and Launcelot stand a little apart, not looking at each other. I cannot speak my heart to Launcelot with Gawain present, nor can I find the words to smooth over an awkward situation. Finally, Gawain gives me a shame-faced smile, and makes a poor excuse about having something to attend to before hurrying away.

"Gawain will see this as yet more proof of my loose morals," I say bitterly, and gesture toward Marie and Guinglan. They appear rapt in each other and oblivious to all else. "You had better pray that he doesn't interfere with this relationship on the grounds that Marie's mother spreads her favors too freely and that Marie is not worthy of his son. I will not see her happiness jeopardized by a lie."

"I will not allow Gawain to think so!"

"You'll tell the truth about your night with Guenevere?"

Launcelot is silent. I know that he cannot, will not, put the queen in danger, nor will he sacrifice his own safety. There is nothing for me here, and I turn to go.

He catches my hand. "Marie said that you love me, and that you love me still," he says softly, in a tone that I recognize from our time together at Joyous Garde when I was so happy; when I thought our love would last forever. It is enough to utterly undo me. I feel tears spring hot and heavy in my eyes, and I cannot speak. He wipes away my tears before they can fall.

"I have been cruel and unkind to you, and very unfair. I was also far too quick to judge you, and I am more sorry than I can say," he tells me.

I gulp and nod.

"But you understand why I need to keep silent now?"

I will not say yes. I will not grant him absolution. I stay mute.

He sighs. "I loved you too, more than you will ever know. After you left I searched for you everywhere, thinking I had been wrong to insist on coming to Camelot alone so that I could give the appearance of being impartial. Because I was not impartial, I was determined to prove you innocent of all charges. After you left, I realized that I should have brought you with me so that we could face your accusers together. That was my first big mistake with you."

I stay silent, consumed with guilt and regret. I can find no words of comfort to say.

"But my biggest mistake was to fall in love with Guenevere. And yet I know not how that came about, because I loved you still." Launcelot's brow creases into a worried frown. "One moment she was just a rather silly young woman, albeit the consort of a king. The next …" He shakes his head. "It's like an enchantment that I cannot escape. I don't know how else to explain it."

Launcelot has explained it perfectly. I am engulfed in misery. I, in turn, should not have been so quick to judge him. I should have listened more carefully to what he was saying; I should not have acted so hastily. I have no one to blame but myself for what followed. Yet I can no more confess the part I have played in our downfall than he can confess his night with the queen.

"I spoke the truth to Marie," I tell him. "Yes, I was angry when I fled Joyous Garde, and yes, I misunderstood your motives for acting as you did. But I have always loved you, Launcelot. And I always will."

"Your beautiful tapestries still hang in my hall, a constant reminder of the love we once shared." He leans down to kiss my cheek. I long to put my arms around him, to draw him closer and show him my need. But I know that to do so will achieve nothing. Nevertheless, for those fleeting moments I relish the smell and feel of him, so familiar and that I have missed for so long.

As he straightens, we become aware of a furious shouting in the distance: screams and wild cries and heartfelt sobbing. "The queen," I say, and he nods. We both know the source of her wrath and her grief.

"I must go to her," Launcelot says, and hurries out of the hall.

Curious, I wait a few moments, and then venture after him. I am just in time to watch him disappear into Guenevere's private solar and the door slam shut behind him. It opens again almost immediately and her retinue of women emerge. They close the door but do not disperse. Instead, they huddle close and listen intently. I join them.

"How could you lie with that whore?" Guenevere screams.

"You will not refer to Morgana in those terms. It is unjust, and I forbid it."

"I'll call her what I will!"

"Do so, and I shall refute your words with the truth of what happened at Meliagrance's castle." There is a moment's silence, broken by a howl of fury.

"I mean it, Guenevere."

"Get out! Get out of my sight! I hate you!"

We hastily disperse, moving away just in time to hear the door open and quietly close, after which a wild sobbing breaks out once more. Guenevere's ladies look at each other, sigh, shrug, and go to do what they may to comfort their mistress. I peep into the hall, where servants are busily clearing up the remains of our feast.

Marie and Guinglan still stand to one side, talking softly. I hope they are making the most of this time together. I suspect Marie has now given up all thoughts of taking her vows—if her threat was ever real in the first place. Smiling to myself, I approach them and give a slight cough to attract their attention.

"May I leave you safely in the hands of Guinglan, Marie? I do not want you wandering around the court on your own." Perhaps Guinglan hears the concern in my voice for he assures me that he will take good care of my daughter until my return.

I venture out into the garden, needing the peace and quiet of nature to ponder all I have seen and heard and felt these past few hours, for in truth I feel as though I have been swept up in a whirlwind, and my spirits are battered and bruised because of it. More than anything, I need to find my calm center once more. And I need to come up with a way to keep my daughter safe.

CHAPTER 16

There is much to bring me joy, and also to cause me worry, in the weeks following Marie's unexpected appearance at court. She has resisted all my attempts to send her back to the safety of the priory and so I have emphasized the unrest and danger here at court, without being too specific as to its nature. I have also instructed her to make sure that she is always in company with others when she is not with me. Although she expressed her surprise, she has given me her word, easing somewhat my fears for her safety. To my joy, she and Guinglan have become inseparable, to the extent that Gawain approaches me with both an apology and some words of the future.

"I have spoken to Agravaine," he tells me. "I have heard what really happened on that night in Meliagrance's castle, and I ask your forgiveness for misjudging you, Morgana."

I nod, knowing it could only have been a matter of time before Agravaine confided in his brothers. He ever loves to garner information, and delights in spreading it.

"The problem is that most of the knights also know the truth now. Probably all of them, in fact, with the exception of Arthur." Gawain's voice is grave as he continues. "Mordred, of course, is using it to his advantage among the younger knights to sow more trouble against the king."

"You must stop him, Gawain. He is a danger to us all."

"I know. And I say what I can, although I suspect that even while the knights listen to me, they reject what I am telling them." Gawain gives an unhappy sigh. "I am sure there is a plot afoot, but I don't know what it is. I suspect Agravaine knows of it, but even he won't tell me."

I remember Agravaine's promise to me. I had almost forgotten it, but now I feel cold tentacles of fear wrap around my body, and I shiver. "I hope they will do nothing rash." The doom of Camelot, foretold by the tablets, comes to the forefront of my mind once more. I vow to increase my efforts to alert Arthur to the danger of his queen's love for Launcelot, and his son's hatred and ambition.

Gawain shakes his head. "It is ever in a young knight's nature to be rash," he says somberly. "They need wise heads to guide them—not that any young person will ever believe it until they themselves have the gray hairs that denote some getting of wisdom." He shrugs, as if mentally freeing himself of a burden. "However, there is one young couple who has my blessing. I believe Guinglan is in love with Marie and serious about making a life with her. Do you have any objections to that, Morgana?"

"None at all!" My heart lifts with joy. "I haven't dared speak to Marie of this, for fear of endangering their romance, but I shall speak to her if you wish?"

"No." Gawain's smile broadens. "Let's not interfere. Let them believe they are the first to ever experience the joy of love and the ends to which that might lead."

"Marie is slightly older than Guinglan, but she is chaste and unworldly, having known only her life in the priory. I trust that he will treat her well, and with honor?" I can't help feeling anxious about my beloved daughter.

"I shall make sure of it," Gawain promises, "and so will his mother."

"And no doubt Marie's father will also watch over her." It is my greatest pleasure to see father and daughter together. I had thought, in view of Guenevere's ongoing fury with Launcelot, that he might spurn his daughter in order to win back her regard, but he has not. I have seen Marie and Launcelot walking in the garden on more than one occasion, heads bent close together and in deep conversation, and I watch them with love and with pride.

It makes my vow to change the future by changing the present even more difficult; more heartbreaking. Nevertheless, I know that I must try. And so, once again, I seek out Arthur. I find him in the garden and I hurry to him, taking his arm. He frowns at me. He has not forgiven me for my disgraceful behavior, as he believes it, at Meliagrance's castle.

"Will you walk with me around the garden, my lord?" I ask. "It is so warm and sunny, it is surely too fine a day for old grievances to come between us."

He hesitates, then falls into step beside me without removing his arm from my grasp. I take this as a most encouraging sign. For a few moments I prattle on about the flowers and herbs that add their scent to the air, admiring their beauty while also reminding him of some of their properties. Finally, when I judge his attitude has thawed somewhat, and he has relaxed in my company, I broach the subject of our son.

"You already know how bitterly I regret what happened between us that led to his birth," I tell Arthur. "But I feel I must warn you that even as we speak he is fomenting trouble among the younger knights." I will not mention, not yet, the reason at the heart of Mordred's troublemaking. "He tells them you are too old now to hold the kingdom in safety. He tells them that he is your rightful heir, and that it is time for you to step aside and let him come into his own. He is trouble,

Arthur—for you, and for the kingdom." In my anxiety, I stop walking and face Arthur. "But it is not too late to act, my lord. Please, put a stop to his mischief, I beg you!"

"And how do you propose I do that, Morgana?"

By acting against him instead of dithering, as usual! The words are on the tip of my tongue, but I am finally learning to think before I speak.

"You sent Gaheris into exile for killing his mother, our sister," I remind him. "Surely you can do the same to Mordred."

"And have half the knights of our country follow him when I do so?" Arthur's quiet comment confounds me. I had not thought that far ahead. I must credit Arthur for more brains and sense than I realized.

"No, Morgana." Arthur resumes pacing. "I would rather have him here, at Camelot, where I can keep an eye on him, and his friends too. I still have knights loyal to me. They tell me what is going on."

Except the most important thing of all. But it is difficult to broach that most sensitive of all topics. And then I have an idea. It wrenches my heart, but I hope it might suffice.

"I understand that Marie's appearance at court has caused the queen much grief, for I know she longs for a child of her own. And perhaps her low spirits have added to the uncertainty and division within Camelot. If Sir Launcelot were to go away for a while, home to Joyous Garde, perhaps she might recover her spirits?"

"Perhaps she might recover them even sooner if I were to banish you instead."

"Perhaps Launcelot and I should both leave your court, along with Marie," I say quietly, determined to conceal how much his words have hurt me.

We walk in silence for a few moments while Arthur thinks about it. "That time Launcelot disappeared, you went missing also. You were with him then, at Joyous Garde?"

"Yes, Arthur. I loved him then, and he loved me."

"But he does not love you now, for I have seen where his affection truly lies."

This is the moment I have been waiting for.

"Then you must take action, my lord, before—" I stop talking. We both halt as Launcelot and Guenevere swing around the corner, arm in arm, their faces flushed with laughter—and something else. They see us, and stop, quickly stepping apart.

"Arthur!" Guenevere runs up to him and gives him a perfunctory kiss on the cheek. "Isn't it the most beautiful day!" She steals a glance at her lover. There is such happiness, such serenity in her expression, that I am immediately suspicious. She links her arm through Arthur's. Her voice chills markedly as she acknowledges my presence. "Morgana."

I step away from Arthur, from them all, and hasten out of the garden and into the fields beyond. I need to be alone, for in those few brief moments when Launcelot and Guenevere thought themselves unobserved, I saw what I have most dreaded. Guenevere has discovered that she is with child, and has now disclosed the news to Launcelot. Their joy is a dagger through my heart. I can scarce keep my tears in check as I move swiftly toward the barns and sheds at the far side of the field. There, witnessed only by the incurious eyes of several cows, I am no longer able to support myself. I sink to the ground, and weep until I can scarcely catch my breath. I cry until my eyes are sore and raw with rubbing; I sob until I am exhausted.

Finally, worry for Marie forces me to stand and attempt to compose myself into some sort of order. I left her in the company of Guinglan, as usual, but that was hours ago. I need to find her, to reassure myself that she is safe. It is an effort to walk; my aching limbs make me conscious that I am no longer a young woman, as I look in the garden and then climb the stairs of the castle to search the rooms there. I can find no sign of either of them.

Becoming worried, I walk upstairs to my small room, hoping she may be waiting for me there. But she is not. I am about to search further when she rushes in. On seeing me, she casts herself into my arms and begins to sob bitterly.

"Marie!" Even while I tell myself that she is alive and apparently unharmed, panic seizes me by the throat. "My darling child, whatever is the matter?"

She doesn't speak; she is so upset she is shaking. I look about for Guinglan, but there is a different young knight standing straight and stiff beside the doorway and looking as if he'd rather be a thousand miles away. They have had a lover's tiff, I think, and she doesn't know how to bear it.

"Have you had an argument with Guinglan?" I ask her tenderly.

She shakes her head vehemently, and draws apart from me. "No. Guinglan was called away. He wanted me to go with him to find you, but the garden was so beautiful and the day so warm and sunny, I insisted on staying out there on my own. There was no one else about; no one to cause me any trouble. But as I was leaving, a man pounced on me and tried to drag me behind a sheltering screen. He put his hand over my mouth to stop me crying out for help. He had a knife, Mamm! I was so frightened, I hardly knew what to do. In my terror I bit his hand, and then screamed as loudly as I could. A party of knights was nearby, and they shouted to let me know they were coming to my rescue. So the man let go of me and ran away."

Shattered, I listen as Marie stammers out her story. I know well the identity of her attacker, but does she?

"Who was he?"

She shakes her head. "He wore a scarf that shrouded his head and his face. I don't know if he was a knight or even one of the servants, for he didn't speak to me at all. He just grabbed me, and tried to drag me away. He was going to kill me, I know it."

My daughter begins to cry once more; I pull her into a close embrace and try to comfort her. "You're here with me now. You're safe." I look at the young knight hovering in the doorway. "Did you not go in pursuit of him?" If Mordred has been captured, Arthur will have to take action against him.

"My companions did, while I stayed with your daughter, my lady. But they could find no sign of the assailant. They said it was as if he'd just vanished into the air." The young man shakes his head. "But of course, the garden's such a maze of little paths ..." He gives me a nervous smile.

"I thank you for looking after my daughter, and bringing her safe to me," I say. The young man bows and withdraws, leaving the two of us alone. As I continue to comfort and console Marie, my head spins with new worries.

Has Mordred acquired some magical powers of his own that he is able to disappear so completely? If so, he is far more dangerous than I suspected. I shudder as I think what might have happened to Marie if her screams had gone unheard. We shall have to leave the court now, just as soon as we can, I realize. But what can I possibly say that might persuade her to leave Guinglan and come back to the priory with me?

It's not only the threat to Marie's safety that troubles me. I am desperate to leave Camelot. I cannot bear to stay and witness Guenevere and Launcelot's happiness. The child could not be Arthur's, that much is certain—but only I have that knowledge. I could not prove otherwise if Guenevere chose to claim Arthur as the father—as indeed she must, and with Launcelot's consent. And would it be such a bad thing to have that child acknowledged as the legitimate heir to the throne?

In all honesty, I would have to answer no. Although based on a lie, an obvious heir, one acknowledged by Arthur, would put an end to much of the trouble within the court. It would also serve to prove Guenevere's fidelity to Arthur, at least in the court's eyes. More than anything, it would negate Mordred's claim to succeed Arthur. I remember the smashed skull of the baby rabbit, and Mordred's threats against Owain. Would Guenevere's baby manage to survive to adulthood? It is a thought too dreadful even to contemplate.

Somehow I must find a way of warning Arthur – or Launcelot – before I leave. I don't want to see this child. I don't want to know anything about it. I would far rather retreat to the priory and hide there, and lead a quiet and contemplative life with my daughter. Yet I also have a duty to fulfill: to Arthur and to his people. What else can I do?

I suspect that we have missed the evening meal. A swift peek out the window confirms that the castle is already cloaked in a dark mantle. It is too late now to think of packing and leaving. A decision must wait until morning, by which time I hope that I may see the way ahead more clearly. I tell myself that I can do no more to unravel and reverse the doom I have foreseen in the tablets. All that I set in motion so long ago, when I set out to seduce Arthur, will inevitably come to pass just as I have foreseen it.

I frown as I reconsider my judgment. There was one small difference in the second reading: a child. I had taken it as a representation of Marie, but there is now Guenevere's child to consider. What role will it have in Camelot's future—if it survives? If I stay, can I make a difference? Or is Marie right in her belief that it is the will of God that dictates our future and that nothing we do or say can influence our destiny?

I shall follow Marie's way, I think. I shall leave Camelot forever.

"But what of the child? Save her, Morgana! Save us!"

The voice seems to come from nowhere. I stop and look for its source, but I can see nothing and no one. It was a voice in my mind—but whose? Too high for Merlin—although I doubt he'd speak to me even if he were still alive. It sounded like the voice of a young woman—but it was not Marie's voice, nor anyone else I know. The girl I saw when first I was able to scry the future in my secret pool? Is Morgan telling me that I must go on as I started?

I am thoughtful as I ready myself for bed and bid Marie goodnight. The questions echo in my mind, along with another. I cannot abandon Marie to the doom I have foreseen, but how can I persuade her to come to the priory with me? She will never agree to leave Guinglan, not even after what has just happened. So can I persuade them instead to marry and make their home somewhere far away from Camelot? Yes, I think. That is indeed a notion worthy of consideration.

I have not practiced my magical arts of late, dismayed by the harm I have already caused but also, I must confess, discouraged by my lack of success at the scrying pool when I most needed guidance. Perhaps I should return to the priory to retrieve my wands and the magical objects stolen from Merlin, and try once more to determine how I may influence the fate of Camelot.

I lie awake as the moon sails high across the heaven and begins to sink to the earth. I try to summon the voice of the young woman to tell me more, to show me the way, but nothing happens and nobody comes. I turn, and shift, and turn again, trying to find ease from the thoughts that torment me. And then I hear shouts, and screams, and the clash of metal striking metal, and I am instantly awake and running toward its source.

The sounds come from Guenevere's bedchamber, and I instantly fear the worst. I push forward in order that I may see for myself whatever trouble has befallen the queen.

What I see terrifies me. Launcelot and the queen are in such undress that there can be no doubting their close and loving relationship. The thought flashes through my mind that not even Arthur can turn a blind eye now. Launcelot has caught up a sword, and is fighting for his life.

"Traitor knight!"

I recognize Mordred, in company with Agravaine and several others. And I understand now the plot they have hatched, the need for secrecy, and the need to wait until "the time is right." No doubt, caught in the joy of Guenevere's news, the lovers have thrown caution out of the window in order to come together to celebrate the fruit of their union.

I watch in fear and horror as Launcelot, greatly outnumbered and at a disadvantage without armor, nevertheless fights with great dexterity, felling first Agravaine and then Gareth and several others. Gawain arrives. Appalled, he takes a moment to assess the situation and then shouts at the knights to sheath their swords. They stand back and, in that instant, Launcelot snatches hold of the queen and whirls her out of the bedchamber and down the stairs. Within the blink of an eye, they have vanished, while Gawain's strong arm prevents any of the knights from following after them.

"Enough," he growls. "Let them go, let them flee the court, and good riddance." And then his gaze falls on his dead brothers, and he opens his mouth in a howl of grief.

I know that the court has lost the last voice that will speak up for unity and moderation when, after he has mastered his emotion, he says, "I shall never forgive him. Never! I shall hunt him down. To my dying days I shall pursue him and wreak vengeance on him for his deeds this night."

Arthur appears in the bedchamber, rubbing his eyes in sleepy bewilderment. Through his tears, Gawain wastes no time in telling him what has transpired; telling him also that the queen and Launcelot have fled. But still Arthur will not condemn them.

"He is the queen's champion. Their friendship was forged right from the start when Launcelot escorted her to Camelot to be my bride. You have greatly mistaken their friendship for something else—and see what damage has been done as a result."

He catches sight of Mordred, and beckons him forward. "Is this your doing? Did you and your fellow conspirators set a trap for the queen, hoping to find her in a compromising position with Sir Launcelot?"

"Yes, we did." Mordred faces Arthur, calm against his father's rage. "And we found them half naked in bed together. There can be no misunderstanding their intention."

Arthur swipes Mordred across the face, a slap that reverberates around the room, and causes several of the knights to draw their swords in readiness. Mordred stays them with a quick movement of his hand.

"You will regret trying to chastise me in this manner, Father."

"Your suspicions are unfounded and unworthy, for our prayers have been answered. Guenevere has told me that she is with child at last, although of course it is early days as yet." He crosses himself quickly, perhaps as a precaution against anything going wrong then glares at Mordred. "Take your friends and leave my court. Begone! I no longer want you here, causing trouble and dissent. I care not where you go, or what you do, just get out of my sight."

Hands on hips, he waits until Mordred and the young knights depart, carrying the slain knights between them. If Arthur is grieving over their deaths, he does not show it. He turns to Gawain.

"I want the queen and Launcelot found and brought back to court."

"No."

Amazed, Arthur steps back, the better to survey his old friend.

"I am afraid, my liege, that you will have to find someone else to carry out your order." It is the first time I have ever heard Gawain refuse the king anything, but Arthur is left in no doubt as to Gawain's resolve when he continues, "Launcelot has killed two of my brothers, and is now my sworn enemy. I will not follow after him and beg him to return."

Arthur is silent for long moments. Then he reaches out and clasps Gawain's arm. "I deeply regret their deaths," he says softly. "And I understand your decision, but I beg you to reconsider. Now, more than ever, I need good knights and true at my side."

I see the anguish on Gawain's face, but also the determination. "My lord," he says, "I cannot. I will not."

There is a long silence. Arthur heaves another despairing sigh. "It is late," he says at last. "Let me sleep on the matter. Perhaps even now the queen and Launcelot are regretting their hasty flight and are on their way home to salvage their reputation. By morning I suspect the situation will seem much clearer."

Personally, I doubt it. If Arthur won't acknowledge the truth now, he never will. But with Mordred banished, and the queen and Launcelot fled, perhaps the doom of Camelot will be lifted and things will come to rights after all. It is on this thought that I once more return to my room and try to sleep. Marie has not wakened, and I am glad of it. She would have understood exactly what her father and Guenevere were doing in the bed. No doubt she will hear about it soon enough, but at least she was spared the sight of their indiscretion. I suspect she will be unable to forgive Launcelot. And with Launcelot gone away with the queen, probably never to return, I feel as though I have lost part of myself. I yearn to be heart-whole once more, but I know that the emptiness caused by his departure will never be filled.

Only one small thought momentarily lifts my despair: they will make all speed to Joyous Garde. I can't help wondering what Guenevere's reaction will be when she enters the hall, and sees my likeness on every wall.

CHAPTER 17

In the days that follow, Arthur asks everyone at court, even me, to go after the pair and bring them back, repeating his reassurance that he understands the true nature of the scene witnessed by Mordred, Agravaine and the other knights. When Arthur talks about the "true nature" of the scene, I suspect he really does know the truth about Launcelot and Guenevere's love for each other but is not willing to split the court further by acknowledging what has been going on. I wish he would rather win the court's respect by denouncing the pair and banishing them from Camelot, but he continues to ask for help in seeking the errant couple.

"Why don't you go yourself?" I ask finally, in exasperation.

"I cannot. I've had word that Mordred is traveling through the countryside, drawing ever-increasing numbers to him. He denounces me now, and I am waiting for an open challenge from him, for he is already promising land and wealth to all who follow him once the kingdom becomes his. I must stay and defend Camelot, Morgana. I must keep our home safe and the throne secure for Guenevere and our coming child."

"What makes you think she will return?" It seems highly unlikely to me that she would give up life at Joyous Garde with the father of her child to return to the sneers and jeers of Camelot.

Arthur shrugs. "She knows her duty," he says, reaffirming my suspicion that in all things, Arthur puts statecraft ahead of emotion.

Meanwhile my time is taken with trying to comfort Marie, who is inconsolable. She has lost her father, and at the same time lost all respect for him. Worse, she now considers herself unworthy of Guinglan, and has told him as much. The pair of them mope about so disconsolately that I feel like giving them both a good kick. Nevertheless, I too mourn the loss of Launcelot, but by myself, in private. I put on a brave face in public, and wish that my daughter would do the same.

To his credit, Gawain is also doing his best to reconcile the young couple, but nothing seems to be working. The court itself is like a hornet's nest, buzzing with unrest. Even though Mordred has gone, there are enough of his followers left behind to continue spreading his poison. The court is now more deeply divided than ever, and it seems to me only a matter of time before what I have foreseen will come to pass.

I worry most particularly about Marie and what will become of her once the last conflagration heralds the end of Camelot. I am desperate to save her from that, for I can't help thinking that in her survival lies the future foretold in the tablets, if I have read them aright. She is the one and only flicker of hope that I have seen: the child who may yet play a vital role in the story of Camelot.

And all the while I try to come up with some sort of plan for the future. When it finally comes to me, I realize I will need Gawain's help for my scheme to succeed. To my relief, he gives it willingly, although he expresses himself mystified regarding my request. I cannot take him into my confidence, I can only hope, and pray to Marie's God and to the old gods I have honored in the past, that what I plan to do will meet the demands of the mysterious voice I heard, and that Camelot's doom may yet be averted.

"Let us go back to Glastonbury for a short while," I suggest to Marie. "I think it will do us both good to leave Camelot until things settle down a little."

She hesitates, tears already glinting at the corner of her eyes. I know only too well what she is thinking.

"It may be a good idea to leave Guinglan alone for a few days—just to give him a taste of what life would be like without you," I urge.

"I am not worthy of him," Marie mutters.

"Your father's sin is not your own," I say wearily. It is not the first time I've pointed this out to Marie, but as always she is blinded by grief and deaf to logic. Indeed, it is my belief that it is Guinglan who is not worthy of Marie, for he seems prepared to let her go without a fight. "Come away with me, my darling. It's obvious that seeing Guinglan every day only serves to reinforce the pain you feel at losing him."

Eventually my daughter agrees to my request. Arthur is too heartsore to question my decision, but instead provides us with mounts and bids us God's speed on our journey. We set out, but Marie keeps turning to look back until Camelot, at last, slips from our view. I am concerned that she might yet change her mind about accompanying me but, once Camelot is behind us, she cheers up slightly and tells me that she is looking forward to seeing her friends at the priory again. I feel a prickle of fear as I consider a new threat: that the sorrow of losing Guinglan will persuade her to make a hasty vow to join the sisterhood of the priory.

More than anything, I long to take her to the sacred pool in the hope that we are blessed with a vision. If we are, I pray that it will contradict the doom foretold in the decorated tablets. But I don't want to scare her off by any talk of magic, at least not yet. Besides, there is still a small hope that I may have regained my powers and shall be able to scry without Marie's help. And so, once we arrive at the priory, I leave her to renew her acquaintance with the good sisters while I hasten to the garden and make my way to the sacred pool by the secret passage.

Once there, I sit silently for a time with my eyes closed. And I pray, I know not to whom, but I ask for a blessing and a return to grace. Merlin had once admonished me to use magic only when it was most necessary. I, in my desire for mastery, and in my childish ignorance, had ignored his advice. As I sit beside the sacred pool I whisper a litany of the harm I have caused, the death and destruction I have wrought through my practice of magic. The weight of it presses so hard on my soul that I find it difficult to breathe. I am truly contrite, and I beg for forgiveness. I hardly dare to hope for anything when at last I open my eyes and gaze into the dark, still pool.

The water ripples gently into life and I see the young woman once more. She bears some resemblance to the illustration on Merlin's wooden tablet. I utter a prayer of thanks for this blessing.

"Morgan?" I ask. Her features resemble mine, but I now suspect that she is someone from a future Camelot—or Glastonbury. She stands among ruined towers of stone, but I recognize the Tor that looms behind her.

She looks at me. I know she sees me as I can see her. She appears afraid, but it is not me who frightens her. "Help me," she says. I hear the terror in her voice. "For God's sake, save us! Save us all!"

"How? Please, talk to me. Tell me what you want me to do!"

The young woman begins to cry. Helpless, I watch her, holding on to her image as it wavers and fades into darkness.

Disappointed, I am about to leave when I hear the same wailing chant that puzzled me so long ago. I listen carefully, trying to discern the words above the cacophony, but I cannot hear them clearly enough to understand their meaning.

A wide river ripples into view. A tower stands beside it, a tower I think I recognize from the time I went to London with my family to pledge our allegiance to the High King, Uther. It seems the same yet it is different, for it is flanked by glittering buildings that line the curves of the river. They are so tall they look as if they might almost touch the sky. Their brilliance is reflected in the water, just as the river is mirrored in their costly facades. I am almost sure that this is the River Thames of London, for I walked along its path with my father when I was just a child, although there were only a few buildings then, and all of them much, much smaller. Now the river is criss-crossed with many bridges, and cluttered with craft of assorted shapes and sizes. I hear great bangs, and shouting, and I see struggling knots of people fighting along the river bank and through the streets nearby. They come together, and clash and part, and come together again. Their dress is unfamiliar, as are the words they scream at one another. Judging from their tone and the actions that accompany them, these are words of war, of hatred and fury, of a lust for destruction.

Some warriors wear only ragged undershirts with short sleeves, and frayed trousers, revealing bare limbs decorated with patterns and words. Jeweled studs puncture eyebrows and lips. There are young women among them, and even children. Their faces are distorted with anger. They hold frames with parchment stretched across them, painted with words I do not understand. They chant as they rush toward their opponents.

These others have a darker skin. Some are bearded and have cloth wound around their heads; their tunics reach down to their ankles. Beside them are smaller, slighter figures; women I think, but it is hard to tell for their faces and bodies are completely shrouded. There are some children present in this group too, boys and girls together. I hear another long wailing cry: "Allah-u-Akbar." Their voices are also full of hate. They, too, carry placards, but the writing looks different. The letters are curled and ornate, something like the ancient scripts of the Arabs that I've seen in the abbey. But I know their message is not of mathematics or astronomy or medicine and healing, for these people are full of anger as they brandish their weapons.

I watch with dread in my heart, for I sense that the sides are evenly matched in their rage and determination to annihilate and silence each other.

The opponents collide and fragment into smaller groups, all of them armed with clubs and knives, or holding unfamiliar weapons that, although small, seem to bring instant death with each reverberating bang. It greatly distresses me to see women and children taking part in a vicious melee; I have never seen such a thing before.

My hope that the women might try to prevent this death and destruction is unfounded, for all wield their weapons with great force. Men, women and even children are dying. Some people are running around throwing small metal objects into the crowds and aiming them toward large metal containers on wheels, causing death and destruction with each explosion. The streets turn into blazing infernos and people scream and scurry like ants in a vain effort to escape.

Horrified, I peer through the flames and smoke, searching for armed knights, for soldiers, for a king—anyone capable of restoring order, and bringing the culprits to justice. But there is no one in control, and the battle rages on. These troublemakers are now joined by several other groups, each tribe different in appearance and dress, so that the streets become jammed with warriors seemingly determined to kill any who stand in their path. I see children cry out in fear and pain. Some are alone and abandoned, desperately trying to escape. Others are being dragged through the throng by their mothers in a bid to flee the danger. But the hatred is so strong that even they are being cut down.

I think of the young woman's plea, but I have tried and I know that I cannot reach across the centuries, I cannot traverse time to make a difference. In the face of this mindless anger, this need to destroy, I am impotent. Is this what I have set in train with my magical arts; this violence, this hatred, this thirst for destruction?

The leaping flames continue unabated. I hear their hungry roar as they consume everything in their path. Is this the end of our world in the future that I am seeing—or is this some other world unknown to me? I become aware of a low droning: objects fall from silver birds and crash into the buildings that line the streets, smashing them into pieces. I duck to avoid the flying, glittering shards, even though I know I am safe and that they can't hurt me. But those who are still standing are flayed like beasts in the butchers' stalls at the markets. There is blood everywhere, dark red rivers of it. And the screaming goes on.

Small silver specks appear in the sky. They look like stars, but it is not night. They seem to hang in an infinity of space. As I pray that they herald deliverance, they begin to float silently down toward the river. A blinding flash of golden yellow leaps across my pool. Even the water is on fire! Fascinated but fearful, I reach out. The water feels reassuringly cold to my touch. I wipe my wet fingertips across my face, and wonder if I am awake or dreaming. I peer through the golden miasma, and try to understand.

When the mist clears there is only a long river that winds and coils through an empty wasteland. Buildings, people—all are gone. But I can still hear the screams of all those who are no longer there. It is a chilling sound that goes on and on and on. I put my hands over my ears in a vain effort to shut out their cries, but I cannot bear to close my eyes in case I miss some hint of how I can make things right again.

The horror fades into silence, the emptiness dissolves into darkness. I stare into the depths of the pool, willing the young woman to reappear, to talk to me, to tell me what's happening and what she wants me to do. She seems to know all about me, she apparently has great faith in me, and yet she is a complete mystery to me. If the prophecy of Merlin's tablets is to be believed, she is vital to our future and the wellbeing of our land—and yet I do not understand how I can help her. I try prayers, and wishes, and even threats, but she has disappeared and I see and hear nothing further.

Finally I leave the sacred, secret place, concerned about what Marie might be doing in my absence, and go in search of her. I find her sitting in the parlor, with two nuns keeping her company. To my surprise Guinglan is also present, sitting at a decorous distance from my daughter. I can tell, from the sly peeks they're exchanging, that only the presence of the good sisters is preventing them from rushing into each other's arms. A weight falls from my shoulders, a weight I was not aware that I was carrying.

"What brings you here, Guinglan?" I ask, thinking this was not part of my plan. I'd asked Gawain to wait a few days, so that the pair could have time to properly miss each other, before divulging Marie's location.

"I beg your pardon if I have acted precipitately and against your wishes, Lady Morgana."

Guinglan has leaped to his feet at my arrival. He smooths down his hair in nervous fashion, and bobs a hasty bow. I smother a smile. No matter how tarnished my reputation at court, it seems that this suitor still recognizes that he must win over the mother of the object of his desire. I warn myself not to appear too keen, and so I take a seat, and indicate the chair so suddenly vacated by Guinglan.

"Pray, seat yourself and let me hear your explanation."

Guinglan gives the sisters an appalled glance before turning to me once more. I recognize his difficulty, and so tell our chaperones that they may leave us.

"Oh, but can't we—" I can tell young Sister Agnes is agog with curiosity, but the older Sister Martha fastens an iron grip on her arm. "Come, Sister Agnes. I am sure you have work to do," she says, and drags her companion away.

Guinglan visibly relaxes once they are gone. In fact, he is so bold, he strides over to Marie, sits down and takes her hand. I note that she does not pull her hand away but instead leans close to him.

"I know all the reasons Marie has given for not wanting to continue our relationship," Guinglan begins, "but no matter how I countered her arguments, she would not listen to me."

Marie nods, and now tries to draw her hand out of his grasp, but his grip tightens and she snuggles into him once more.

"It was only when I learned that you had left Camelot that I realized I could not let Marie go. I badgered my father for information and, as soon as I knew your likely destination, I followed after you on the fastest horse I could find. And here I am."

"Here you are indeed," I murmur. "And what do you propose to do about it, young man?"

"I will marry Marie tomorrow, if she will have me. Even today, if it can be arranged. That is, if I have your permission," he adds hastily.

"Please, Mamm," Marie adds softly. It is a wrench, I confess it, to hear my daughter so determined to pledge her life and her love to another, and I hesitate for long moments.

Their faces grow anxious. Guinglan pats Marie's hand as if gentling a nervous horse. He is a fine young man, and with the best of bloodlines. Now that he has shown courage and determination, I cannot fault him. And so, finally, I say, "Yes, of course you have my blessing."

The next few hours see a whirl of preparation as Marie plunders the gowns I have left in storage at the priory, seeking something fit to wear for her wedding ceremony, while the nuns splutter and squawk like hens at feeding time as they plan a feast in celebration.

As evening falls and candles and lanterns are lit, my Marie comes to the side entrance of the small chapel where her love awaits her. In front of witnesses, the couple make their vows.

It is done. My child has grown and flown away, I realize, as we sit down to celebrate their nuptials after the ceremony. I watch them watching each other while everyone else feasts and drinks their health, and I am happy for them. I have done what I can to secure the future, but already I feel my daughter's loss, for I intend to send them both to my Castle Perilous, and keep them safely away from Camelot and Mordred's plots.

As soon as it is polite to do so, the couple bid us all a good night and, with glowing faces and hand in hand, they hurry away to consummate their love.

How I envy them their first night together! Memories of Launcelot torment me and keep me awake through the long dark hours. To take my mind off my heated imaginings, I think instead of the woman in my scrying pool, and try to fathom what she wants. At once, all my doubts and fears come rushing back, along with a deepening sense of doom that I cannot shake. I relive the terror of the burning citadel that in the end vanishes as if it has never been, and I hear again the screams of the dying and the damned.

I am filled with the sense that I need to do something more if I am to answer the unknown woman's plea for my help. But what is it she wants from me? The night seems endless as I think of first one plan and then another, only to discard them all. Finally, I sense the glimmering of an idea—but I reject it utterly. And yet it sits like a burr in my brain, fretting me until I can no longer ignore it but must examine it more carefully. I don't like it; I'm not sure I'll have the courage to see it through. But I cannot think of anything else that might suit the purpose.

*

The twittering and warbles of birds as they practice their morning songs heralds the pale light of early dawn. It is time for me to act, but I am conscious that it will take Marie even further away from me, and that it may earn me her enmity forever. Nevertheless, it is the only way I can keep her safe while at the same time I try to fulfill the young woman's request and bring about the destiny foretold in Merlin's tablets.

Before I go to Marie, I venture into my secret garden once more to gaze into the sacred pool. I wish that Marie was with me. I am so afraid. My one desire is to receive a blessing, some confirmation that what I propose is the right course of action. I am almost sure of it—but not entirely. But although I linger, the waters stay dark and still, portending death and destruction.

Finally, hunger drives me back to the priory to break my fast. There is no sign as yet of Marie and Guinglan. Once more I am stabbed with envy as I imagine their bed games, their pleasure in the discovery of each other's bodies. I am sure they will be late rising and I resign myself to a long wait. While the hours pass, I conjure up a pretty woven bag and place into it my most prized possessions: the ancient book I stole from Merlin so long ago, and the wooden tablets that have spelled our doom. After some hesitation, I also add the amethyst crystal. I know that I am taking a risk with this and can only pray that I'll be able to find a replacement once I have need of it. All these I seal into the bag with an incantation that will keep them secret and invisible to all but Marie, and I finish my task with a prayer of love, and of hope that my daughter will come to understand the true purpose of my gift. With the decision made, and now irrevocable, I feel easier in my mind for it seems to me that I have done what is right.

It is mid-morning before I catch sight of the young lovers. Arm in arm, they are walking in the direction of my garden, and I know I shall never have a more perfect opportunity. I pick up the bag and hurry toward them to give them my morning blessing.

They are heavy eyed, and drunk with desire. They can hardly keep their hands off each other, and I know that I'll not succeed in keeping them with me unless I act quickly to distract them.

"I designed that garden when first I arrived at the priory," I tell Guinglan.

"It's very beautiful," Marie adds. "I'd like to show it to Guinglan."

"But first let me show you a part of it that no one but me has ever seen. Not even you, Marie."

She regards me thoughtfully. "How has it stayed secret all these years, Mamm?"

She is sharp as a needle, my daughter! I pat her cheek, and notice that my hand is shaking. "It is set apart in a private place. It's where I come to meditate—and to pray. And now I want to share it with both of you. But before I do, I want to give you a gift to honor your marriage and your new life together. Not knowing what was about to happen and its happy outcome, I came to the priory empty-handed, so I have nothing to give you now but my jewels. However, they are your heritage, Marie, and I want you to have them. A beautiful young woman deserves beautiful adornments." As I speak I am stripping off all the rings, bracelets and brooches I've brought with me, every costly thing I possess, and piling them on top of the bag's secret contents.

Finally only Launcelot's gold band is left. I hesitate. The ring came from Marie's father, after all. But I cannot bear to part with it and so I keep it, the only adornment I have left, but the most prized.

"No, Mamm!" Marie throws up her hands in protest. Even after her time in court, she still follows the sober and devout ways of the priory nuns.

"I want you to have them, Marie," I say, and fold the bag into Guinglan's careful grasp. "They are costly, so guard them well." I can only hope that the couple will remember my words in the days to come. I wish I could also give them the small purse of silver coins that I brought along for our traveling expenses, but to do so would excite their suspicion, and so I keep it for my own use. As for what else is in the bag: will my daughter be angry with me when the contents are revealed, or will she understand that what I have given her is also part of her heritage? I can only trust that she will accept the gift, and value it accordingly.

Unsuspecting, they follow me through the portal in the bramble hedge. I already carry an oak leaf while, unknowing, Marie carries Merlin's crystal. The youngsters do not hear my silent chant that I pray will set us on the secret way toward that Otherworld where, so many years ago, I ran away from Merlin and heard the jongleur tell his stories in the marketplace. I have chosen this world because it so closely resembles our own. I do not want to excite their suspicion until it is too late for them to retreat. At all costs, I intend to keep them safe from the doom of Camelot that I fear I may not be able to prevent.

The narrow path is hedged with tall trees; their foliage interlaces over our heads so it is as if we are walking through a leafy green tunnel. But once we emerge, Marie turns to me, puzzled as she surveys her new surroundings.

"But where is your special garden, Mamm? Where is your secret place?"

I give a nonchalant shrug and look about me. "It must have been destroyed during my long absence from the priory. But see, the priory garden lies before you. Why don't you and Guinglan explore it on your own? I am quite sure you don't need my company. Besides, I must return to the priory; there is much to do before I return to Camelot." I long to take my daughter in my arms, to bid her one last farewell, but I dare not.

They move away, arm in arm. With a heavy heart, I watch them go. They are so rapt in each other that they pay little attention to their surroundings, which is a blessing, for sooner or later Marie will realize that this garden is not the same as the one at the priory, nor is the abbey the same, and she will come looking for me.

As soon as they vanish behind the high hedges that mark the garden's boundary, I retreat down the secret path and close the portal. Silently, I send my blessing after them and hope that they will be able to live comfortably in their new surroundings, with my jewels to pay for food and shelter and whatever else they might need while they are there. I have done what I may to keep them safe from the doom of our world, and have also given them the means to protect themselves should protection become necessary. I try to comfort myself with the thought that this separation is not forever, and that in time, I shall be able to explain everything. Even so, I tremble as I imagine Marie's reaction when she understands my betrayal, and can only pray that I shall have my daughter's understanding when next we meet.

Once back at the priory, I tell the good sisters that Marie and Guinglan have asked me to pass on their gratitude and good wishes, and that they have now gone to Castle Perilous to start their new life. I sweeten my own farewell with the small bag of silver coins, for I am anxious to return to Camelot to do whatever I may to avert what is about to befall us all.

*

On my return I sense an air of tension, for it seems that the knights are more divided than ever now. Small knots huddle in corners, casting furtive glances over their shoulders to make sure no one can overhear what they are saying. As I approach there is always a too-obvious attempt to change the subject. The weather, in particular, seems to be a constant source of wonder and amazement. I go in search of Gawain, and tell him the same story I told the nuns at Glastonbury: that Guinglan and Marie have gone off to Castle Perilous to start their new life together.

Gawain frowns. "It is as well they are away out of danger, Morgana. Arthur is still looking for someone to fetch Launcelot and Guenevere home, while Mordred's poison grows and festers. I cannot—I will not—go to Launcelot, for he has become my sworn enemy. I cannot forgive him for killing my brothers. And yet Arthur needs the strength of the knights who are still loyal and true behind him for I fear there will be a confrontation sooner or later. While none of us wishes to support Mordred, it will be impossible to support Arthur if those two return. The king has lost the respect of the court because of his refusal to condemn them. I wish you would talk to him, Morgana."

"I have tried, but he will not listen to me. But he might pay attention to the Lady Viviane. Is she here?"

Gawain shakes his head. "That is a good suggestion, Morgana, but where she dwells is something of a mystery. Perhaps you might try to seek her out?"

I agree. I just wish I'd thought of it while I was still at Glastonbury, and before I'd given my gift to Marie. But

Viviane has come to Camelot before, when she felt there was a need—perhaps she might come again, even without my summoning? Nevertheless, I make preparations to return. But before I leave, something happens that puts the whole castle into an even greater uproar: Guenevere returns to Camelot of her own accord.

She is alone and looks disheveled, as if she has been sleeping in ditches on her journey. Her face is drawn, her eyes red and swollen from crying. I wonder what can possibly have gone wrong but I say nothing, only make myself unobtrusive as Arthur welcomes her tenderly, sits her down beside him, and calls for food and wine to be brought.

"My love," he says. "I am overjoyed to see you, yet you look so sad. Pray, tell me what is wrong. And why have you traveled alone? Where is Launcelot?"

At once Guenevere breaks down in a storm of tears and stammers out the somewhat incoherent explanation that Joyous Garde was not to her liking and that she became fearful for her virtue once she was alone with Launcelot. I hear the words "God's curse" before she doubles over and gives herself up to such bitter sobbing that she is rendered speechless.

But I can fill in the gaps well enough, beginning at the moment she stepped into the hall at Joyous Garde and saw the tapestries, proof of Launcelot's love for me. What rage, what sulks must have followed. Launcelot must rue the day he brought her to his home, or alternatively, cursed the love he bore me that left such a tangible mark on Joyous Garde. He would have done his best to appease her fury, and I suspect he would have prevailed if, in the end, she had not lost the tie that would have bound them together forever. "God's curse," she called it, and that's how it must have seemed to Guenevere: her longed-for baby lost because of her betrayal of her husband and king.

I feel sorry for her, and I take great care to stay well out of her path. I have no doubt that she will blame me for her loss if she catches sight of me. And indeed, I am to blame, and for so much more than she knows. But I already feel guilt and sorrow enough without having to listen to her venting her wrath and pain on me.

Arthur appears to swallow the story whole and treats her tenderly while vowing to seek revenge on Launcelot. The only good thing to come out of this tangle is that he and Gawain are reconciled once more, along with many of the other older and wiser knights. The time of reckoning is near. We all sense it. And I know that we all fear that this will mark the end of everything, including Camelot.

CHAPTER 18

The first inkling of danger comes when I am confronted by Mordred. I have been walking alone in the garden, lost in thought, when he steps out seemingly from nowhere and stands in my path.

"Where is she, Morgana?" he says pleasantly. His cold gaze belies the affability of his words.

"Where is who?" I ask, giving myself time to think.

"Don't play games with me. My half-sister, who else? I know she is not at Glastonbury, and neither is Guinglan."

"You've been to Glastonbury?"

Mordred's smile chills me to the bone. "I have indeed. The good sisters were delighted to see me after all these years. 'So grown up and so handsome,' they said. They made me very welcome—at least at first."

Fear turns my bowels to water. "What have you done?" I whisper.

Mordred's smile grows broader. "You will never again use your dark arts against me or anyone else, Morgana," he taunts. "I have taken steps to ensure it."

"What have you *done*?" In my fear, I shout the words. I grab hold of his arms and shake him, until he effortlessly twists out of my grasp.

"Where is she?" It is his turn to grip my shoulders. His hands tighten, hurting me. I am unable to free myself, but I muster all my courage and glare at him.

"She is safe where you cannot reach her," I say, while silently I thank the gods for giving me the wisdom to follow my instinct.

"I shall hunt her down," he says. "Owain, too. The kingdom will be mine and mine alone, Morgana. My time will come." He lets go of me, gives me a contemptuous shove, and walks off, whistling nonchalantly. I stare after him, wishing I had the powers to strike down this child whom once I loved so dearly.

I send a message to Owain, bidding him stay up north and out of reach, and to be on his guard at all times, and then I ride back to Glastonbury at speed in the hope of reaching Viviane. I am aghast at what I find there. The priory has been burned to the ground, and my garden along with it. The ashes have grown cold, but there is still the acrid stench of burning in the air. Fearing what I may find, I walk through the charred debris. There are no bodies among the ruins. It seems that the nuns have escaped with their lives, and I give heartfelt thanks for it, and for the fact that, unknowingly, Mordred has also destroyed the one means he had of finding Marie and Guinglan.

And with that realization comes another, far worse: I shall never see my daughter again, never be able to explain to her why I abandoned her in an unfamiliar world, with no chance of ever finding her way home. I crumple and clutch my arms tight around my body in a vain effort to hold myself together. I am too shocked, too distraught to cry. I can hardly believe the full extent of my loss, but I know that I am punished now for all the harm that I have done. The pain is excruciating; I can scarcely breathe. Only my hatred for Mordred stops me from losing my mind altogether. The need for revenge is visceral; a furious rage brings a rush of heat through my body, enabling me to stand upright once more, and give some thought to the future.

I am still able to utilize the magical arts of the mind, those that do not depend on what I have given to Marie, and I pray that they will be enough for my needs. It is reassuring to recall how I defeated Merlin, and how I also evaded Gawain and his brothers. An eagle with talons to disembowel my son? A fire-breathing dragon? That would scratch the smile off Mordred's face!

Before I have time to try out my skill, for it's been so long I am not sure if I still possess the ability to shape-shift, I am hailed. I turn and see the Prioress walking toward me.

I wait, wondering how much she knows, or guesses, of what has transpired. "I am so grateful to see you alive and well, Prioress," I tell her. "I was fearful you and your companions might have perished in the fire."

"No, Dame Anna, we all managed to escape, thanks be to God, but some have severe burns while others are coughing and in great distress after inhaling so much smoke." She frowns at me. "I should tell you that we believe the fire was set by your son Mordred."

How can I deny it? Sadly, I tell her that I believe her, and that I deeply and humbly apologize on his behalf should it prove to be so.

"The sins of the child can often be blamed on those who influence his upbringing," she says tartly.

I press my lips tight to refrain from pointing out that the sisters, too, had an influence on Mordred's early years. But while I deplore my son's actions, I know that the blame rests largely on my shoulders, and I accept responsibility for it.

"He said at first that he was looking for your daughter, so we told him she and Guinglan had gone to make their home at Castle Perilous—that is correct, is it not?"

I nod. "When was he here?"

"He arrived some days ago, but left almost at once. I presume he did not find your daughter, for he was very angry on his return. I must confess that I was pleased he was unable to locate our sweet Marie, for I was sure, then, that he meant her harm. Unfortunately I made the mistake of telling him as much. He accused me of hiding her and scoured every inch of the priory in search of her. I did not like his attitude, Dame Anna. Indeed we were all fearful and very relieved when he finally left—or so we thought. The priory, and your beautiful garden, went up in flames that same night."

Her words confirm my suspicions. As well as trying to locate his half-sister, Mordred must also have hoped to discover my books and the magical possessions that help me practice my craft. He, more than anyone, would know that a knowledge of the magical arts would give him powers that no one in our kingdom, save me, would be able to match. Not finding what he desired during his search of the priory, he had resorted to their utter destruction—or so he thought. No wonder he'd threatened me with such confidence. It frightens me to think of the havoc he would have wrought if I had not removed both my daughter and my most prized possessions out of his reach. I can only thank the gods that circumstances prevented me from showing him any of my magical practices before I became aware of his true nature.

"I am so very sorry for the trouble my son has caused you," I tell her. Fortunately I still have Launcelot's gold ring, although it takes all my courage and will to pull it off my finger and hold it out to the prioress. Profit from its sale will be some recompense for the destruction wrought by Mordred, although losing it feels worse than would losing the hand it came from. "Please put this to use when rebuilding your priory."

The prioress brightens and wastes no time in snatching it from my grasp. "I thank you in the Lord's name." She hesitates a moment. "The brothers have given us shelter in the abbey until such time as our priory is rebuilt," she continues. "I am sure their Guest-Master will find a room for you, should you wish to rest and refresh yourself after your journey?"

It is late and I am exhausted. I am tempted by her offer, but it seems more urgent that I should return to Camelot. The destruction of my garden and its secret paths means the way to Viviane is barred to me now. There is no more I can do here. And so I bid her farewell, and turn my tired mount in the direction of Camelot.

*

Upon my return, I discover Mordred has sent a challenge to Arthur to meet him at the field of Camlann. He has asked Arthur to name him king in his place, and is prepared to wage war to achieve his ambition. Arthur has replied that he would like to meet in peace in order to discuss Mordred's proposition. The date has been set for a few days' hence. Despite the so-called truce, the castle is abuzz as squires prepare the knights' armor and all make themselves ready for battle.

I hurry to Camlann to find Mordred, hoping I may be able to avert the doom I have foreseen. Once there I am aghast at the huge army he has managed to gather to his cause. His soldiers far outnumber Arthur's army, although I know my brother has sent out scouts to scour the countryside for men willing to come to his aid. Owain was not among Arthur's soldiers and, to my infinite relief, he is not at Camlann either. I can only pray that he stays safe in the north.

I transform myself into a tiny sparrow, and hop about among Mordred's men, hoping to hear something—anything—that Arthur might use to his advantage. I hear a cacophony of different languages, and realize that these are mercenaries, men hired by Mordred to fight on his side. Might they be turned to Arthur with the promise of more silver? It is a thought worth considering, if I fail in what I am attempting to do. But I cannot fail. There is far too much at stake here for failure.

I transform myself into an eagle. I wait and watch, hoping to catch Mordred on his own, and defenseless. With him dead, or horribly injured, I know that the men will desert him and his plans will fail. He has gathered his men together and is talking to them. My confidence wavers as I hear their cheers and whistles of support. These are not men to be bought. Mordred must have promised more than payment, should his bid for the throne succeed.

The men disperse, and Mordred wanders off alone, perhaps to think, to plot and plan, to savor his coming victory.

He looks up as I approach. There is something in his gaze that alerts me to danger, but even so I swoop down with talons outstretched, readying myself to claw at his eyes and render him blind. Within a heartbeat his sword is drawn. He awaits me, smiling, as he anticipates my death.

Panicking, I beat my mighty wings in a desperate effort to avoid that shining blade. I swoop over his head with only a hair's breadth to save me from slaughter. His mocking laughter follows me as I fly higher, away from my shame and from danger. He might not have mastered the trick of transformation, but I know now that any form I take will find him armed and prepared to defend himself. I am impotent against the implacable ambition of my son.

It seems clear to me now that Marie is wise to say I should leave matters to God to either save or destroy Camelot. Weary and fearful, I stay on at Camlann to witness the outcome of this meeting between Arthur and Mordred. Knowing that, as a woman, I would not be allowed near the field, I transform myself from eagle to harmless sparrow once more, and take shelter in a copse of trees. I am close enough to the field to see what transpires, but far enough away and so insignificant that Mordred will not notice me—or so I hope. And there I wait until I hear the sound of a horn ring out, and the clinking of armor and the tread of horses' hooves as Arthur's men approach Camlann. They are far fewer in number than Mordred's men, and my heart sinks in my feathered breast as I see my son's eyes narrow in swift calculation. He smiles.

I fly as close as I dare, and watch as Mordred brings his men into formation behind him. Both sides stop while still some distance from each other. There is a tense silence as Mordred and Arthur step forward, ready to parley. Arthur holds out his arms, palms upraised in a gesture of friendship, wanting a truce. But Mordred takes a step back and folds his arms across his chest.

A flicker of movement catches my eye. A small brown snake has emerged from a patch of dry grass and is weaving its way toward one of Arthur's men. Instantly I understand the danger, but I am unable to call out a warning. The adder strikes the soldier. He feels the sting and at once draws his sword to kill the serpent.

A great roar arises from Mordred's men. They have seen the action, and misinterpreted it. Taking the drawn sword as a sign of Arthur's treachery toward their leader, they rush upon Arthur's men who, almost before they have time to draw their own swords, find themselves fighting for their lives.

Sick at heart, I watch them from my perch. Watch as men wield swords and battleaxes, cutting down opponents as lightly as reapers scythe hay. The ground darkens with the blood of the wounded, the dying and the dead. Shouts, curses and the prayers of the dying fill the air, along with the clash of metal on metal, and the wild squeals of destriers that lash out with their hooves at the enemy, but are inevitably cut down. It is a bloody scene, a field of carnage, a careless destruction and waste of life.

Through it all, I keep an anxious eye on Arthur and Mordred. They, too, are intent on massacring as many of each other's soldiers as humanly possible. It seems that Arthur's men, trained fighters as they are and with so much more to lose, are winning the battle, for Mordred's men, those who have not been killed, are now in retreat. I suppose, having been promised an early and easy victory, they now realize that their lives might well be forfeit if they tarry longer.

Mordred looks about him, surveying his dead. His shoulders sag in acknowledged defeat. Arthur too, is looking around, assessing the damage. So many men have died, including Gawain and other knights of the Round Table. But loyal Bedivere is still standing, and it is he who shouts a warning to Arthur as Mordred rushes toward him.

With a roar, Arthur snatches up a spear and throws himself at Mordred, slicing the sharp spear through his armor and deep into his son's body. It is a death blow, and I feel an overwhelming sense of relief.

But it is not over. Mordred's eyes widen in anticipation of one last act of revenge. As Arthur turns, he lunges forward over the spear and, with sword upraised, strikes Arthur such a blow on the back of the head that he cleaves through his helmet. Arthur drops instantly. It takes Mordred a little longer to die, but die he does, and painfully.

A great silence falls over the battlefield. I am filled with shame, and remorse. If I had not thrown away the magical scabbard that protected Excalibur—and Arthur's life—he would have survived this day. Truly I have caused more harm than ever I could have imagined when first I embarked on my quest to reclaim my realm. I have destroyed everything.

I fly down to the ground, ready to transform myself and go to my brother's aid. But before I can do so, I am aware that Arthur has not died after all. Bedivere kneels beside him; they are talking together. I fly over to them and hover above, hoping with all my heart that all may yet be well.

"Take my sword and throw it into the lake," Arthur tells Bedivere. I am intrigued. This was once a ritual observed by all warriors in our land in a time long ago. Upon their death, and sometimes even before it, perhaps in hope of a boon, warriors would throw their swords into a lake or the sea, or a spring perhaps, to appease the gods and guarantee a safe passage to the afterlife. This practice is still observed in the Otherworld of the Druids, but I have not seen it at Camelot since the court turned to the way of Christ. It seems now that my brother is not quite so devout a Christian as I had once thought.

Nor, it seems, is he so badly wounded as I had feared. And so I leave him and follow Bedivere to a lake some little distance from the battlefield, for I am curious about Arthur's request. It seems so out of character for him to revert to the old ways. But then I remember that the sword was a gift from Viviane, and she might well have instructed Arthur regarding its use.

Bedivere comes to the lake and raises the sword, ready to throw it in. He hesitates, and then lowers it and thrusts it into a thicket of bushes to hide it. He returns to Arthur. I fly after him.

"Have you done as I asked?" The king's voice is weaker, but still steely with purpose.

"My lord, I have," Bedivere answers.

"And what saw you when you threw the sword into the lake?"

"Nothing, my lord. It fell with a mighty splash and sank straight away, leaving only ripples to mark its passing."

Arthur rears up, terrible in his wrath. "You have not obeyed me," he thunders. "I command you to do as I ask."

"But my lord, the sword has served you for so long, and may well serve you again in time to come."

"I am dying, Bedivere; I shall not have need of it again. I bid you, grant my last request or your soul will be forever forfeit, in this world and the next."

Exhausted, Arthur sinks back onto the ground. I am torn between wanting to follow Bedivere and staying to tend Arthur's wounds, for I am sure that he has suffered a mortal blow. But I have no herbs with me, no potions to heal him or even to ease his pain. I can do nothing for him here. Reluctantly, I leave him and fly after Bedivere.

The knight casts a quick look around. Fancying himself alone, he retrieves the sword from its hiding place and once more raises it above his head. He stops, perhaps reconsidering his actions. And then he throws it right into the middle of the lake.

I watch, fascinated, as a hand rises up out of the water to catch the sword. The fingers lock onto it in a firm grasp and then, slowly and gently, the sword is lowered until it disappears under the water, leaving barely a ripple in its wake to mark its passing.

Viviane? Or someone else from a different Otherworld? Cold shivers run through me at the thought that even I, with all my magical powers, have not yet fathomed all there is to know about our world and the magic of the worlds beyond. It is as well Bedivere has obeyed Arthur's command, I think, as I change into my real guise and hurry back to the battlefield behind the knight.

"Is it done?" Arthur's voice is very weak now.

"Yes, my liege."

"And what saw you?"

Bedivere recounts what we both witnessed. And Arthur is satisfied, knowing that his last wish has been obeyed.

I kneel at his side. He manages to smile when he sees me. It is the smile of the little boy he once was; the child going into the dark and fearing what he might encounter there, but trying, so bravely, to hide that fear.

"Have courage, Arthur." I take his hand. "All will be well." He knows he is dying, and so do I now. All I can do is hope to ease his passing.

"Hurry to the castle and fetch my medicaments," I tell Bedivere, and I give him detailed instructions as to the things I need and where they might be located. "Bring also a litter and men to carry the king." An image comes into my mind; it is an image once seen in my scrying pool but not understood until now. "Send someone to the river to find a sturdy and comfortable boat for hire," I add, and the knight hurries off to do my bidding.

Once he is safely out of hearing, I sit down beside my dying brother and confess all my sins, and earnestly beg his pardon. I have greatly feared his wrath, but now, when it is too late, I need his forgiveness. But he does not give it to me. He stays silent and withdrawn, ignoring my pleas. It is no comfort to me to think that perhaps he has gone beyond earthly emotion and instead is composing himself to meet his God.

But then he sighs, rousing himself a little. "I truly loved Guenevere," he mutters. "But no matter what I did and however hard I tried, I could not satisfy her, neither as a lover nor as a husband. I think, from the very first, she was enchanted by Launcelot. In truth, I should never have married her. But I always hoped, loving her as I did, that she would come to look beyond him and see me, especially if we could make a child together. And so I stayed quiet, both for the love I bore Guenevere but also for the sake of keeping unity in my kingdom."

Arthur's confession is a scourge on my heart for it was I who, by enchantment, ensured that Launcelot reciprocated Guenevere's love, with all that followed on from that. Too late now for regrets. Too late to try to change the doom of Camelot. Nor can I cheat what the tablets have foretold.

I shake my head, trying to clear the thick fog of misery that shrouds my brain. What can I do to ease my brother's pain other than try to reassure him? "I shall take you across the water to the magical Isle of Avalon," I tell him, hoping that I can trust the image that I saw, and that I shall be able to find the means to bring it about. "The island is a center of sacred healing, and Viviane is there. If anyone can save you, she can. Have courage, Arthur. Don't give up hope. You may yet come again to Camelot and unite the kingdom to create an even mightier empire."

He makes no response. I don't know if he has heard me, or if he believes me. I'm not sure if I believe it myself. But he is still alive when the men sent by Bedivere gently place him on the litter and carry him, with the greatest care, to the river side. There, we find a barge awaiting us, with a bed hastily fashioned out of cushions and covered with a silky black curtain on which to place the dying king. This is the barge I saw in my scrying pool, before I went to Arthur in disguise to make a child, the instrument of his undoing. It was a warning, and I did not heed it, for I had not understood that if I went ahead with my plan to seduce Arthur, I would destroy everything and break my heart. A surging tide of regret leaves me feeling sick and shaken.

Once Arthur is settled, I am at a loss as to which direction to take. The barge in my scrying pool had been sailing upriver. I remember also Arthur's comment that Viviane had come downriver to see him at court. While I had devised my own way of visiting Otherworlds, I know that Merlin found another, and perhaps Viviane has too. I can only hope that I have read the signs aright as I give the boatmen their instructions and point them upriver.

A great wailing lament of loss and grief accompanies our passage as people hastily gather along the banks to mark our passing. The boatmen ply their oars and the river winds on, but thick tendrils of mist are reaching out to us now, enveloping us in their damp, clammy arms. The boatmen stop rowing. I see the fear in their eyes, but I command them to keep on. And so they do as the mist grows thicker, until we have no way of knowing the direction in which we are heading or even if we are turning in circles. Once again the boatmen stop rowing, but this time I leave them be for there is magic here, I am sure of it. The boat continues to move of its own accord, slipping swiftly and silently over the water. Arthur's eyes are closed. I take his hand, squeeze it, and feel a slight answering pressure. I bend over him, and kiss his cheek.

The mist clears, and I realize that it is night. The black velvet sky is brilliant with stars, the same stars that shine over Camelot. I wonder if we are in Avalon, or merely further upriver at some new settlement. I discern the faint outlines of buildings, pricked with lamplight at their windows. A procession is wending its way to the wooden pier where we have berthed. At sight of it, the boatmen cross themselves in terror. I wait, holding Arthur in my arms, to see who comes.

It is Viviane who leads the procession. Several women hurry forward, bearing a litter. They carefully lift Arthur onto it and begin to make their way back to the settlement. I stand up, ready to follow them, but Viviane will not allow it.

"You are not welcome here, Morgana."

I have not bid Arthur farewell. I cannot bear to let him go without a final word. I need to sing to him the lullaby that comforted him in his childhood. I need to sing my brother into the dark. I try to push past her, but Viviane is stronger than me, and she bars my way.

"Go back to Camelot," she orders. "You may tell those few who are left behind that Arthur has gone to the sacred Isle of Avalon for his wounds to be healed."

"When shall I say he'll return?" I ask, accepting defeat.

Viviane scrutinizes me carefully for some moments, then looks off into the distance. I realize she is seeing things that I cannot see when she continues, "The day will come when Britain is divided and is once more under siege from within. There will be a great need for a wise and courageous leader, someone able to bring the tribes together and unite them in the quest for common ground."

"That time is now," I tell her. "Few have survived the battle between Mordred and Arthur. Now, more than ever, are we in need of a strong ruler."

"And that would surely be you, would it not, Morgana?" Viviane's voice is cool, tinged with dislike. "Have you not worked your magic for this outcome all along?"

I blush with shame that she has read my heart and my mind so clearly.

"So many knights dead, and Camelot in ruins. But surely you, with all your magical powers, can save Camelot and make it great once more?"

Defeated, I shake my head. I can find no words to defend myself against Viviane's scorn, for everything she knows about me is true.

"Go away, Morgana. It is too late for Camelot. You must look to your own salvation now." And she turns on her heel and strides away.

After a few moments of shocked silence, the boatmen set up a furious rowing, desperate to leave this haunted place. They say nothing of what they have overheard, and I am grateful. I have no way to defend myself, and no idea of what to do next.

Once more we are enveloped in mist, but the boat travels quickly now, caught in the current that takes us down to Camelot and will ultimately flow on to meet the sea.

CHAPTER 19

This is a true account of the part I played in the doom of Camelot. This must serve also as my confession for I am weary beyond bearing, and know that the sand in my glass must soon run out.

After the battle of Camlann I returned to Camelot to find Guenevere fled to the abbey at Amesbury and the rest of the court dispersed. I heard later, from a traveler visiting the abbey here at Glastonbury, that Launcelot had heeded Arthur's call, but had come to Camelot too late to fight at his side. Would that he had arrived in time! How different the outcome might have been—for all of us. The traveler, who had come from Amesbury and who had seen Guenevere there, said that she and Launcelot had bid one another a tender farewell, for it seems he plans to take holy orders in an abbey across the water in Brittany, place of his birth. For me, this news marked the end of a dream. I had long hoped that one day my potion would lose its power and Launcelot would come for me. I had to accept then that I would never see him again.

Of Marie, stranded in another world and in another time, I have had no news at all. I pray that she and Guinglan are safe, but suspect I shall never be forgiven by them for they will not understand the danger from which I saved them, or hear of the long, slow death of Britain that has followed the battle at Camlann.

After the fall of Camelot no one traveled very far at all. With Arthur gone, and so many of his knights either dead or dispersed, marauders from across the ocean flocked to our shores, fighting those few of our people who dared to show themselves, and stripping them of their land and possessions. It was a great grief to me to learn that Owain, too, had been killed while trying to protect his father's estate from the usurpers. By then, I had taken refuge at the priory once more, all of us living in fear of our lives through those dark days. The invaders, while killing any who stood in their way or who did not bend to their will, left alone those who served God although they stripped the abbeys of all their wealth and most of their land. And so we live in poverty, tilling the fields and feeding ourselves as best we may. Our land is crumbling into decay, dying from within.

It has been a long journey from the daughter of a king to a humble daughter of Christ here at the priory—for I, too, have dedicated my life to God, the sisters would not have let me stay here otherwise. There is no other refuge open to me. Throughout Britain I am blamed for the fall of Camelot, my name linked with that of my son, Mordred. I am called witch and sorceress, whore and succubus. The name Morgana is associated with all that is evil. And so I shall be judged by all who follow, even until the end of time. The voices of those I have harmed, and those who are dead at my hand, haunt my days and disturb my nights. Despite confession, and multiple penances for my sins, I have found no relief. I am riven with remorse. And I ask myself: Why did I not have the wisdom or the sight to see that in taking that first small step, I would bring such misery and devastation to our land?

If the prioress knows of the part I have played in Camelot's downfall, she is kind enough to say nothing about it. Everyone else knows me only as Anna, and if there are any doubts, or rumors, they are muttered quietly and in secret. Our days are spent toiling in the fields and doing what we may to keep our bodies together and our souls alive.

We are no longer able to house guests in comfort here, for there was only money enough for the smallest part of the priory to be rebuilt. But travelers still come and, if we have room and pottage to spare, we take them in.

On a day in early spring, a jongleur arrives at the abbey from across the water in France. In return for a meal and a bed, he entertains us with a *lai* that tells of the deeds of a knight from King Arthur's court, called Lanval. I listen in amazement as the story unfurls, for it seems to me that it bears a strong resemblance to the love affair between Launcelot and me, as it might have turned out if I had not spoiled everything with my meddling. I question the jongleur afterwards.

"'Lanval' was composed by a woman known only as Marie of France," he tells me.

Marie? I hardly dare to hope, yet my ancient heart dances a jig inside my breast. "Who is she? And how does she know this story of Arthur of Britain?"

The jongleur shrugs. "No one knows much about her, other than that she once resided at the court of a king named Arthur, and that she was wed to a man named Guinglan."

"Guinglan!" This must be my own Marie he is talking about! I am so filled with gratitude to have news of her I can scarcely speak. "Are they not still wed? What became of Guinglan?"

"I believe he died of a fever. Marie travelled to France after his death, along with their child. I heard she'd gone in search of her father, who is said to reside somewhere in Brittany. I know not if she ever found him, but her stories and songs have found favor everywhere in our land."

Marie has a child! The blessings pile one on the other; I am suffused with happiness.

"Do you know aught of her child? Is it a boy or a girl?"

The jongleur looks somewhat confused by my interest.

"The child is a girl, I believe. She and her mother live within the royal court, for Eleanor of Aquitaine takes a great interest in Marie's poetry. Indeed, the queen is renowned for the encouragement she gives to artists, scribes, musicians and poets such as Marie. To my great regret I have not yet been invited to perform at her court, so all I can repeat is gossip and hearsay from the common folk."

"And I am truly grateful for your charity in passing it on." I wish I had a coin to give the fellow. Instead, I make sure he has an extra helping of pottage for, by the look of him, he is in need of a good meal.

As I serve him, my joy gives way to questions. How is it that this man has been able to cross from Marie's world to our own? By his account, that Otherworld is stable and prosperous, whereas our world has become so poor, so riven with strife, that I wonder if it is coming to an end. I resolve to question the jongleur further, but carefully, for I must not give any hint of magic or witchcraft. It is no longer safe to do so.

It seems that the sisters of the priory have so enjoyed the jongleur's performance that they have begged him to stay on for another night to give another recital. I am pleased, for it gives me a little longer to formulate my questions so that they do not arouse suspicion.

This time he recites another *lai*, "Le Fresne", about a young woman who is raised in an abbey and is unaware of her true birthright. Is this Marie's own story, but woven anew into what she most desires? I listen, enthralled, as the jongleur recites her love and dependence on the king who takes her in, and her joy when, at last, she is reconciled with her contrite mother and sister.

Does Marie long to come back to Camelot, where she is known and recognized for who she truly is? The thought that she wishes to be reconciled with her mother stabs me through the heart.

I waylay the man after he has finished his meal. "How did you come to travel our way?" I ask innocently. "Is it chance, or did you choose to come here?"

The jongleur smiles. "Not chance, my lady, but a happy circumstance for me, nevertheless. I have been reciting the *lais* of Marie of France for some time now, for they are extremely popular with the common folk at fairs and in the marketplaces; even barons occasionally invite me to perform for them and their friends after they have dined. On one such occasion I was told that a woman named Viviane wished to speak with me. It was she who promised me a purse of silver if I would come here to your priory. She asked me to recite these *lais* to the community here, although I'm not quite sure why." His gaze is inquisitive as he continues, "I was also told to ask for the Lady Morgana, but it seems she is not here."

"Yes, she is." Interfering Viviane! My lips twitch in a smile as I tell the man, "I am known only as Anna in the priory, but before I came here Morgana was my name." I am suddenly anxious. "But you must tell no one, for my life might be forfeit if my true name becomes known."

He nods. I wonder what, if anything, he has been told about me. His expression is unreadable, although he bows courteously enough. "I am pleased to meet you, my lady. I have a message from Dame Viviane. She says to tell you that she sends you both a lesson and a blessing. She says also that your daughter thrives, and that she is content."

For a moment I am speechless with joy. "And I beg you, give her a message in return," I say, when I am able once more to put my thoughts into words. "Please tell her that I am grateful to have news of my daughter. Will you also ask Dame Viviane to pass on to her my love, and tell her that I wished only to keep her safe?"

"I am pleased to be of service to you, my lady. But I confess, I am not sure why the dame suggested I come here to ply my trade for ours is a prosperous and settled kingdom, whereas it seems to me that your land is dying, and that people here live in fear and despair. I do wonder how I shall eke out a living while I am here."

"How came you to Glastonbury?"

"Dame Viviane sent me downstream in her barge, and I was left on the riverbank." The jongleur brightens somewhat. "She did say that if I was unable to find a patron, I should wait there and the barge would come for me, and that I would find the promised payment on board."

He has said all I need to know. I wish him well, and apologize for not being able to reward him for his pains. He looks around our poor priory. "I realize how things are here," he says. "So I shall ask you instead to please pray for me, pray for my soul."

I assure him that I will do so, and that I will also pray for his safe return to the world that he knows. His gaze sharpens with interest, but he does not question me—which is fortunate, perhaps.

The jongleur has set my mind at rest about Marie, but it has also prompted me to think anew about our own fate. And so I convince him there is nothing more for him here and I personally escort him to the river. He accompanies me willingly enough, having seen for himself his lack of future prospects, while I ensure that he speaks to no one who may tell him of the events that have brought us into such a parlous state. I am reassured that the story of Camelot lives on with Marie, but I am determined now that my part in its downfall must be hidden and forgotten. And so, once we catch sight of the barge, I bid him farewell and hurry back to the priory.

I pray that my waning powers will be equal to the task as I weave the spell that I once used to seal Merlin into his cave. In so doing, I hope to ensure that our world will be lost forever, and my shame will die with me.

The spell is successful, but it has taken its toll both on my body and on my ability to practice any magic at all. Over my years in exile at the priory, I have attempted to rebuild my once beautiful garden, although I was unable to restore the secret ways without the magical tools at my disposal. But I still take comfort in nature, and in my resurrected garden, poor imitation though it may be. The flowers that bloom are still magnificent. Trees still cast their shade in summer, lose their leaves in winter, and promise new life in spring. Everywhere I look I see an affirmation that no matter what has happened in the past, plants keep on growing, babies are born, and the great cycle of life continues. There is a comfort in that thought.

The news that Marie is safe and well, and has a royal patron, was balm to my soul, but the hunger to see her again, awakened by the jongleur's words, is a constant ache. I long to see her one last time, just once before I die, for I suspect that my end is near. I resolve to go out into the garden to say farewell while I still have breath in my body.

It is a fine day. The sun shines warm on my shriveled limbs as the good sisters carry me outside and into the garden. At my wish, they seat me on a turf bench close to its center, where I have fashioned a small enclosed pool that is fed by the ancient spring with its rusty water the color of blood, the same spring that used to run into the sacred scrying pool in my secret garden.

I ask the sisters to leave me alone by the pool. There is some concern but when I insist, they agree on the understanding that it will be only for a short while, and that they will return soon to make sure that I am comfortable.

I wait until they have gone. Slowly, I pull myself up from the bench and stumble toward the pool. I fall to my knees beside it, and look into the water. This is my last, desperate attempt to see my daughter.

The water stays dark. I close my eyes, and pray to the gods that I may be granted a last vision. When I open my eyes once more, I find I am looking directly into the face of a woman I am almost sure I have seen before.

"Morgan?" I ask. She looks some years older now. It comes to me that in fact there is a striking similarity between her and the illustration of the woman holding the crystal on Merlin's tablet. A man sits beside her; he bears such a strong family resemblance that they might even be twins. They are seated at a round table, surrounded by a sober group of men and women who are nothing at all like the wild rabble I witnessed in the streets of London. Yet there is some similarity to those warring tribes in the differing styles of their dress and skin colors.

Great windows of glass set along the walls give a view of the Tor standing like a sentinel beyond, with the ruins of stone towers and walls scattered among the grass at its feet. Is this the Glastonbury of our world, or is this the Otherworld I chose for Marie? And why has the abbey been destroyed? This must surely be a vision of the future.

Morgan and her brother, if that is who they are, appear to be in deep discussion with their companions. It is a serious debate, but I sense there is no anger among them. There is tension, but not the overwhelming fear I felt before, when I witnessed the streets of London erupting into fire and vanishing as if they had never been. These people seem to have come together for a common purpose, a purpose I can only guess at: how to overcome the threat to their kingdom, the threat that has already caused so much devastation.

The woman looks at me. "Thank you, Morgana," she says.

With her words, I come to understand that by saving my child from the dying days of Camelot I have done what she asked. I remember Viviane's words: *The day will come when Britain is divided and is once more under siege from within. There will be a great need for a wise and courageous leader, someone able to bring the tribes together, and unite them in the quest for common ground.*

I remember the fiery scenes from my scrying pool: the rampaging tribes, the rage and hatred of warriors who seemed intent on the mindless destruction of everything and everyone. I remember also that final, awful, screaming.

Not our world but a future time in the Otherworld that resembles our own so closely. And Morgan? I'd wondered at first if perhaps she was my counterpart in that Otherworld, a reflection of me as I could have been if only things had turned out differently.

Now I know the answer. We have come full circle, and I pray to the gods that Marie's descendant—and her brother—will have the courage and the wisdom to unite this other Britain, and save it from those bent on destroying it from within; save it from total annihilation.

It is time for me lay down my quill, and I pray to the gods for peace—and forgiveness. I gaze into the pool, but there is nothing now to see, only a gathering darkness that spreads out and folds around me like a soft night blanket, and wraps me safe into its cold, clear silence.

ACKNOWLEDGMENTS

My thanks to the Waratahs for their interest and feedback while I was writing *I, Morgana*. Thanks also to Dr. Gillian Polack, Isolde Martyn and Laurine Croasdale – your input was invaluable. Special thanks to Molly Talbot for sharing with me her knowledge of the Tarot, and for helping me devise the "reading" for Morgana. Finally, my thanks to the team at Momentum for all their expertise and care.

Printed in Australia
AUOC02n0703290914
263467AU00001B/3/P

9 781760 081393